Hell's Bell

A LIZZIE GRACE NOVEL

Also by Keri Arthur

With thanks to:
The lovely ladies at Hot Tree Editing
The Lulus
The ladies from Central Vic Writers
And finally, Damonza for the amazing cover.

CHAPTER
one

I woke abruptly, my heart hammering and a scream dying on my lips.

For several seconds, I did nothing more than stare into the darkness of my bedroom, trying to find a reason for the fear that pounded through my veins. Though I'd rather weirdly become prone to prophetic dreams of late, it wasn't a dream that had woken me. The source of the fear was external, not internal.

Aside from the usual creaks and groans of an old building, the apartment above the café I owned and ran with my best friend and fellow witch, Isabelle—or Belle, as she preferred to be called—was silent. Nor was there any noise coming from the street outside, but that wasn't really surprising given this part of Castle Rock was mostly retail, and everything here had shut down by nine.

I pulled my phone out from under my pillow and checked the time. 12.25. Which was almost smack bang in the middle of witching hour—a time when those on the spectral edge of the world were thought to gain substance and reality. As a witch—even if a somewhat underpowered one—I knew the truth lay not so much with the time, but rather the position of the moon. Midnight was when she reached her highest point in the sky, and was therefore at her most powerful.

Did that mean some sort of supernatural activity had woken me?

I seriously hoped not. Only a couple of weeks had passed since we'd gotten involved in the hunt for a vampire hell-bent on revenge, and I'd only just recovered from the injuries received in that final bloody battle.

The last thing this reservation—or, indeed, Belle and I—needed was another force of darkness finding its way here.

And yet, Castle Rock was a place filled with wild magic. While such a force was in itself neither good nor bad, without a proper, fully vetted witch here to protect and channel it, it would inevitably draw those who followed the darker paths—or those who coveted such unrestrained power. And the werewolf council was—as far as I could tell—willfully ignoring the danger it represented.

Either that, or they simply didn't believe in a force they were physically incapable of seeing.

I scrubbed a hand across my eyes, then flicked the bedcovers off and got up. The night was cold despite the fact Christmas was now only three weeks away, and I shivered my way into track pants and a sweater before walking across to the door.

There really wasn't that much living space up here on the first floor. Belle and I each had our own bedroom, and there was a separate toilet and bathroom. Beyond that, there was a small kitchenette, and a living area that held a two-person sofa and a TV. At the far end of the room were glass sliding doors that led out to a balcony that extended out over the sidewalk. It provided us with much-needed extra space while giving weather protection to café patrons who preferred to use the sidewalk tables.

I glanced to the left, studying the shadows that concealed the stairs leading down to the café. There was no sense of wrongness coming from that area, and the wards and spells I'd placed around the inside perimeter of the building were untouched and untroubled.

I frowned and headed right, silently making my way across to the balcony door. The night air condensed my breath, and my shivering increased. I hugged my arms across my chest and walked to the railing, my gaze drifting over the silent street and the nearby buildings.

Castle Rock was the capital of the Faelan Werewolf Reservation, one of only seven here in Australia. It had initially been the sole province of the O'Connor pack, but some long-ago human government had decided the three Victorian packs held too much land—and therefore too much wealth and power—between them, and had decided all three need to be on the one reservation—this one. Of course, the Marin and Sinclair packs had been as unimpressed with the idea as the O'Connors, and the resulting turmoil was the reason werewolves today were basically self-governing. Witches had been the driving force behind that peace deal, which was perhaps why some packs remained unhappy about a witch's presence on their land.

But there wasn't much any of them could do about it—at least when it came to government-assigned witches. Aside from providing magical assistance when needed, reservation witches were also the government's mouthpieces and rule enforcers.

Which made this reservation's lack of an assigned witch all the more surprising. Granted, Gabe Watson might have disappeared after apparently murdering his wife, but that didn't explain why he hadn't been replaced. No matter how hard the werewolves here might have protested, the High Witch council had the law behind them. And they surely knew—better than anyone—just how dangerous unguarded wild magic could be.

And while I might have been born into a royal witch family, I'd never gone through the vetting system and I certainly didn't have the power to protect the magic in this place.

Even if the magic here seemed to have a strange affinity with me.

I frowned and glanced up at the moon. Though a cloak of clouds hid her presence, her power nevertheless sang through the deeper recesses of my soul. It was a force often used to bolster the strength of spells, but I had no sense that anyone was using her to perform magic. At least not in the immediate surrounds, anyway.

So what had woken me?

I scanned the silent night for a few more minutes, then cursed softly and pushed away from the railing.

Just as I did, I heard it.

The distant ringing of a church bell.

Once.

Twice.

Thrice.

Then silence.

A silence suddenly filled with an odd edge of malevolence.

Trepidation stirred even as the need to track down the source of that ominous ringing hit. I didn't question it; I simply turned and ran back inside, pausing long enough to lock the door before racing toward my bedroom.

And almost collided with Belle as she came out of hers. It was only thanks to her jump back into her bedroom that we didn't come to grief. For someone who was just over six feet tall with the physique of an Amazon, she was amazingly quick on her feet.

"What's wrong?" she asked, her voice sharp with concern.

"I don't know. Something."

"And apparently you're in a hurry to investigate it." She followed me into my bedroom. "Do you want company?"

I hesitated. Belle wasn't only a witch, but a spirit talker and a strong telepath. Of course, she was also my familiar—something that had apparently never happened before in all witch history. It had been the subject of much gossip amongst the six witch houses when we were children, and had caused more than a little shame to my blueblood parents.

"Your parents have their noses stuck so far up their own asses," Belle commented, obviously catching my thoughts, "that they wouldn't know a good thing if it hit them in the face multiple times."

Belle's tone was tart, and I chuckled softly, even if it was a rather sad truth. There were three so-called "royal" lines of witches, all of which were considerably more powerful than the other, more "common" lines. Over the centuries, the royal three had so ingratiated themselves with rule makers that they were now considered vital aides to governments across the world. Both my parents were high-ranking—and therefore highly sought after— members of the Council of Advisors. Or had been when Belle and I had fled Canberra and my family twelve years ago. For all I knew, my father might now be the head of the council; it wasn't like I kept up-to-date on witch happenings, be they local or national. And although my family could probably have found me if they'd truly wanted to, I nevertheless preferred to keep my profile low, and did my best to avoid not only anything to do with the witch council but most things magic.

Which had certainly become harder since we'd set up shop here in Castle Rock, as magic and we seemed to be on an unavoidable collision course.

"It might be safer if you do come along," I said. "I think there's some sort of spectral presence out there, and that means I might need guidance from you and the spirit world."

She pushed away from the doorframe, a smile on her lips. "The spirit world just went into shock at hearing you say they might be useful rather than annoying."

"Hey, they do have a habit of dishing out dire warnings without actually providing a source or a reason." I zipped up my jacket. "I'll meet you downstairs."

She nodded and disappeared into her bedroom. I switched on the hall light and clattered down to the café. The Christmas lights strung around the dining area filled the room with color and cheerfulness, and I couldn't help smiling. Belle and I had opened—and closed—a few cafés over the years, but this was the first one that truly felt like home.

I turned and headed into the small reading room at the rear of the building. The air sparked briefly as I entered, a clear indication the spells encircling and protecting the room were active. A simple wooden table sat in the center of the small space, along with four mismatched but comfortable chairs. A large rug covered the floor, and bright lengths of material were draped across the ceiling, both of which not only provided the otherwise drab room with some color, but also hid the ramped-up spellwork painted onto the floor and etched into the wooden ceiling. Only an entity of extreme power would ever get into this place.

We might not have come to Castle Rock with the intention of doing much more than spiritual and psychic readings, but the advent of the vampire and the knowledge that we were all that stood between the wild magic and those who would use it for ill had made what most witches in our line of work would consider an overload of protections totally necessary.

I walked across to the full-height bookcase that lined the right wall, moved a gorgeously ornate pottery fairy, and then I placed my hand against the bookcase's wooden back. Energy immediately crawled across it, and a heartbeat later, the wooden panel slipped aside to reveal an eight-inch-deep compartment. It wasn't the only hidden compartment in the bookcase—there was one behind every shelf. A witch could never be too careful when it came to protecting magical items and potions.

I grabbed Belle's silver knife, because mine was still being held at the ranger station, a couple of bottles of holy water, and my spell stones—or warding stones, as they were sometimes known. Once I'd secured them into a backpack, I opened another compartment to get a couple of ready-made potions to ward off evil, then slung the pack over my back and headed out.

The faint caress of energy swirled around me again as

I joined Belle outside. It wasn't magic; it was the spirits, communing with her.

Once I'd locked the door, I shoved my hands into my pockets and headed left. After a moment, she joined me.

"I'm told there's something rather odd happening near the botanical gardens."

"I don't suppose they could define the term 'odd.'"

Her lips twitched. "Apparently, it's not odd in the way you are."

"Which, as usual, clarifies things greatly."

"They do not wish to provide a clear answer because it would cause you great shock." Her silvery eyes shone with amusement. "And they feel it's better for you to remain capable of tackling whatever it is both you and they are sensing."

"Is there a reason behind their high form tonight?" I asked mildly. "Because it's a little unusual for them to be this backchatty."

"I think it's the energy of this place. They like it." She hesitated, eyes narrowing as she listened to the other side. "Dispensing the truth is not being backchatty, apparently. And they suggest we get a move on."

I snorted, but nevertheless increased my pace. I wasn't foolish enough to ignore a suggestion from the spirit world—not when it meshed with my own need to investigate, anyway.

We made our way down Mostyn Street until we reached the far end, and then swung right onto Kennedy. It probably would have been quicker to drive, but the nebulous part of me that had woken filled with fear wanted to be on foot.

As we drew closer to Lyttleton Street, I couldn't help but glance at the white weatherboard house across the road. Did Marjorie's soul remain there, eternally locked in grief for the daughter who'd been turned by a revenge-seeking vampire?

"Her grief will probably stain the atmosphere of that place for many years to come," Belle said softly. "But her soul has moved on. The spirits say it was her time."

"Meaning we couldn't have saved her no matter what we did?"

"No."

Which at least went some way to easing the vague sense of guilt that had lingered since that horrible night—even though the logical part of me knew we'd done everything we possibly could. "And Karen?"

"Has also moved on, but her path is not one of light."

I frowned. "But it wasn't by choice that she murdered her mom—"

"No, but it was her decision to share blood with a vampire. Gran's book was very specific about that."

Belle's grandmother Nellie might have been one of the so-called "common" Sarr witches, but she'd held a vast collection of books on magic and the supernatural. Belle had inherited a good percentage of that library, although we'd had no real cause to use them for anything more than an occasional charm spell until recently.

"But Karen was still only sixteen," I replied. "It's hardly fair that she should suffer an eternity of hell for the unthinking selfishness of youth."

Belle shrugged. "You always pay for the choices you make, be it in life or in death."

"That might be true, but it doesn't mean it's always fair."

"Life is never fair—what happened to you after your

sister's death is evidence enough of that."

Another true statement, and a hurt that still festered in the deepest part of my soul. But then, it wasn't often your parents held you responsible for the death of the sister you'd tried so desperately to save.

We ran on, our footsteps making little impact on the hush that controlled the night. Fog appeared, thick patches that drifted along the street, masking the glow of some lights while leaving others free.

But as we neared the park, all the lights became so heavily shrouded it plunged the entire area into foggy darkness. My trepidation increased; that masking—and maybe even the fog—wasn't natural.

And yet there was no sense of magic touching the air.

"It might be too far away—or too faint—for either of us to detect," Belle commented.

"Maybe." I paused briefly at Walker Street, glancing left and right before racing across. "I don't suppose the spirits have any information yet on what might lie ahead?"

"Only that it's not a spirit, as such."

Which ruled out ghosts, but left the door wide open for all other manner of ghouls and demons—although it was rather hard to imagine a demon being paired with the sound of a church bell.

I hauled myself over the old metal fence that surrounded the park, and ran on. Clammy fingers played across my face and swirled heavily around my body; it almost felt like the fog was trying to push me away.

Ahead, on the ground and barely visible, lay something white. It wasn't moving and appeared to have arms but no body or face. I slowed instinctively, my breath hitching in my throat.

"What on earth is that?" Belle's voice was little more

than a croak of fear.

"I don't know." The charm at my throat—one designed to ward off evil—wasn't reacting, but that might simply be because we weren't close enough.

As I edged forward, I silently began the incantation for a repelling spell. Better to be safe than sorry....

The white thing became clearer, and amusement washed away the gathering dread. It was a shirt. We were scared of a damn shirt.

Belle's silent laughter bubbled through my mind. Although I wasn't telepathic, the ability to share thoughts was one of the many benefits that came with her being my familiar.

Your ranger would have a field day if he ever discovered we were both scared witless by an innocuous men's shirt.

Aiden is hardly my anything. We haven't even gone out yet.

I squatted next to the shirt and reached out—but didn't quite touch the crisp material.

I didn't need to.

Evil rolled off it.

Evil and hunger.

Whether the source was the owner of the shirt, or a companion was what we now needed to uncover.

And fast.

I hesitated a second longer, and then grabbed a fistful of the material and reached down to that place deep inside where my psychometry skill lay leashed and waiting. While it usually worked better with possessions worn close to the skin that weren't washed—things like necklaces, rings, or watches rather than items of clothing—it was still possible to track someone through clothing if the item had only recently been discarded. This shirt had been—it was still damp with perspiration.

But I didn't open the door to my abilities very wide. Given the foulness emanating from the material, the last thing I needed was to slip into the mind of the stranger as I'd slipped into the mind of the teenager when the vampire had first killed her. I didn't need to experience whatever hell was being inflicted on him. I just needed to find him.

The shirt led us left, toward the lake and a barely visible strand of trees.

You know, it might be wise at this point to ring Aiden, Belle said.

And tell him what? That I've found an evil-feeling shirt? That'll go down well at this hour of the night.

Her grin flashed. *If that man is asleep, I'll eat my hat.*

You don't wear them.

Well no, because they mess with the hair. But the sentiment nevertheless applies.

I snorted softly. *If and when we find something to ring him about, I'll do so. Not before.*

Besides, I was a little peeved at the man. Though he'd come into the café regularly for coffee, cake, and a chat, he'd yet to make any further moves when it came to us going out.

He did say the date could wait until you'd fully recovered, Belle said mildly. *It's possible he's simply waiting for you to say you are.*

Anyone can see that I am. He can't be that daft.

He's a man. They sometimes have to be clubbed over the head with the obvious.

I snorted again and continued to follow the shirt's weakening vibes. We neared the barely visible grove of trees, but weren't led into them, as I'd half expected. Instead, the shirt tugged me around their left edge. About halfway down the grove, sitting rather neatly side by side, was a pair of black shoes, complete with socks tucked neatly inside.

This is seriously weird. Belle stopped beside me. *If it weren't for the evil rolling off that shirt, I'd think we were tracking nothing more than a werewolf who's decided to go for a midnight run.*

Werewolves don't need to strip off to shift shape. The shifting ability was an inherent DNA mutation rather than a form of personal magic, but the latter *did* rather conveniently take care of their clothes and everything they might be carrying.

I know that, but maybe this fellow is drunk or something.

Maybe. I doubted it, though. This whole situation felt darker than that.

We stepped over the shoes and continued on toward the lake. The black water was still and quiet, and, rather strangely, clear of fog. Which meant if the fog was connected to whatever was happening, the lake was not our final destination.

We were guided around the water's right edge, and soon discovered another item of clothing.

Dress pants, Belle said. *I'm betting undies are next.*

I think that's a given at this point.

Three minutes later that proved to be the case.

This time, I didn't bother stopping. The vibes coming from the shirt were fading fast; either the owner's presence was leaving the material, or his life was slipping away.

I hoped it was the former.

I suspected it was the latter.

Urgency beat through me and I quickened my steps. Up ahead, the vague outline of a building appeared through the gloom. I knew by its position it was the recently renovated rotunda, but it certainly didn't look anything like that right now.

But there was one thing I was sure of: whatever was happening—whatever it was that I was sensing—it was waiting for us in that building.

How do you want to play this? Belle asked.

I hesitated. *While I really don't want to go anywhere near that building alone, it makes far more tactical sense if I go in and you hang back to keep an eye on things out here.*

She nodded. *Just don't get dead or anything like that.*

I'll certainly try not to.

Good. She paused. *The spirits inform me there's something on the move ahead.*

My gaze jumped back to the rotunda. Nothing stirred the heavy fog; if someone was moving, then they weren't coming toward us. *Seriously, can they be a little less enigmatic on this one occasion?*

They would if they could. They can see movement. They just can't see what lies behind it.

I frowned. *It's hiding its presence? Because I'm still not sensing any magic.*

They're not sure if it's magic, or simply an ability to use the fog as concealment. There are spirits who can do that, apparently. She paused. *It's now running, so it's obviously sensed either them or us.*

I swore, swung the pack off, and pulled out the silver knife. Anything that could hide from the eyes of spirits was not something I wanted to confront unarmed. And while I did have the beginning of a repelling spell threaded around my fingers, it would still take time to complete— and time was something I might not have if the unknown entity decided to attack.

I'll chase the spirit or whatever the hell it is. You go check the rotunda. But use the warding potions around that building, and be damned careful.

I handed her the pack, and then bolted after the spirit. Even though I hadn't yet gone that far, my heart was racing so fast it felt like it was going to tear out of my chest. Fear, not exertion.

The closer I got to the rotunda, the deeper the fog became, and the more certain I was that death and violation waited within its shrouded walls.

But that was not my discovery to make.

I took a wide path around the building, but my boots sank into the soft soil near the lake's edge, momentarily robbing me of speed. I swore and lunged back up the bank in an effort to reach more solid ground, but thick ropes of ethereal dampness swirled around me, pushing me back, impeding my progress. It was only when the charm sitting around my neck flared to life that I realized it was also attempting to bind me.

Even though neither the spirits nor I could feel the presence of magic, it was certainly here. I finished the repelling incantation and, with a flick of my fingers, thrust it out into the night. The fog immediately retreated. I ran on, every sense I had—both psychic and magical—searching the night, trying to find some hint of a creature who seemed as ethereal as the fog.

But there was absolutely nothing out there. Nothing except the thick gray blanket that crept ever closer again, and the vague hint of wrongness.

I began another repelling incantation, but before I could finish, insubstantial matter twined around one leg and yanked it out from underneath me.

I twisted as I fell, landing on my back rather than my stomach in an effort to avoid skewering myself with the knife. My breath escaped in a short, sharp wheeze of pain and, for a moment, stars danced in front of my eyes. I wasted more breath cursing, and then slashed at the fog with the knife. It instantly recoiled from the silver blade, and I was free again.

But as I pushed upright, something splashed in the lake. Something large. I spun around, my grip on the knife so fierce my knuckles were white. With the dark water free from the fog, it was easy enough to see the ripples rolling away from a spot at least twenty feet out from the shoreline. But there was nothing else to see, and certainly no indication that anyone—or anything—might be hiding beneath the lake's surface.

Had it been a fish? Did they even jump at night?

I really had no idea, although that splash had sounded a whole lot larger than the type of fish generally caught in this lake.

I stood and watched for several seconds longer, but there was no further movement. Uneasy of the water—or perhaps of what might now be in it—I spun around and continued following that faint wisp of wrongness. But I'd barely taken a couple of steps when my tenuous hold on it snapped and died.

Whoever—whatever—it was, it was no longer within the range of my senses. Had it used the water to escape? My gaze swept across the lake's dark surface, but there was nothing to indicate movement. Nothing to suggest anything untoward had happened within its boundaries.

I cursed again, then spun and stalked back to the rotunda. The fog was already beginning to lift, all but confirming my suspicions that it was linked with whatever had been in this park. Up ahead, the simple wooden structure reappeared; its sides were open and its tin roof shone dull silver in the night. Belle stood unmoving on the far edge of it, but I could feel her horror as strongly as if it were my own. And part of me really didn't want to confront whatever might be causing it.

But instinct had led me here for a reason, and no good ever came of ignoring it.

I slowly climbed the steps, felt the light caress of energy as I crossed over the barrier of the warding potions, and then stopped. The man who'd scattered his clothing through the park lay on his back in the center of the small building. He was lean rather than muscular in build, and was probably about six feet tall, with reddish-brown hair and brown skin—all of which suggested he might be a member of the Marin wolf pack. Even from where I stood, it was obvious he was dead, but it rather weirdly looked as if he'd simply lain down and gone to sleep. His arms were crossed across his chest, and neither terror nor fear lingered on his face.

And yet, a deep sense of violation and utter, *utter* agony rode the air. One that chilled me to the core.

I rubbed my arms, but it didn't seem to help. "Why isn't his soul rising?"

"Because it can't."

I frowned and studied the stranger with my "other" senses. And, thanks in part to my connection with Belle, saw what she'd meant.

His soul really *couldn't* rise. Not because he was in any way reluctant to accept his death and move on, but because that choice had been taken from him, and in the most violent way imaginable.

Someone—*something*—had ripped it from his flesh while he was still alive.

CHAPTER two

My gaze rose to Belle's, and in those silver depths I saw echoes of the shock and fear that coursed through me.

This wasn't an ordinary evil spirit.

This was a goddamn *soul* eater.

Which was the worst of the worst. At least most evil spirits only killed you in *this* lifetime. They didn't utterly destroy any possibility of reincarnation and *future* lives.

"I think I'd rather be dealing with another damn vampire." Belle thrust a somewhat shaky hand through her thick black hair. "We're not equipped to deal with this, Lizzie."

"And even if we were, I sure as hell don't want to." My gaze returned to the naked stranger. How could he look so peaceful when his last minutes must have been utter agony? I shivered and added, "Aiden will have to call in the local RWA representative."

The Regional Witch Association was the overriding governmental body that dealt with all situations involving witches within regional communities, with each witch having a set district to look after. But they were also often called in on investigations that involved supernatural criminality.

Such as a vampire running amok.

Or a soul eater setting up shop in an unprotected reservation.

"The trouble is," Belle said, "we're all this place has until that representative gets here."

"It surely wouldn't take them more than a day to do so."

And while I had no idea how often soul eaters fed, it didn't think it would be a nightly occurrence. Not even vampires fed that often.

"Even my guides aren't willing to take a punt on *that* question." Belle's nose wrinkled. "I'm guessing the speed with which RWA gets here will depend entirely on whether they've employed a temporary replacement for Anna."

Anna Kang was the RWA witch who'd taken the brunt of a spell explosion that had been meant for me. Though she'd received what had looked like serious burns, we'd heard on the local gossip grapevine—who apparently had first-rate contacts—that she was recovering better than expected and would thankfully be back on the job within a month or so.

"It's too big a region to go without a witch for more than a week."

Belle shrugged. "Who knows how that mob works? It's not like we've ever had much contact with them."

And for a very good reason—my parents. Or rather,

my probably absurd fear that they would one day come for us. It was the main reason behind our change of surnames and the invention of backgrounds that would stand up to fairly close scrutiny.

Of course, it *was* a High Council ruling that all witches moving into a new area inform local authorities of their presence, but we never bothered. Both of us were unvetted, which technically meant the rules didn't apply. If it hadn't been for that damn vampire, the RWA would have remained unaware of our presence here.

"Just in case there is a delay," I said, "it might be worth hunting through your grandmother's books and seeing what she's got to say on the subject."

"That might be a little hard, given we have no idea what type of spirit we're looking for aside from the fact it feeds on souls."

I blinked, and glanced at her. "There's more than one type?"

"So the spirits say."

"Isn't *that* just fantastic." I thrust a hand through my hair, but my fingers snagged in a tangle. When I pulled them free, a little ball of crimson floated away on the breeze. In the darkness, it almost looked like twined strands of blood, and I couldn't help but hope it wasn't an omen of what was to come. "In that case, look for one whose foul deeds are foretold by the ringing of a church bell."

Belle's eyebrows rose. "Is that what woke you?"

"Yep. It rang three times, and then stopped."

"And when the bell rings thrice in the middle of the night, death this way comes.... I remember reading that somewhere as a kid." She stared down at the stranger for a second. "You know, this thing could have at least waited until Christmas was over before it started causing mayhem."

"I'm thinking soul eaters *really* don't care much about anything other than their own wants or needs." Not that I'd ever had any dealings with them, but it did seem to be the creed of evil spirits in general. "While I call Aiden, can you look around for any spell remnants or magic paraphernalia? We might be dealing with a spirit capable of doing nothing more than compelling fog, but it's better to be safe than sorry."

And I'd rather *not* leave anything magical lying about for some kid to either stumble over or get caught in.

She nodded and quickly left. I didn't have to read her thoughts to know she was more than happy to get away from the heavy emotions and taint of evil that still lingered here in the rotunda.

I pulled out my phone, scrolled through the contacts list until I found Aiden's number, and called him.

He answered on the third ring, which suggested Belle had been right—he wasn't asleep.

"Liz? Why are you ringing at this hour? What's wrong?"

His reply was soft, and there was someone speaking in the background. I couldn't hear what was being said, but the voice was definitely feminine rather than masculine in tone.

That thin thread of annoyance grew stronger, which was utterly stupid given we hadn't even gone out. "I've just found a body in the small rotunda at the botanical gardens."

My voice was, thankfully, free of any sort of emotion.

He swore, and the background speaker fell silent. I wasn't entirely sure whether to be pleased about that, if only because silence didn't give me any clues as to where he was or who he was with.

Not that I had a right to know either.

A serious case of attraction does tend to short-circuit the rational sections of the brain, Belle commented dryly.

I did not request a comment from the peanut gallery, thank you very much.

Her laughter drifted through my thoughts as Aiden said, "I'll call Ciara and get her out there immediately. I'll be there in about half an hour." He paused. "Are you able to stay until then?"

Ciara wasn't only the coroner, but also his sister. The fact that she could get here far sooner than him suggested he was somewhere other than his pack's home compound on Mount Alexander. It had only taken him ten minutes to run from there when I'd called to say I'd found Anna burned but alive, so he was obviously well outside the Castle Rock district.

"Why don't you just call in Tala or one of the deputies?" I replied. "It'd save me freezing my butt off, and you leaving your company."

"Because I'm on call tonight, *not* them." There was a slight edge in his voice. "Can you stay?"

I sighed. "Yes, but only if you bring me a bucket of coffee to unfreeze me."

"Deal. Don't disturb the crime scene any more than necessary," he said, and hung up.

I stared at the phone for a moment, then shoved it back into my pocket with perhaps a little more force than was necessary.

Belle, are you finding anything untoward out there?

Not a goddamn thing. I'm on my way back.

I knelt beside the stranger but didn't touch him. I

really didn't need to at this point—the emanations of what was basically a metaphysical rape still rolled from his skin. The horror of it continued to push at my mind, but it was fading as fast as his flesh was cooling.

If I wanted to find out what had truly happened here, I needed to use my precognition and psychometry skills before the heat totally left him. The brain didn't die the minute the heart stopped—generally; there was up to a six-minute window of survival, after which deterioration began if the heart wasn't restarted. Even then, some levels of memory *could* be affected, particularly short-term.

Reviving him was out of the question in this particular case, as no one could survive without a soul. No one except zombies, that was, and their survival was reliant on the strength of the sorcerer who raised them.

The longer I delayed reading this man, the less chance there was of uncovering what had gone on here. But, at the same time, I wasn't about to attempt reading a dying mind without Belle here to watch over the whole process. I'd heard plenty of stories about psychics being ensnared by the death of another while psychically connected, and while I had no idea if they were true—or even if such a thing was possible—it wasn't something I wanted to risk.

I glanced up as Belle came back into the rotunda. "We can't wait for Ciara to get here."

"No, but we can always record the reading on our phones—that way, they'll at least have something for their records." Belle slipped off the backpack. "I'll start preparations for a protection circle."

I frowned. "Do you really think that's necessary? I mean, he's dead—"

"*And* a victim of a soul eater." Her expression was

grim. "Given how little we currently know about them, I don't think a precaution or two is out of the question."

I raised my hands in acquiescence and stepped out of her way. She was totally right, especially given what had happened to Anna. While I doubted the soul eater had that sort of power, I had no idea if consuming this man's soul gave it some sort of connection to his dying flesh. The last thing *I* needed or wanted was my attempt to read this man's memories coming to the attention of this thing.

I crossed my arms and watched as she made the preparations and then began the incantations that would produce a secondary protection circle. It still wouldn't be full strength, given we neither had candles nor our athames here, but it would at least prevent whatever other evil might linger in the park from being drawn here.

The sound of a car's engine caught my attention and I glanced around. Headlights briefly swept around the far end of the park and came toward us.

"I'm guessing that's Ciara." I flexed my fingers, trying to ease the tension that rode me. Trying to gather courage for what I now had to do. "And just in time, too."

Belle wove the final exception into her spell—one that allowed me to cross over the barrier she'd raised around the stranger, but no one and nothing else—and then met my gaze.

"She still has to collect her kit and whatever else she might need—do you really want to wait for her?"

I grimaced. "You know we can't."

As much as I'd rather do *anything* other than read a dead man's mind, we were already on the cusp of time limitations.

She got out her phone, took a couple of photos of the stranger's position, and then said, "Right then, I'm recording. Good luck."

"Thanks."

I took a deep breath, released it slowly, and then stepped into the circle of her magic. The spell stones that encircled the stranger's body flashed silver and blue, and their energy spun around me and then faded as the spell registered and then accepted my details.

I squatted behind the stranger and placed a hand on either side of his head. After another of those breaths that didn't do a whole lot to ease the tension surging through me, I closed my eyes and lightly pressed my fingers against his skull.

For several seconds, nothing happened. The utter foulness of his death crawled across my senses and dragged tears from my eyes, but there was no immediate sense of anything else. No indication of where he'd been and who he'd been with before his death.

Which was decidedly weird.

Unless, of course, the lack was *my* fault. It had been a long time since I'd tried to use my psychometry skills in such a direct way, and I was somewhat rusty. For the most part, using personal items rather than direct touch made the whole process less... confronting.

Of course, there were never any guarantees when you worked with psi powers; sometimes the connection simply wasn't there, and sometimes it was so damn strong it dragged you deep into the mind of another. Which was exactly what had happened when I'd tried to find Karen for Marjorie, and I certainly didn't want to relive this man's last minutes as I'd lived the teenager's.

Images began to flicker through the deeper recesses of his mind, but they were extremely fragile things. The minute I reached for them, they fragmented and spun away into the gathering darkness in his head.

I frowned and went even further. His surface memories might be beyond reach, but there was still a chance deeper memory remained.

The darkness that was both brain death and something else—something I'd never encountered before—fought my invasion for several heartbeats. Then, with an abruptness that tore a gasp from my throat, I was beyond it, and right in the middle of events from a few hours ago. But these, too, were fading very quickly—it was a little like watching a badly degraded movie that flicked abruptly from one scene to another.

You nevertheless need to say aloud what you're seeing, Lizzie, Belle said. *We need it recorded.*

"His memories are almost *too* fractured." I hesitated. "There's a woman, tall and pale. A short red dress that sparkles brightly under muted lights. Laughter and warmth and alcohol. Teasing touches that promise much...."

Careful, Lizzie, Belle warned. *Don't go too deep.*

No, I said, even as I did. "There's a car—a sports car. White, with black leather seats. Caresses that tease and kisses that taste like ash. And heat, so much heat. Desire burns and I chase her, capture her, and there is bliss and then...."

I stopped, simply because the memory reel did. Not because his brain was dying, or because death had snatched away whatever had followed that brief, blissful moment.

The memories simply *didn't* exist.

It was as if someone had taken a knife and sliced them away.

I released my fingers from either side of his head and pushed out of the protection circle. I landed on my butt, and for several seconds, didn't move. I simply sucked in air and tried to make sense of what I'd felt at the very end.

While telepaths certainly *could* erase or rearrange memories, I knew from Belle it wasn't possible to create such an utterly clean break. There were always tells—memory fragments and odd bits of fuzziness that gave the game away.

But this man's memories hadn't been erased—they simply *didn't* exist.

"Which suggests," Belle said, "he was unconscious when his soul was ripped from him."

"But if that were the case, there shouldn't be so much horror and pain in the air. An unconscious mind isn't capable of feeling, and surely wouldn't emote as strongly as this man has."

"Under normal circumstances, that's probably true, but this situation *isn't* normal. I'm betting his soul would have fought like hell even if his flesh couldn't."

"Who fought like hell?" Ciara said, as she stepped into the rotunda. "It certainly wasn't this wolf, from the look of him."

Like most wolves, she was tall and rangy in build. Her short blonde hair gleamed silver against the night's shadows, and her eyes were—like Aiden's—a deep blue rather than the usual amber of a werewolf. But then, the O'Connor pack were also gray wolves, a color that tended to be somewhat rarer amongst Australian packs. Most were brown, red, or black; the O'Connors ran the full gamut from silvery white to a blond so dark it was almost a dirty brown.

"Looks can be deceiving," I replied, even as Belle hastily deactivated the protection circle.

Ciara stopped near the stranger's feet and frowned

down at his body. "What were you doing to him?"

"I was trying to read his memories before death claimed them."

"You can *do* that?" She glanced at me, her tone incredulous. "Seriously?"

"Sometimes, if the death is fresh enough." I pushed upright. The rotunda briefly spun, and an ache started in the back of my head, one fierce enough to make my left eye water. A result of reaching too far, I knew. At least my stomach remained steady; I suspected neither Ciara nor Aiden would be happy if I puked all over the body. "We recorded the whole thing, so we can post you the file if you want."

"Aiden will want it. I'll rely on more old-fashioned methods to find out what killed him."

"Good luck with that," Belle murmured.

Ciara raised her eyebrows. "Meaning what?"

"Meaning the reason this man died is because his soul was stolen from him, and I'm doubting science has yet devised a means of uncovering an event like that."

"How on earth is something like that even possible?"

"Simple—we're dealing with something that's technically *not* of this earth."

"Meaning what?" she snapped. "At this hour of the night, I'm really not in the mood for games."

I couldn't help the smile that touched my lips. In that brief moment, she sounded scarily like her brother.

"It means this reservation seems to have gained a soul eater."

Her gaze went from me to Belle and back again. "You're serious."

"Totally." Belle's voice was flat. "If you thought a vampire wanting revenge was bad, you ain't seen nothing yet."

"*Fuck*." Ciara's gaze swept the darkness beyond the rotunda. "Is it still nearby?"

"If it was, we sure as hell wouldn't be standing here yakking to you."

"Are you *sure*?"

"Yes." I rubbed a hand across my forehead, but it didn't really ease the strengthening ache. "Whatever did this is long gone."

For now, at least.

"Good—although I have to admit, I'm finding all this a little hard to accept." She hesitated. "But if we do have something like that on the reservation, how the hell do we stop it?"

"*We* don't," I said. "The RWA does."

"More fucking witches is just what we need here." She hesitated. "Present company *not* included in that comment, of course."

Belle snorted softly. "You know, one of these days, your damn pack will have to—"

The O'Connors have a good reason to hate witches, I cut in. *We don't need to do or say anything right now to get them offside again. Not when things have started to thaw out.*

One witch's actions should not *brand an entire race*, she fired back. *We had nothing to do with her sister's death.*

No, we didn't, as it had happened over a year before we'd arrived in Castle Rock. But I could nevertheless understand their pain, as well as their need to pin blame. In many respects, their situation was similar to my own, even if the only person I could blame for my sister's death was myself.

Ciara studied Belle for a moment, and then said, "I've a feeling you were about to say a whole lot more than that."

"I was, but it doesn't matter."

Ciara grunted, and glanced at me. "I'll have to ask you both to wait outside while I start proceedings in here."

"I'm afraid I can't wait. I have to go home."

She frowned. "Aiden wants to speak to you—"

"And he knows where to find me."

"But he said—"

"I don't really care what he said, or what I might have agreed to when I rang him," I snapped, and then drew in a breath, trying for calm. "Unless you want me puking all over your crime scene, you'd better just let me go."

"Reading the dead isn't a pleasant thing to do," Belle said. "And believe me, the projectile vomiting that often follows isn't an easy thing to clean up."

Ciara's gaze briefly swept me, and then she waved a hand. "Fine. Go."

Meaning, perhaps, I looked as ill as I was beginning to feel.

I turned and quickly left—catching Belle somewhat flat-footed. She caught up with me in a couple of strides, and we continued in silence. By the time we'd reached the café, my head felt like it was going to tear apart, and my stomach was a couple of churns away from surging up my throat.

"Go climb into bed," Belle ordered, in a voice that would brook no arguments. "I'll make you up a potion."

I grimaced. Belle's strengthening and revitalization potions might be the reason why many incantations—and psychic shit like I'd done tonight—didn't affect me as badly as they did other witches and psychics, but they were also the foulest goddamn drinks ever created.

Her grin flashed. "Says the person who gave me a

potion not so long ago that hands down beat *anything* I've ever made over the years."

"You only have yourself to blame. You're the one who taught me how to make them."

"That is, rather sadly, very true. Perhaps I'll make an exception and be kind this one time."

"Good, because you might just get the lot puked all over you otherwise."

"You forget how quickly I can move when I need to." She pushed me lightly toward the stairs. "Go, before you collapse and I have to carry your butt up there."

I dragged myself up the stairs and started stripping off the minute I reached the landing. My bedroom's darkness wrapped around me, warm and secure thanks to all the protections around it, and yet goose bumps nevertheless raced across my skin.

I wasn't entirely sure either these spells or the exclusion ones we'd placed around this building would be enough to deal with something that could steal souls.

And yet, they did pretty much cover most types of evil spirits; the only real worry was if this thing was also capable of magic. It might then be able to see and maybe even unravel the spell threads that protected us—something the vampire had come very close to doing.

But *that* was something I could worry about when we knew for sure what sort of soul eater we were dealing with. And it wasn't as if I was capable of bolstering the protection spells in any way right now.

I climbed into bed, tugged the blankets up to my nose, and promptly fell asleep.

I woke who knew how many hours later. Though my door was shut—something I couldn't remember doing—noise still drifted up from downstairs. It sounded as if there were a lot of people down there, and it made me wonder what time it was.

One in the afternoon, Belle said, amusement evident. *To say you slept the sleep of the dead would be an understatement.*

Seriously? I threw the blankets to one side and scrambled out of bed. *Why the hell didn't you wake me?*

Because you needed the sleep. Now shut up and drink the potion that's waiting on the bedside table.

I glanced to my left. The glass was large, and the potion a rather sludgy greeny-brown color. Even from where I stood I could smell the thing. *I thought you said you were going to be kind?*

That was last night, when your stomach was fragile.

How do you know it still isn't?

Because I've been hanging around you long enough to know the only thing your stomach will be doing after such a sleep is rumbling with hunger. So drink that shit, grab a shower, and then get down here. Your ranger is getting antsy.

Feed him another brownie and tell him I'll be there in ten minutes.

He's already had three. At this rate, he'll be eating our profits.

Says the woman who feeds her wolf all manner of goodies.

The difference, Belle said, her amusement increasing, *is that he needs the sugary energy boost because he has a woman with a healthy sexual appetite to look after.*

Thanks for the cheery reminder that I'm in a drought, I replied. *Appreciate it.*

She laughed. *So get your butt down here in something sexy, just to remind Aiden what he's missing out on.*

I snorted and headed for the shower. *Yeah, right.*

When I did get down there nearly fifteen minutes later, it was in jeans and a tank top, with a checked shirt over the top of that.

Oh, that's really putting it all out there, Lizzie. Good job.
Belle, go suck a lemon.

She burst out laughing, a good-natured sound that rolled across the chatter and had people looking around with a smile.

I've ordered you some lunch, she said. *I'll have it brought over when it's ready.*

Ta. And you might as well join us, given you're the local expert on spirits.

And spoil your time with the man?
I'm thinking he'll be all business.
Maybe. Maybe not.
Belle, you haven't read him... have you?
Maybe. Maybe not.

I snorted again, but didn't bother questioning her any further. Even if she had read him—and I doubted she had, given she generally believed everyone had a right to privacy unless or until they in some way provoked her— she obviously wasn't about to tell me.

Aiden sat at the table in the corner of the room, one that had, over the last few weeks, become "our" table— the one we always used whenever he came to the café.

The sunlight streaming in through the nearby window had streaks of silver glimmering through his otherwise dark blond hair, and highlighted the somewhat sharp planes of his face. He was nursing a mug between his hands, and watched me approach with an intentness that had heat rising to my cheeks.

"I'm sorry I couldn't stay behind last night." I pulled out a chair and sat down next to him. "But I really wasn't in a fit state to be questioned."

"So I gathered." His gaze briefly swept me, and his expression gave little away. "Are you feeling any better?"

I nodded. "Did Belle send you the recording we took?"

"Yes, as well as the photos. Thanks for that."

Despite the earlier intentness, he was being overly polite, which worried me somewhat. "Do you know who he was?"

"Yeah—Aron Marin. His father is one of the pack's alphas." He hesitated. "Ciara said you believed his death was caused by an evil spirit—one that ate his soul. Are you absolutely positive about that?"

"As positive as we can be without actually confronting the thing." I frowned. "Why?"

"Because Rocco was having problems within the pack, and very recently his family was threatened."

My eyebrows rose. "I wouldn't have thought the person behind such a threat would have lasted long within the pack."

Aiden's smile held little in the way of humor. "She didn't—"

"She?" I cut in, surprised. "Do female wolves often go about threatening the hierarchy?"

He raised his eyebrows. "Isn't it almost a rite of passage that young adults fight back against the restrictions of their parents? Didn't you?"

My smile held an all too familiar edge of bitterness. "Not really." I'd simply run away rather than keep uselessly flinging myself at walls that would never come down, and accusations that would never cease. My parents might have had three children, but my sister had been their golden child—and my brother came in a close second. As my parents had told me multiple times, either were worth a trillion of me. "But if it was only a teenager who'd threatened the alpha, why was the threat taken so seriously?"

"Because the woman in question was twenty-three, and the somewhat troubled daughter of a lower-rank pack member."

I frowned. "I still don't get why it was taken seriously enough to banish her."

"Larissa has a string of minor and major assaults behind her, stretching back to when she was barely twelve." He grimaced. "Her behavior of late has been escalating."

"But still—"

"She's a *werewolf*." His voice was blunt. "And a strong one. She might never have beaten Rocco, but there's no doubt in my mind that she'd hold her own against Aron."

"Except he wasn't physically attacked."

"On first appearances, that appears to be the case. But until the autopsy is done and we get the tox results back, nothing is certain."

Including my claim that evil had dined on his soul, I suspected. It would only be the *lack* of any other cause that would allow him and the other rangers to actually contemplate the impossible. "So why did she threaten the pack's alphas?"

"Because Karla Marin refused permission for her to marry Garrett, their youngest son."

I blinked. "Do alphas often go about doing things like that?"

"Yes." He hesitated. "It's often necessary, as many within his pack are blood-related."

"But wouldn't that be a problem for all three packs here? The reservation certainly isn't the largest."

"Again, yes, which is why we long ago started an exchange program—with packs both here in Australia and overseas—that allows those seeking mates to investigate options elsewhere."

"So Larissa is related to Garrett?"

He nodded. "A second cousin."

I frowned. "It *is* legal for second cousins to marry in Australia."

"Yes, but it's a practice that's banned on most reservations, except under exceptional circumstances. As I said, the bloodlines are too close, especially when it comes to smaller packs such as the Marins, or even the O'Connors."

"Which is a problem the witch families share."

It was also why half-breed witches were supposed to be registered. It might be rare for such children to hold any true witch powers, but if they did, then it could add fresh blood into the older lines.

He nodded. "But I suspect that in *this* case, it wasn't the only factor. There's also a five-year age difference—Garrett's only eighteen—and the fact she's from an omega-class family."

I raised my eyebrows. "I didn't realize wolves were so rank conscious."

"I think it was more a reflection of their dislike for her family than their actual ranking within the pack." He raised an eyebrow. "But aren't the royal witch houses just as picky?"

"Yes, and for many of the same reasons." I wrinkled my nose. "Which is why the rather medieval practice of arranged marriages is still somewhat prevalent, despite it being outlawed."

He blinked. "Seriously?"

"Totally." I ignored the questions I could see in his eyes. "Is Karla's refusal the reason you believed this was a retaliatory attack?"

"And the reason why the council won't allow us to contact the RWA until we get the autopsy results back." He finished his coffee, then crossed his arms on the table—an action that brought him slightly closer, and allowed his warm, somewhat smoky musk scent to tease every breath. "But if Aron's soul *was* stolen, it couldn't have been Larissa."

"That's not exactly true, Ranger." Belle deposited a huge plate of steak and vegetables in front of me, and then sat down on the chair opposite. "A strong enough witch can certainly call and command such spirits, and if Larissa or her parents had enough cash, then the witch world is their oyster."

He frowned. "I wouldn't have thought calling on an evil spirit to destroy another was within the rules of the witch creed."

I picked up my cutlery. "It's not, but not all witches are vetted, and there are those who walk grayer paths and don't really care about the rules or the creed."

"Have either of you sensed that sort of magic being performed in the last few days?"

"No, but that doesn't mean anything given we'd only sense it if the spell was being cast nearby." I tucked into my meal. "And I would have told you if we had, Aiden."

It was a rebuke, even if gently said, and he smiled somewhat ruefully. "I know, but the question nevertheless had to be asked."

"Have you notified the RWA about the kill?" Belle asked.

"No. As I said, the council wants to wait until the autopsy results come back."

"Because they don't want any more damn witches on

the reservation?" I couldn't help the tartness in my tone as I echoed Ciara's words.

"In part." He grimaced. "But it's more that they don't want to be seen acting hastily."

"I hardly think warning the RWA you might have a soul eater on the reservation is *hasty*," Belle retorted. "It's more a precautionary measure, given we're not equipped to deal with something like this."

"And no one's expecting you to. In fact, while I'd appreciate your advice, I'd really prefer it if you keep your noses out of the physical hunt for whoever—whatever—is behind this murder."

"Consider our noses out." Belle picked up his empty plate and rose. "Just don't blame us if things go to hell in a handbasket."

Aiden's eyebrows rose as she walked away. "She doesn't look or sound happy."

"It's hard to be either when your spirit guides keep emphasizing just how dangerous this thing is." I mixed some veggies into the mashed potatoes and then scooped up a forkful. "Especially when this thing appears able to hide from *them*."

He scrubbed a hand across his chin. "Look, I'm not doubting you, but—"

"But you're nevertheless finding it hard to believe in spirits, let alone soul eaters." I shrugged. "I get it. But I still think it's a fool's move to wait. You should at least contact the RWA, explain the situation, and ask for their advice."

"If Ciara hasn't got an answer in twenty-four hours, I will." He paused. "Can I ask why you were out in the gardens at that time of night?"

"Because the ringing of a church bell woke me up,

and then my instincts kicked in and discovered evil." I met his gaze evenly. "Trust me, I'd rather have been partying or otherwise enjoying myself than following that thing's foul trail and finding a body at the end of it."

"I can imagine." He paused again. "Can I also ask if you've changed your mind about going out with me?"

"No." I couldn't keep the surprise out of my voice. "But I thought *you* might have."

The smile that teased his lips was decidedly sexy. "And why would you think *that* when I've been in this café nearly every single day since you got out of the hospital?"

"Well, we do have the most amazing brownies that you seem to have developed a strong addiction to."

His smile became full-blown, and it swept his features from ordinary to extraordinary in a heartbeat. "The brownies, as amazing as they are, do not hold half the appeal of a certain crimson-haired witch."

"Ah," I said, with a silly grin. "Good. But why would you think I'd changed my mind about our date?"

"Because in the many weeks that I've been coming here, you made no mention of it."

Told you, Belle said. *He was waiting for you to make the next move. He's a patient man, this wolf of yours.*

I glanced up with a smile of thanks as Penny, our waitress, deposited a pot of tea and a cup in front of me. Like most of the items in the café, we'd salvaged them from various secondhand stores, and they all had a history and a presence the sensitive could feel. While most people wouldn't believe something as simple as a cup could make any sort of difference to a person's mood, I knew from experience the wrong choice could swiftly change a situation from good to bad. In this particular case, however, Belle's cup of choice was a Christmas one decorated with mistletoe—a not-so-subtle hint to the ranger that he should just get on with kissing me.

I poured my tea and then said, "That's because I was waiting for you to say something."

"Why? I took the initial step. You're supposed to take the next one."

I grinned. "Except I'm an old-fashioned type of girl."

"Meaning a little pursuit never goes astray?"

"Indeed. A girl likes to be sure there is true interest, especially when the man in question has an acknowledged hate of witches."

"One that seems to have dissipated rather quickly since your arrival on the reservation." He caught my hand in his, raised it to his lips, and kissed it. It was little more than a tease—a brief brush of lips across my palm—and yet it promised so much. He almost immediately released me, but the heat of it lingered.

"Well then," he said, "let the hunt begin."

I licked my lips—an action his gaze followed rather avidly—and said, "When?"

"Tonight? I'm feeling the desire to make up for wasted time."

A desire I could *totally* get behind. "What time?"

"I'm rostered on until eight, so around nine? There's a lovely bar in—" He hesitated, his gaze moving past me. "Can I ask why Belle is currently grinning like a Cheshire cat?"

"Because," I said, without even looking at her, "she was saying only last night that men sometimes needed to be clubbed over the head with the obvious. I think she's feeling vindicated."

"Ah." His watch beeped, and he glanced down at it. "I've got a meeting I have to get to. Will you be able to come to the station sometime this afternoon and make an official statement?"

"I can once we close here."

"Thanks. Tala will be around to take it if I'm not there."

Tala was from the Sinclair pack, and his second-in-command. She was also a woman unafraid of being forthright with an opinion, and one I suspected you wouldn't want to be on the wrong side of.

But then, that could be said of most werewolves.

Not to mention quite a few witches, Belle said. *You and I just happen to be extraordinary exceptions.*

My parents might disagree with that.

Belle didn't comment, but then, it was hard to be snarky against an undeniable truth—and one that Belle had, in many ways, paid a deeper price for than me. After all, she'd had to drop all contact with her own family when we'd run from mine. She hadn't talked to or seen her mom and her five siblings in over twelve years now, and I knew that hurt her, even if she never said anything.

I picked up the teapot and poured the hot liquid into my cup. Orange teased the air, a scent designed to arouse and attract—Belle was still playing games. Aiden's nostrils flared, but there was no immediate indication the warm rich aroma had any effect.

Which wasn't surprising when werewolves were generally very good at keeping their emotions in check.

Only in certain situations, Belle said. *You just haven't found this one's right situation.*

I restrained my grin, and watched as he rose.

"I'll see you tonight, then." He hesitated, as if he wanted to say something else, then simply nodded and walked away.

My gaze followed him; like most wolves, he moved with the lithe grace of a predator. Unlike most, his shoulders were nicely wide, and his arms had just the right amount of muscle. My gaze slipped down his spine... and he did look particularly fine in a pair of jeans.

They all do, came Belle's comment. *You just happen to be hooked on this one's pheromones more than the others.*

That is an undeniable truth.

I finished my meal and cup of tea, then got up and dumped the dishes in the kitchen for Frank—our dish hand—to wash. For the next couple of hours, I helped Belle and Penny in the café and tried to ignore my gathering excitement over the evening's possibilities.

Once we'd finished cleaning up and everyone else had gone home, Belle said, "You'd better go make that statement. I'll head upstairs and do some research."

Though I hadn't thought much about the soul eater since Aiden had left, uneasiness stirred once again—and I wasn't entirely sure whether it was intuition or simply fear. I really didn't want to be dealing with this thing, and yet I couldn't escape the notion that we would be.

"I don't suppose the spirits have been able to come up with anything useful since last night?"

"Only that this thing has not finished." She paused, her gaze remote as she listened to her guides. "They said they're keeping an eye out for any unusual activity, but they're not sensing anything as yet."

"Would they normally sense it?"

"Depending on the spirit involved, yes. But there are many who can not only hide their form, but also their presence."

"Last night suggests we're dealing with one of those."

"They tend to agree."

"Then I'll keep my fingers crossed it doesn't take a second victim tonight." I grabbed my keys. "I won't be long."

I locked the door behind me and then headed right. The ranger station was located near the corner of Hargraves and Templeton Streets, and was one of those grand old colonial buildings that spoke of majesty and money—the total opposite of what you'd expect of a ranger or police station.

I went through the rather ornate wooden door and into the main reception area. Maggie, the dark-haired receptionist and ranger in training, glanced up as I entered. Her expression was polite, which was something of an improvement from the last time I'd talked to her.

"Hello, Ms. Grace," she said. "How may I help you?"

"I've come to make my statement on last night's events."

"Ah yes, Aiden mentioned you might be here. I'll go get Tala."

I leaned on the counter and briefly wondered if Aiden's meeting had anything to do with wherever he was last night. Instinct suggested it was, but that didn't mean it was right.

Or that I had the right to ponder such things.

I frowned and looked around. As had been the case the last time I'd come here, there was no one else in the station's main room, and the half dozen desks and multiple filing units didn't go anywhere near to filling the huge space. A large whiteboard dominated one wall, and beside it was a smaller one on which there was a roster with seven names—the total number of rangers on the reservation. Aiden was one of four on patrol duties, and one had the day off.

After a few moments, Maggie returned. Behind her was a woman with silver-shot, black hair, and skin that was the same rich ebony as Belle's.

"Maggie, could you please buzz Ms. Grace in?"

The younger woman did so, and Tala led me across to her desk in the corner of the room. Unlike some of the other desks, hers was incredibly neat. She sat down, opened up her laptop, and then glanced at me. "Right, just tell me everything that happened last night. No detail is too small."

My statement was recorded and then printed. Once I'd checked and signed it, Tala slipped it into a folder, and then said, "Do you honestly believe we're dealing with a soul eater?"

"Yes. And I think delaying calling in the RWA is a bad move."

"Off the record, I tend to agree, but we are bound by the council's ruling."

There was an edge in her voice that had my eyebrows rising. "Did you know the victim?"

"We all knew the victim. He was, after all, the son of a pack alpha." She rose. "Thank you for coming in so promptly. And if those psychic talents of yours happen to—"

"The talents you don't believe in?" I cut in mildly.

"The same," she replied, without even the hint of a wry smile. "If they do happen to send you on another midnight chase, it might be wise to call one of us in on the action beforehand."

"Why? Bullets and teeth don't work against spirits."

"No, but having a ranger present to witness events means we have a greater chance of motivating the council into immediate action."

Which again suggested they mightn't ask for help if Ciara's report came back inconclusive. "I'm actually hoping not to be visited by any more premonitions, but I will call if I am."

"Good. Thanks."

I was let out of the office area, but as I trotted down the steps and swung right, an odd sense of being watched stirred.

I paused and looked around, but couldn't see anyone who appeared to be taking undue notice of me. I frowned and kept walking, but the sensation grew rather than eased. I flexed my fingers, trying to ease both the gathering tension and the urge to prepare another repelling spell.

Then, from out of the vague shadows that clustered around a small lane dividing an art supply shop from the nearby real estate agency, stepped a man.

A man who had pale skin, pale hair, and eyes that were a weird milky white. He wasn't human and he wasn't a werewolf. He was something else altogether.

Something that was—according to the books I'd been reading since our paths had crossed with not one vampire, but two—commonly known as either a thrall or a drudge. Basically, they were human ghouls—neither fully one nor the other—who both protected and ran errands for their masters during the daylight hours.

This particular thrall belonged to Maelle Defour, the vampire who owned the recently opened Émigré nightclub. And while the council was fully aware of her presence here in the reservation, Aiden and his rangers were *not*.

I stopped and eyed him warily. "Can I help you?"

"Yes." His voice was cool, polite. "My mistress wishes to see you."

And I *so* did not want to see her. Still, I suspected it would not be wise to refuse. "I can come around tomorrow, if she—"

"Tomorrow is not soon enough," he cut in politely. "She wishes to see you immediately."

"I'm afraid I—"

"And I'm afraid it would not be wise to delay," he cut in again. "She is a very old vampire, and well used to getting what she wishes."

One way or another.

He didn't actually say that, but it nevertheless hovered in the air between us.

He smiled and stepped to one side. "Please," he added, with a wave toward the lane.

I hesitated, but it seemed I had little other choice but to do as he—and Maelle—wished if I wanted to remain on pleasant terms with the local vampire.

I turned and headed down the lane. And hoped like hell whatever it was didn't take too long, given I finally had a date to get ready for.

But even as that thought crossed my mind, another rather scary one rose.

Maelle wasn't only a very old vampire, but one who'd admitted to dabbling in the darker arts.

What if *she* was the reason for the soul eater being on this reservation?

CHAPTER
three

I stopped so abruptly that the silent man-ghoul had to do a quick sidestep to avoid running into me.

"Tell me one thing before I go any further." I clenched my fingers against the need to start a truth spell. "Is your mistress in *any* way involved with dark magic?"

He raised an eyebrow. "Given she's my mistress, I'd hardly answer in the affirmative if she was."

"I want a guarantee that she's not. Otherwise, I'll not step one foot inside her nightclub."

"That would be unfortunate indeed, given how often your friend is there of late."

While it was no surprise she knew about Belle dating Zak Marin, who worked as a bartender at her nightclub, it was nevertheless an ominous statement—one that suggested Maelle knew enough about us to understand a threat to Belle would be far more effective than one directed at me.

"Answer me truthfully, or I go no further." I hesitated. "And please believe that I will know a truth from a lie."

Which wasn't exactly correct given I hadn't raised such a spell, but I was hoping he wouldn't know that.

He considered me for a moment, and then said, "Why is this information so important?"

"Because a soul eater hunts within this reservation, and there's a theory it's here under the invitation of a dark practitioner."

"Ah." His expression became oddly amused. I had a vague suspicion it wasn't his, but rather Maelle's. "As my mistress has already mentioned, she *has* dabbled in the darker arts, but she is in no way capable of creating a spell that could call or command such a spirit."

Which didn't mean she wasn't capable of magic, and that was yet more unsettling news.

"But she nevertheless guarantees she is not in any way connected to whatever or whoever is responsible for the dark spirit being here," he continued. "May we move on now?"

I swung around and walked on. While I normally wouldn't trust a vampire's word, Maelle was of the *Defour* line, which, if she were to be believed—and the council certainly did—meant that once she'd given her word, she was incapable of breaking it. The binding was one of magic, a curse that had been given long ago by a Marlowe witch—a fact that initially had me wondering if she'd had some inclination of my true identity, however unlikely that might be.

A black sedan waited at the end of the lane. As we approached, a gray-clad driver got out and opened the rear door. I climbed in. Émigré was situated on Richards Road, which was within walking distance, but it would have far taken longer to get there than I really wanted to waste right now.

The driver closed the door once we were both inside and, within moments, we were underway. Maelle's servant didn't move; he barely even breathed. He simply stared directly ahead, his expression devoid of life or animation.

"Tell me," I said, more to break my gathering tension rather than from any real need to know. "Do you have a name?"

He blinked and then glanced at me. "Roger."

"Really?"

His eyebrows rose. "Why are you surprised?"

"I guess I was expecting something more... exotic."

"Roger *was* exotic in my time."

"Oh."

You need to get with the times, Lizzie. Renfield is so yesterday.

It's not like I've had much to do with thralls before now. I paused, watching uneasily as the animation left Roger's face again. *Has your gran's book on vampires anything about them?*

Haven't checked, but I will. Are you okay? Do you want me to wander over to Émigré, just in case you need help?

I hesitated. *She said she's not involved with the spirit, and she's guaranteed the council not to take blood from the unwilling, so I think I'll be relatively safe.*

It still might be wise to have a spell or two ready to use, just in case.

Given her admitted knowledge of the darker arts, that's probably not a good idea. There's the risk of her sensing it and getting annoyed. And I very much suspected it would not be wise to get on the wrong side of Maelle Defour.

Better to be on the wrong side than to be dead.

I don't think she wants me dead, Belle.

Well good, because seeking revenge isn't on my to-do list today.

I grinned, but it quickly faded as the car came to a stop and the driver opened my door. I climbed out and looked up at the building. In the waning light of the afternoon, it looked almost otherworldly, especially against the very ordinary buildings on either side. The entire thing had been painted matte black—even the windows—and the walls were decorated with weird, almost alien-looking biomechanical forms. It looked like something that belonged in a science fiction film rather than out here in the middle of the Victorian countryside.

"This way, please."

Roger motioned me toward the main entrance, which had been styled into an air lock. He unlocked the door and then ushered me inside. The second set of doors that led into the main area were open, so I continued on.

The room beyond was huge, and had been painted battleship gray rather than black. The arched ceiling was adorned with more of those biomechanical and alien forms, but in the cold light of day, this vast room held none of the heat, energy, or intrigue that it did at night. In fact, it looked and felt rather soulless. Which, considering a vampire owned the place, was rather apt.

Of course, the whole "did vamps possess souls" debate was still very much ongoing. Not even the books we'd gotten from Belle's gran could answer *that* particular question.

I paused at the top of the steps that led down to the lower-tier dance floor. It was empty, which was no surprise given the place didn't open its doors until the sun had begun to set, and at this time of year that was generally around eight. But there was also no one behind the bar that dominated half of the upper area, nor was there anyone replacing the tea candles in the grotesquely shaped lanterns that adorned the table in every seating pod, or otherwise getting the area prepared for use by guests.

Which was decidedly odd—in a place this big, I would have thought it'd be safer to allow more time to prepare rather than less.

My gaze rose to the ceiling. Maelle had built a dark glass and metal room into the point where all the arches met, and though it was obvious right now, at night it disappeared into the darkness and was all but invisible. Only the occasional glimmer of a strobe flickering across its surface gave its position away, and I doubted many of those who frequented this place would have noticed. The only reason I'd done so was thanks to the sensation of being watched.

Which once again I *was*. Maelle made no acknowledgment of my presence, however, and after a second or two, disappeared into the darkness behind the glass.

"Would you care for a drink, Ms. Grace?" Roger moved past me and walked across to the bar—a vast twisted metal and glass construction. "My mistress will be down momentarily."

"I wouldn't mind a sparkling water." I perched on the nearest barstool—which, following the theme of the entire place, was shaped like an alien's head—and watched him move across to get my drink. "Where are all the staff? I would have thought they'd be here by now to get things ready for opening."

He placed the opened bottle and a glass down in front of me. "Normally that would be true, but we had to delay opening this evening."

I nodded my thanks and then said, "And has this delay anything to do with my reason for being here?"

"Indeed it has," a soft and slightly accented voice said. "And I do appreciate your promptness in answering my request to see you."

I swung around and watched Maelle approach. She was once again wearing what looked like an eighteenth-century riding gown, although this time it was dark green rather than brown. Her rich chestnut hair had been plaited and curled around the top of her head, and under the bar's cool lighting rather looked like a crown. Her skin was porcelain perfect, and gave no hint of her age. But she was old.

Very old.

"Let's be honest here," I said, my tone as neutral as I could manage. "It wasn't an invitation. It was more a demand."

A small smile touched her too-perfect lips. "That is very true, but I do have my reasons and they are quite urgent."

"Something I gathered from your thrall, and the only reason I am here." I hesitated, and then added bluntly, "And I do *not* appreciate the threat against my friend. You were the one who said you'd prefer a relationship based on respect rather than one mired in animosity and distrust. Threats are more likely to garner the latter, Maelle."

"Another truth, and I do apologize for falling into habits of old."

She sat gracefully on the stool beside mine, a far too close position that had my "other" senses flaring to life.

Maelle Defour was *hungry*.

Dangerously hungry.

My pulse rate jumped into overdrive, which was very unwise given the waves of hunger washing from the other woman. But it wasn't like I could control either my pulse or the fear that accompanied that jump.

"What do you wish of me, Maelle?"

Her gaze met mine, and though no heat flared in the pale depths of her eyes, I knew she was aware of my accelerated heart rate.

Aware, and wanting.

She smiled. It was a cool and very controlled motion that held nothing in the way of warmth. "I wish you to find someone for me."

"Who? A friend? Or another servant?"

Did she—or any other vampire, for that matter—even have friends? Everything I'd been told about them suggested they were loners—a necessity, given they were generally an unwanted addition to any community—and Maelle herself, for all her politeness, wasn't the warm and friendly type.

"She would perhaps consider herself a friend."

"But you do not?"

"No. She is simply an attendant—one who caters to my physical and nutritional needs."

It took a moment for that to sink in, and my heart rate unwisely shifted up another gear. "I thought that was the role of a thrall?"

Roger laughed and, just for a moment, a glimmer of amusement broke the ice in Maelle's eyes. "No—not when it comes to the latter, at any rate. Not unless it was an absolute emergency, and even then, it would have unfortunate consequences."

I glanced at him. "Like what?"

"Death," he stated, his expression neutral, "would be

a welcome option if I was so used."

"And also very unlikely in such a case," Maelle added. "But we are not here to discuss that, but rather Marlinda's disappearance."

Leaving me wondering what fate could be far worse than death. "Are you sure she *has* disappeared? She's not homesick or something?"

"No. When she did not show at her assigned feeding time last night, I sent Roger around to check her apartment. She wasn't there."

I frowned. "Is it possible she simply decided she no longer wished to be an attendant?"

Just for an instant, something very old—and very inhuman—flashed in her eyes. It was all I could do remain still and not edge away. Or, better yet, run.

She's a vamp, Belle said. *They're supernaturally fast. She'd be on you before you took two steps.*

Thanks for that cheery reminder. Needed it.

It is the task of every good familiar to anticipate the needs of their witch, she said cheerfully. *I'm hovering nearby if you need help.*

Good. I felt safer, even if that feeling was nothing more than an illusion.

"No," Maelle said softly. "It is not."

For one confused moment, it almost seemed as if she was answering my reply to Belle rather than the question I'd asked her.

I hesitated, and then very carefully said, "Please don't take offense, but why are you so sure?"

"Because the nature of being an attendant gives rise to a connection. If she was unhappy—or in any way contemplating leaving this life—I would have known."

Did her use of the term "this life" simply mean being

an attendant, or did it in fact mean exactly what it sounded like—that death awaited anyone who did decide to leave?

"What sort of car does she drive? I could ask the rangers to run a check—"

"I would prefer it if the rangers are not involved," she cut in. "And she currently has use of a Mercedes AMG Sports car."

Foreboding stirred. "A white one? With a black interior?"

Maelle's gaze narrowed. "Yes. You've seen it?"

"Kind of." I took a long drink of the fizzy water, but it didn't really ease the dryness in my throat. "I caught glimpses of a car fitting that description when I was doing a reading last night."

"Who were you doing the reading on?"

"Aron Marin." I hesitated, but the grapevine would have undoubtedly latched on to the news by now, and it would be common knowledge soon enough. "He was murdered last night."

She absorbed this with little emotion. "Marlinda is not responsible. It is not in her nature to kill."

And yet she was consorting with a vampire, and that to me suggested a darker nature. Which might be doing Marlinda an injustice, but still…. "Do you know if she has a red sparkly dress in her wardrobe?"

"Undoubtedly. It is this season's fashion accessory. But she did not make this kill. I guarantee you that."

Maelle could guarantee however much she liked, but I seriously doubted it was a simple coincidence that Marlinda owned a car and probably a dress similar to what I'd seen in Aron's thoughts.

"And how is it," she continued, "that you did a reading on Aron if he was murdered last night?"

"Because memory doesn't die as soon as flesh." I paused. "Are you sure you want me to find Marlinda given the possibility—however remote you think it might be—that she was with him last night?"

"I'm sure. She was a favorite of mine."

Suggesting Maelle had other attendants to call on—but if that were the case, why was she so hungry?

"Well, I'll need something of hers—"

"Roger can take you to her apartment. I cannot leave this place until the sun sets, so he will be my eyes and ears on this quest."

And wouldn't *that* be fun? But I didn't say anything, and simply nodded in agreement.

"If you go there immediately—"

I glanced at my watch. "I do actually have a later appointment—"

She raised an immaculately groomed eyebrow. "Then you had best hurry along, hadn't you?"

I opened my mouth to protest and then shut it again. While I doubted there'd ever be a good time to antagonize her, doing so when her hunger was so tangible probably wasn't the wisest move. She might have promised the council not to dine on the unwilling, but history was littered with the carcasses of broken promises.

"Fine." I finished my drink and rose. "But please don't expect miracles. Psychometry is not always reliable—"

"All I ask is that you try."

I nodded and glanced at Roger. He immediately said, "This way please, Ms. Grace."

I followed him from the building, but as we hit the sunlight, my legs went to water and it took a whole lot of determination to keep upright. I hadn't really realized how tense I'd been until I was actually beyond Maelle's reach.

Although in reality, I wasn't. Not when Roger remained by my side.

As the driver climbed out of the black car and moved around to open the rear passenger door, I casually glanced over my shoulder. Though there were a number of people moving up and down the street, I couldn't immediately see Belle. But I knew she was down there—I could feel the caress of her magic.

I'm using a glamour. Didn't want to alert our vamp or her people that I was near.

Your skills are definitely improving—I didn't even sense you creating it.

That's because you were concentrating on not getting bitten or otherwise antagonizing our bloodsucker. Do you want me to keep close? I can go get the car and follow from a distance.

I really don't think it's necessary at this point. I'll see you at home.

No probs.

I climbed into the car. The driver closed the door behind the two of us, reclaimed his seat, and drove out of the parking spot. He seemed to know where we were going without being told, which made me wonder if he was another thrall, or simply in telepathic contact with either Roger or Maelle.

It turned out that Marlinda lived on Forest Street, in a building that had obviously started out life as a pub. While there were still retail premises at the ground level, the first floor had been converted into a number of apartments. Hers was at the front of the building, overlooking the roundabout and the park opposite.

Roger opened the door and then waved me inside. The apartment was far more spacious than the one above our café, with a full-size kitchen and a large open living room. There were two doors leading off this—one was a bathroom and the other a bedroom.

I headed across the white carpet—which was a rather odd color choice for someone who was a vampire's meal ticket—and went into her bedroom. If I wanted to find Marlinda, then I needed to find something she wore often enough to hold some hint of her presence.

The bedroom was again white, but the floral cushions adorning the bed provided much-needed splashes of vibrant color, as did the deep blue curtains. The room itself was extraordinarily neat; even the jewelry on the dressing table was arranged in precise lines rather than being thrown into a somewhat jumbled pile—my usual habit when undressing.

I raised a hand and skimmed it over the various chains, watches, and earrings on the dresser, but there was nothing that even remotely stirred my psychic senses. I frowned and swung around, pensively studying the rest of the room. There was no jewelry on either bedside table, and she certainly didn't look the type to place anything inside her pillowcases, which had been the teenager's hiding place of choice. My gaze stalled on the wardrobe, and instinct stirred. I walked across and slid one of the doors aside. There, on the floor, was a small safe.

I glanced at Roger. "I don't suppose you or your mistress know the code?"

His gaze went inwards for a moment, and then he said, "Five-three-nine-one."

I bent, tapped in the code, and the door opened. Inside was an assortment of shiny boxes and silken pouches, the contents of which were no doubt worth more than our entire damn building.

I reached into the safe and skimmed them. At the very back, I got a response. I pulled the blue silk wrap free, and then walked over to the bed to unroll it. Inside were four diamond necklaces; I touched each one, but it wasn't until I got to the last—and smallest—that I had a response.

But it was a cold, somewhat murky sensation that had trepidation stirring anew.

"You found something?" Roger asked.

"I found something that's responding to my psychic senses," I replied. "Whether it will lead to anything is another matter entirely."

I plucked the necklace free, then rolled up the rest and placed them back into the safe. Once it was locked, I took a deep breath, and then closed my fingers around the pendant and *reached*.

The response remained muted—vague—but there was at least enough of a connection to follow.

"This way." I headed out of the apartment.

Roger locked the door and then followed me down the stairs, his steps so light they were barely audible.

"Do you wish to take the car?" he said, once we were again outside.

I hesitated. Given the sensations coming from the pendant, Marlinda was either some distance away, or this necklace simply hadn't been worn enough to maintain a strong connection. If it was the latter, then Maelle was out of luck. But if it was simply a faint connection, then I risked trudging about all night in an effort to pin down her location—and that wasn't something I wanted. Not when I had better things to do.

"Car," I said. "But we may have to go slow."

He nodded and motioned me toward the vehicle.

Once we were inside, I said, "Continue up Forest Street until I say otherwise."

The driver nodded, slipped the car into gear, and carefully pulled away from the curb. We passed a couple of streets and a small reserve before the pendant again pulsed against my hand. "Right at the next street."

"Gingell," Roger said, more for his mistress's sake than mine, I suspected.

We swept around the park, and the road straightened, following the rail line up toward Walker Street and the botanical gardens.

The foreboding that had stirred earlier found new life, although it wasn't really a surprise that I was being drawn back to the park.

"Stop," I said, and climbed out the minute we had.

It was late afternoon and the sun shone brightly. Nothing tainted the air other than the scent of eucalyptus, and the merry sound of children playing intermingled with the constant flow of traffic—sounds that spoke of life and happiness.

But that's not what we were about to find.

I took a deep breath, released it slowly, and then walked on. Into the park, past the grove of trees, around the edge of the lake, and then beyond the rotunda.

It was only at the point where I'd heard the loud splash and seen the ripples spreading out across the still, dark water that I stopped.

"Have you lost the trail?" Roger immediately asked.

"No."

"Then why do we stop?"

"Because the trail leads into the water."

"Ah." He contemplated the lake for a moment. "At what point of the shoreline does your talent suggest you enter?"

My gaze shot to him. "I'm not entering that lake at *any* point."

"Nor did I mean to suggest that," he said. "Show me where."

The sensations emanating from the pendant were becoming fainter, the diamond cooler, despite the heat of my grip. I pressed the stone deeper into my palm, trying to eke out an exact location. After a moment, I walked to the bank's edge and said, "Right here."

He stopped beside me, his gaze sweeping the dark, still water. "How deep is this lake?"

"I have no idea. Nor do I have any idea whether this is merely a false lead. It's entirely possible that Marlinda simply tossed something of hers into the lake."

"And there is no way to uncover if that might be the case?"

"No. As I said, psychometry isn't always reliable."

He sighed and then stripped off his shoes and socks, and rolled up his pants. His legs were thin, bony, and white. Very white. Obviously, his mistress wasn't the only one who avoided sun exposure.

He waded carefully into the water. Mud stirred, blooming around his ankles and concealing the glow of his feet. He inched farther in, carefully sweeping the lake's bottom with each foot before taking the next step. The water slowly climbed past his ankles and up his calves. I wondered how far he'd be willing to go—and if he even had a choice in the matter.

He slowly moved deeper; the bloom of mud got thicker, and every step sent bigger waves rolling away.

One of those waves very briefly revealed a flash of red.

"Did you see that?" I asked.

"I did." His voice was cool, without emotion. "It might not be who we seek though."

I had no idea who that comment was aimed at—his mistress or me.

It didn't really matter either way.

He took two more steps, and then stopped. "My toes have just touched something."

I crossed my arms against the chill racing across my skin. "It might be wise to call the rangers before we do anything further."

"No. Not until we are sure what it is we've found. It's pointless getting involved with an investigation if we have found nothing more than a discarded dress."

While that flash of red had undoubtedly been a dress, we both knew what else was down there—Marlinda's body.

And the part of me that was inclined to guilt certainly didn't want to know if I might have been able to save her life last night if I'd only done a more thorough investigation of that splash.

He reached a hand down into the water and, after a second or two, grunted and tugged something upright.

That something was a red dress.

A red sparkly dress.

Inside of it was a woman.

CHAPTER
four

I briefly closed my eyes and swore internally. This wasn't how I'd wanted the hunt to end.

"Is that Marlinda?" I asked softly.

"Yes." Roger's tone was without inflection, but weirdly echoed Maelle's. "I think it best you ring the rangers now. But this evil will be avenged."

"We have no real idea what happened here, Maelle. I wouldn't be making hasty threats—"

"There is nothing hasty about the threat," he said, the tone still his mistress's. "Whatever help you need to track down the thing responsible for this murder, I will give."

"Except I'm *not* tracking it. If we're dealing with a soul eater, the RWA will be called in. I'm not a strong enough witch to even contemplate such an action."

"That is a statement I seriously doubt, but nevertheless, my offer stands."

"Then make it to the rangers and the RWA."

"I do not wish to deal with the rangers more than necessary. Nor do I believe that you will be allowed to stand apart in this fight. Like it or not, you are this reservation's witch, and the task will fall on your shoulders."

"This reservation deserves better than an underpowered witch."

"This reservation seems to think otherwise, if the wild magic is anything to go by."

Unease stirred. "What do you know about the wild magic?"

"Only that it exists here, and seems to have an unusual... sentience."

That it did... and I had some theories as to why that might be the case, especially given there was a distinctly feminine feel to that awareness. But I'd been putting off confirming or denying those theories, simply because it meant asking Aiden to take me to the place where his sister had been murdered—and I really hadn't wanted to dredge up those painful memories. Not when his aura still ran with the heavy weight of his sorrow.

"*That* magic seems intent on protecting this reservation," I commented. "I hope you don't plan to use it, as you might not like the resulting push back."

"My mistress holds no designs on the magic," Roger said, his tone his own and his expression amused. "She certainly has no need of its power."

Because she had enough of her own? That was a somewhat scary thought, and one I hoped wasn't true.

I dug out my phone and called Aiden. He answered on the second ring. "Every time you call me out of the blue like this, you've found a body. Please don't tell me that's the case again."

"Then I won't tell you."

He swore softly. "Where?"

"In the lake, near the rotunda."

He was silent for a moment, and then said, "Is there a connection to last night's murder?"

"Yes."

"I'll call the crew and be there in a few minutes." He paused. "Please wait this time."

"I will."

I hung up. Roger no longer held the small section of red dress, and Marlinda's body had sunk back underneath the water.

"What are you planning to do?" I asked. "Stay or go?"

"Given there are plenty of people who have seen me accompany you here, it would seem suspicious if I now left." He walked out of the lake but didn't bother putting his shoes or socks back on. "Cooperation with the ranger will also ensure easier access to information."

I wasn't entirely sure about that, given the rangers tended to play their cards—and information—very close to their chests, but I was more than happy to let him and Maelle find that out for themselves.

I rubbed my arms and watched the ripples slowly die away. Roger was once again statue-like, and it was rather unnerving. It was almost as if he shut himself down to conserve energy.

It took less than ten minutes for Aiden to arrive. With him was Bryon, a ranger I'd only met once and had never been officially introduced to. He was wearing a wetsuit under his jacket, and was carrying scuba gear.

Aiden stopped beside me, one arm lightly brushing mine as he offered me a take-out coffee cup with the other. "Figured you might need this. Who's your friend?"

"Roger Smith," he said, before I could. "My employer—Maelle Defour—asked for Ms. Grace's assistance in finding a friend who was missing. This is not the result we'd wished."

"I can imagine." Aiden's voice was neutral. "I gather you went in?"

"Indeed. It was the way to uncover what, exactly, we might have found."

"How far in from the bank did you discover the body?"

"About twenty feet."

Aiden grunted and glanced at the other ranger. "Byron, you want to get ready?"

As the man obeyed, I said, "Sorry about messing up our plans like this."

He glanced at me, his expression a mix of amusement and frustration. "As dates go, this wasn't exactly what I had in mind."

"Nor I. But you can always drop by the café once this has been wrapped up."

"I've no idea how long we might be here—it could be late, as the lake will have to be swept."

I shrugged. "It would appear I've nothing else better to do tonight."

"Good." Amusement creased the corners of his eyes. "I'd hate to think I could be so easily replaced."

"And I'd hate you to think I've nothing better to do than wait around for you," I mused. "Perhaps I *should* go out."

He grinned. "Says the woman who waited several weeks for me to ask her out again."

"Smugness is not an attractive trait in a man."

"It's not smugness. More a confidence in a mutual attraction." His amusement died as Bryon moved toward the water. "I'll have to ask the two of you to move back to the rotunda. Once Jaz has taped off the immediate area, she'll take your statements."

I hadn't even noticed the other ranger's arrival. As Roger and I made our way back to the rotunda, I saw the brown-haired woman reeling out the blue-and-white tape. I ducked under it and then climbed the step and sat on the bench with my back to the lake, and sipped my coffee. I didn't need to witness Marlinda's body being dragged out of the water—not when I was still struggling with nightmares after witnessing a zombie's head being blown apart.

Roger, it seemed, *did* need to watch events unfold. Or maybe Maelle did. Maybe she simply wasn't willing to accept the truth without seeing it with her own eyes. Or, rather, Roger's.

Once the area was secure, Jaz—who was tall and slender, with lightly tanned skin that suggested she wasn't from one of this reservation's packs—stepped into the rotunda and took our statements. With that done, we were released.

"My mistress wishes to thank you for your assistance tonight," Roger said, as we walked back to his car. "And also wishes to reassert her offer of help should you need it."

"I won't, because I'm hoping this is the end of it, but thanks."

"There is no ending, not until the person responsible for this murder is caught," he replied.

"Not to belabor the point, but *that* is a task for the rangers and the RWA, not me."

"If you truly believe that you will not be called into this hunt, then you are a fool." His tone once again echoed his mistress's. "And we both know neither is the case."

I didn't say anything, even though I very much suspected she was right. I drained the last of the coffee, then dumped the cup into the nearby bin. Roger and his driver returned me to the café, and Belle had a large glass of wine waiting for me as I stepped through the door.

"Thought you might need to drown your disappointment," she said.

I took a drink and then said, rather glumly, "It'll take more than one glass to do that."

"Which is why I have left the bottle uncorked and waiting on the table."

"You think of everything." I moved across the room and sat down. "How did the research go?"

She wrinkled her nose as she claimed the chair opposite. "I found a couple of mentions of soul eaters in one of her books, but there's nothing of a specific nature. I'll dig some of her older books out of storage. I did uncover some interesting facts about your man ghoul, though."

I raised my eyebrows. "Like what?"

"Like the fact they don't share the blood of their masters, but rather their energy."

"So they're some sort of zombie?"

"No, because they're alive, and zombies are dead." She took a sip of her wine. "From what Gran noted, a thrall is created in a magic-based ceremony that involves the swearing of allegiance and consuming a bloody piece of the vampire's flesh."

A shudder ran through me at the thought. "Why flesh and not blood?"

"Because eating the flesh, when combined with magic, makes master and thrall one. He's given eternal life in return for eternal service."

"Which is not something I'd imagine most sane people would ever contemplate."

She shrugged. "I suppose it depends on who your master is. Maelle seems sane enough—for a vampire, at least."

"Or she's simply putting up a very good front." I leaned back in my chair and swirled the wine around in the glass. "She all but admitted she's capable of quite powerful magic."

Belle frowned. "You don't think she's behind the murder last night, do you?"

"No, if only because the woman who was with Aron last night was one of her feeders, and Maelle's seriously pissed about her now being dead."

"Do you think their deaths are connected?"

"Yes, though I have no idea how. Marlinda obviously *wasn't* a soul eater, given Maelle is alive and well."

"Presuming, of course, vampires do have souls."

"Even if they don't, I suspect Maelle has enough magical nous to sense that Marlinda was no longer present in her flesh."

"Which means the soul eater must have killed Marlinda before it feasted on Aron."

"Aron wouldn't have looked like he'd simply gone to sleep if he'd witnessed his companion being murdered."

"True." Belle finished the remainder of her wine and then topped up both glasses. "More research is required, it seems."

"I might do that while I'm waiting for Aiden to arrive." I paused and glanced over at the clock. "Aren't you meeting with Zak in ten minutes or so?"

"Yes, but we're only going over to his place to watch some movies, so he's getting my regular fabulous self rather than the dolled-up version." Her grin grew. "Of course, my normal self is more than most men can handle."

"Amen to that, sister." I clinked my glass against hers. "So, have you progressed beyond the city pad yet?"

Werewolves, we'd discovered, either had their own place or a place they co-owned with others in order to get around the severe restrictions placed on non-werewolf lovers entering pack compounds.

"No, and I'm unlikely ever to be invited into the inner sanctum, given we're only casual."

"And you're human besides."

"That too." She shrugged. "Their loss, not mine. You want me to bring down some books, or are you going upstairs to wait for Aiden?"

"Given he could be hours, I think I'll head up. Might as well read in comfort."

She nodded and pushed up from the table. "Zak will be here in a sec—can you keep him entertained while I go grab some shoes?"

"Sure."

She'd barely padded up the stairs when the chime above the door rang and Zak stepped inside. He was maybe an inch or so shorter than Belle—who was a towering six foot one—and he had the brown skin, red-tinged brown hair, and deep amber eyes that were common amongst the Marin pack.

"Lizzie," he greeted warmly, stooping to drop a kiss on my cheek. "How come you're sitting here drinking? Weren't you going out with Aiden tonight?"

"I was, but ranger business intervened."

He grabbed a chair, swung it around, and sat astride. "Well, there goes my five quid."

"And what is a comment like that supposed to mean?" I knew what it sounded like, but I was hoping I was wrong.

He grinned. "Didn't you know? There's a betting pool running amongst some locals as to whether you two will actually ever go out on an official date."

"Seriously? Have people got nothing better to do with their time?"

"It *is* a small town, remember. Nothing much ever really happens around here."

Nothing much except a vampire going on a bloody rampage, a teenager being forced from his grave as a zombie, and now a soul eater on the loose.

But I guess it was a good thing the general population didn't know about any of *that*.

"Tonight's events also lost me a fiver," Belle said, as she clattered down the stairs. "Which will teach me not to use insider knowledge to gain an advantage."

"And how come you failed to inform me about this?"

"Because it would have placed undue pressure on you, and what sort of friend would I be if I did that?"

I snorted and took a drink. "It's nice to know my love life—or lack thereof—is the subject of speculation."

"It's more Aiden's love life than yours," Zak said. "He's been something of a loner since his sister's death."

Something I was both pleased and saddened to hear. I pushed up from the chair. "If you do make another bet, I expect a cut of the winnings."

"Only if you give us an inside tip." Zak caught Belle's hand. "Shall we go?"

"As long as we can get a pizza on the way there. I'm starved."

"And not just for pizza, I hope." Zak winked at me. "Catch you later."

"*Much* later," Belle said, as they headed out.

I locked the door behind them, but their mention of pizza had my stomach rumbling, so I headed into the kitchen and cooked myself a meat pie and some chips for dinner before heading upstairs. Once I'd finished, I grabbed one of the old books sitting on the coffee table— one marked *Dark Spirits, volume 2*—and started to read. It was rather scary just how many different types of evil were sitting beyond the folds of the wider world, waiting to be called into action. Scarier still was the fact that—at least with some of them—the call to action didn't actually require magic, but something as simple as a heartfelt wish for revenge.

Was that what we were dealing with here?

Had Larissa done nothing more than desire revenge against Aron's parents?

I hoped not, if only because I hated the thought that such anger and bitterness could bring something like a soul eater to life.

I continued reading, but didn't really find anything concrete about which type of soul eater we were dealing with, or what might kill it.

I gave up at ten thirty and headed over to the kitchenette to make myself a coffee. As the machine began to splutter, my phone pinged. I pulled it out of my pocket and saw it was a message from Aiden.

Waiting outside the door if the offer for coffee still stands, it said.

I grinned, and all but bounced down the stairs.

"Hey," I said, as I opened the door. "How'd things go?"

"As well as you can expect given we've two bodies in as many days." He looked and sounded tired, but that wasn't really so surprising given he wouldn't have had much—if any—sleep last night. "Ciara's doing the autopsy as we speak, but it could take a day or so to get the toxicology results back."

I locked the door and led the way toward the rear stairs. "And Aron's results?"

"His autopsy didn't reveal a cause of death. She's expecting bloods and toxicology back tomorrow."

"Hopefully they'll uncover why he died looking so peaceful, because I really don't want to discover we've got a dark spirit capable of magic or hypnotism on the reservation."

"Personally, I'd rather it not be a soul eater at all. Are we heading up to the inner sanctum?"

"Yes." I flashed him a grin over my shoulder. "It's a rare event, so I hope you feel honored."

"Oh, I do." His voice held a note of amusement. "Although I rather suspect the real reason is the brewing coffee I can smell."

"You could be right." I clattered up the stairs. "Would you like plain black or something more exotic?"

"Plain is fine, the stronger the better, as I've a council meeting to get to."

I glanced over my shoulder again as disappointment slithered into my heart. "Do they often hold late night meetings?"

"No, but they wanted an update on the investigation." His gaze went past me. "This place really *is* small, isn't it?"

"Small but perfectly formed, as the saying goes. Grab

a seat, and I'll bring your coffee over."

He touched my arm, holding me still as he brushed past, and sending a rush that was all desire through my veins. His nostrils flared and a smile tugged at his lips— both indications he'd scented that rush—but he said nothing as he walked over to the sofa. I made our coffees, sliced up some of the Jaffa cake we had sitting in an airtight container for emergency cravings, then picked up the tray and walked over.

"You know," he said, his voice wry as he picked up a piece of cake, "it's just as well a werewolf's metabolic rate runs higher than that of humans, because otherwise, I would have gained several kilos over the last couple of weeks."

"The wolf doesn't have to eat the cake, you know."

"Refusing cake is something no sane man who loves his food would ever do."

"Which confirms the rumor that the best way into a werewolf's good books is via his stomach."

He laughed. "It isn't the *only* way into our good books, but it's a damn fine start." His gaze fell on the pile of books. "Research?"

I nodded and sat down beside him. It was only a two-person sofa, so we were close enough that our thighs touched. It felt intimate even if it really wasn't, and it had me hankering for a whole lot more. "We were curious as to what sort of soul eater we might be dealing with."

"A statement that suggests there's more than one type."

"According to Belle's guides, there is, but so far we've only found vague mentions." I hesitated. "There's something I need to talk to you about."

He raised an eyebrow. "This sounds serious. Have

you done the finances and decided you can't afford to keep giving me free cake?"

"Idiot." I nudged him with my shoulder. "It is serious, though—remember how I said that the source of the wild magic was within the O'Connor compound?"

The amusement faded from his expression. "Yes."

"I need you to take me there. Whether or not you believe a soul eater is behind these recent murders, they've only reinforced our need to protect the wellspring."

He hesitated. "I'd normally have to seek formal permission from the pack elders, but I can circumvent that by saying it relates to our current investigation."

I half smiled. "And here I was expecting an argument."

"I may find it hard to believe that something like wild magic can spring up in the middle of nowhere—"

"It's not always nowhere," I cut in. "It does sometimes happen in city centers, but such events are much rarer. Something to do with all that metal and concrete providing a barrier."

Or so one of my long-ago teachers had once said. Of course, no one was really sure why the wild magic—which was said to develop close to the heart of the earth's outer core—became a collective force in the first place, let alone how or why it then found its way to the surface. But there was no argument about the danger such wellsprings represented if they were not appropriately protected and monitored.

"Fascinating," he said, voice dry. "When do you want to go?"

"Tomorrow morning?"

He hesitated, and then nodded. "I'm on afternoon shift this week, so that works."

"Thank you," I said. "I appreciate you humoring me like this."

"It's not humoring, not really. I did as you suggested, and requisitioned the reports on the High Ridge Massacre. I'd rather not chance that happening here."

The High Ridge Massacre was what happened when a wellspring was too new or left too long without protection. Dark forces had invaded the town and basically wiped out the population in one brutal night. But there'd been warning signs—a gradual increase in crime and murder rates over the previous few months. The cops there had just failed to put two and two together until it was far too late.

"Have you actually mentioned the wellspring to your pack's alpha?"

"Elders, as there's more than one alpha. And yes, I did. Last I heard, they were still arguing about whether or not they needed to call the RWA in to properly protect it."

"I'm surprised the RWA hasn't ridden roughshod over pack sensibilities and just done it anyway."

"A regional association hasn't the power to overturn pack rulings. The order would have to come direct from the state or maybe even federal government."

Which was the perfect opening for the *other* thing I'd been putting off. And yet, part of me still resisted. Sitting here with him so obviously relaxed, and with a good percentage of his aura gleaming orange—a color that not only spoke of high intelligence, vitality, and excitement, but also warm emotions—was nice. Did I really want to risk sending him spinning back into grief by mentioning his sister?

"I can see from your expression something else is troubling you," he said. "Whatever it is, just say it, Liz."

I wrinkled my nose. "I just... I think we also need to drive to that spot where your sister was killed."

His expression closed over, and black once again pulsed through his aura. But it didn't take over, and that suggested he might be finally coming to grips with his grief.

I hoped so, for his sake as much as any relationship he might want in the future. With the weight and depth of his grief, there was little hope of other emotions surviving—which could well explain his lack of emotional attachment over the last year.

Although it didn't really explain the apparent lack of sex. Men generally didn't need emotions to be involved to engage with someone sexually.

"So you really still think Gabe is there?" he asked eventually.

"I honestly don't know what to think." While I did agree that it was highly unlikely that Gabe—if he *was* alive, as Anna had suggested—could have avoided any wolf sensing his presence for so long, there was something strange going on here. Something that, at the very least, had resulted in his magic remaining active within the reservation even if he *wasn't*. "I just know that I have to go there."

"Is this an intuition thing, or something more?"

"Intuition, mainly. I've had no dreams, and Belle's guides haven't mentioned Gabe's presence."

"Would they?"

"If asked a direct question, maybe." I shrugged. "They can be spectacularly unhelpful when they want to be, though."

"Here's to spirits being as ornery as the rest of us." He lightly touched his coffee cup against mine. "It's oddly comforting to know the afterlife actually *has* life."

"It's generally only those who have chosen not to move on and be reborn, or those who are chosen to be familiars, who remain."

"So ghosts are the former?"

I nodded. "Generally, yes."

"Have you sensed many around here?"

"I don't actually go looking for them. And for the most part, they're harmless." I studied him for a moment. "Do you need to ask permission from the Marin pack to go into St. Erth forests tomorrow?"

He sighed. "No, because if Gabe *is* there, it's once again ranger business. They can't stop me."

"Good."

I drank some more coffee, and the silence stretched on for several minutes. And while there was a definite undercurrent that spoke of desire, the silence was nevertheless a comfortable one. Wolf or no, this man was happy to simply sit here, and that was something of a rarity in a world that seemed intent on instant satisfaction.

Although if I was being at all honest, a little instant satisfaction would *not* have gone astray.

But maybe he was still waiting for me to make that first move.

My gaze fell to his lips. What would he do if I simply leaned forward and kissed him? It wasn't really an appropriate time, but was there ever going to be? Especially if fate continued to crap all over our plans?

I sipped some coffee, torn between desire and my natural tendency for caution—at least when it comes to the opposite sex. Eventually, I said, "Can I ask how a pack works with more than one alpha?"

Heat stirred in his eyes, and a smile tugged at his lips.

He might not be a telepath but he obviously knew what my thoughts were.

"Proper wolf packs are usually one family unit. Ours consists of *many* family units, so naturally, we're going to have a number of both alphas, betas, and omegas within each pack."

Betas being second-in-command, and the omegas the lower-ranked members of the community. It was a system that ran against what generally happened with real wolves who, in the wild, tended to live in packs that centered around a breeding pair and one or more generations of their offspring rather than multiple families. "And the alphas rule the pack jointly?"

"Yes. And there's a vote every five years for the pack's three positions on the reservation council." He paused. "My father and his two brothers have won that vote the last five times."

If his father and uncles had been on the council for twenty-five years, they were either very popular or had very powerful personalities. "What happens when an alpha dies? Does one of his direct family group step up into that position, or does it go to a vote?"

"It's usually taken by the oldest alpha sibling, be they male or female."

I raised my eyebrows. "There're women representatives amongst both the elders and the council?"

"Of course. Werewolves might have a macho reputation, but every family group is run equally by an alpha male and female."

"Here's to social equality," I said, and repeated the coffee cup tap. "Are you the oldest in your family?"

He shifted slightly to look at me directly. Which only made it easier to lean forward and kiss him.

And I did want to.

Badly.

Especially when his very next question was the one question I'd been hoping to avoid until we knew each other far, *far* better.

"I'll answer your questions about my family if you answer mine about yours."

"I haven't seen my family for years, so I really can't tell you all that much about them."

I didn't want to lie to him, but by the same token, I really couldn't afford to be totally honest. Not when there was still a niggle in the back of my mind that my parents would—sooner or later—come hunting for us.

"Why? Did you have some kind of falling out?"

"You could say that." I paused. "My hair coloring, and the little magic I possess, both came from my grandmother, who was the result of a brief dalliance with a blueblood. Neither of my parents shared her attraction to witches or magic, and they spent my growth years trying to smother the skill."

Though I'd told that story often enough, this time the lies tasted very bitter. It wasn't a great way to start a relationship, no matter how inconsequential it might be.

"When was the last time you saw them?"

"Answer my question," I said primly, "And I'll answer yours."

He laughed—a warm, rich sound that caressed my senses as sweetly as honey on the tongue. I put my coffee cup back on the table and tucked one leg under my body so that I was fully facing him. Not only because I wanted direct eye contact, but also because it would make it even easier to kiss him.

"I am indeed the oldest. I've five sisters and a

younger brother."

I blinked. "There are seven children in your immediate pack?"

"*That* is another question." He paused, and a devilish light appeared in his eyes. "If you want me to answer it, there has to be a penalty. Rules are rules."

"More than happy to oblige," I murmured. "What shall it be? Another piece of cake, a coffee refill, or perhaps...?"

I didn't finish the sentence. I simply leaned forward and kissed him.

And oh, what a kiss it was.

It was everything our very first one had been and far more besides, because this time, it wasn't fleeting and he didn't pull away. Instead, he slipped his hand around the back of my neck, holding me gently as the kiss deepened into a slow and passionate exploration, one that was restrained and yet hinted at a far deeper desire—one that was only a touch away from exploding. It left me breathless, giddy, and had me wanting him with a fierceness that I hadn't felt in a *very* long time.

Except time was the one thing we didn't have a lot of. Not tonight, anyway.

As his phone began to buzz, he groaned softly and then said, "Never have I cursed the council and their damn meetings as much as I am right now."

His breath teased my lips and sent a shiver of delight down my spine. "You're not alone there—especially given I've been waiting weeks for a proper kiss."

He chuckled softly and brushed his lips across mine a final time before he pushed back. His blue eyes glimmered with the same sort of heat that pulsed through me.

"Next time, just ask. Or, better yet, just do. More

than happy for a woman to take the lead."

"Sound advice I'll definitely follow if I feel things are progressing a little slowly." I took a deep breath in an effort to calm my racing pulse, but it was filled with the musky, smoky scent of him, and really didn't help.

"So, tomorrow—what time?"

He grimaced. "My shift is supposed to start at eleven, but I'll ring Duke and see if he can swap. That'll give us a couple of hours to check both locations."

"Eleven is an odd time to start, isn't it?"

"We generally stagger starting times so that there's someone manning the station until fairly late." He silenced the reminder chime on his phone. "It's only when we've a few people either off sick or on holidays that the night shift ends earlier, but in those cases, I'm generally on call."

"Which kind of explains why you were in sweats but carrying a gun when we first met."

He reached out and lightly tucked a stray strand of hair behind my ear. "A day I will never forget, for many various reasons."

Though I wanted nothing more than to lean into his touch, I resisted. I didn't want to be the reason for him being late—especially given the council's edict of no witches on the reservation. We might already be walking a tightrope when it came to remaining in Castle Rock. I didn't need to be giving them additional reasons—however inconsequential—to boot us out.

Unease rose at that thought, and I wasn't sure if its cause was pessimism, or my hit-and-miss precognition skills coming to life.

"Well," I said, keeping my tone light, "it isn't every day you discover the body of a teenager who'd been seduced onto the dark path by a vampire capable of blood magic."

"That is something of an understatement." He pushed to his feet and then caught my hand and tugged me up. "I enjoyed tonight, even if our time was severely restricted."

"Me too." I rose on my toes and dropped a quick kiss on his lips. And fought the desire to do more. "I'll see you tomorrow morning."

"Indeed." His expression was a mix of amusement and frustration. "I'll be here at ten thirty."

"I look forward to it."

He hesitated, then turned around and headed for the stairs. I followed him down to the front door and held it open as he stepped through. The cool night air caressed my skin, but it didn't do much to ease the inner heat.

Lights flashed amber as he pressed the truck's remote, and then he glanced back at me. "I'd normally kiss you good night, but I don't think that would be wise. The council does not appreciate tardiness."

"Then you'd better get your butt into gear, instead of lingering on the sidewalk."

"Indeed I must," he said, and then did precisely what he'd said he shouldn't, and kissed me again.

Briefly, but urgently.

Then, with another groan, he broke away and stalked over to his truck. I stayed where I was, and watched until he was well out of sight.

And knew I could get into very big trouble if I didn't watch myself—and my emotions—around him. I'd fallen for the wrong type of man once before, and I really didn't want to go through that sort of heartache again. It wasn't as if my heart didn't have ample enough warning about the foolishness of such a leap; he was a werewolf, after all, and they rarely got emotionally involved with anyone *other* than another werewolf. His sister had been a rare exception, and even then, her marriage to Gabe had only been granted as a dying wish. As the eldest in his family—and therefore heir to his father's position—Aiden wasn't likely to go against pack rules, even when it came to matters of the heart.

Besides, not only was I a witch, but a lying one at that. He could only *ever* be a good time, not a long time, no matter what sparks might fly between us.

Of course, there was one other point I needed to remember—the fact that I was getting way, *way* ahead of myself with these sort of thoughts. It wasn't as if we'd done anything more than kiss, for heaven's sake.

I closed the door and headed back upstairs. After cleaning up our cups and putting the leftover cake back in its container, I wrote a note for Belle, letting her know about the visit to both the clearing where Aiden's sister had died and to the wellspring, and asking if she'd mind coming along. Then I went to bed.

And if my dreams were haunted by the specter of a blue-eyed werewolf, I certainly didn't remember it.

"So, what happened last night?" Belle leaned against the countertop and gave me a somewhat speculative look. "Your thoughts are all sorts of happy."

"I don't always wake up grumpy, you know."

Amusement twitched her lips. "Granted, but this is more than just an I-had-a-great-night's-sleep happy."

I raised my eyebrows. "Maybe I had a great night's sleep filled with good dreams rather than ominous ones for a change."

She snorted. "The delaying tactics won't work. Give, woman, or I shall ferret."

"I'm surprised you haven't already."

"Hey, I only ever mine thoughts when absolutely necessary." She paused. "Or in cases like your ranger, when it's hard to know what the man is thinking from his expression or body language."

I gave her a long look. "You haven't read his mind— have you?"

She merely grinned. "You answer my question, and I'll answer yours."

Which was an echo of what I'd said to Aiden last night, and one that had my eyes narrowing. Her grin grew.

"You're a tart," I said.

"And you love me. So give, or I will dig deeper."

I rolled my eyes. "Aiden came here for coffee last night. Trust me, you probably got a whole lot more action than I did."

"Zak and I just cuddled and watched a movie." Her smile flashed again. "Shocking, I know."

"What, have you worn the poor man out already?"

"Nope. I just didn't feel in the mood last night."

"I do hope you're not coming down with something." I reached across the counter and pressed the back of my hand to her forehead. "No temperature—"

She laughed and slapped my hand away. "Now who's the tart? Just give with the information, woman, because something obviously *did* go down between the two of you."

I snapped the lids on the three travel mugs and handed one to her. "We kissed. Nothing more, nothing less."

"And?"

"And that's it." I picked up the other two mugs and walked around the counter.

"So how was it? On the scale of okay to oh-hell-*yeah*, where did it fall?" She picked up the backpack at her feet, swung it over her left shoulder, and fell into step beside me as I walked toward the door.

I gave her the look—the one that told her to mind her own business. She only grinned at me.

Meaning she'd keep on asking until I answered. I rolled my eyes and said, "The latter. The man can kiss."

"And you're going out again when?"

"Today. In a few minutes, in fact."

"Idiot." She nudged me as we walked toward the door, sending me staggering sideways. "I meant on a date."

I shrugged. "We didn't really get around to discussing that."

"Seriously? Why not?"

"Because he had to run off to a council meeting."

"That's rather inconsiderate timing by the council."

"I agree." I opened the door and waved her through. "And I have a rather weird feeling it might have had something to do with us, even though he said he merely had to update them on the murder."

She glanced at me sharply. "Why would they be discussing us?"

"Because we're witches on a reservation that's banned witches, remember?"

I locked the door and shoved the keys back into my pocket. The wind stirred around me, its touch biting, and the sky was gray. I shivered and contemplated going back for my coat, but decided unlocking the door and racing upstairs was too much effort.

No doubt I'd regret that laziness when I was freezing my butt off in the forest.

"Yeah, but as far as anyone is concerned, we're only capable of minor magic, and we advised the council about our intent to make charms before we opened the café." Belle paused and frowned. "You don't think Aiden's said something to them, do you? He's the only one who really knows we're capable of far more."

I shook my head. "No, but it's likely the RWA might have. They would have mentioned us in any report they made."

"But why would they submit a report to the council? They're only answerable to the witch High Council and the government."

"Yes, but we're on a semiautonomous reservation, and I'd imagine there'd be a rule that states any report made by outside sources on events that happen within the reservation has to be copied to the council."

"Possibly." She wrinkled her nose. "I'm not sure we really need the council finding out about us so soon. Not when we've had so little time to prove we're worthwhile additions to Castle Rock."

"That's precisely what I'm worried about."

Her expression became even more concerned. "Normal type worried, or I've had a premonition and this is definitely going to happen type worry?"

I hesitated. "Neither. It's just another of those niggles."

"Like the one that says your parents are going to find us?"

I nodded. "Which means it may be based on nothing more than fear."

"Hopefully, because I'm getting rather attached to this place, and I don't really want to leave it."

I glanced past her as Aiden's truck came around the corner and walked toward the curb. "I've answered your question, so time for you to answer mine."

"Yes, I did," she said. "But it was only a light run through his thoughts. Nothing too in-depth."

I frowned at her. "Meaning what?"

"Meaning I wanted to know if he was coming to the café for the brownies or the woman."

"He answered that question last night."

"But was he honest? Because that man is seriously in lust with our brownies."

I laughed and nudged her, returning the favor and sending her staggering. "You're an idiot."

"Well okay, he's seriously in lust with you, too, but it's a close-run thing."

My grin grew, but I didn't reply as Aiden stopped in front of us and then leaned across and opened the door.

"Morning, ladies." He sounded far too cheerful for someone who probably hadn't had that much sleep—although the tiredness had at least left his eyes.

We both climbed into the front of the truck. I handed him the two travel mugs, did up my seat belt, and then retrieved my drink. My fingers brushed his, the brief contact sending warmth tingling through me.

"Were you held up long with the council last night?" I asked.

"Only for just over an hour, thankfully." He glanced past me. "Belle, do you want to buckle up?"

"Getting there, Ranger." She dumped the backpack at her feet and then handed me her mug. "How did they react to the possibility of a soul eater being on the reservation?"

"They didn't, because I haven't told them." He pulled away from the curb and continued up Mostyn Street. "Until we've ruled out all other possibilities, I'm not going to."

I handed Belle's mug back and said, with just a touch of annoyance in my voice, "Then how did you explain the two bodies?"

He shrugged, a small movement that nevertheless had his shoulders brushing mine. "Murder suicide."

Belle snorted. "Oh, how I wish that was true."

"Me too." His voice was flat. "Because, seriously? I don't want to even contemplate the possibility of soul eaters. I mean, how do you even stop something like that?"

A smile twitched my lips, despite the lingering annoyance. "Very carefully, I'd imagine."

His quick grin momentarily lifted the gloom of the day. "And from as far a distance as possible, no doubt."

"Indeed."

He turned left into Barker Street and accelerated away from the city center. "If no obvious cause of death can be found in either Aron's or Marlinda's tox results, I'll call in the RWA." He hesitated. "Will they have the skills to deal with a soul eater?"

"Yes," Belle said, before I could. "Unlike us, they're fully trained. Plus they have full and immediate access to the council if necessary."

"Given the somewhat dodgy phone reception in some parts of the reservation, I wouldn't count on immediacy unless we're talking about a landline."

I half smiled. "RWA witches don't really need phones. Not to contact each other, anyway."

"They only use phones so as to not scare regular people," Belle added.

He swung onto the Pyrenees Highway and then gave us a narrow-eyed look. "I can't tell if you're being serious or not."

"Totally serious," Belle said cheerfully.

"Does that mean *all* full witches are telepathic?"

Belle reached past me and patted his knee. "Don't worry, Ranger. As I've already said, we realized long ago that the thoughts of most men are not worth the trouble of checking."

His expression was a weird mix of uncertainty, disbelief, and concern, and I laughed. I couldn't help it.

"No, most witches aren't telepathic. But there *are* spells that can instantly deliver a message from one place to another, be it verbal or written."

"That's a relief. One person messing about in my thoughts is more than enough, thank you very much."

Belle grinned. "I promise I've done nothing more than check which you like more—our brownies or my crimson-haired friend here."

"I've already told her it's the brownies, but only by a smidge."

I laughed again, and took a sip of coffee. "So where exactly are we going?"

The amusement left his expression, leaving me mentally kicking myself. "The Marin pack's territory is the St. Erth forests, which basically rings Maldoon. The clearing in which we found Kate lies at the source of one of Manton's Gully creek tributary feeds."

Which didn't tell me a whole lot given I didn't know the Maldoon area at all. "Will there be much walking involved?"

"Yes." He glanced down at our feet. "But you're both wearing sensible shoes, so you'll cope."

"Hey, you've witnessed the level of my fitness when it comes to walking, so don't be so certain of that."

Bet he was too busy witnessing said action from behind and not really paying too much attention to anything else, Belle cut in, and then grunted when I elbowed her. Hard.

"Yes," he said, with an amused glance our way. "Which is why I've brought along a backpack with water and energy bars. It's a bit of an uphill hike."

"Great." *Not.*

Silence fell as we continued on up the highway, but in little more than twenty minutes, we were approaching Maldoon. Aiden turned off onto a gravel road before we got to the township, and the small suburban houses gradually gave way to acreage. Eventually he turned right onto a tiny dirt road and drove up into the scrub-covered hills until we came to a dead end. I frowned as Aiden stopped. The path beyond seemed little more than a damned goat track.

Goats and werewolves would certainly be the only ones comfortable using it, Belle grumbled.

She grabbed our backpack, and then opened the door and climbed out. The wind that whipped past her was icy, and I shivered. I really *should* have brought my coat.

"If you're cold, there's a couple of spare coats in the back seat," Aiden immediately said. "But to be honest, you'll probably only be wearing it for ten minutes or so given the climb."

"I'll grab it anyway, just in case it rains." I undid the seat belt then twisted around and spotted the two lightweight green wind jackets. "Belle, do you want one?"

She hesitated and glanced upward. "Yeah. That's sky

is not looking promising."

"It's not supposed to rain until this afternoon, so we should be right," Aiden said.

He climbed out and then held out a hand to help me. His touch lingered perhaps a little longer than necessary and it had both anticipation and frustration stirring. I really, *really* hoped fate didn't conspire to interrupt any more of our dates, because one kiss and brief touches were never going to be enough.

A sentiment *he* shared if the flare of desire in his eyes was anything to go by.

We put on the coats while he grabbed his pack and slung it over his back. "This way, ladies."

We followed him around the dead-end barrier, then up the goat track. It was as rough as it looked and the incline grew steadily steeper, until my legs started to burn and my breath was little more than short, sharp pants for air. I tugged off the coat and tied it around my waist, and, a few minutes later, did the same with my sweater. Thankfully, I was wearing a tank top underneath—though I'm not entirely sure I wouldn't have done the same if I'd only been wearing a bra.

If the rasping coming from behind me was anything to go by, Belle wasn't faring much better, despite being far fitter than me.

Aiden did at least take pity on us unfit souls, stopping twice so that we could catch our breaths and grab some water. He even resisted teasing us, though the amusement crinkling the corners of his bright eyes suggested it might have been a hard task.

The scrub and trees became denser the farther we moved away from any sort of habitation. Unlike the forests around Castle Rock, this area didn't appear to have much in the way of old mines or tailings. There *were* animals here though, if the occasional rustling of unseen creatures scurrying away from our presence through the undergrowth was anything to go by. For the most part, though, the area was so quiet that I could clearly hear the soft bubble of a creek some distance away.

I was just about to call for yet another break when the path started to level off. The trees around us were thick and tall, and shut out much of the wind as well as the light, leaving the path in deep shadow.

But shadows weren't the only things here.

There was also magic.

Wild magic.

A force that not only felt feminine, but also had an odd sort of cognizance.

Both had been evident when I'd first called to the wild magic for help in dealing with Waverley—the vampire who'd tried to drain me and who'd left me with a neck scar to forever remind me of my brush with death—but *not* in the force I'd used to finally kill him. There'd just been power. Mind-blowing, incredible power.

Which made me wonder if we were, in fact, dealing with a *second* wellspring—one that was far younger in creation than the one in O'Connor territory.

It'd be a rare occurrence, Belle said. *But it's certainly not beyond the realm of possibility.*

If this reservation has a second wellspring, then we need to call in the RWA, even if the council won't. My mental tone was grim. *Our magic will never be enough to protect two such forces, especially if this second one is still developing.*

Yes, although I can't believe that they haven't pressed the matter of having a witch on the reservation, given they are aware of the unguarded nature of the first wellspring.

Except that, according to Anna, Gabe is still here, and his magic is protecting the place.

Aiden doesn't believe that's possible, she said. *And I tend to agree.*

So did I. There was no way known Gabe could have killed his wife and escaped the notice—and the noses—of three werewolf packs for well over a year now. Even if he'd called upon every ounce of magical skill in his arsenal, he simply wouldn't have had the strength to maintain those as well as his protections around the main wellspring. Not even a blueblood could do that.

We continued to follow the weaving path through the trees, and the sting of magic got stronger with every step. Whether or not this wellspring was young, it was giving every indication it would end up being as powerful as the other.

From up ahead came glimmers of sunlight, suggesting we were finally nearing the clearing in which Aiden's sister had been murdered. My gaze fell to his back, and though there was no outward tension evident in the set of his shoulders, it was nevertheless visible in his aura. In the dark swirl of grief and the flashes of red that indicated heartbreak.

I clenched my fingers against the desire to reach out and comfort him. A touch, no matter how well-meaning, wouldn't ease his pain. Especially when that touch came from someone who was still, in many respects, a stranger, and a witch besides.

We reached the edge of the clearing and stopped. It wasn't very large, but it was strewn with rocks and other debris. Directly opposite us was a sharp cliff face—the rubble scattered around the clearing had obviously come from a long-ago landslip—and at the base of this was an ankle-deep rock basin. Water bubbled up close to the cliff's face, lapped over the edge of the basin, and then wound its way down the gentle slope, where it would no doubt join forces with the stream we'd heard but hadn't seen further down the mountain.

That tiny well was also the source of the wild magic; the air shimmered with the force of it, and the hairs on my arms stood on end. And with it came the thick sense of presence—of awareness—that I'd felt both in the forest above Castle Rock, and in the cemetery when it had angrily snatched my spell and twisted it into something so much more powerful.

Whatever the awareness was—however it had come to be a part of the wild magic—this was where it had been born.

Or, perhaps, died.

Because given the overtly feminine feel to the sentience, I very much suspected that its source was none other than Aiden's murdered sister.

CHAPTER
five

You can't infuse someone's soul into wild magic, Belle said. *You simply can't.*

That we know of, I replied. *But it's not like we've had anything more than rudimentary learning when it comes to the stuff.*

True. She frowned and studied the small clearing. *There is something else here, though.*

I studied the clearing for a moment, but couldn't feel anything more than the wild magic. *Like what?*

If I knew, I'd say.

Have you asked your guides if they're sensing anything other than the wild magic?

Yes.

And?

They can't even get into the clearing. Something is not only blocking them from doing so, but also preventing them from seeing what might lie within this place.

It takes pretty powerful magic to do something like that, Belle.

I hesitated. *Or is the wild magic itself blocking them?*

They were able to enter the area holding the original wellspring easily enough, so it's not that.

Meaning Gabe must have placed a spell around the area. Odd that neither of us sensed it.

Not really. Not given our less than stellar capabilities and the fact he's a vetted, RWA approved witch.

Maybe, but if the spells protecting this place are active, it means he is still alive. Spells only very rarely outlasted the death of their creator.

Unless he's somehow leashed it to the wild magic and—if you're right about the sentience we're sensing—Kate's presence here.

"I've a sudden feeling you ladies are having a very private conversation." Aiden's tone was edged with annoyance. "And while I appreciate you're used to communicating that way, I'd really like to be included in *all* conversations relating to this clearing and the events that went on here."

"Sorry." I wrinkled my nose. "We were just discussing the fact that there's something in this clearing."

He raised an eyebrow. "Define 'something.'"

"We can't as yet." I hesitated. "Where, exactly, was your sister killed?"

Though his expression didn't change, his grief surged, spilling darkness across his aura. "Over near the spring's source."

Which also happened to be the wellspring's source. I doubted that was a coincidence.

I followed him into the clearing, and with every step the caress of wild magic grew stronger, until my entire body thrummed with its power. But there was nothing threatening in its touch; in fact, it seemed oddly welcoming.

It was almost as if it had been waiting for us.

Waiting for you perhaps, Belle commented. *I can certainly feel the wild magic, but there's no sense of welcome within it.*

I frowned. *But you can sense its awareness, can't you?*

Yes, but there's nothing more distinct than that, she said. *You merged with the wild magic to defeat that vampire. Maybe it created a permanent connection. Maybe that's why your eyes are now ringed with silver.*

My eyes had been—up until very recently—pure emerald green rather than the silvery-gray of a full-blooded witch. It was a major reason why few people questioned my carefully reconstructed background.

If such a connection was even remotely possible, don't you think the High Council would be doing more than simply guarding the wellsprings?

Well, yes, but just because it hasn't happened before doesn't mean it's imposs— The rest of her sentence was cut off by a loud gasp.

I immediately swung around. I couldn't see anything threatening, and her thoughts showed no sign of fear. Just… surprise.

I frowned, definitely not understanding the latter. "What's wrong?"

"There's a ghost here."

"Whose?" Aiden's voice was harsh and yet edged with trepidation. "Kate's?"

"No." Belle hesitated. "It's male. I suspect it might be Gabe."

"How is that even possible when his remains have never been found?" Aiden all but growled. "Aren't ghosts pinned to the area in which they died, or have I got the facts wrong?"

"You haven't," I said, "Which means either his body

is well hidden or something stranger is going on."

"There is no way *known* his fucking body could have gone undiscovered for over a year. Not here; not within the Marin compound—or any other one, for that matter." He stopped, and chagrin touched his expression. He took a deep breath and then added, "Sorry, that was uncalled for."

This time I didn't resist the urge to touch him, but his arm felt like steel under my fingertips. "We understand, Aiden, probably more than anyone outside your family ever could."

He placed his free hand over mine, squeezed it lightly, and then released me. "Is there any way we could talk to his ghost, and uncover what really happened in this place?"

And why he killed my sister.... He didn't actually say that, but the words nevertheless hung in the air.

"Yes," Belle said. "But it could be a dangerous thing to do."

"Why?"

"Because this clearing isn't only a tributary source for the creek," I said. "It's also the location of another wellspring."

His gaze swept the area before coming back to mine. "I can't feel anything."

"You wouldn't, given you're not sensitive to magic. But it's here, and while it's nowhere near as powerful as the wellspring within the O'Connor compound, it's still young and growing."

"Which doesn't explain why it would be dangerous to speak to Gabe's ghost, given that's a psychic skill rather than magical," he said. "And ghosts can't hurt the living, can they?"

"That," Belle said gravely, "not only depends on the ghost, but also on what else might be here."

"So do a protection circle or whatever else it is witches do in these situations." He hesitated. "You are capable of that, aren't you?"

"Yes." It was pointless saying anything else, given my oft-expressed desire to place such protection around the original wellspring. "But using *any* sort of magic within the presence of wild magic is dangerous. You saw what happened to my spell in the cemetery."

"We could just use the stones," Belle said. "If we're both inside the circle, you can react if anything goes ass-up."

I hesitated, and then nodded. Hopefully, things wouldn't go awry, but it was better to be safe than sorry. Especially when we were dealing with the ghost of a witch and very possibly the wife he'd murdered.

Belle handed me the pack, and then walked over to the spring. I followed, but she stopped in front of the small well and studied the ground. After a couple of seconds, she moved over to the left edge of the spring, close to the cliff face. "Whatever happened in this place to Gabe, it happened here."

Aiden frowned. "We found Kate's body on the other side of the well."

"Which means," I said, "it's very possible he *did* include the wild magic in whatever spells he raised in this place."

Belle nodded in agreement and sat cross-legged on the ground. "I'll prepare to contact him. You raise the shield."

"What about me?" Aiden said. "What do you want me to do?"

I undid the backpack and fished around for the small silk bag that contained my spell stones. "There's nothing you can do, I'm afraid."

"Other than making sure neither of us gets attacked by whatever wild things might inhabit this area," Belle added.

Aiden smiled, though it didn't really lift the tension in him. "The only wild things in these parts are rabbits and the occasional kangaroo. Neither is particularly dangerous." He hesitated. "Is it possible to repeat what you did in the rotunda, so that I could record it?"

"I can certainly ask questions and, under normal circumstances, Belle can reply for the spirit." I opened the silk bag and poured the stones into my hand. These particular ones were rough-cut clear quartz, which were a whole lot cheaper than diamonds and yet had very similar properties. "But neither of us know what sort of spell restrictions Gabe might have placed around this area, so you may or may not be able to hear us once we get in contact with him."

"Let's hope that's not the case, because I'm going to need recorded evidence to take to the council."

Because they wouldn't believe him without it, obviously. And part of me couldn't help wondering if that would have changed if we'd been proper RWA witches.

"Whatever happens, do not approach the circle or attempt to help either of us until we say otherwise."

"Sure, but why would I even need to?" he asked. "You've done this sort of stuff hundreds of times, haven't you?"

"Yes, but this time we're dealing with the ghost of a witch who may or may not take over Belle's body. And if that's the case, she might need to pull on my energy to maintain physical status quo."

He frowned. "Why? And how is something like *that* even possible?"

"She's my familiar, remember." I started placing the stones into position. "And while a familiar is tasked with providing additional physical strength for their witch whenever necessary, Belle's *also* a witch, and *that* means the ability to do so goes both ways."

But only thanks to the strength of our connection and friendship, Belle commented.

Aiden's expression remained confused. "That still doesn't explain why it might be necessary."

"Contacting spirits can be physically demanding," Belle said. "Which is why true spirit talkers often restrict the time they spend with the other plane."

Not to mention the fact that some spirits were so strong they could not only inhabit the body of the talker, but try to oust the witch's own spirit and permanently take over their body. *That* was one of the reasons why we had so many protections around our reading room at the café, and why only using spell stones in this instance might be dangerous. We had no idea what Gabe's state of mind had been when he'd killed his wife. If grief had tipped him over the edge, then he would have carried that into the afterlife, and who knew what madness he might attempt once we were in contact with him.

I can feel him, Belle said. *He's near, and waiting. I don't think he's crazy, though his grief is so black it's a cloud that surrounds him.*

Which means his grief could be preventing you from seeing his madness.

True. She paused. *He's also a very strong spirit. I suspect he'll be one of those who takes over.*

If you have any *trouble getting him out, scream mentally.* No matter how strong Gabe might be, even he couldn't erase her spirit, the control she had over her thoughts, or my link with her. We knew *that* from experience.

I will. Loudly.

Good.

I positioned the last stone, then stepped inside the circle, sat down opposite Belle, and inched close enough that our knees touched. With our energies so connected, I glanced at Aiden. "Start recording once Belle starts speaking, not before."

He nodded and got out his phone. I lit some sage to cleanse the area, and then started the spell, carefully layering in as many protection threads as I could. With that done, I attached the spell to each of the stones, and activated it. The air thrummed with its power, and, once again, it was far stronger than I'd intended or even should have been capable of. And that suggested the wild magic had threaded its way into the spell even if I'd had no sense of it. I took a deep breath to wash away the vestiges of nervousness, and held my hands out to Belle.

We'd done this many times over the years. There was nothing to fear except fear itself.

And maybe a crazy witch with far more power than either of us.

She placed her fingers in mine and then closed her eyes. While some spirit talkers used the spirit's personal items to contact them, or objects such an Ouija board or even a spirit pendulum to provide simple answers, Belle had no need. The High Council might not hold psychic skills in high regard, but she was one of the strongest spirit talkers out there—or so my mother had said, in a moment of rare kindness toward Belle.

Though our hands were only lightly touching, I nevertheless felt the moment she silently began summoning Gabe's spirit.

He didn't just answer. He entered her body and seized control.

"You took your time coming here, young Elizabeth."

Though the voice was Belle's, the rhythm of her words and the pronunciation was not.

"It's not my task or duty to come here," I said. "I'm not the reservation witch."

"Then why are you here?"

"Because thanks to your actions in this clearing, the reservation council has banned all witches. Belle and I are only here because we're trinket sellers with a little magic capability and knowledge, nothing more."

"Oh, you are both more than mere trinket sellers, even if you do not hold the power of bluebloods." He paused, and Belle's frown deepened. "Why would the council risk such a ban? Surely they know the danger an unprotected wellspring represents."

"Why did you murder your wife?" I countered. "There was no justification—"

"I did *not* murder her!" The words exploded from Belle. "How dare you—"

"Your prints were on the knife," I cut in. "Yours, not hers. That is pretty clear evidence in anyone's book."

"Of course my prints were on it. It was my athame."

"Which you shoved through her heart in the middle of a pentagram."

"Not to murder her!"

There was so much anger and grief in those four words that I rocked back slightly. "Then tell me what *did* happen."

Belle took a deep breath then released it. It was a shuddering sound of sorrow. "She was dying—"

"From leukemia." One that had been detected far too late for the treatments to be of any use.

Belle nodded. "She was so sick of the treatments, and wanted to give up. I tried to convince her to stay the course, but she'd had enough. She was dying, and we both knew it."

Belle's fingers twitched against mine, but she wasn't yet pulling on my strength, and there was no indication that she was ready to end the session.

"And if she'd died, she would have moved on, as is the way of all souls."

All souls but his.

"But she didn't want to move on. She wanted to remain here, with her family, for all eternity."

I frowned. "Why would she give up the chance of rebirth and future lives to remain in this life—in this place—forever?"

"Katie was a pretty special lady." Just for a moment, Belle's silvery gaze glittered with tears—both his *and* hers, given she was very connected to his emotions right now. "It's unusual for werewolves to have any type of psychic ability, so she was never tested, but I swear to every god out there she had at least some precognitive skill."

"Is that why she was so sure she would die?"

"I believe so." He paused, and again tears rose. "It is also why she wanted to remain here. She said it was her destiny to protect this place."

"What made you believe her? It could have been nothing more than the ramblings of a sick—"

"No," he cut in. "I did a scrying. It confirmed what she saw."

"So what sort of magic did you raise that she ended up in a pentagram with your athame stuck in her heart?"

Belle's fingers twitched again, and the flow of strength from my body to hers began. We needed to end this soon—it took a lot of energy to maintain two souls in one body, and while it was extremely rare, if she was drained too far, it could lead to death.

And if she drained me too far, we'd both die.

"I found the remnants of a spell," he said. "A very *old* spell—one that, if the notes were to be believed, could bind a soul to a place of power."

"Such as a wellspring?"

"Yes. There was no guarantee it would work, of course, and I told Katie that, but she was adamant." Belle paused again, and again her fingers twitched.

"Gabe, you need to hurry. Belle can't take much more."

"I'm aware of her strength, and I will not push her beyond her boundaries, I can assure you of that."

I wasn't assured, and frustration stirred, but there was little I could do to speed things along. Little except cast him out of her body, and I knew from her thoughts she didn't want that to happen yet.

After a moment, he continued, "I studied the spell, prepared as much as I could, and we came to this place. This wellspring had only broken to the surface a few days before, and I hadn't reported its presence because the binding spell could only be used when the power was very new and raw."

"Did it involve a ritual sacrifice?" Because if it did, it could stain this place for eternity, even if neither Belle nor I could feel the slightest tendril of darkness within the clearing.

"Not as such, no. I raised the spell; she spoke the words of binding and commitment, and then the three of us—me, Katie, and the wild magic—picked up my athame, pressed it to her heart, and finished the binding."

"Then why were your prints the only ones on your athame?"

"Because Katie placed her hands *over* mine, and, of course, wild magic has no prints. But I daresay its power resonates on the steel even today."

That I couldn't say, given it was undoubtedly still locked up in an evidence box somewhere. "What happened then? Why are you dead?" I hesitated. "Did you take your own life?"

It would certainly account for his ghost being here, but *not* for the lack of a body.

"No. Not deliberately, anyway." Belle's smile was full of sadness. "Both the spell and the wild magic were far more powerful than I'd expected. The binding consumed both my strength *and* my flesh, but I do not mind, given I now live in this place alongside my love, even if we can never be together as we once were."

"So the spell was successful? She's the presence we can sense in the wild magic?"

"Only in some of it. The protections I'd put around the old wellspring were in place when we unleashed the magic here, and it prevented a total fusion."

"Meaning the wild magic from the old wellspring is now unprotected?" I already knew it was, but given he was here—if only in spirit form—I couldn't help the vague hope that at least *some* of his magic remained to protect it.

Belle nodded. "The spells I placed around that area to protect it died when I did."

I frowned. "So why does your magic linger here?"

"Because it is tied into the magic here, through Katie's presence. But the magic of *this* wellspring and even Katie can only do so much—and neither she nor the wild magic here can react against the living. Not without some form of direction—"

"Such as what I did in that clearing against the vampire?"

"How you survived infusion with the larger wellspring, I'll never understand." He paused. "Regardless of that, the fact remains that the larger wellspring urgently needs full protection, and neither you nor your friend have the knowledge to do that. You must convince the council to bring in a council-approved witch."

Which was *exactly* what I'd been saying to Aiden.

Belle's weariness was now beating through me, and the flow of strength down the link between us was gathering pace. "I wish you peace, Gabe, and whatever happiness your situation allows, but it is time for you to leave this plane."

"Yes." He hesitated. "May the gods grant you both safety in this reservation."

I frowned. "What have you sensed to say something like that?"

"Nothing more than you, young Elizabeth. But a major wellspring has been left to its own devices for over a year. Even if it *is* quickly protected, those aligned to the dark path will know of its presence and be lured to this place. Trouble is coming, if it is not already here."

And with that almost ominous warning, he departed. Belle took a deep, shuddering breath and released it slowly. Her weariness was as strong as my heartbeat, and I thrust as much strength through to her as I could without completely draining myself.

After several more seconds, she squeezed my hands and then released them as she pushed away from my knees, thereby severing our connection. I silently dismantled the protection spell, and then carefully gathered my spell stones and placed them back into their bag.

Only then did I look up at Aiden.

His face was pale and his expression haunted. His eyes glimmered in the sunshine, and his long lashes were wet. He might have stopped the tears from falling any further, but they remained in his eyes.

"So she's here?" he said softly. "Katie's here?"

"Within the wild magic, yes."

"Can you talk to her?"

"I don't know enough about either the spell or the wild magic to say either yes or no." I got to my feet, then offered Belle a hand. "We'll have to ask Gabe if it's possible, and Belle's too weary to attempt that right now."

"Why can't you speak to her as you just did with Gabe?"

"Because she's not a ghost. She's not even a spirit." Belle grabbed my hand and hauled herself upright. "She's something more."

I could feel his frustration even from where I was standing, but little of it showed on his expression. It wasn't evident in his aura either—that still ran with grief.

"It's entirely possible that she's beyond any form of communication," I said gently.

He thrust a hand through his short hair. "Even with the video, the council is going to find this all very unbelievable."

"But you do believe."

It was a statement rather a question, and he half

smiled in response. "Yes. I suspect most of my family will, as she always did have a tendency to think about others more than herself."

The wild magic stirred, and an odd feeling of contentment and perhaps even joy rolled across my senses. Belle, it seemed, was right yet again. I might not have any connection to the wild magic radiating from the original source, but I'd definitely formed one with *this* wellspring.

I grabbed Belle's arm to steady her as she rather wonkily turned around, and then said, "I might not be able to converse with her, Aiden, but I can tell you she has no regrets, and that she's happy to be here, protecting the place and the people that she loves."

"How do know when you can't talk to her?"

"Because I'm sensitive to the magic here, and can feel her within it. To some extent, I can also feel her emotions." I smiled. "It was her anger that warped my spell in the cemetery. She was rather pissed that someone was attacking her big brother."

He laughed, even though those tears once again glimmered in his eyes. "She always was a fierce little thing." He looked around the clearing, as if trying to see his sister's presence. But werewolves, while often sensitive to emotions, were no more likely to sense the presence of a ghost or a spirit than the average human. And in this case, Kate was neither. After a moment, he added softly, "Thanks, Katie. And while I'm tempted to say you shouldn't have sacrificed your future for us, I'm well aware that once you put your mind to something, there's no dissuading you."

Again the magic stirred, and this time it was filled with amusement and love.

He took another deep breath—visibly controlling his

emotions—and then looked at Belle and me. "We'd better get back to the car. Belle, you're looking rather unsteady on your feet—are you going to able to get down that hill okay?"

She raised her eyebrows. "Why? Are you offering to carry me?"

"I could," he all but drawled, "but I'm thinking Zak might not approve of us getting that close."

She snorted. "He has no more right to tell me who I can and can't get close to than I have him. Besides, werewolves play, not stay, with folks like us."

"True enough," Aiden said, his gaze briefly meeting mine.

A silent warning that he was no different in that regard, I thought, although my amusement was perhaps touched with a thread of annoyance. After all, it wasn't as if we'd even done the short-term thing yet.

"Does that rather snarky reply," he continued, "mean that you want a lift? Or not?"

Belle glanced at me. *You won't be offended?*

I'd be offended if you fuck the man. Anything else, go for it. Permission to kiss granted!

I mentally snorted. Loudly. She winced, and then added, *Bitch.*

I grinned and kept my hand under her elbow as we walked over to Aiden. Talking to Gabe really had drained her, and that meant she'd probably sleep for the rest of the day.

And probably much of the night, she replied.

So you're canceling your date with Zak?

Sadly, I think I'd better. I'm not going to be much fun for the next twenty hours or so.

I could always make you a potion—

I'm not feeling that *bad,* she replied hastily. *Seriously, I'm not.*

She obviously *was,* but I didn't press the point. Aiden handed me his pack and then turned around. Within a few seconds, he was piggybacking Belle out of the clearing and down the hill.

It might be far easier going down the mountain than coming up, but the path hadn't magically smoothed out, and I had to keep grabbing at nearby branches to stop sliding into Aiden and Belle. Of course, it was also partially due to tiredness. Belle might have restrained from draining me too fully, but my strength was nevertheless half of what it should have been. Which meant Belle mightn't be the only one sleeping.

As I slipped again, Aiden commented, "I'd greatly appreciate it if you'd avoid falling over and breaking something. I really can't carry two of you down the hill, and I don't think Belle would appreciate being dumped."

"At least I know where I stand in the scheme of things," Belle said, voice dry.

"Sorry, but I want to go out with Liz, and that's mighty hard to do if she's in the hospital with a broken something."

"I rather suspect you want to do a whole lot more than just go out."

"Also true, but I was being polite."

"Not sure why," Belle commented. "We're underpowered witches, not undersexed ones."

He laughed; the warm sound echoed across the forest and momentarily stilled the chatter of nearby birds. "I'll make a note of that for future reference."

"You might also want to note that it has been a long time since she's had decent sex," Belle continued sagely.

"So if you don't hurry yourself up, she might just have to go looking elsewhere."

"Ignore her," I commented, even as I mentally scowled at her. "She's just trying to win a bet."

"Do I dare ask what sort of bet we're talking about?"

"One that at least half the town is apparently taking part in."

"Ah, *that* one. I learned about it this morning, after I'd overheard Tala commenting that she'd lost a tenner on us."

Belle snorted. "At least Zak and I only lost five each."

"I hardly think it fair you two are betting with insider knowledge."

There was something in his voice that had suspicion stirring. "I hope you're taking your own advice there, Ranger."

"Maybe." His voice ran with amusement. "And maybe not."

I couldn't help grinning, even as anticipation stirred. "Then what day have you placed money on?"

"I can hardly tell you that when I'm carrying a competitor."

"Hey, I'm the other half of this bet, remember," I grumbled lightly. "Besides, a girl does need advance warning so she can get ready."

"That depends on where we might be going," he said. "And whether the girl is pretty perfect as she is."

"Oh, very smooth, Ranger," Belle said, even as she silently added, *if that doesn't make you believe the man is seriously into you, nothing will.*

I never doubted the attraction, Belle, just his willingness to get over me being a witch.

And last night—and our kiss—had certainly squashed any fears in *that* regard.

We finally came out of the shadowed forest and the chill wind once again hit. The clouds had grown much darker during our time in the forest, and the smell of rain filled the air. A storm couldn't be too far away.

Aiden stopped at his truck and carefully deposited Belle on the ground. She dropped a quick kiss on his cheek and said, "Thanks."

He grinned. "I'd say anytime, but you're not exactly a lightweight."

She snorted and lightly punched his arm. "I'll have you know this beautiful body is *all* muscle."

"And muscle weighs more than fat." His gaze skimmed her. "You certainly haven't much of that, but I do prefer my women a little more rounded."

I thrust my hands on my hips and said, with mock sternness, "Meaning what, Ranger?"

He raised his hands, his smile growing. "Hey, no insult intended, because blind Freddy can see your weight distribution is in all the right places."

"Meaning mine isn't?" Belle said, rather mildly.

He glanced at her and slowly backed away, blue eyes sparkling in the growing darkness of the day. "I think I'd better shut up before I get myself in deeper trouble. Ladies, the truck is open and the seats are awaiting."

Once we'd both stripped off his coats, I shoved them and his pack onto the rear seat along with ours, and then climbed in. As we were heading back down the dirt road, the clouds finally unleashed, and the rain was so heavy the wipers couldn't cope.

"Isn't it supposed to be summer?" Belle grumbled. "Or does that whole season skip this area entirely?"

"Our hotter months tend to be January and Feb," Aiden said. "Although that's extended into March and April in more recent—"

He stopped as the incoming call sign flashed up on the truck's computer screen. He pressed a button on the steering wheel and said, "What's up, Tala?"

"Everything." Her voice was grim. "We've got another goddamn body."

CHAPTER
six

A iden swore softly and then said, "Where?"

"Just beyond the boundary of the Marin compound, over at Picnic Point."

"Any idea who?"

"No. The report came in from a couple of sightseers. The body is in the water, from the sound of it." She paused. "Are you still in the area?"

"Yes. I'll head over there now to begin prelims. Liz and Belle can drive my truck back." He glanced at us briefly when he said that, eyebrow raised in query. When I nodded, he added, "Have you called in Ciara?"

"Yes, and she's not amused."

"Given her recent workload, I'm not surprised. Can you contact Byron and ask him to bring along his scuba gear? We'll have to do a search of the lake."

"Will do."

As the call light on the screen went out, he glanced at

us and said, "Sorry about this, ladies. Will you be all right finding your way back to Castle Rock from this area?"

"Shouldn't be a problem," I said. "But if it is, we've Google Maps on our phones."

There was satnav in the truck, but I had a suspicion he wouldn't be happy if we started playing about with the onboard computer.

"Good. I'll come by sometime later today to pick the truck up."

Silence fell after that, although between the pelting rain and the siren there was little point in trying to talk. Aiden obviously knew this area well, because we were driving along the old dirt road far faster than I would have thought wise given the lack of visibility.

We sped along several more roads—although some of them were little more than rough muddy lines—before we reached our destination. As Aiden slowed, I spotted a red SUV parked to the right of the track, though it was little more than a bright flicker in the wet gloom of the day. Beyond it was the faint outline of what was probably a barbecue hut, given this area was called Picnic Point. If there were people inside either the vehicle or the hut, I couldn't see them.

Aiden halted beside the SUV, shoved his truck into park, and then twisted around to grab one of the coats. "I'll get my gear out of the back, and then you can head home. Just take it easy until you get onto the main road, because the tracks will have deteriorated rapidly in this storm."

"We will." I hesitated, only barely resisting the urge to drop a kiss on his cheek. "Talk to you later."

"Yes." His smile flashed, but it was all too fleeting.

Once he'd climbed out, I undid my belt and slid

across to the driver seat. When he'd retrieved his kit, he hit the side of the truck a couple of times. I watched him walked around the front of the vehicle, and then slipped the gears into reverse and got out of there.

"Let's hope this body isn't connected to either the other two *or* our soul eater," Belle commented.

"I'm betting we've got Buckley's chance of that being the case."

She grimaced—something I felt through our connection more than saw, given my attention was solely on keeping the truck straight on the increasingly shitty road.

"And I'm betting you're right. It doesn't stop me from hoping otherwise though." She yawned hugely. "Do you mind if I nap?"

"Go for it." I paused, but couldn't help adding, "If I'm going to slide us into a tree or something, it's probably better not to see it."

"Thanks for that rather cheery thought."

"You're welcome, my friend."

She shook her head, amusement teasing her lips as she grabbed the remaining coat, folded it up to form a pillow, and then shifted to a more comfortable position in the seat. Within minutes, she was fast asleep.

I not only managed to stay awake and not run us into a tree or worse, but also find my way back to the main highway without resorting to Google for help. Visibility remained poor, however, so I kept well below the speed limit—no doubt frustrating those who were caught behind me for however many minutes it might have taken to reach a passing point. It took me almost an hour to get back to Castle Rock and, by that time, I was battling to stay awake as tiredness pulsed through me.

I pulled up in front of the café and lightly nudged Belle. "Crap," she muttered. "We here already?"

"Yeah. Are you going to be okay to get inside while I park the truck around the back, or do you want help?"

"I'll manage."

She dumped the coat on the seat then climbed out and staggered more than walked across to the door. I waited until she'd disappeared inside, then drove around to the rear of the building and the parking area we shared with all five businesses along this section of the street. Once the truck was safely tucked behind our old wagon, I shoved Aiden's coat on, grabbed the backpack, and then ran like hell for the rear access door—one we generally used only when we needed to dump the waste in the nearby bins. But in the few seconds it took me to open it, my hair was running with rivers and the bottom half of me was soaked through.

I stripped off in the small, rather cold corridor that held both our walk-in fridge-freezer and the storeroom, and then grabbed a bag from the latter to shove in the wet stuff so I didn't drip into the main part of the building. Once upstairs, I dumped my clothes into the wash basket, hung Aiden's coat up to dry, and then checked on Belle. She'd managed to strip off, but had hit the bed fast asleep. I tugged the blankets over her and got muttered at for my trouble. The spells we'd placed around the room to give Belle a break from the constant barrage of my thoughts prevented me from understanding the content of that mutter, but it didn't really matter. Her tone told me it wasn't a "thank you" but rather something along the lines of "bugger off and leave me alone"—only less polite.

I grinned and headed into the bathroom, where I grabbed a quick shower to warm up. Once I was dried off and dressed, I headed downstairs to make myself a potion and some lunch.

And discovered Roger standing in the middle of the café, looking around with interest.

I stopped abruptly. "We're closed—and how did you even get in?"

"The door was open."

Meaning Belle really *had* been out of it when she'd come inside, because checking we were secure was normally the first thing she did. "Which doesn't mute the point that we're closed. It even says that on the door."

"Yes, but I am not here for sustenance." He paused, and half smiled. "Although if you were to offer me a piece of that rather delicious-looking orange and walnut cake, I would not gainsay you."

I snorted, but nevertheless walked around the counter. "Why are you here, Roger? What does your mistress want?"

"She wishes to know what you have heard about Marlinda's death."

I retrieved the orange cake and cut him a slice, then opened the drawer beside the cake fridge, grabbed a paper bag, and slid the slice of cake into it. I wasn't about to encourage him to stay and eat.

"Haven't the rangers spoken to her yet?"

"Yes, but only in her capacity of Marlinda's employer."

"If she wants to uncover the reason behind Marlinda's murder, it might have been wise for her to mention they also had a relationship beyond the boundaries of employer and employee. After all, no matter how careful she might be, someone in this reservation is likely to have seen them together at some point."

He accepted the bagged cake with a somewhat amused smile. "Which is why she *did* tell them they had an intimate relationship."

That raised my eyebrows. For some reason, I hadn't expected Maelle to be gay, although there was no reason for a vampire not to be, given their sexuality didn't change when their bodies did.

"I see surprise in your expression." His tone and pronunciation told me I was now speaking to the woman in charge rather than her servant. "You did not expect me to be so crude as to take my pleasure without also giving it, did you?"

"Given how little I know about vampires and their feeding habits, I can honestly say I didn't know what to expect."

The smile that teased Roger's lips was almost predatory, and a chill raced down my spine. Not because I in any way feared him, but rather the anticipation evident in his expression. It imbued me with a deep sense that if I didn't play my cards right, Maelle would loom far larger in my life than I wanted or needed.

"Oh," he all but purred, "I'm sure we can fix that if you so desire."

"I don't desire," I replied evenly, somehow resisting the urge to step back and run like hell from this half human and the woman who sustained him. "And never will."

"Shame," he murmured, even as Maelle's presence leached from his features. He blinked and added, "Even with that information, the rangers have not told my mistress much about how or why Marlinda might have died."

"That's probably because they don't know anything

more, thanks to the fact they haven't gotten the autopsy results back as yet." I studied him uneasily. "And why would you think I'd actually know anything?"

Amusement touched his expression, though his eyes remained cold. "Come now, it is quite common knowledge that you and the ranger are... perhaps not bedfellows, but close to."

I laughed. I couldn't help it. "You and your mistress need better sources, because we are not—much to my chagrin, admittedly—even *close* to being bedfellows. We haven't even gone out on a goddamn date yet."

"That *is* a surprise, given what we've witnessed."

That had my amusement fading, and fast. "You've been watching me?"

"We keep an eye on all the main players in this reservation," he said. "It pays to be up with current events when you're a vampire."

"I wouldn't have thought that necessary given the council does know you're here—"

"And they are well able to revoke that permission at any point," he cut in smoothly. "We have not lived this long by being caught unawares."

Which was basically confirmation that he *was* far older than he actually looked—though probably not as old as his mistress. His speech patterns might be a little old-fashioned, but I'd hazard a guess he'd at least been born in the twentieth century. If Maelle wasn't far older than even that, I'd be very surprised.

"The point remains the same—I don't currently know any more than either of you."

"Perhaps, but we were wondering if you would be willing to share any information you do get." He paused, and then added, with odd emphasis, "My mistress would not only be *most* appreciative, but she would also be in your debt."

That, his reverence suggested, was not only rare, but could be highly beneficial. And I couldn't help but agree, especially if Gabe was right about the darker forces being drawn to this place even if the original wellspring became fully protected.

"I very much doubt Aiden will tell me too much about the investigation," I said. "Especially if the coroner's report proves there's no connection to the soul eater's presence on the reservation."

"Even so, we'd appreciate any information you do get."

I hesitated. "Okay, but I won't share anything that could jeopardize the ongoing investigation. Is that clear?"

He inclined his head, the movement almost regal. "That is acceptable."

Too bad if it isn't, I wanted to say, but wisely kept the words inside. I walked back around the counter and motioned him toward the door. "If there's nothing else, I've got work to do."

"Thank you for the cake and your time," he said, and left.

I locked up after him, and then headed into the kitchen to make my shake. Between it, and the steak, chips, and salad I had afterward, the lingering tiredness that was a result of my supporting Belle began to fade. The coffee and double chocolate cheesecake that followed washed away the remainder.

I spent a couple of hours in the kitchen doing prep for tomorrow, and then headed upstairs to relax and read some more of Nellie's old book on darker spirits.

The rest of the afternoon drifted by without any

major revelations as to what sort of soul eater we might be dealing with, let alone how to stop it killing, and banish it from the reservation.

Belle came out just as the clock downstairs started chiming. She yawned hugely and then somewhat blearily glanced my way. "Is that six AM or PM?"

"The latter. Why aren't you still asleep?"

"Because I forgot to call Zak and cancel our date, and he just sent a text saying he'll be around in half an hour to pick me up." She wrinkled her nose. "I said I needed an hour *and* a very early night, so we're just going to the pub down the road for steak and chips."

I raised an eyebrow. "You can get that here."

"Yes, but it would mean me cooking, and that's not going to happen on my day off."

"Fair enough." I bookmarked the page I was on, and then pushed upright. "You want a coffee to wake up a bit more?"

She hesitated. "Nah, the shower should be enough."

I made myself an espresso as she pottered about getting ready. Zak arrived right on time, and I couldn't help the wisp of... not envy, but certainly longing that stirred as he tugged Belle into his arms and kissed her soundly. I really wasn't sure Aiden and I would *ever* get to the point of being so open and easy when it came to desire.

I locked the door again once they'd left, and headed into the kitchen to make myself something for dinner. The rest of the evening passed uneventfully—which I supposed was a good thing even if it was utterly boring.

I'd just about given up hope of Aiden dropping by when, at ten thirty, my phone rang.

"Didn't wake you up, did I?" he said, by way of

greeting.

"The only reason you'll ever find me in bed this early is if I'm sick or having sex."

He chuckled softly, the sound so low, and warm desire stirred. "I hope the latter activity is not just confined to the bedroom."

"If you play your cards right, you might just find out."

"I'll be seriously disappointed if I don't." He paused. "I know it's late, but do you want to go out for coffee?"

No, I want to stay in and play. But with Belle due home at any minute, that really wasn't an option. Magic might be able to stop her hearing my thoughts, but I wasn't aware of any spells capable of stopping sound—which didn't mean there weren't any. Still, while it might be considered rather old-fashioned in this day and age, we'd long ago made a rule not to bring our lovers home unless the other was staying elsewhere. So I simply said, "There won't be much open at this hour, will there?"

"There's actually a little twenty-four-hour place just off the freeway that does surprisingly good coffee."

"By your standards or mine?" I asked, amused. "And does this count as a date?"

"I think I can manage a classier first date than mere coffee."

"Which suggests you've placed your bet on a different day."

"I certainly have. Next Sunday, to be exact."

Meaning I had to wait *six whole days* before I got any serious action? That was almost cruel....

"Is there any reason we're waiting so long?"

He chuckled again. "If I said better odds, you'll probably never speak to me again."

"You may well be right."

"In truth, I have Monday off. Given the café is also closed, I thought it'd be nice if I picked you up for dinner on Sunday night, after which we can then retreat to my place." He hesitated. "There're two bedrooms, so there are no expectations, and you can sleep alone if you so desire."

"I think you can guess the response to *that*—especially given Belle's comments this morning."

"Perhaps, but I learned a long time ago to never presume." His smile was evident in his voice. "I'll finish locking up the station and be there in ten minutes."

"I'll be waiting."

I hung up and then raced upstairs to put on some fresh clothes and makeup. Belle still wasn't home by the time I clattered back down with his coat, as well one for myself, so I left her a note, collected my purse and his keys, and then headed for the front door. He was striding down the street as I stepped out, and the warmth in his smile had my toes curling. He was wearing dark jeans that hugged his long, strong legs, and a rich blue sweater that emphasized his shoulders and brought out the color of his eyes. He was, I thought idly, a rather good-looking man.

I held his keys up and said, "Your truck is parked around the back."

"Thanks." His fingers brushed mine as he took them from me, and heat curled through my body. "But I'm afraid there's been yet another change of plans."

I valiantly pushed down the sliver of disappointment and said, "What's happened?"

"I got a call from Ciara. She needs to discuss the autopsy results on Marlinda Brown."

"At this hour? Isn't it a bit late?"

"I asked her to do overtime to get the autopsies

done, as we need to present the prelim findings to the council ASAP." He grimaced. "It's hardly fair for me to expect that of her and not be willing to put in extra time myself."

He'd already put in plenty of overtime from what I'd seen, but it wasn't like I had any right to comment on that. "And today's body? Was it connected to the other two murders?"

"No—not unless our murderer has gained a sudden desire to kill cows."

I blinked. "How on earth did the witnesses mistake a *cow* for a human?"

"They were city folk," he replied, amused, "and it had floated out a bit from the shore and did look body-like in the rain."

"I still suspect the witnesses might need to their eyesight checked." I crossed my arms against the chill of the night and thwarted expectations. "Do you know how it died?"

"Ciara thinks it slipped down the slope when it was trying to get a drink, broke its leg, and drowned."

"Poor thing." I hesitated. "I guess we'll do coffee another time, then."

"Yes." He brushed a finger down my cheek. Though the touch was light, it nevertheless caused havoc inside. "I'm sorry."

I smiled as he dropped his hand and stepped back. "So am I."

His fingers twitched, then clenched, and I had a suspicion he was barely resisting the urge to reach for me. So I did what any sane, sensible woman would in that situation—I stepped closer, rose up on my toes, and kissed him. I kept it light and sweet—made it a tease more than a declaration. But the minute I tried to step back, his arms went around me, the kiss deepened, and it became that declaration of intent I'd been trying to avoid. It left me aching and hungry for more, and while the sane, sensible part of me cursed my impulsiveness, the rest at least had something to dream about in the long hours ahead.

"You," he said, as he eventually—and somewhat reluctantly—released me, "have totally ensured I won't sleep easily tonight."

"Good, because that was the aim, Ranger." My tone was filled with mock outrage. "Consider it payback for making our first official date nearly a *week* away. And all to win a ten-dollar bet!"

"It was twenty, and you have *no* idea how little I care about that damn bet right now."

I let my gaze drift down his length and then said, somewhat cheekily, "Oh, I think I do."

He laughed, a warm, rich sound that stirred me almost as much as his kiss. Almost. "Then how about we still keep Sunday's date, but do something a whole lot earlier?"

"Earlier as in, straight after your meeting with Ciara you'll pick me up and we'll head to Argyle?"

He raised an eyebrow. "Don't you have to get up early and run the café tomorrow?"

"I do, but I'll take eye bags and tiredness over unquenched desire any day."

"A sentiment I can certainly agree with." He caught my hand, tugged me closer again, and dropped a quick kiss on my lips. "But it could be close to midnight."

"And?"

"And I'll see you then."

With that, he left. I crossed my arms again, this time

trying to contain the warmth of his body more than anything else, and watched until he'd disappeared around the corner. Then went back inside, a silly grin on my lips and anticipation singing through my veins.

I ran upstairs to get some essentials packed, and heard Belle come in about ten minutes later. Even without connecting to her thoughts, I could feel her buzz of contented happiness. Hopefully, it was a happiness I'd share in another couple of hours.

I zipped up the bag, shoved my coat over the top of it, and then walked over to the stairs and leaned over the railing as she started up. "My, don't you just look like the cat who got the cream."

"And good cream it was," she replied, with a happy sigh.

"So much for having no energy to do anything other than eat."

"It's truly amazing just how invigorating a good steak and a good man can be." She paused, her eyes narrowing. "It would seem I'm not the only one in this outfit who's buzzing with happiness. Did Aiden pop by while I was out?"

"Sort of. Do you want a tea or coffee?"

"No, and don't change the subject."

I grinned and pushed away from the railing. "We were going to go out for coffee, but he got a last-minute call from his sister. He had to go see her about the autopsy results."

"This calamity does not explain the happiness." She paused. "I take it he's coming back?"

"Yes." I filled the kettle and flicked it on. "We're going to go back to his place in Argyle. Apparently, he decided he couldn't wait for our first official date—which was Sunday night, by the way."

"The man must have masochistic tendencies if he was intending to wait that long."

"I think he took my comment about a little pursuit never going astray a little too much to heart."

She snorted softly. "Given he was more than ready to take you out last night, I doubt that. He probably just got better odds for the Sunday."

I grinned as the kettle began to whistle softly. "That is also possibly true."

She shook her head, a smile on her lips. "Tuesdays are usually pretty slow here, so if you want to stay a bit longer with him, feel free."

I squeezed her arm in appreciation. "Thanks, but I'm not going to shirk my duty here just because hot sex is in the offering."

"I certainly would if my sex life had been as sparse as yours over the last few months."

She wouldn't, and we both knew it. I made myself a strong coffee in the vague effort to stave off the tiredness that would undoubtedly hit the longer I had to wait for Aiden, and then said, "I'm just hoping that sparseness is remedied rather than being sidetracked yet again."

She frowned. "Meaning your witch radar is sending you vibes?"

"No, not really. It might be just pessimism."

"But you don't think it is?"

"Who knows? It's not like we've found a whole lot information on soul eaters."

"I'm sure it'll be in Gran's books somewhere—we just need to find the right one."

That we did. "Anyway, forget me and my pessimism, and go get some sleep. One of us needs to be reasonably intelligent tomorrow during service."

"I'm not sure why that task always falls to *me*." Her amusement faded. "If those vibes do turn into something, you'll call me, won't you?"

I gave her the look—the one that said "don't be daft." She scowled in response and added, "You can't handle that thing alone."

"I know that, and I have no intention of doing so. But I also know it's going take both of us at full strength to deal with this thing—and right now, you're not."

"That *doesn't* answer the point of you rushing off alone if the eater appears tonight."

"I won't be—"

"Aiden hardly counts given bullets don't harm spirits."

I hesitated. "What about a compromise, then? I'll head downstairs now and pin a containment spell to your silver knife, so that it's ready if the vibes do become reality. If I can trap this spirit in whatever body it's using, then I'll call you in so we can jointly figure out a way to banish it."

"Deal," she said immediately. "But in all honesty, let's hope it doesn't get to that. Let's hope the goddamn council get their act together and calls in a proper witch to deal with the thing."

"Amen to that," I muttered, then gave her a quick hug. "Go. I'll see you tomorrow morning."

"Replete with satisfaction, hopefully."

"Amen to *that*, too."

She laughed and disappeared into her bedroom. I grabbed my coffee and headed downstairs to make good on my promise. It took nearly an hour to create and place the spell on Belle's knife, and I had no idea if it would actually work. In theory, it *should*. In theory, the spell would activate the moment the knife was lodged in flesh, and thereby trap the dark spirit. Trouble was, I'd never actually done anything like this before.

Hell, the only reason I even *knew* about the spell's existence was thanks to the abuse—to put it mildly—that my parents had flung my way over *not* trying a very similar spell in the tumultuous nights that had followed my failed attempt to save my sister's life. Never mind the fact that, as a sixteen-year-old, I'd only *just* started learning about the higher-level spells such as sorcerer immobilizations and dark spirit containment, and certainly hadn't gotten as far as practicing them yet.

I'd made damn sure I'd learned about them afterwards, of course; it might have been altogether too late to save Catherine's life, but I wasn't about to risk the life of the only other person who'd meant anything to me—Belle. Especially since we had no idea—either then *or* now—if the dark sorcerer who'd killed Cat was actually dead. Given the amount of blood and the lack of a body, it had been presumed that the dark spirits he'd used had literally come to claim their pound of flesh, but no one could say with absolute certainty that he'd died.

In the darkest of my dreams, I saw him coming for me. But whether that was simply the lingering fear of the teenager I'd been, or a premonition of a future event, I couldn't really say.

I frowned and placed the knife securely into a backpack, then gathered a few other potions and magical items, including two of the strongest charms we had on hand. They were both made of tawny agate, which was the strongest of the protective agates. We'd magically enhanced its natural ability to drive away spirits, protect from psychic attack, and stop most minor magics, and had then encased them in a cage made of two old iron nails, which also had protective qualities. We'd created them a few days after the vampire's death, even as we'd vaguely hoped they wouldn't be necessary. But with a large wellspring still unprotected, *that* was always going to be unlikely.

With everything done, I walked back upstairs to replace my half-drunk and very cold coffee, and then headed over to the sofa to pick up the book I'd been reading earlier. Ten pages in, I found the first true mention of soul eaters—and a handwritten note on the side of the page indicating what book to grab to uncover more. According to the text, there were several German legends about the *Nachzehrer*, a soul-consuming monster who rose from the grave to devour his or her own kin. It was also believed that anyone hearing the ringing a church bell at midnight would be subsequently doomed to die under the *Nachzehrer*'s hand.

Not something I really wanted to know.

But it wasn't like the rest of it exactly applied to our situation, given none of our victims were in any way related—unless, of course, "related" also meant lovers and friends. Still, it was a start, and maybe once I read the book the note mentioned, we'd find out more.

I kept reading, but there was nothing else about soul eaters. It was just a whole lot of random information about other evil spirit types I could only *hope* never found their way here. I bookmarked the page so I could find the reference once Belle was awake, and then rose to grab another coffee.

And that's when I heard it—the church bell, ringing three times before falling into a silence filled with evil and death.

Which, if the last time was anything to go by, meant the soul eater was not only *out* there in the darkness, but about to take another life.

If I wanted to stop it, I needed to be fast. As I rattled down the old wooden steps and headed for the reading room, I dug my phone out of my pocket and called Aiden.

He answered on the second ring. "Impatience. I like it."

"I really wish that was the reason I'm ringing." I opened the storage locker and grabbed the pack. "Our soul eater is out hunting."

He swore. "Can you track it?"

"Yes."

"Be there in five." He hung up.

I grabbed the backpack, shoved on my coat and checked the keys were still in its pocket, and then headed out. The night air was icy and still, and other than the rumble of an approaching truck, there was little in the way of noise. It was almost as if the regular sounds of the night had been silenced by the thread of evil creeping like a thief through the darkness.

It was a thief that was hungry.

Very hungry.

I shivered and moved across to the curb as twin beams of light swept into Mostyn Street and raced toward me. Once Aiden's truck had stopped, I climbed inside.

"Where to?" he asked, even as he pulled away from the curb.

I shoved the pack at my feet and wound down the window; the icy air slapped my face and drew a soft gasp from my lips, but I ignored the discomfort and reached with that psychic bit of me able to sense these things.

"Straight ahead, and then left."

Tires squealed as we took the corner at speed. I held onto the handgrip to steady myself, and tried to concentrate on the tenuous thread that pulsed through the night.

"Turn right at the next road."

"That's the Pyrenees Highway." His voice was grim. "Looks like we're heading to Maldoon and the Marin reservation."

"It can't just be about the Marins," I said, "because Marlinda wasn't a werewolf, let alone a Marin, was she?"

"No, but she did have a rather long relationship with Luc Marin, Aron's older brother, so there *is* a connection."

"Meaning this still could still be about revenge." I paused as the thread tugged sideways. "Right at the next road."

"We're definitely heading back to Maldoon." He slowed just enough to take the corner safely, and then accelerated away again.

I didn't say anything. I simply concentrated on the steadily strengthening thread of evil. This thing *wasn't* in Maldoon.

But it wasn't the pulsing that told me that.

It was the faint wisps of fog that were beginning to sidle across the road. It was the same sort of fog that had been present with the first murder. Now, as then, the patches gradually got thicker, until both the road and the land beyond either shoulder were nothing more a wasteland of white.

The soul eater was here somewhere.

"Slow down," I said.

He immediately did so. "There's nothing out here but scrub."

"Maybe." And maybe not. I flexed my fingers, but it did little to ease the growing tension. Ahead, at the very edge of the headlight's reach, was a vague and rather squat outline. "What's that?"

"It's one of the old brick cottages that are scattered all around this area. Many of them belong to—or are leased by—the Marin pack, even though they're outside pack ground."

"We need to check it out." The evil I was sensing might not be coming from within that cottage, but it *was* very close to it. I dragged up my backpack and quickly undid it.

"I'll continue on and turn around at the next farm gate. That way, we'll hopefully allay the suspicions of anyone who might be in that building."

He turned off the headlights once we were past the cottage and, at the next farm gate, turned around and then stopped. We were near enough that the cottage was visible despite the fog, but hopefully not so close that whoever was inside would have taken much notice of the truck's engine.

I pulled the charms from the backpack and handed him one. Aiden slipped it over his neck without comment and tucked it out of sight under his sweater. I couldn't help the smile that touched my lips despite the seriousness of the situation.

"What?" he immediately said.

"I was just thinking how much things have changed. A month ago you would have distrusted *anything* to do with witches and witchcraft."

"*That* still lingers. I just happen to trust you." He paused. "I'm gathering the stone offers protection against the soul eater or whatever other kind of evil spirit we might be dealing with?"

"Yes." I slipped the second charm over my head and let it rest beside the minor warding charm I wore every day. "Though how much protection it'll provide, I can't say, because it's a general charm rather than one aimed at a specific spirit."

"And therefore not as strong?" When I nodded, he added, "Then I'd best get my gun."

I smiled. "A gun won't kill a spirit."

"But it will kill the flesh it's wearing, right?"

"In this case, we need to restrain the spirit within the body before we do anything like that, and then find a way to completely banish or destroy it."

He raised an eyebrow. "I doubt you'll be given time to construct a pentagram."

"No, and they're not something I can make on the fly anyway."

"Then how are you going to deal with it?"

"I shouldn't *have* to be dealing with it," I bit back somewhat testily, and then took a deep breath to calm the tension. "I've pinned a restraint spell to a silver knife. The combination should work."

"And if it doesn't?"

"Then pray like fuck the charms work."

"Right." He hesitated, his gaze sweeping me. "Ready?"

Not really, I wanted to say, even as I climbed out of the truck. I slung the pack over my shoulder and then caught the door with my fingertips to ease it close. Aiden grabbed a gun and a flashlight from the locked box in the back of his truck, and handed the latter to me. I didn't bother turning it on. The fog was a wall of white, and it was unlikely the flashlight's beam would do much more than reveal our presence to whatever waited ahead.

We walked back down the road, keeping to the bitumen rather than the road's stony shoulders in an effort to cut down our noise—or rather, my noise. He was as silent as a ghost. But given how little we knew about soul eaters, it was totally possible that it would sense our approach in much the same manner as vampires could, only via our life forces or souls rather than the pulse of our blood.

The old building began to loom out of the fog. It was small and rectangular, with a wooden door facing the road and two single-sash windows on either side of this. The roof was tin, and some sort of creeper climbed over the gable end closest to us. A chimney rose from the other end, but despite the chill of the night, no smoke rose

The closer we got to the building, the greater the pulse of evil became, until its force was so strong my skin crawled.

Then I felt it—the specter of death, approaching fast. It wasn't coming for Aiden or me, but rather whoever was inside the building.

I fought the desire to run and instead silently began a repelling incantation, letting it gather around my fingers in readiness. I had no idea what might wait inside that building, but I'd yet to come across an entity that could *not* be forced away by such a spell.

And I hoped, even as the thought crossed my mind, that it wouldn't change tonight.

Aiden slowed as we approached the end of the building. He motioned me to the far side of the door, but I shook my head, stepped closer, and whispered, "Magic before gun."

He hesitated and then nodded. "On three, then."

We crept forward in single file, ducked under the first small window, and stopped either side of the door.

He reached for the handle and tested it. It turned. His gaze rose to mine and he silently began the countdown.

He didn't get to one. He barely got to two.

From inside the cottage came a bloodcurdling scream that abruptly cut off.

Death had just claimed her prize.

CHAPTER
seven

Aiden immediately thrust the door open. I threw the spell into the cottage, spread it as wide as I could, and then directed to our right, as far away from the door and us as possible. Something heavy hit the chimney end of the cottage and then screamed. This time, it was a sound of anger, not agony, and male rather than female.

The air rushed out the cottage, as if it couldn't wait to escape in the presence of the thing inside. It was filled with a thick mix of anger, evil, and death, and the force of it so strong that for several seconds, I couldn't even breathe. Whoever—whatever—the stranger might have once been, he was now little more than flesh controlled by the spirit who had both ended his life and was now extending it.

And that spirit was *foul*.

Aiden stepped into the cottage, his gun aimed at the utter darkness to the right, and his stance wary. "Keep your hands up and don't move, or I *will* shoot."

Another scream was the only reply, and a heartbeat later, Aiden followed through with his threat. Two shots rang out, the sound echoing harshly across the silence. Then he swore and leaped sideways, away from the door and me. A flash of pale skin followed his movement and the smack of flesh against flesh and heavy grunts began to punctuate the air.

Aiden's grunts, not the creature's.

I flicked the flashlight on, desperate to see what was going on. The powerful beam banished the darkness and revealed Aiden fighting a monster of a man. It also revealed a woman lying naked on the double bed that rested against gable end wall to my left, a look of horror frozen on her face.

My gaze flicked back to the two men. Aiden's teeth were bared and his arms thrust out straight as he battled to keep the stranger away from his throat. Though his sweater hid the charm I'd given him, its force burned across my senses, a clean, bright energy that was barely keeping the darkness at bay. The fact that the charm was active suggested the stranger wasn't *only* punching Aiden in an effort to break the lock of his grip, but also reaching for Aiden's soul.

I quickly created a spell to force the stranger from him, but didn't release it. Given the fierceness of Aiden's grip on the monster, there was every chance the spell would affect them both. The last thing I wanted was to break the current status quo in the stranger's favor.

I swore and swung the flashlight around, looking for some nonmagical means of distraction. From just under the edge of the old wrought iron bed came the gleam of metal.

Aiden's gun.

The creature must have torn it from Aiden's grip, because I doubted he'd have lost it otherwise. I quickly placed the flashlight just inside the door so that it spotlighted the two men, and then dove for the weapon. Aiden must have caught the movement because, even as I twisted around, ready to fire, he bucked hard to unsettle the stranger's balance and, at the same time, heaved him upright.

As he released him and fell back, out of the way, I fired. The first one missed. The second one didn't. It blasted into the stranger's upper chest, and he howled in response. Again, it was a sound of fury rather than pain, but one that was abruptly cut off as Aiden's fist smashed into the stranger's face, flattening his nose and sending blood and gore flying. Another blow followed, and the big man's head snapped up and back. As he began to topple backward, I released the spell, tore him from Aiden, and flung him out the door. Aiden scrambled upright, grabbed the gun from me, and followed.

Two more shots echoed, and then silence.

I ran to the doorway. Aiden stood on the shoulder of the road, his gun raised and body tense. The big man lay facedown on the other side, his outline barely visible through the wall of white between us. I couldn't see if he was breathing or not, but he certainly *was* moving. It was little more than a series of jerks and shudders at first, and reminded me somewhat of a broken marionette being slowly brought to life by a determined puppet master. Which, given the situation, was nothing more than the truth.

"How the fuck is that even possible?" Aiden said, as the big man's body heaved upright. "He's been shot *six* times, including two into his fucking knees. At the very least, he should be rolling around in agony, not climbing to his goddamn feet."

"As I keep saying, I'm no expert when it comes to these things." Nor did I ever want to become one. I swung the pack around and grabbed the silver knife. The thick fog swirled around it, and blue fire flickered briefly along the blade—a reaction that confirmed this fog wasn't natural. "Stay here while I try to stop this thing from escaping."

"Be careful."

"Always." I hesitated. "If the host attacks, go for a head shot."

I had no idea if even *that* would actually stop the big man, but it should at least make him pause. Which, in turn, should give me enough time to shove the knife into his chest and pin the spirit.

Which was at least one too many shoulds for my liking.

I carefully moved forward. Just as I reached the halfway point, the spirit must have sensed me, because, without any sort of warning, the big man was in the air and arrowing straight at me.

I reacted instinctively and threw myself sideways, out of his way. Gunshots bit across the night, but if they had any effect it wasn't obvious. I'd barely caught my balance when the big man's fingers latched on to my sweater and yanked me backward. I slashed wildly with the knife, catching my arm even as I severed two of his digits. Blood spurted over my sleeve as blue fire began to crawl across the remains of his hand, but he didn't release me. Instead, he gripped the blade with his other hand, wrenched it from my grip, and tossed it away from us both. The agate charm came to life, burning fiercely against the darkness gathering around me. I swore, twisted fully around, and kneed him as hard as I could in the balls. He might be little more than dead flesh controlled by a spirit, but there were some things that remained instinctive.

The pain of crushed nuts was one of those things.

As he doubled over, I hit him as hard as I could with both hands, breaking his grip on my arm and forcing him away from me. As he staggered backward, failing for balance and screaming in fury, another shot rang out. The man's head exploded, showering me in blood, bone, and brain matter. My stomach heaved but I bit my lip, fighting for control as I raced toward the fiery glow of the knife.

But even as I picked it up, the soul eater fled, and the big man crumbled to a lifeless, bloody pile in the middle of the road.

Almost immediately, reaction set in. I stumbled over to the nearest tree and was totally and violently ill.

Aiden appeared beside me a few minutes later. He tucked a couple stray strands of hair away from my face, his fingers so warm against my cheek, and then offered me a bottle of water. Once I'd rinsed out my mouth, he handed me a dampened handkerchief. I wiped the bloody remnants of flesh and bone away from my face, but the feel of them lingered. My stomach heaved again; I swallowed heavily and somehow managed to control it.

"Are you okay?" he asked softly.

"No, I'm fucking *not*. You need to get a proper witch here, Aiden, because I can't do this—" A hiccup cut the rest of my sentence off, and the tears started to flow.

He didn't say anything. He just gathered me in his arms and held me tight. And lord, it felt so damn safe, so damn comforting, tender, and *right*, that it only made the tears flow harder.

Because no matter what happened between us in the future, it was never going to be "right."

Not because of what I was, not because of any lies I might have told or might still tell, but because of what *he* was.

I'm not sure how long we stood there in the middle of the road. Long enough for the tears to stop falling. Long enough for his warmth and closeness to be causing all sorts of other problems—the least of which was the desire to remain locked in his embrace. But he had a job to do; staying here like this certainly wasn't an option.

I pulled back and hastily wiped away the lingering tears. "I think I've utterly soaked your poor sweater."

"It's not wool, so it's in no danger of shrinking." He half smiled, though it didn't reach as far as his eyes. "I need to call in the troops. Why don't we get you back to the truck—there's an old sweater and a pair of track pants in the back. They'll swim on you, but it's still a better option than remaining in your current clothes until I can get someone to take you home."

I crossed my arms and tried not to think about the goop. "Meaning you're not entrusting me with your truck a second time?"

"It's not a reflection on your driving skills but rather a necessity. I need it to block off the road."

Of course he did—especially with the big man's body still in the middle of it. I glanced past him and studied the small cottage. With the soul eater gone, the fog quickly dissipating, taking with it the lingering remnants of evil.

But not the feel of death.

I started to rub my arms, but stopped abruptly when I felt wetness. I swallowed heavily and said, "I need to look at the body of the woman inside."

He hesitated, and then nodded. "Wait for me to get back with the truck, and we'll go in together."

As he jogged back to his vehicle, I walked around the body of the big man to retrieve my knife, and then went back to my pack and secured the blade. The last thing I wanted to risk was one of the other rangers confiscating it. By the time Aiden returned, the fog had completely cleared. The red and blue emergency lights at the front and rear of his truck washed across the darkness, casting grotesque shadows around the body on the road.

Aiden pressed a hand against my spine and lightly guided me inside. "What are you hoping to see?"

"Whether she died the same way as Aron."

I stopped and crossed my arms against the chill in the air. Unlike Aron, there was no hint of peacefulness in her expression, but rather shock and growing horror. Whether that meant we'd interrupted the soul eater before he'd fully consumed her soul, I couldn't say. Belle could have told me, but I was loath to reach out to her.

Except I'm awake because I had to pee, she said. *What do you need?*

Can you merge with me briefly, and tell me what you see?

Hang on while I move across to the sofa. There was a brief pause. *Right. You might want to warn Aiden first though.*

I glanced at him. "I've just asked Belle to mind merge with me, so that she can see the victim and tell us what happened."

He blinked. "She's taking you over?"

"No, it's more—" I hesitated. "It's hard to explain, but she'll see what I can't, so if you've any questions, she can answer them through me."

"It's not a body swap thing, is it?"

I smiled and touched his arms. "No. Our souls are staying right where they belong. Ready?"

He hesitated, and then nodded. I closed my eyes and reached psychically for Belle. Her mind closed around mine and the two fused—not so deeply that she became a part of me, but deep enough that she could use her talents while seeing through my eyes.

A shudder went through her—through me.

"Her soul was only half torn from her body," she said. "She's dead, and yet not."

Aiden's confusion echoed my own. "Meaning what?"

"Meaning the soul eater consumed enough of her soul to kill her flesh, but left enough behind that her awareness lingers within the boundaries of this place."

"I can't feel a ghost, Belle," I commented.

"You wouldn't," she replied. "Because what remains isn't really a ghost. It's merely a shade—a remnant of what she was. Shades have neither consciousness nor any true ability to interact with this world."

"Have you any idea why her expression is so different to Aron's?" I asked. "He looked as if he'd been asleep when it happened. This woman looks as if she was in the middle of sex."

"She was," Aiden said. "The scent of arousal and desire lingers in the air, but not completion."

"Then perhaps your arrival on the scene is the difference," Belle said. "Maybe our soul eater normally only dines *after* its victims have fallen into a contented sleep. You might have forced it to do otherwise."

"I wouldn't have thought a soul eater would care one way or another about whether its victims were aware or not," Aiden said.

"There's plenty of spirits who feed on souls during

the act of sex," I said. "But maybe this one has learned that the best way to avoid detection is to make it look like nothing untoward happened."

"After all," Belle added, "would you be considering either of these deaths murder if we hadn't said anything?"

"Probably not." His voice was grim. "And the council still mightn't."

"Then the fucking council are fools," Belle said.

"No," he bit back. "They're merely cautious, and rightly so, given up until now we've had no confirmation that these murders are a result of supernatural interference."

"It's a shame we didn't think to record what happened out on the road, because *that* would certainly prove someone beyond the norm is happening here proof."

"I did record it—that's why I turned the truck around to face the cottage. Whether anything will be visible through the fog is another matter."

"And if the council decides there's not enough proof?" I asked. "What then? How many more people have to die before someone will pick up the phone and call the RWA in? Or do we have to do it?"

"That's the one thing you shouldn't be doing—your position here is tenuous enough."

"Meaning what?" I said, my voice sharp.

"I'll tell you later. Right now, I've another murder scene to lock down." His expression was grim. "But I promise you this, if the council doesn't make a decision, I'll call in the RWA myself."

"Good," Belle said. "Do you need anything else? Because if not, I'm off back to bed."

"No," Aiden said, even as I added, "Thanks, Belle."

Her thoughts disconnected from mine and tiredness washed through me. I scrubbed a hand across my eyes and then said, "Do you know who the victim is?"

"Yes." He caught my elbow and gently—but firmly—led me out of the cottage, grabbing my backpack on the way through. "Her name is Teresa White. She works part-time at the bakery up near the ranger station."

"And the monster of a man?"

"I'm not sure, but he does have the coloring of the Schmidt pack, who hark from South Australia."

I frowned. "What's he doing here, then?"

Aiden shrugged. "He could have come here under the exchange program I mentioned earlier. It would explain why he was here with Teresa."

"Were they an item?"

"I have no idea. They might have simply come here to relieve tensions. These old cottages are often used by those who don't as yet have a place of their own but who want to escape the prying eyes of the pack. If Schmidt was here under an exchange, he'd have usage rights."

"If that's the case, then maybe revenge isn't the primary motivation behind these attacks, given Schmidt isn't in any way related to Aron."

"Possibly. Right now, we're not discounting *any* theory."

I glanced at him and raised an eyebrow. "Meaning there are other theories?"

"Yes, but Larissa remains our number-one suspect." He opened the truck door and helped me up onto the seat. "She might not be directly responsible for these murders, but I can't discount the possibility that she hired a witch to bring this evil into the reservation."

"When are you meeting with the council?"

"Tomorrow morning." He paused. "Ciara got Aron's tox results back. There were no drugs or alcohol in his system, and no conclusive means of death."

"Good." When he raised his eyebrow, I added, "It means the council doesn't just have to rely on your word or even mine. They now have an inconclusive autopsy result and whatever the dash cam might have caught tonight. Surely *that* will be enough."

"I would think so. They're not fools, no matter what you and Belle think." He lightly squeezed my leg, and then stepped back. The warmth of his touch lingered, chasing away much of the chill that still rolled through me. "There's a blanket in the back if you need it. It shouldn't be too long before someone gets here to drive you back."

"Thanks." I hesitated, but couldn't help adding, "This is so *not* how I'd envisaged spending the midnight hour."

"Me neither." He grimaced. "Fate does seem intent on keeping us apart right now."

She certainly did. "We'll just have to make a more determined effort tomorrow night."

His smile crinkled the corners of his bright eyes. "Indeed we will."

He slammed the door shut, got his kit out of the back of the truck, and then headed back to the cottage. I twisted around, grabbed the shirt and pants he'd mentioned, and swiftly changed. They did indeed swim on me but I didn't really care. Not when they filled my nostrils with his musky, smoky wood scent.

I settled down in the seat and must have slept, because the next thing I knew, the door opened and an altogether too cheery voice said, "Right, Ms. Grace, let's get you back home."

"Please, call me Lizzie," I muttered, as I pushed

upright and scrubbed a hand across my eyes. "What time is it?"

"Close to one," the woman at the door replied. It took me a moment to realize it was Jaz. "Do you need a hand out of the truck?"

I shook my head, gathered my discarded clothes, and jumped out. She led me across to one of the green-and-white SUVs the rangers generally used, opened the door, and offered me a hand up.

I stepped away from her reach and said, with some amusement, "I'm not an invalid."

"The boss said to look after you," she replied equably. "So look after you I will. There's a hot chocolate sitting in the center console with your name on it."

I climbed in, and then picked up the chocolate and peeled off the lid. Steam rose, suggesting it had only recently been made. "Where did you get hot chocolate at this hour of the night?"

Her cheeks dimpled as she started up the car and pulled away from the cottage. "My man is a barista. I booted him out of bed to make them for us while I got ready."

I grinned. "I'm sure he was happy about *that*."

"Oh, totally." Her laugh was bright and warm. "But we haven't been married for long, and we're still in that honeymoon phase of trying our best to please each other."

I raised an eyebrow. "Meaning you don't expect it to last?"

"The honeymoon phase? Hell, no." Her grin flashed. "The Marins have a reputation for being a little more staid when it comes to traditional roles than most other packs."

"I take it you're not a Marin, then?"

"Nah, I'm one of the Rankin mob, out of New South

Wales." She grabbed her chocolate and took a sip. "It was his skill with hot chocolate that first attracted me to him."

"He does make a good chocolate."

Her cheeks dimpled again. "It's one of his many talents, I've since discovered."

We chatted on, and by the time we'd reached Castle Rock and the café, it really felt like we were old friends rather than two people who'd only just met. I drained the last of my chocolate, placed the cup back, and gathered my bundle of clothes.

"Thanks for the lift and the hot chocolate, Jaz." Cold air whipped in the minute I opened the door, eliciting a shiver from both of us. "If you and Levi are in the area, drop by. We may not be able to match the hot chocolate, but we do have some pretty awesome cakes."

"So I've heard," she said. "See you soon, then."

I slammed the door shut and headed into the café. I didn't bother putting my clothes into the wash basket—I just dumped them straight into the bin. I doubted I'd be able to wear them again without memory rising.

I had a quick shower to wash away any bits of the man monster that might remain, and then crawled into bed and went to sleep.

The café was busy from the get-go the next morning, with a steady stream of customers filing in and out. Most of them were sit-downs, but there were plenty who came in to take away cake, biscuits, or hot drinks—which was good for our bottom line.

It wasn't until after two that things began to ease. As I walked into the kitchen with a stack of plates, Mike—our chef—said, "Lizzie, can I talk to you for a moment?"

"Sure." I put the plates on the bench to the right of the dishwasher, and turned around. "What about?"

He hesitated, a hint of uncertainty touching his eyes. While most werewolves—aside from the O'Connors—had amber eyes, there were lots of color variations between packs. Mike's eyes were a light honey gold in color, which suggested that although he hailed from the Sinclair pack, he'd originated from outside this reservation.

"Do you mind if we go out the back, where it's a bit more private? It's a personal matter."

"Sure." I motioned him to lead the way and then followed. Belle glanced at me, eyebrows raised in silent query. I shrugged and said, *Why don't you come with us?*

She was, after all, co-owner of the place, and if there was a problem then we both needed to deal with it.

I'll keep in light contact. If it's something serious, I'll come out. Fair enough.

Mike pushed the rear door open and stepped out into the parking lot. I grabbed a coat from the nearby hook and shoved my hands through the sleeves as I followed him out. It was, I was relieved to discover, a whole lot warmer than it had been last night. There was even some blue sky beginning to appear, which gave me some hope that the summer weather that had so far been absent mightn't be too far away.

When Mike didn't immediately speak, I stopped and said, "What's the problem?"

"No problem." He hesitated. "But I'd like to ask you a favor."

Caution immediately stirred. I'd gotten myself into trouble more than once for offering to help someone out before I actually knew what they wanted, and I certainly didn't want step straight into a similar situation here. Not with everything else that was currently going on.

"What do you need?"

He scrubbed a hand across his chin and glanced across the lot. Aside from the vehicles and a lone blackbird pulling rubbish out of a nearby bin, the place was empty. After another second or two, he somewhat reluctantly said, "I was wondering if you'd meet with my sister. Her daughter has gone missing, and she'd like your help to find her."

The last time I'd tried to find someone's daughter, it hadn't ended well—and Mike was well aware of that. Maybe that was why he was so hesitant. "Has she filed a missing person's report?"

"No. I told her to, but she refuses."

The stirrings of caution became trepidation. "Why?"

"Because my sister is Meika."

The heaviness with which he said that implied I should have been familiar with her name and that only strengthened the trepidation. "I'm afraid I don't—"

"Her daughter's name is Larissa," he cut in. "Larissa Marin."

No wonder he'd wanted to speak out in the parking lot. While I had no doubt plenty of people were aware of their connection, he certainly wouldn't want to be discussing something like this in hearing distance of others.

"I didn't know that, Mike. I'm sorry if we've inadvertently said anything over the last few days that upset you."

"You and Belle have treated me no different than before all this mess, which is more than can be said about some in the reservation." A grim smile touched his lips. "I know what they're all saying, but she didn't do it. She didn't kill Aron."

I hesitated, but there was no point in pussyfooting

around. "She did threaten his family, Mike, and she does apparently have a reputation for violence."

"She's a wild one, to be sure, but I promise you, murder isn't her style."

It was natural for them both to believe that, but if she'd gone on an alcohol or drug-fueled binge, anything was possible. And while I certainly didn't believe she was directly responsible for the murders, she was still a suspect when it came to bringing the soul eater into the reservation.

"Neither you nor your sister can be absolutely sure of that."

"But we can, because she went missing two days *before* Aron's death. She didn't do it. She wasn't around to do it."

"She wasn't missing from the compound; she was banned. I know that much, Mike."

"Banned from there, yes, but she was staying at her mom's place in Guildford. But she hasn't been sighted for several days now, and with these deaths and all, we're both worried." He paused. "She'll pay your regular fee, of course."

I waved the offer away. "I'll do it as a favor to you, but be warned—if I do find her, I'll be obliged to tell the rangers."

"That's fine, because that's exactly what Meika wants to convince her to do anyway. I'm not sure she'll be successful, though. Larissa can be somewhat... stubborn."

More than stubborn, from what Aiden had said. "There's also no guarantee I'll find her. You've heard me talk about psychometry enough to know it can be hit-and-miss."

"I know, and I told Meika that." He grimaced. "She still wants you to try."

"Okay. I can book her in tomorrow—"

"Can you do it this afternoon? At her place?" he cut in. "She doesn't want to come into town if she can help it, what with all the gossip that's currently about."

I hesitated. *Belle, what do you think?*

If Larissa's desire for revenge is the reason the soul eater is here, then she may be tainted by its darkness, she said. *So while I think you should attempt to find her, I'd be creating a protective circle around yourself before you try it.*

Good idea. If she was tainted or otherwise linked to the dark spirit, however lightly, the circle would at least prevent it from sensing my attempt to find Larissa. And that, in turn, might just save Larissa's life.

If she was still alive to save, that was.

I frowned and hoped like hell that wasn't a premonition coming through. There'd been enough deaths in this reservation already.

"Okay," I said, "I'll go there once we've closed the café."

"Thank you." He gripped my arm lightly and then released me. "I'll come with you, though, if you don't mind. I also want to be there if you actually go look for her. She's more likely to talk to me if she's in a mood than a stranger."

I hesitated again and then nodded. It wouldn't hurt to have him along if and when I found Larissa, and not just because he could talk sense into his niece. Larissa was a werewolf, and a strong one at that, going by what Aiden had said. I might be able to protect myself magically, but physically I'd be very much at the other woman's mercy. *That* was a risk I had no intention of taking.

"Fine." I glanced at my watch. "We'll leave at three thirty. Can you ring your sister and let her know we're coming?"

"I will, and thanks again."

I nodded and followed him back inside. Belle raised an eyebrow and silently said, *Are you going to call Aiden?*

I shook my head. *Not until there's something to call him about. It may amount to nothing.*

It won't if that vague premonition proves to be correct.

I seriously hope it isn't. I don't need to see or find any more dead people, Belle.

On that, we are agreed.

Once we'd finished clearing the café and cleaning up, I grabbed my backpack and purse, then headed into the reading room to grab my spell stones.

"Did you bring in your car or did you walk today?" I asked Mike, as I followed him out into the parking lot.

He smiled, though it did little to hide the tension in him. "It was too bloody cold to walk this morning. I biked it over."

Meaning a motorbike, not a bicycle. "I'll follow you around to your sister's, then."

He nodded and walked across to the far side of the parking lot. I jumped into our old wagon and turned her around. Mike—now riding a bright red-and-white motorcycle—couldn't be missed, and not because of its size or color, but because of the sheer volume of noise it made.

We headed out of Castle Rock on the Midland Highway, going toward Argyle rather than Maldoon. I guess that was to be expected, given what he'd said about his sister's reluctance to meet anywhere too public. Undoubtedly the Marin pack's gossip brigade was just as fierce and nosy as those here in Castle Rock.

We slowed down as we approached Guildford, and

turned right at a general store that looked to have been around since the gold rush days. About halfway down the street, Mike pulled into a graveled driveway and stopped. I did the same and grabbed my coat and purse before climbing out. The house was only a little larger than the cottage we'd been at last night, and looked to be about the same vintage, even though it was weatherboard rather than brick. The lace curtains covering the window to the left of the blue-painted door twitched, indicating we'd been seen.

"This way." Mike led me up the somewhat rickety wooden stairs to the porch. The door opened as we approached, and a thin, somewhat haggard-looking woman with a surprisingly lush mane of black hair appeared.

"Oh, Ms. Grace, I'm so glad you were able to come here." Her golden eyes briefly glimmered with tears. "It's so unlike Larissa to be gone this long. I fear—"

She stopped and drew in a deep breath. I smiled, but resisted the urge to touch her arm in comfort. Though I'd been well enough trained that everyday contact with people posed little threat, there were nevertheless some situations—such as when I was caught by surprise or when, like now, the emotions were so very strong—that no amount of safeguards could stop them from affecting me.

She blinked back tears and added, "Thank you."

I nodded and followed Mike into the cottage. It was nominally larger than it had initially looked, consisting of a small hallway from which there were three doors—two bedrooms and living room—and a kitchen/dining area that ran the length of the back room. There was a small covered porch beyond the rear door that connected the house to another building—the bathroom and laundry, I suspected.

Mike waved me toward the old wooden table to the right of the door. "Would you like a cup of tea or coffee?"

I walked over but didn't sit down. Despite the crowded hominess of the place, desperation, fear, and something else—something that needled my senses and made my skin crawl—touched the air. I really didn't want to stay here any longer than necessary, and I certainly wasn't about to try and find Larissa without making a protection circle. I might be using psychic rather than witch powers, but if something went wrong—if my attempt to find her became either a full-blown connection or somehow alerted the dark spirit—I wanted to ensure I was utterly safe.

He filled up the kettle and put it on anyway. Meika came in a few seconds later with something silver dangling from her left hand. "This is Larissa's," she said. "Mike said you needed something of hers to focus on."

"I do." I held out my hand and she dropped the chain and small pendant into my palm. Though I had my psi skills locked down fairly tight, I still should have felt a tingle if there'd been a recent connection to Larissa. But there was nothing. The small Celtic cross felt inert. Dead.

I tried not to think about what that might mean and glanced around. The long kitchen was rather crowded, and between all the tubs filled with what looked like material and cotton reels, and the sewing machine table set up in the far corner, there was little room to truly move.

"Do you mind if I go into the living area? I need to sit down within a protection circle to try this."

"Sure," she said, and stepped to one side. "It's the door on the left."

I made my way back down the hall and walked into

the front room. It was simply furnished, with a long sofa under the window and a well-worn chair to the left. A TV dominated the wall directly opposite the window, and the outside wall was lined with bookcases that were filled with DVDs and Blu-rays rather than books. There was a coffee table in the center of the room, but aside from that, the room was surprisingly free of clutter.

I glanced around as Meika and Mike appeared at the doorway. "Do you mind if I move the coffee table?"

"Feel free." She hesitated. "Are we allowed to watch?"

"Aside from when I'm creating the protection circle, there won't be much to see other than me silently sitting on the floor."

"I'd still like to be here, just in case."

Just in case you find her and she's dead. She didn't say those words but they nevertheless hovered in the air. I wasn't sure how being in the room when or if I discovered that was going to help, but I guess it was a natural desire.

"I've no problems with either of you watching, but once I set up the stone circle around me, you mustn't come near me or the stones," I said. "That will break any connection I might have with her."

Which was a lie, but it was far better she believed that than me admitting I was worried about a soul eater attacking me through her daughter.

"I'll just sit over on my chair, then," she said, and did so. "This is okay, isn't it?"

I nodded and moved the coffee table closer to the bookcases. Then I sat down, placed the necklace in front of me on the floor and pulled the small silk bag from my purse. Once I'd freed the stones, I silently began the protection spell, placing each stone down on the carpet as

I wove the spell threads onto them, until the circle was complete and the energy of the spell flowed around me so strongly that the hairs at the back of my neck rose in response. While it wasn't the strongest protection circle I'd ever created, it was as encompassing as I could make it under the circumstances. I breathed deeply to calm my nerves then picked up the necklace and pressed the Celtic cross into my palm. The metal was cool against my skin. Cool and lifeless.

Without allowing myself to dwell on the possible reason for that, I closed my eyes and reached down to that place deep inside where my second sight lay leashed and waiting.

For several seconds, nothing happened. The metal remained cool and inert. Then, gradually, warmth stirred within the cross's cold heart. It was a distant thing, but it did at least mean that, as of this moment, Larissa was alive—that she, unlike Aron, hadn't met her death at the hands of our soul eater. The pendant would have remained inert if it had been otherwise.

I reached deeper, trying to connect with that faint flutter of heat, and drag from its heart some idea of location. It didn't work—and that perhaps meant Larissa hadn't worn this necklace very much in recent weeks.

At least, that's what I hoped was happening.

I opened my eyes, scrubbed my free hand across my eyes, and then looked around at Meika. "I can't grab a connection with this pendant. Do you have anything else she might have worn more recently?"

Meika shook her head. "Not here, but there's probably something up at her place on the reservation. I could take you there now—"

"No," I cut in, gently but firmly. "It'll take more time

and strength than I currently have."

"Oh." She clasped her hands together, her expression one of disappointment and desperation. "Tomorrow, then?"

I hesitated. I was more than happy to try and find her tomorrow, but there was no way I could do so without informing Aiden. "I can, but I'll have to bring one of the rangers with me. There'll be hell to pay if I don't."

"Is that really necessary? Larissa will just run the minute she spots one of them. She's never trusted them."

The feeling was completely mutual, I was sure. But all I said was, "People are dead, Meika. Larissa may well be innocent, but she needs to come forward and talk to the rangers to prove that. Until she does, she'll remain their number-one suspect."

"But if I could talk to her first, reassure her—"

"It's better if it's done this way, Meika," Mike said gently. "People can see we're doing the right thing, and have nothing to hide or fear."

"The gossips don't care about right and wrong—not as long as they've a juicy morsel to sink their teeth into." She paused and took a deep, shuddery breath. "But okay, we'll play it your way. Can you come to the reservation tomorrow morning? Around ten? The worst of the gossips will have moved into Maldoon for their morning tea bitch session by then."

"Sure," I said, barely restraining my grin.

"Good." She thrust to her feet. "Are you sure you don't want a cup of tea?"

"Yes. Thank you."

She nodded and left. I deactivated the protection spell and carefully placed my stones back into their silk bag.

Mike stepped forward and helped me up. "Is she alive?" he asked softly. "I know you can sense things like that, and it looked to me like you were holding something back."

I hesitated. "There was a pulse within the heart of the cross, which suggests life. But I can't guarantee it, and I can't tell you what state she's in or where she might be, because the connection was so damn faint."

He drew in a breath, and then released it slowly. "That's at least something. To be honest, I'd actually thought she might have been dead."

I frowned. "Why?"

"Because even at her wildest, she'd always come home."

"Which suggests she has something to fear by doing so."

"I know it looks that way, but I just won't believe she'd kill Aron. They were longtime friends." He ran a hand through his close-cropped hair. "And she certainly had no reason to drown Marlinda."

"Maybe friendship became something more. Maybe she saw them out together and went after them in a fit of jealousy."

He was shaking his head even before I finished. "It was Garrett she loved, not Aron. And Marlinda was a friend of them both—they went to school together."

I frowned. "Marlinda was older than either of them, wasn't she?"

"Only by six months or so."

Meaning either her family was rich, or becoming Maelle's blood supplier had been a *very* profitable deal for the young woman.

"Did they hang around together much?"

He shrugged. "That I couldn't tell you, but I could ask Meika, if you want."

I hesitated, and then nodded. Aiden had undoubtedly checked any connection between the three of them, but it wouldn't hurt to ask anyway. It was always possible—though also very unlikely—that I'd nugget out something he'd missed.

I followed Mike back into the kitchen. "Sis, has Larissa been seeing much of Marlinda in recent weeks?"

Meika's golden gaze immediately shot past him and hit mine. "My girl didn't kill her. She wouldn't. They were good friends."

I held up my hands. "I'm not suggesting she did, but it's possible there's a connection between Larissa's disappearance and the murder of her two friends. Maybe she *is* involved, but not the way everyone is thinking."

Tears gleamed briefly in her eyes and she blinked rapidly. "You mean she could be another victim?"

I hesitated, torn between not wanting to upset her or to give her false hope. Mike placed a hand on her arm and said, "That's not what Lizzie meant, but it's nevertheless a possibility we have to be prepared for."

"She's not dead." The older woman crossed her arms, her stance defiant. "I'd know if she was."

"Has she been in any trouble of late?" I asked. "Had any arguments with anyone other than Garrett's parents? It's possible she's hiding from whatever—whoever—killed her friends."

And if that were the case, the next question had to be—if she wasn't the reason for the soul eater's presence here, who was?

If the part of my soul that had prophetic dreams had an answer to *any* of the current crop of questions, she certainly wasn't saying so. But then, she did tend to prefer the midnight hours to hit me with her dire portents.

"No." A somewhat wry smile touched Meika's lips. "And while threatening his parents wasn't the wisest move she'd ever made, it was done in the heat of the moment."

I didn't say anything to that, because there was really nothing I could say. So I simply nodded and glanced at Mike. "Do you want to be there tomorrow? I can ring for a temp to cover your shift."

He hesitated, and then shook his head. "With the rangers there, there'd be no point."

"Cool." I returned my gaze to his sister. "I'll see you tomorrow then."

She nodded. I gathered my purse from the living room and then left. Mike followed me out. "Thanks for trying. I appreciate it."

"No probs, Mike." I threw my purse onto the passenger seat and then glanced at him. "Just make sure your sister isn't expecting miracles. Larissa might not have worn *any* of her jewelry often enough to leave a resonance, and if that's the case, I won't find her."

"She knows, but you can't blame her for holding out hope."

No, I guess I couldn't. I waved goodbye, then got into the car and reversed out of the driveway. I'd just turned back onto the Midland Highway when my phone rang. The number that flashed up on the console screen told me it was Aiden, and a silly smile touched my lips.

I pressed the answer button and said, "What's up, Ranger?"

"I'm due a dinner break, and I'm feeling like some company. Care to join me for something to eat?"

"Sure," I replied. "But be aware the gossips will

consider it a date and you'll lose your twenty quid."

"Not if you come to the station and we order in."

"A cop shop is not the most romantic location for a first date, but it's certainly better than nothing. I'll be there in about fifteen minutes."

"Meaning you're not at the café?"

"No, I'm just coming back from Guildford."

"Why on earth are you there?"

"Meika asked me to find her daughter."

"And did you?"

He didn't seem surprised that she was missing, but I guess that was natural given she was their number one suspect and they would have been looking for her. "Not tonight, but I'm trying again tomorrow. Thought you might like to come along."

"You thought right." He paused. "What do you want to eat?"

"Surprise me."

He chuckled softly. "That could be an unwise decision on your part, given I'm a werewolf and we do have a taste for steak that's more than a little on the blue side."

"Then order mine well-done, and all will be good."

"Done deal." I could hear the smile in his voice. "See you soon."

He'd no sooner hung up when energy stirred across my skin. Not dark energy, but wild.

And there was an odd sense of warning to its touch.

I frowned and glanced around. I was about halfway between Guildford and Castle Rock, in an area that was all gently rolling hills dotted with trees. Aside from the cars on the other side of the road, the area was practically deserted. If there was a threat out here, as the wild magic seemed to imply, then it wasn't evident.

I drove on, but the pulsing beat of wild magic got stronger, until my skin burned and my heart raced.

Then, without warning, something hit the rear of the car, the windshield shattered, and I was spinning out of control.

CHAPTER
eight

My first instinct was to hit the brake, but some distant voice in the back of my brain screamed *"No,"* and told me to steer out of it instead. But that was a hard thing to do when the windshield had become a spiderweb of long cracks. I swore and peered between two of the veins, looking for the road as dust and stones flew high, distorting my vision even more. I caught a glimpse of a speed sign and steered toward it, figuring the road would be somewhere between it and me.

Then the wild magic stirred and the curtain of dust parted, allowing me not only a clear view of where I was in relation to the road and that sign, but also the trees I was rapidly sliding toward. I resisted the urge to wrench violently on the wheel, and instead kept the nose pointed in the direction I wanted it to go. Slowly but surely, I got the vehicle back under control. Once it was, I pulled over to the side of the road and stopped. For several seconds, I didn't do anything more than shake.

You okay, now? Belle asked eventually.

Yeah. I sucked in a deep breath to chase away the lingering remnants of fear, then released my fierce grip on the steering wheel.

Then what the fuck happened? Why did you lose control of the car?

My gaze went to the cracks and the small hole in the center of the windshield that was their source. *One of the cars coming the other way must have thrown up a stone. It cracked the damn windshield.*

That doesn't explain the spin.

Maybe I blew a tire. The rear end slid out before the windshield shattered.

Meaning the stone might have been thrown up as a result of the oncoming cars off-roading to avoid you.

Possibly. And yet that didn't explain the overt sense of danger in the wild magic, or why it was now absent. I climbed out of the car and walked around to the rear. None of the tires had blown and there was no obvious reason—either on the road or the car—as to why I'd been thrown sideways. I frowned and glanced around. The nearby hills were empty of anything other than cows, trees, and the odd rock outcrop. There was absolutely nothing to suggest anything untoward had happened, and yet a niggle remained that this wasn't an unfortunate accident. But I couldn't say if that was merely a lingering effect of the wild magic's touch, or my psychic skills kicking in a little too late.

I frowned and walked back to the front of the car. The hole in the windshield was actually quite small, and while there was indeed a spiderweb of cracks radiating out from it, they didn't cover the whole thing. Which meant that while the windshield would need replacing, the car was probably safe to drive back to Castle Rock as long as I didn't do insane speeds.

You just don't want to miss your dinner date with Aiden. Amusement ran through Belle's mental tone.

True that, I replied cheerfully. *With the way fate and this goddamn soul eater are messing with us, it might be days before we get another chance.*

The council's reluctance to call in the RWA is putting everyone in danger.

Aiden said he was going to talk to the council this morning, so I'm hoping someone official will be here ASAP.

If neither he nor the council has called, I'm going to do it myself, she said. *Anonymously, of course.*

That's not likely to help, given only the rangers, the council, and the two of us know the true reasons for these deaths.

Well, our position here is already tenuous according to Aiden, so what more can they do to us?

I don't know. In truth, I really didn't *want* to know. *Until the worst actually happens, I'm thinking we're better off not stressing about it.*

She snorted. *And I'm thinking it's a little late for that sort of advice.*

Also true. I laughed and got back into the car. *I'll ask Aiden about it. That way, we'll know, one way or another.*

Talking about business rather than pleasure—way to spend an evening with a luscious man, Lizzie. Belle's mental tone was dry.

He's at work, I reminded her. *And call me old-fashioned, but I'd rather not be doing the wild thing in a workplace environment.*

Especially when the werewolves who worked with him would be able to smell the scent of sex the minute they walked into the room.

Belle's laughter ran through my thoughts. *You're all adults, so what does it matter?*

It's a matter of decency, I said, somewhat primly, *and not wanting the whole bloody reservation knowing when I do and don't have sex. It's bad enough that they're placing bets on when we go out.*

Small-town minds do have to amuse themselves somehow, she replied. *Be careful driving. If any of those cracks start growing, stop and call the auto club. We've windshield replacement in the policy.*

I know, but it'll take too long to get someone out, and I'm not missing my dinner.

She snorted, the sound lingering as her thoughts left mine. I started the car and pulled back onto the road, carefully increasing the speed until I reached sixty kilometers. The window remained stable. I probably could have gone faster, but decided one scare a day was more than enough.

I made it back to Castle Rock without incident, and found a parking spot not far from the ranger station. Aiden opened the door as I walked up the steps, his smile wide and welcoming. He didn't say anything—he simply grabbed my hand and tugged me inside. Once the door was closed, he pressed me back against it and kissed me, with all the passion, heat, and urgency I could possibly want. It left me breathless, and hungry, and wanting so, *so* much more.

"You have no idea just how much I've been looking forward to doing that." He lightly rested his forehead on mine, his warm breath teasing my lips. "What took you so long to get here?"

I laughed softly. "A stone hit my windshield and sent the car into a spin. You're lucky I even arrived."

He pulled back and scanned me somewhat critically.

"You're okay?"

"As Double-O-Seven would say, shaken not stirred."

"Good." He twined his fingers through mine and then tugged me into the main office area. "What sent you into the spin? Was it the shock of the stone smashing the windshield?"

"Weirdly, I went into the spin before the stone hit. It felt like I'd blown a tire, but they were all intact when I checked."

"Maybe you hit something."

"If I had, there would have been some damage on the car or a dead animal on the road. But there was nothing."

We went through the door into the area that held the interview room, cells, storeroom, and who knew what else. He led me into the former, which hadn't changed since the last time I'd been in here. At least this time I was neither tied up nor about to be questioned as a suspect. The basic table that sat in the middle of the room held several take-out containers, a couple of bottles of drink, and some glasses.

"I decided on Chinese." He pulled out a chair and grandly seated me. "So we have crispy duck served with pancakes, several types of dumplings, beef with black bean sauce—which is all meat, no veg, because I can't stand too many vegetables—chicken with cashew, honey king prawns, and of course, fried rice."

I laughed as he sat down next to me. "There's enough food here to feed a damn army."

He shrugged. "I wasn't sure what you'd like, so I got a bit of everything. What we don't eat I'll put in the fridge for lunch tomorrow." He motioned to the soft drinks. "Alcohol would have been nicer, but I'm on duty. So,

Coke, lemon squash, or bubbly water?"

"Water would be good, thanks."

He picked up the bottle and started pouring. I tugged the containers closer and pulled off the lids.

"How come you're the only one here? I thought you said the shifts were staggered so that there were always a couple of people on duty?"

"They're out on patrol." He handed me the glass of water, then clinked his Coke against it. "To the voyage of discovery ahead of us."

"*If* fate ever actually gives us time."

"To fate being less of a bitch, then." He lightly touched my glass again, amusement crinkling the corners of his bright eyes. "Unfortunately, that time is not later tonight."

I reached for the steak, scooped some onto my plate, and then handed the container to him. "After the last few late nights, I'm not surprised you've run out of steam."

"Oh, trust me, there's plenty of steam left in the tank." He accepted the container and tipped the rest of it onto his plate. "But the council have asked me to meet with them again when I finish work."

"Why?" I frowned as I helped myself to the rice. "I thought you met with them this morning?"

"I did. They agreed it was time to call in the RWA."

Relief slithered through me. At least the pressure would be off Belle and me once he or she arrived here. Last night had proved that I didn't have the power to fight the soul eater. If it had knocked away the charm as easily as it had knocked away the spelled knife, I would have died out there.

"When are they due to arrive?"

"Tomorrow, apparently." He hesitated. "They'll

probably want to talk to you."

I wrinkled my nose. "I suppose I've no choice, given the situation."

He shifted so that he was looking at me more fully. "Why do you and Belle want to avoid any sort of witch authority?"

I smiled even as my heart began to race. I started eating, more to buy thinking time than because I was hungry. "The High Council doesn't like having unvetted half-breeds like me and Belle running around willy-nilly."

"Why?"

I shrugged, a casual movement that belied the tension growing within. "Because half-breeds can be born with full witch power, and if it's uncontrolled, it's dangerous."

He frowned. "But you and Belle are in control of your abilities, which means you must have undergone some training."

"We did, but even underpowered witches don't go through the official appraisal process until they're eighteen. If they're deemed powerful enough, they go on to full training at the Halden University—"

"That's the witch one, isn't it?"

"And the only one in Australia." I grabbed the chicken and cashew, and scooped some into my almost empty plate. Not because I really wanted it, but because it was the only way to not so obviously avoid his gaze.

"So why didn't you and Belle go there?"

I smiled, though there was little in the way of amusement in it. "Aside from the fact neither of us are powerful enough, we weren't around at eighteen to be tested. We skipped out on our parents at sixteen."

"How do you know you weren't powerful enough if you weren't appraised?"

"Because, as I've already said, I had a lifetime of my parents either telling me that I wasn't good enough, that I'd never make it through regular witch school let alone university, or trying to force me—" I broke off and took a deep breath in an attempt to calm the bitterness before I said too much. It might have all happened a very long time ago, but it was a wound that had never really healed. "So when we could, we got the hell out of there."

"I didn't think your parents were witches."

"The witch blood came down the line through Gran, so Mom did have witch blood in her." I grimaced. "I'm the one who got the watered-down powers, though."

Most of which was true enough, but the words still tasted bitter on my tongue. I hated not telling him the entire truth, and yet I simply couldn't. I might like and trust him, and I was definitely attracted to him, but that wasn't enough to counter the last twelve years of caution. Only when I found the man I wanted to spend the rest of my life with would I finally admit who I was and what had really happened to make us both run.

And Aiden wasn't that man. As Belle had said earlier, werewolves were a fun time, not a long time.

"Is that why the RWA mentioned the fact you're not registered with them?" he asked eventually. "Because you're unvetted?"

"We're not registered with them because it's only full-blood witches who are supposed to register on entering the areas of the various regional associations." I ate some chicken and then glanced at him. "And you've neatly avoided answering my initial question—why do the council want to meet again tonight? Surely it would be better now to wait until the RWA witch gets here?"

His gaze met mine, and there was something in his

eyes that made my breath catch in my throat. Its cause wasn't desire. It was uncertainty. Maybe even trepidation.

"They're making a decision about Belle and me, aren't they?" I all but whispered. "That's why you warned us last night not to do anything to jeopardize our position here."

"Yes. They received a copy of the RWA's final report on the vampire event. It included advice that the council asks the High Council for tenders to be sent out to fill the position of reservation witch, otherwise they'll force the issue by notifying them we have a large, unprotected wellspring."

"It's rather unusual for the RWA to give them that option—especially given it's now been a year since there's been a full witch on the reservation."

"I suspect they still believe Gabe is here somewhere, but know they can't risk leaving the wellspring without an official protector any longer." He half shrugged. "It's their butts on the line as much as ours if something does go wrong, given they *should* have forced the issue when Gabe first disappeared."

"But how does any of that relate back to Belle and me?"

Even as I asked the question, I knew. *Any* official report would have to mention our presence here. And while I very much feared the werewolf council's reaction to us being called out as witches rather than psychics, I was even more worried about the report finding its way into the wrong hands up in Canberra. It was unlikely anyone on the council or even my direct family would be the ones checking it out, but I certainly had plenty of other relatives who worked with lower government departments. Two witches bearing the coloring of the Marlowe and Sarr lines but *not* their surnames might just raise some unwanted flags.

Whether those flags would result in the action I feared was another matter entirely. One I'd probably have nightmares about.

"The report finished with the comment that while the two unregistered witches currently on the reservation were quite capable *and* did seem to have an affinity with the wild magic," Aiden said, "it would not be enough to either protect it or the reservation from the darker forces that will be drawn here."

So the truth of what we were—that we weren't just psychics capable of minor magic—was officially out. I scrubbed a hand across my eyes and then met his gaze. There was no sense of recrimination or anger in his expression, and that made me feel even worse. "So the council is currently deciding what to do with us?"

"The council has apparently decided. Tonight's meeting is to inform the pack elders and me as to whether I'll have to evict you or not."

I didn't know whether to laugh or cry. "For fuck's sake, it's almost *Christmas*. It takes a special brand of bastard to do something like that at this time of year."

"I know, and I'm sorry, but I have no say in council matters." He caught my hand and squeezed it lightly. His fingers were warm against mine, and yet I found no comfort in his touch. "A number of us spoke up in favor of allowing you to remain. And your assistance in stopping the vampire will play in your favor."

"*You* spoke in our favor?"

"I may have been a bit of a bastard when we first met, but why would you think I'd do anything other than that now?"

"Because we lied about the extent of our abilities."

"That was pretty evident from the beginning." There was something in his tone that suggested he remained suspicious about certain aspects of my story. But then, he was both a ranger and a werewolf. They had excellent instincts when it came to things like that. "But at least the RWA backed up your statement that neither of you are capable of protecting the wellspring. That will count in your favor."

"I can't see how."

"Small lies are infinitely better than bigger lies." Amusement briefly shone in his blue eyes as he added, "And I did remind the council that the best cakes and chocolate brownies anyone in this reservation has *ever* tasted were in danger of being evicted right alongside the pair of you."

"Idiot." I nudged him with my shoulder. "Did you show the council the recording you did when we contacted Gabe, or the one from the truck last night?"

"Yes. I think some of them struggled to believe the authenticity of the spirit talking, and last night's tape was, as I'd feared, hampered by the fog."

I wasn't surprised by the former. Even in this day and age, where spirit talking—and even spirit walking—were recognized and well-studied psychic talents, there were still plenty of people who refused to believe in the existence of such things as ghosts and spirits.

That the fog had obscured the video footage was simply frustrating. If anything could have convinced the council of the need for witches in this reservation, it would have been a dead man with a hole in his chest, no knees, and half his head blown away trying to kill me.

"Do you have any idea which way the decision will

fall?"

"No. They play their cards very close to their chests."

I blew out a frustrated breath, but it did little to ease the sick tension growing within me. "We seriously cannot afford to be run out of another town."

"The council would offer compensation. They're not that cold."

I snorted. "The fact they're even considering this action right before Christmas says otherwise."

"The report only arrived a couple of days ago. Had it arrived sooner, it would have been dealt with sooner."

"Does our possible eviction mean they're going against the RWA's recommendation to bring in a replacement for Gabe? Because they might not like the outcome if the government forces the issue."

"I won't know that until tonight, either." He paused, and then added softly, "We can still date even if you're not on the reservation. There's no rule against that."

"Except if we're kicked out there's no guarantee we'll even remain in this state." I pushed away my plate and then rose. "I think I'd better leave."

"Don't." He caught my hand. "Please."

I gently pulled free of his grip. "I can't. Not until I know, one way or the other, whether I can still consider Castle Rock my home come tomorrow."

He swore softly and rose with me. "Right now, I fucking hate the council and their damn ruling."

I raised my eyebrows. "It's a ruling you agreed with until very recently."

"Yes, but I was looking for someone to blame for my loss, and Gabe was the obvious and easy answer. If I can change my opinion, they certainly can."

"I guess we'll find out in a couple of hours." I walked

around the table and headed for the door. "Will you ring me the minute you know? No matter what the time?"

"Even if it's late?"

"Yes. It's not like I'm going to sleep either way."

He didn't reply. He keyed open the door into the main area and then led the way across the room, his movements filled with repressed frustration and anger. Once we were outside, I got my keys out of my purse and walked down to my car.

"You're going to have to replace the windshield. It's not safe to drive it too far with it like—" He paused, leaned closer to the glass, and then swore. "It wasn't a damn stone that caused *that* hole."

I frowned. "If it had been anything larger, I would have seen it."

His gaze came to mine, and the fury I'd sensed earlier was now full-blown.

"What?" I said, my heart beating somewhere in my throat.

"If I'm not mistaken, that hole was caused by a goddamn bullet." His expression was fierce. Angry. For me, not *at* me. "Someone was trying to kill you."

CHAPTER
nine

"No way," I retorted, not attempting to control my disbelief. "And even if it *is* a bullet hole, wouldn't I have been hit? Or at least have heard it hitting something inside the car?"

He stepped around me and opened the car door. "Given the car was out of control and spinning at the time, probably not."

"I still don't get why you'd think someone was trying to kill me." I crossed my arms against the chill gathering around me, and watched as he began checking the inside of the car. "You said yourself not so long ago that some farmers within the reservation were granted special rifle licenses to shoot vermin. Maybe that's what they were doing, and a shot simply went astray."

"Where were you when the accident happened?"

I shrugged, a movement he had no hope of seeing given he was currently inspecting the side of the driver headrest. "About halfway between Guildford and Castle Rock."

"So plenty of rolling hills and rocks?"

"Yes, and if there'd been anyone close enough to shoot at me, I would have seen them."

"Exactly. The fact you didn't suggests they might have been using either the rocks or trees as cover." He glanced at me, a slight smile teasing his lips despite the sternness of his expression. "Unless, of course, the reason you didn't see them was that in your anxiety to make our dinner date, you were dangerously over the speed limit and the landscape was little more than a blur."

"I like you, Aiden, but I'm not willing to risk my life for you."

"Your actions against that vampire say otherwise—which is something else I reminded the damn council about." He pulled a glove out of his pocket. "You got a pen in that bag of yours?"

I fished one out and handed it to him. "Why on earth would you carry silicone gloves and not a pen?"

"Because I don't write up scene reports. I record them and then download them onto my computer via an app. I will always need gloves, however."

He dug the pen into the side of the headrest, and after a moment, something plopped into his right hand. He grunted and held it up for me to see. It was indeed a bullet.

I rubbed my arms, but it wasn't doing much against the damn chill. "I really can't believe it was deliberate. No one here has any reason to want me dead."

Although I guess I *was* helping to hunt down the soul eater and the witch responsible for his presence here. Still, it was unusual for a witch to use such a mundane means to get rid of a foe.

"If it had been a stray shot from a farmer, they would have seen your near accident and reported it." He pulled off his glove, enclosing the bullet within it. "I'll need to impound your car for a day or so; we'll have to go over it and check if there were any more shots taken. I'll get the windshield fixed when we're finished."

"Except we'll need the thing if we get booted out tomorrow."

"They'll give you time to pack everything up, Liz. As I said, they're not heartless. However, you'll need to be careful until we discover why someone took a potshot at you." He slammed the door shut and plucked the keys from my hand. After taking the car keys off the main ring, he handed them back. "Let's get you home."

I raised an eyebrow. "I thought you were on station duty?"

"I'm there in case something comes up. Something did." He waved me forward and then fell into step beside me. "It might be better if you call off trying to find—"

"No," I said, before he could finish. "Even though I'm not convinced Larissa and her need for revenge are the reason the soul eater is here, until we find her, we simply can't be sure. And given she's managed to avoid all your efforts to locate her, using psychometry is our only other option if we want a fast resolution."

"The RWA witch will be able to do a finding spell—"

"Yes, and if he or she gets here before I've arranged to meet with Meika, great. If not, then we need to make the attempt. If the current pattern holds—"

"It will attack again tomorrow night," he finished for me.

"Yes."

The thought had horror creeping through me, and I shivered. Aiden's arm slipped around my waist and he tucked me close to his long, warmth length. But, as nice as it was, it didn't stop the chills.

"I'm not meaning this as a criticism, but let's hope the RWA witch is more knowledgeable on these types of spirits than you and Belle."

"That wouldn't exactly be hard." I hooked my fingers into the back pocket of his jeans and couldn't help but be aware of the play of muscles under my fingertips, and just how little material now separated my hand from his rather well-formed butt.

There was nothing like a little badly timed lust to take your mind off more serious matters, it seemed.

We walked the rest of the way to the café in silence, reaching it without incident. I somewhat reluctantly stepped away from him and said, "I'll undoubtedly be awake if you want to drop by for a drink later. Bad news is always better done face-to-face rather than over the phone."

"Being the bearer of bad news is a task I absolutely hate, so let's hope we'll be having a celebratory drink rather than drowning our sorrows." He brushed his fingers down my cheek, a tender touch that had my hormones skipping about again, and then stepped back. His fingers, I noticed, were again clenched. "I'd better get back to the office. Lock the door, and keep well away from the windows."

"I seriously doubt anyone is going to have a go at me in the middle of—"

"If they want you dead seriously enough, they just might. So stop arguing and just do as I ask."

The ranger is very worried about your safety, Belle

commented. *Which is rather nice, is it not?*

He's a ranger. It's his job to be worried about things like this. To Aiden, I added, "Just this one time, I will. But don't expect such easy compliance on future orders."

Oh, this is more than professional worry. Trust me on that.

Stop skimming his thoughts, Belle. Just leave the man alone.

It is my duty as your familiar to look after you—not just physically, but mentally and emotionally. It is a job I take very seriously.

I mentally snorted. *It has nothing to do with looking after me, and everything to do with being a stickybeak. And we both know it.*

"Oh, if there's one thing I never expect from you," Aiden said, amusement in his tone, "it's certainly compliance."

"Good, because it's always better going into any sort of relationship with that understanding on the table." Of course, after tonight, it might not matter.

His amusement faded but he didn't say anything. I opened the door, stepped inside, and then glanced back. "Talk to you later."

"Indeed," he said. "Now lock the damn door and go upstairs."

I did. Belle met me at the top of the steps with a very large glass of whiskey on ice. "I thought you might need this."

"I do. Thanks." I downed half of it in one gulp; the fiery liquid burned all the way down my throat but didn't immediately make me feel better. I rather suspected it would take a whole lot more than one large glass. I followed her over to the kitchenette and topped up my drink. "So what do you think?"

"I tend to agree with you—I can't see the witch

bothering to use a gun when her magic is strong enough to control the soul sucker."

"I meant about the council and their upcoming decision."

"I have faith that common decency will prevail in our favor." She paused, her expression distracted. "The spirits say common decency should never be relied on."

I snorted. "Says the crowd who never have the decency to answer a direct question."

"The fault is apparently yours—you never ask the right question." Her amusement faded. "What the hell are we going to do if they throw us out?"

I sighed and slumped back against the counter. "I really don't know." I took a sip of whiskey, and then added, "If we're given compensation, I guess we won't lose money, but it really feels like we're meant to be here. I don't want to leave."

"Me neither." She propped beside me. "We could always appeal the decision. People have."

"But have they ever won?"

"No, but that doesn't mean we won't."

"Appealing their decision would mean revealing a little more about ourselves than I'm comfortable with right now."

"And yet you're not comfortable with lying, either, if the unhappy vibes I was receiving earlier are anything to go by."

"The worst of it is, he's well aware that I'm still not telling him the whole truth."

"That's why he's the ranger, and Zak is a bartender." Belle pushed away from the counter and plucked the empty glass from my hand. "Look, why don't you go grab a sleeping draught and catch up on some of the sleep you've missed over the last few nights. Aiden's not likely to get here before midnight, so that at least gives you a couple of hours."

I hesitated, and then nodded. If my gut was right, I'd be missing more sleep tomorrow night thanks to the soul eater, so it was infinitely better to grab some sleep while I could. And it sure as hell beat hanging around for hours on end worrying about the council's decision and what it might mean for us—especially when there was nothing either of us could really do to change it.

I went back downstairs to make a gentle sleeping potion. Once I'd thoroughly washed out the containers and stacked them away again, I hit my bed. The good thing about sleeping potions was they also stilled your mind, giving you a dream-free sleep. Given the fact that I woke in the exact same position that I went to sleep in, I evidently didn't even stir.

For several minutes, I listened to the creaks and groans of the old building, finding an odd sense of comfort and peace in them. In the street outside, magpies warbled, and that had confusion stirring. Why the hell were they up and active at night?

"Because it's not night," Belle said, as she came into the room. She'd obviously just woken, as her hair was messy and she was still in her nightie. "It's seven in the goddamn morning, and your ranger didn't drop by last night, as he promised."

I closed my eyes and swore softly. "It's obviously bad news then."

"Probably." Belle sat on the edge of the bed, then reached past me and pulled my phone out from its usual position under my pillow. "You need to call him, because we fucking need to know what's going on. It's not just us they're affecting, but our staff as well."

I accepted the phone somewhat reluctantly. My heart raced and sweat was beginning to trickle down my spine. Anyone would think I'd just run a marathon.

"High stress levels can do that." Belle's tone was grim. "Make the call. I'll go downstairs and make a couple of Irish coffees. No matter which way it goes, I've a feeling we'll need the alcohol."

She rose and left. I took a deep breath in an effort to calm my churning stomach, and then made the call. The phone rang several times before it was answered.

"Liz," he muttered, his voice husky with sleep. Sheets rustled as he moved, and I had visions of cotton sliding over skin.

I closed my eyes against them and bluntly said, "Are we in or out?"

"In. At least for the moment. And I'm sorry I didn't call in, but when I came past, the place was dark. I didn't want to wake either of you."

I closed my eyes against the tears suddenly prickling my eyes... and heard an echoing whoop from downstairs. But that didn't mean we were out of the woods yet—not given that "for the moment" comment. "You should have at least sent a text, Aiden, because I woke up believing the worst. And you need to explain that rider."

"Yes." He paused. "I'd rather not talk over the phone. If the offer of coffee still stands, I can be there in ten minutes."

"I might even offer you breakfast if your explanation is reasonable enough."

"That would be appreciated. I'll see you soon."

He hung up. I threw the phone onto the bedside table, then collapsed back onto my pillow. Tears continued to prickle, and my body was shaking, a reaction akin to shock and evidence of just how much the decision had meant to me—to us. I rubbed a hand across my eyes, smearing moisture, then got up, pulled on a sweater long enough to hang down to the middle of my thighs, and padded bare legged down the stairs. Despite the fact the sun had risen an hour or so ago, the café remained in shadows.

"I pulled the blinds down." Belle came around the counter and handed me a tall glass filled with delicious-smelling coffee and a mountain of cream. "I figured it not only met Aiden's order to be careful, but stopped the inhabitants of Castle Creek enjoying the glorious sight of us parading around in our underwear. They've done nothing to deserve it."

"They have supported the café."

"True, but they remain undeserving in my eyes—especially if some of them still think we need evicting."

"It's the council who are deciding that, not the everyday folk who come in here." I sat down at the nearest table and sipped the coffee—and felt the warmth burn all the way down. Belle really *had* ramped up the alcohol content. It was probably just as well I couldn't drive anywhere today.

"How can you be sure the various council members aren't amongst our customers? It's not like they walk in here and announce who they are."

"That's true." I watched the play of sunbeams across the wall for a moment, then said, "I don't suppose you found the reference I bookmarked?"

"I not only found it, but I found the book it was referencing. It was in one of the boxes we haven't unpacked."

"They always are. Did you find anything interesting?"

"I haven't tracked down the type of soul eater we're dealing with, but it seems your guess that we need to pin them in flesh to deal with them is spot-on—although the book does advise that we do so within a protective circle. Then it's simply a matter of banishing them back to the dark realm."

"None of which will be easy if the man mountain was anything to go by."

"Well no, because any living thing, be it flesh or spirit, is going to fight like hell to survive. Let's just hope the RWA witch arrives today, and that we're not the ones who actually have to deal with the thing."

"Amen to that." I clinked my glass against hers. "I don't think it'll be that simple, though."

She all but groaned. "Don't tell me you've had another of your dreams?"

"No. It's just a feeling."

"They're almost as goddamn bad." She wrinkled her nose. "What else is this vague premonition saying?"

"That we'll have to finish what we started."

She grunted. "I'd better keep reading the damn book then, just in case there's something we've missed."

"And I'll make another agate charm for you, just to be safe."

"Good idea. The last thing I want is to end up on a soul eater's dinner menu."

"It wouldn't overly please me, either."

She grinned. "If you'd said anything else, I would have hit you."

"To do so you would have had to release your grip on your coffee, and we both know that isn't going to happen until it's finished."

"You know me too well." She cocked her head sideways, her expression intent. "Aiden's approaching, and he's on foot."

I frowned. "Wonder why, given we're supposed to be going to the Marin reservation this morning?"

"I can't answer that without reading his thoughts, and you keep telling me to stay out of them." She rose. "I'll head upstairs and leave you two lovebirds alone. At least until I get dressed and breakfast is ready."

"I hope you don't want anything more serious than a toasted sandwich this morning, because I'm not going into the kitchen barefoot, and I'm not in the mood for shoes."

"A toastie would be perfect." Her dimples appeared as her grin flashed. "He's almost here."

As she went upstairs, I got up and walked over to the door. The small bell chimed merrily as I opened it. Aiden was standing on the other side, one hand half raised.

"I'm guessing Belle told you I was approaching." His gaze skimmed me and came up heated. "And you have great legs. You should unleash them more often."

"I will if we ever get some decent hot weather." I stepped to one side to let him in. "Why are you walking?"

"Because the council meeting was held on O'Connor grounds last night, so I left my truck at the station and stayed up there last night."

"Meaning you ran here?"

"Both last night and now." His nostrils flared. "That's a decent amount of alcohol you've got in that glass."

"We felt the need for it—would you like one?"

"I have to be sober enough to drive you to the Marin reservation, so no. But a regular coffee would be awesome, as would breakfast if that offer still applies."

"As long as you don't want anything more strenuous than a toastie, yes it does." I locked the door and followed him across the room. He leaned against the counter while I walked around to make his coffee and then the toasted sandwiches. "What did you mean this morning when you said 'for the moment'?"

He sighed and crossed his arms. I couldn't help but notice just how well the shirtsleeves defined his arms. "There are some members of the council who believe it's something more than a coincidence that these supernatural events coincided with your arrival in the reservation."

I blinked, not sure whether to laugh or cry. "They think we're *behind* it all?"

"Yeah." He shook his head. "Let's just say that common sense and some of the older members of the council aren't always good friends."

"That's putting it far too politely, in my opinion." I slid his coffee across the bench, then turned on the sandwich press and got out the bread and butter. "What's their reasoning behind such a warped opinion?"

"That you were aware of the witch ban and have been creating these supernatural events to provide a reason for your presence in the reservation."

I snorted. "I'm guessing it escaped their notice that we applied for permission to open this café as psychics, not witches."

"No. In fact, they're using that subterfuge as more evidence to back their argument."

The fuckers behind this warped view wouldn't want to be coming into the café, Belle commented. *Because they will very quickly find themselves marched right back out.*

Whatever happened to forgive and forget?

In this case, it's well and truly forgotten.

"I'm gathering," Aiden said, his tone dry, "that you and Belle are having a conversation."

My gaze rose to his. "Yes. How can you tell?"

"Your expression gets distracted. Dare I ask what she was saying?"

"She was contemplating what she'd do to those councilors if they ever stepped foot in this café."

He raised an eyebrow. "I thought it was witch creed to do unto others?"

"It is, and given they're contemplating kicking us out, her actions would be rather fitting. Do you want chicken, beef, turkey, or strasburg on your sandwich?"

"Would it be pushing it if I said one of each?"

I snorted. "Don't they feed you back home?"

"Mom keeps stating I'm old enough to make my own damn breakfast."

"Which you are."

"Yeah, but it's still nice not to have to cook for yourself occasionally."

"Does that mean you'll return the favor and cook breakfast for me one day?"

"Love to."

"Good." I finished putting together his four sandwiches, and placed them under the press. "So why aren't we being kicked out immediately if that's their view? What are they waiting for?"

"Two things, the first being the arrival of the RWA witch today."

I opened the press and flipped his sandwiches over. "What the hell have they got to do with the situation?"

"They wish to question him about the wellspring situation, and how it could possibly be the source of the evil finding its way here."

"Good, because whomever the RWA send will certainly put the bastards straight about the danger they've put everyone in." I grabbed a plate, stacked up his sandwiches, and handed them across. "What was the other thing?"

I glanced over my shoulder when he didn't immediately answer; he was contemplating the chicken, avocado, mayo, and cheese toastie with something close to bliss on his face. "This is amazing."

I laughed. "If you've never had a chicken avo toastie before, you've been seriously deprived."

"It would appear so." He all but inhaled the rest of it, and then said, "The other thing they've done is send a request up to the High Witch Council for information about the two of you."

My heart began to beat a whole lot faster. Such a request, along with the RWA report, might just gain the very interest we were trying to avoid. "The council won't be able to tell you much more than the RWA. We're not vetted, as I've said."

"I did mention that." He picked up the ham and cheese sandwich and started in on that.

"And their response?"

"Was to remind me that I also suspected you weren't telling the entire truth when it came to your background." His gaze rose to mine. "Which you aren't."

If ever there was an opening to be honest, this was it. My gut twisted, but I just couldn't force the truth out of my mouth. I flipped our sandwiches over, and then said, "The secrets Belle and I keep aren't dangerous. We're not criminals on the run, and nothing in our past should hold any fears for anyone in this reservation."

Aside from Belle and me, that was.

His gaze held mine for too many minutes; seeking the truth, judging my words. Judging me. "Do your secrets revolve around the problems you had with your parents?"

"Yes." I took the remaining toasties out of the press and silently added to Belle, *Your breakfast is ready.*

On my way down, she said. *But I'll eat it on the way to the gym. I need to punch out some angst.*

Throw a few punches for me while you're there. I grabbed a brown paper bag to put her sandwich in, and then held it out as she rattled down the stairs, a towel thrown over her right shoulder and her gym bag in her left hand.

"Thanks." She grabbed her breakfast, and then glanced at Aiden. "I hope you reminded that council of yours it's not wise to piss off witches—even underpowered ones."

He raised his eyebrows. "Are you saying we're about to experience an influx of rats?"

She grinned. "Let's just say they're on standby."

With that, she departed. Aiden glanced at me. "I'm never sure if she's serious or not."

"Most of the time she's not." I picked up my toastie and took a bite. "And it was me who called the rats into Peak's Point, not Belle."

"But she's still capable of it?"

"Yes."

He drank some coffee, contemplating me over the rim for several seconds. "Why won't you confide in me, Liz?"

I smiled, though it held little in the way of amusement. "Aside from the fact our relationship hasn't even gotten off the ground yet, you've warned me a couple of times that nothing serious will ever happen between us. Why would you then expect me to tell you my deepest secrets?"

"You'll have to trust someone eventually," he commented. "You and Belle can't keep running forever."

"We're aware of that." I grimaced. "We had thought Castle Rock might be a place we could settle in. Your council would seem to have other ideas."

"It's not the whole council," he said. "And it's certainly not the whole reservation."

"It's a historical fact that the minority often spoil things for the majority."

He frowned. "Does that mean you and Belle will leave, regardless of what decision the council comes to?"

I sighed. "I honestly can't say."

He didn't look happy, which made two of us. We finished our toasties and coffees in silence. Once I'd cleaned up, I glanced at the time and said, "Is it worth heading over to the Marin reservation a little early?"

"You're not waiting for Belle to get back?"

"She'll be here well before any of our staff get here."

"Then yes, we can head over now. But I'd suggest putting pants on first."

I raised an eyebrow. "Not so long ago you were all for me getting my legs out."

"Oh, I still am." His tone was somewhat droll. "But the wolf in me has no desire to share the lusciousness that is your bare butt. Not when I've had little more than teasing glimpses."

I grinned. "Glimpses are all you're likely to get given our current track record."

"Believe me, I'm painfully aware of that." A mischievous gleam appeared in his eyes. "But I could come up and help you dress."

"And here I was thinking you'd prefer to undress

me."

"To do one, you must first do the other. More than happy to help with that."

"Sadly for you, Belle and I have this rule about bringing lovers home. As in, we don't do it when the other is likely to arrive home at any moment."

"I'm destined to be a monk forever."

His woebegone expression was somewhat spoiled by that gleam, and I laughed. "Does that mean if we ever do manage to have sex, I'm to expect nothing more than a short, sharp explosion?"

He raised an eyebrow. "I do have a little more finesse than that."

"Well, if it's been over a year—"

"If rumors are true, it's been longer than *that* for you."

And those rumors would be right. "Seriously, has this reservation got nothing else to do but talk about other people's sex lives?"

"Apparently not. Go get ready. I shall help myself to another coffee and mourn the continuation of my monk status."

I grinned, then spun around and headed up the stairs, aware all the while of his gaze following me; if the groan that chased me up the stairs was any indication, he was both enjoying *and* additionally frustrated by the flashes of bare butt.

I quickly swapped the oversized sweater for more figure-hugging jeans and a long-sleeved T-shirt that had a deep enough V-cut to show the swell of my breasts—I certainly wasn't above showing off what the man would be missing out on if we got kicked out. After slipping on my boots, I grabbed my purse and headed back downstairs.

"Shame about the lack of legs on display," he murmured, delight etched across his features. "But I'm liking the fit of that top."

I grinned. "I gathered that by the swirl of appreciation and desire in your aura."

His eyebrows rose. "You can see desire?"

"I can see auras, and if the emotion is strong enough, it'll certainly appear in the aura."

"So the world is a rainbow of color to you?"

I smiled. "No, because I mostly have the ability switched off. It's only when the emotion is very strong that it slips past my guard."

"Ah." He rose and pressed a hand against my spine, lightly guiding me toward the door. "Does that mean you were well aware of my hatred for witches the minute you set eyes on me?"

"It was more your grief I saw," I said. "Your aura was almost black with it."

"And now?"

"The grief is still there, but it's not dominating."

"I have you to thank for that," he said softly. "You made me confront it; made me see that what I was doing wasn't healthy."

I didn't say anything and, after a moment, he touched my back again and guided me up the street. It didn't take us long to reach his truck, which was parked in the locked lot behind the ranger station, and we were soon on the way to Maldoon and the Marin compound.

"Have you discovered who the man mountain was?" I asked, as we once again approached the small cottage.

"No one in the Marin camp recognized him," he replied. "But the background check hit pay dirt. His name was Gerry Schmidt, and he arrived at the reservation a year ago. He's been working at Émigré for the last six months."

Meaning he'd probably known Marlinda. And while it might have been nothing more than a coincidence that the two had worked at the same place, I very much suspected it wasn't. "Have you talked to the owner of the club?"

"Maelle Defour," he said, voice oddly neutral, "has been faultlessly cooperative, and I don't trust her at all."

I shifted in my seat so I could study him properly. "You don't think she's involved, do you?"

"No. She's very obviously annoyed by Marlinda's death."

But not by Schmidt's, I gathered, although that was no real surprise if Maelle preferred her donors to be female rather than male. "Do you ask if she was aware of any connection between Marlinda and Gerry?"

"Yes. She said they were often on the same shift, but she couldn't say if they were friends outside of work."

"I gather you've searched his home?"

"Of course." He cast an amused glance my way. "Anyone would think you were the ranger here, given all the questions."

"Sorry." I gave him a lopsided grin. "But I've a long history of sticking my nose where it doesn't belong."

"In this case, and until the RWA witch comes along, your nose is actually welcome. It's not like I've got a whole lot of knowledge about spirits and magic." His amusement faded. "We haven't yet found a connection between him, Aron, and Larissa. We can't even find anyone who saw him and Teresa together, and her family said she never mentioned him."

"You wouldn't expect her to if he was just a one-night stand. And she *is* human, not wolf, is she not?"

"Yes."

My gaze was drawn to the side of the road up ahead, and the small cottage that was now ringed by police tape. Gerry's body was long gone, but the stain of his blood remained. As did, undoubtedly, Teresa's shade.

Belle, I asked, *is there anything you can do for her?*

According to my guides, it would depend on just how much of her spirit was consumed before the two of you spooked the soul eater.

So if her shade has some form of awareness, you could move her on?

Possibly. We'll have to wait until it's no longer considered a crime scene, though. She paused, and amusement crept into her mental tone as she added, *You and Aiden certainly timed your departure well.*

Why? What's happened?

The RWA witch has arrived and, oh boy, is he a piece of work.

In what way?

Picture your grandfather, and then imagine him two times worse.

That's not possible. If my father was ice, then my grandfather would have been fire. He'd never been afraid to call anyone out on their bullshit, and he'd had a very, *very* short fuse. But, weirdly enough, he and I had gotten on rather well.

That's because he saw something of himself in you.

I'm neither fiery nor short-tempered, I retorted.

Except when the right occasion comes along. Her amusement ran through my mind. *But I meant more in the lack of power. Like you, your grandfather never had the power to meet his dreams.*

That was probably true, although my dreams had never amounted to anything more than wanting to be something other than an utter disappointment to my parents.

Why is he at the café?

He wanted to talk to us about the dark spirit. I told him what I could, but he still wants to talk to you. She paused, and her amusement grew stronger. *Tala is looking a little like a deer in the spotlight.*

"Care to share?" Aiden said mildly.

I jumped slightly and then glanced at him. "Sorry. Belle was just informing me that the RWA witch has arrived."

"And? Because I'm sensing there is an 'and ' after that statement."

"Apparently, he's old, crusty, and short-tempered. And Tala is looking rather shell-shocked."

Aiden swore. "What the fuck were they thinking in sending someone like that? They know the situation here is somewhat tenuous in regard to witches."

"Regional centers are often only staffed by a couple of people. Maybe with Anna out of action, they haven't much other choice."

"They could have brought someone more suitable in from one of the other areas." He shook his head. "This is not going to sit well with the council."

"And yet he could be *exactly* what they need. Maybe if they're told in no uncertain terms the true depth of the danger they're placing everyone in by someone who knows, they might finally get off their butts and get a replacement witch here ASAP."

He raised an eyebrow. "And if he can't convince them, maybe you should get up there and have a go."

"As if they'd listen to someone they want to banish from the reservation."

"Not all of them want to evict you, but all of them

will hate a recalcitrant old fart treating them like errant children."

Which in many ways was exactly how they needed to be treated, given their somewhat childish attitude toward the wellspring. In this day and age, there was no excuse for such willful blindness.

But there was little point in saying any of that, because Aiden basically agreed with me. We turned off the main highway onto another of those goat tracks that paraded as roads within the reservation, and then went right into another one. But just as the track started to climb, Aiden pulled off the road and stopped.

I glanced around. The area was a mix of open space and thick trees, and there was absolutely no sign of habitation.

Aiden must have sensed my confusion, because he said, "The gates into the Marin compound are up ahead. We have to formally seek permission before we can enter."

I peered up the road, but couldn't see anything resembling gates. Just two huge old gum trees guarding either side of the goat track. Were they the gates he meant?

"Why?" I asked. "You're a ranger—surely that means you can move through the entire reservation without restriction."

"I can—especially if it's life and death—but this is more an official courtesy. It's an acknowledgment that we're entering sacred home grounds, and all three packs have the same rules and entry procedures."

"They can hardly consider it their sacred home considering this whole area was once O'Connor territory, not Marin or Sinclair."

His smile twisted. "Yeah, but that was long enough ago that they now consider this land theirs. So we shall be respectful and obey the rules."

I held up my hands. "I'm all for obeying rules."

"Only when it suits you, I suspect. You'll have to come along—you'll need to sign in."

I frowned, but nevertheless climbed out of the car. "Neither Mike nor Meika mentioned any of this when I was talking to them yesterday. If I hadn't insisted you come along, I would've blundered up here and gotten myself into a world of trouble."

"They wouldn't have done it deliberately. It's a procedure that's used in all compounds throughout Australia, so they probably thought you'd be aware of them."

I walked around the front of his truck and fell into step beside him. "Presuming someone knows something is never a good idea. Maybe your council needs to provide a reference sheet of dos and don'ts for those of us who have never lived in a reservation before."

"That's probably a good idea." His gaze met mine. "So if you've never lived in a reservation before, why choose this one?"

"As I've said, the fact this is a major tourist area was part of the reason." I hesitated and then shrugged. "But it also felt right and, according to Belle's guides, the omens were good for settling here."

"Who or what are her guides? Are they spirits or ghosts? Or are they one and the same?"

"Ghosts are generally the souls of those who were taken before their time, or those who, for whatever reason—be it revenge, confusion, or a simple unwillingness—refuse to move on to their next life. Spirits are from the realm beyond ours—supernatural beings that were never human even if they can attain that form."

His eyebrows rose. "So Belle's guides come from the same world as the soul eater?"

"No, because spirit *guides* are a different beast altogether. For the most part, guides are powerful, knowledgeable witches who have either decided to dedicate their *after*life to the council of other witches, or those whose path it was always destined to be."

"Do all witches have them?" He glanced at me. "Do you?"

"No, thank God. I get enough crap from Belle's guides without having my own to put up with." My gaze swept the area ahead, but I still wasn't seeing any gates. Those trees *had* to be it. "Of course, it's extremely rare for someone from the Sarr line to have guides—it's generally only the highborn witches who get them."

"Sarr?" Aiden said mildly. "I thought her name was Kent?"

I silently cursed the slip. That's what I got for endlessly weaving lies and being too comfortable around someone. "It is, but she obviously has Sarr witch blood in her. You only have to look at her to know that."

"Indeed," he said, even as his tone suggested disbelief.

Which meant it was time for a little up-front honesty—though not, perhaps, the type he was looking for. "Can I ask you a rather personal question?"

"Sure. No guarantee I'll answer it, but feel free."

"If you're so convinced Belle and I are lying about our past, why the hell do you still want to fuck me?"

He laughed, a warm and oddly surprised sound that echoed loudly. Something stirred in response, something that was dark and angry. I frowned and swept my gaze across the mix of rocks, trees, and open ground that surrounded us. I couldn't see anyone out there, but then, this was Marin territory; in wolf form, their red-brown coats would very much blend in.

"Like any regular man, I'm quite capable of separating logic from desire. In your case, the latter has little hope against the former." Despite the lightness of his tone, his expression, when his gaze met mine, was deeply serious. "You're lying about your past, Liz. I'm sure of it. I'll find out why eventually. But I also trust my gut, which is telling me you have a good reason for the lies. So until you either trust me enough to confide in me, or I ferret the information out, I can see no reason *not* to pursue you sexually."

I half smiled. "At least we both now have our cards on the table in that regard."

"Indeed." His answering smile faded as he looked back up the road. "That's odd."

Even as he said that, the feeling of wrongness increased. I flexed my fingers, trying to ease the tension gathering within me. "What is?"

"Our presence should have been acknowledged by now." His nostrils flared as he drew in a deeper breath. "Someone *is* there."

I studied the trees ahead with a frown. "There is?"

His grin flashed, though it held little in the way of amusement. "All buildings within werewolf compounds work with nature rather than against it. Look up."

I did so, and saw what he meant. A small tree house sat in the canopy of the tree on the left, one that very much looked as if it had grown out of the tree rather than built onto it.

"You all live in trees?"

"Of course not. But we do build our homes both

around nature, and from nature, which means logs, stone, and earth. Wait here."

I stopped immediately, my tension level ramping up several more degrees. He'd barely taken three steps when he stopped abruptly and cocked his head.

A second later, I heard it.

A short, sharp noise that sounded like a car backfiring.

But there were no cars nearby and no cars approaching, from either up ahead or behind us.

And in that instant, between one heartbeat and the next, I realized what it was.

A gunshot.

CHAPTER
ten

Aiden swore and dove at me, twisting around as he caught me around the waist, so that his back was toward the sound. We fell as one, hitting the ground hard enough for dust to plume, and my breath to escape in a painful whoosh. A heartbeat later something burned across my thigh; I yelped, but the sound was smothered by Aiden's growl. It was a deep and angry noise, one that had come from a wolf's throat more than a man's.

But he didn't say anything else, and he didn't release me. Instead, he rolled me over his body, and then repeated the action, until we were barrel rolling toward his truck. Dust flew, stones embedded into my back and sides, but it didn't matter. Nothing did, except the fact that the sharp noise of that car backfiring was chasing us, biting into the roadside, missing us by inches. I caught brief glimpses of the truck's underbelly and tire as we passed them, but Aiden didn't stop. Not until we'd reached the rear tire.

Even then, he didn't immediately move, but remained as he was, his body lying over mine protectively, his expression intent and his gaze scanning the area. Two bullets pinged off the front bull bar, and then silence fell.

But not my tension level.

And not his, if the quivering in his limbs was anything to go by.

His gaze dropped to mine. His eyes were bright, fierce, and almost otherworldly. He was caught between worlds, I realized—between the human need to ensure I was safe, and the wolf who wanted to hunt.

"Go," I said. "I'm okay."

"No, you're not—I can smell blood."

"Then you'll know it's nothing major. I'm fine—really. Go."

"Get into the cab, but keep low." His voice was losing its clarity, becoming a growl. The wolf within wanted to run, to chase.

"Go," I repeated yet again.

He rolled away from me and sprang to his feet, the movement fluid and beautiful. In three strides he went from human to wolf, although a shimmer of energy hid the actual change. His wolf was as lean and powerful as his human, and his coat rippled silver in the morning sunshine.

As he disappeared around the front of the truck, I carefully pushed onto my hands and knees, and crawled to the passenger door. I reached up, grabbed the handle, and hauled the door opened, my heart hammering and every sense I had attuned to the silence around me, waiting for the sound of another bullet being fired.

When it didn't come, I climbed into the truck, keeping low as ordered, then closed and locked the doors.

That's when the shaking began. I lay across the bench seat, my head on the driver side and my arms crossed across my chest, fighting the urge to cry.

Who the hell could want me dead? It couldn't have been the witch—not this time, not here on Marin grounds. I may not know a whole lot about werewolves, but if they had guards on their main entry point, then they'd run regular patrols around the rest of it.

So if not the witch, then who? No one else on this reservation had any reason to hate me.

They may not be on the reservation, but the Fitzgeralds certainly do, Belle commented. *Maybe that little rat infestation you left behind when they ran us out of town pissed them off so much they've decided payback is required.*

I snorted. *Those boys are gutless wonders. They used the local cop and innuendo to do their dirty work; I can't see them suddenly gathering the courage for more direct action.*

It doesn't take courage to hire a hit man. Are you okay?

Yes. The ache in my leg amplified even as I said that. I twisted around and saw the tear in my jeans and the blood seeping around it. *Although it would appear I've been shot.*

What!

It hurts, but not that much. I gingerly pulled the material away from the wound, but instead of the hole I'd been expecting, I discovered a shallow scrape. *It's a flesh wound, and nothing serious.*

She says with utter authority, because she's seen so many flesh wounds in the past.

Trust me, some of the wounds I received in knife spelling class were far deeper than this. Not that they were supposed to be dangerous, but knives and me hadn't been a great combination in those early years—and I still had some of

215

the scars to prove it.

Having seen some of those wounds, I'm now comforted. Amusement ran through her mental tone. *I'd still recommend bandaging it, and then getting a doc to check it as soon as you can. Or I will nag.*

Which you do so well.

A familiar does have to look after her witch, even when the witch doesn't like it.

And a witch had to look after their familiar, or they'd be lessened by their absence. That was something they'd ingrained into us from a very early age. *Is the RWA witch still hanging around the café?*

Yeah. He's currently studying the spells protecting the place. I think he's impressed.

Anna thought their informal construction was dangerous.

He's certainly intrigued by their construction, but I'm not getting the impression he thinks our magic is dangerous.

Meaning you haven't read him?

No. You know how those two IIT officers were wearing a device to stop me reading their thoughts? I think he's got one.

The IIT—or Interspecies Investigations Team, as they were officially known—were legally required to be called in whenever there was a murder on a reservation that involved humans. Whether they would be called in on this case now that Teresa White had been killed, I couldn't say, although I rather suspected it would be the RWA's call if they were.

Why would a witch be wearing an electronic device like that? Surely it'd interfere with his ability to sense the natural energy of the world.

You might be right. Maybe it's a charm of some kind.

Possibly. It's not like we've kept up-to-date with recent spell developments. And if the High Council's spell development team could create magical fingerprint locks, it was certainly possible they'd found a way to stop telepathic intrusion.

I could probably get past it, but it's really not worth the effort given he has absolutely no problem telling the world at large exactly what he's thinking. She paused. *I'd better go. He's heading into the reading room, muttering something about ley lines and wild magic and why didn't the bastards in Canberra know that.*

Know what?

I have no idea. But I daresay he'll tell us sooner rather than later.

I couldn't help grinning. He really *did* sound a hell of a lot like my grandfather.

"Lizzie?" a familiar voice said from outside the truck. "You there?"

I rose up on my elbows and warily looked out the windshield. Zak and a man who was almost a carbon copy of him, but with slightly fuller cheeks, were standing at the front of the truck.

"I'm not entirely sure where else you'd expect me to be," I replied. "Has the shooter been caught?"

Zak grinned. "Yeah, Aiden got her. He's asked us to escort you up to the compound proper."

"I have to walk?"

"No. The council gave you special dispensation because you're shot. Jak and I will drive you."

I sat up and unlocked the doors. Pain slithered up my shot leg, and I winced. "Jak and Zak? Seriously?"

His grin grew as he climbed into the driver seat. "For some weird reason, Mom likes names that rhyme. So aside from the two of us, there's Nick and Mick, and Jen and Wren."

I laughed. "Are you all twins, or just born close together?"

"Twins," Jak said, and handed me a bandage. "Wrap that around your leg. The medic is on standby in the meeting hall."

"Why are we going there rather than to a surgery?"

"Because it's the elders' right to be present when Aiden questions Larissa." Zak started the truck and reversed out of the parking spot. "And he also wants you to be there."

I blinked. So it was Larissa who'd shot at me? Why on earth would she want to kill me? Then a chill crawled across my skin as another thought stirred—what if she was under the soul eater's control? If Aiden was still wearing the amulet I'd given him, he'd be safe enough, but everyone else in that room certainly wasn't. They had, quite literally, invited death into their presence.

I shivered and rubbed my arms. That thought was probably nothing more than just paranoia; there had to be easier ways to access a meeting of the elders—especially given they apparently had regular pack meetings. But that still didn't discount the growing conviction that both the soul eater's presence and these murders were something *other* than Larissa needing revenge.

"You cold?" Jak said.

"No, just uneasy." I lifted my leg up as best I could and started bandaging the wound. "Can we hurry this up a bit? I need to get up to that meeting and check Larissa out."

"She's no danger to anyone now," Zak assured me. "She's trussed up tighter than a turkey at Christmas."

Even so, he planted his foot on the accelerator and we shot up the old track at a faster pace than was probably wise.

As we wound our way up the mountain, the track

grew increasingly narrower, the forest darker, and rock outcrops bigger and closer. Eventually, the truck could go no farther. Zak pulled into a small clearing off to the right of the track, and stopped. "We'll carry you from here."

"I'm not an invalid—"

"Aiden said you'd say that," Jak interrupted cheerfully, "and he gave us strict instructions to ignore you."

"And," Zak added, as he climbed out. "The only way you're going to get up there is if we carry you. Otherwise, we've orders to keep you here, and the medic will be called down."

"I'm going to have a serious word or two with that man when I get the chance," I muttered crossly.

Jak grinned and offered me a hand to get out. "He also said you'd probably say that."

Aiden might not yet know me on an intimate level, but it certainly appeared as if he'd otherwise gotten my measure. I carefully climbed out of the truck, but couldn't put a whole lot of weight on my leg. I might not want to admit it, but the damn man was probably right about my inability to walk very far.

Zak stopped on my other side and, in very little time—and with very little fuss or effort—they were quickly chair-carrying me up the narrow path. It soon began to flatten out, but the trees and the rocks remained prolific. In amongst them, buildings began to appear, some of them hewn out of the earth, and many of them built around both the trees and the rocks. There was nothing basic or crude about any of these structures, however. Their design might be unusual, their construct might be from nature itself, but there were also necessities such as windows and heating—if the many chimneys were anything to go by—as well as the latest in green technologies such as wind turbines and battery storage. The farther we moved into the encampment, the larger and grander these houses became, until we reached a vast clearing. In the middle of this sat a huge wooden hall that very much looked like a relic from medieval times. Around the perimeter were a number of buildings both ornately decorated *and* huge; not so much in height—although some were a good thirty feet tall—but rather in square footage. Though I suppose large residences would be needed if generations of werewolves lived together.

The door to the old hall opened as we neared, and we were quickly ushered in. The building looked as old on the inside as it did outside. The frame was built of sturdy tree trunks that curved toward each other, and rather looked like a series of connected wishbones. A long ridge beam ran the length of the building. The outside walls were braced with more wood, and the rooftop—at least from the inside—looked like shingles, and was held up by more wood and braced. The only part of the building that wasn't wood was the far end—it was a massive rock construction that held a fireplace big enough to party in. Or, as it was currently doing, roast a kangaroo in.

Seats ran around the three other sides of the building, and a smaller selection of seats clustered in a semicircle around the fireplace. Aiden stood in front of the fireplace, facing them, and the woman I presumed was Larissa was beside him, securely bound to a metal chair.

The elders—seven men and five women—glanced around as we entered, but they didn't offer a greeting, and their expressions gave little away. Only Aiden gave me a quick smile, but it did little to ease the tension I could see both in his aura and his stance. There was a large bloodstain on his leg, another on his left arm, and a newly gained but almost healed scratch that ran from the edge of his right eye to his chin. Larissa had obviously put up a hell of a fight.

I was deposited in a chair to the left edge of the semicircle, not far away from bound Larissa. She glared at me balefully, her golden eyes narrowed and glittering with anger. Anyone who didn't know the true situation might have presumed that I'd done her wrong, not the other way around.

Once Zak and his brother had left, the door was once again closed and a thin, elderly man with thick gray streaks at his temples rose and walked toward me. "I'm Harry Marin, the healer around here," he said. "How's that leg of yours?"

"It's sore, naturally enough, but it's really only a flesh wound."

"I think I'd better be the judge of that, young woman." He knelt in front of me, put on a pair of glasses, and then pulled on some gloves. "You want a painkiller?"

I hesitated. "If you're going to sew it up or something, yes. If you're just going to inspect and treat it, no."

"I can't say what I'll do before I actually look at it."

His tone was tart, but I held back my smile. Given the stern atmosphere of the room, I didn't think it would be appreciated.

As he started unwinding the hastily wrapped bandage from my leg, I glanced over at Aiden. "Has she said anything?"

"The only things to come out of her mouth are obscenities." Aiden's tone was annoyed, even if his expression was as controlled as everyone else's in the room. "I was hoping you might have a trick or two up your sleeve that might loosen her tongue."

"There are a couple of spells I could try." I switched my gaze to hers. "Anyone know if she's afraid of spiders? Or maybe even rats? I dare say a nibble or two from either might loosen her tongue."

"You're talking *shit*," Larissa all but spat. "You're a psychic and charm seller. You ain't no witch."

"Actually," Aiden said, "Ms. Grace does have some magical abilities. I can assure you, having researched her background, that she is quite capable of spelling rats to obey her orders."

"Maybe so, but I'm betting the elders wouldn't appreciate an influx of rats."

"That," a deep voice said, "very much depends on which elder you're talking about. I, for example, could think of nothing better than watching you be smothered in rodents who eat away at you piece by tiny piece."

The man who spoke was of average height and looks, but there was something in the way he held himself that was not only dignified, but also spoke of someone used to being obeyed. Combine that with the vehemence in his words, and I had no doubt this was Rocco Marin—Aron's father.

Larissa didn't say anything, but her expression remained thunderous, and her aura was basically all red. While it was often a color associated with passion, success, and strength, it was also nature's warning color and could represent negative emotions just as much as positive. And that was the case here—the red in Larisa's aura represented a mix of rebellion, aggression, anger, and hate.

All of which was to be expected from the person who'd just tried to shoot me. And yet, despite the anger in her aura, it didn't feel murderous—at least, not when she was looking at Rocco anyway.

"It would appear you're right," Harry said. "It is only a flesh wound. I'll wash it down and rebandage it, if you'd like."

He proceeded to do so without waiting for the go-ahead. Once he'd finished, he added, "Just don't be running any marathons for the next few days."

I grinned. "I can absolutely guarantee I won't be doing that, Doc."

"Liz, do you think you can make it over here, or do you need some help?"

I hesitated. The doc immediately rose, offered me a hand, and then pulled me easily to my feet. He kept hold of me until I was steady, and remained close as I hobbled over to Aiden, before he moved back to his own chair.

Larissa's lip curled into something resembling a snarl, and she made a hawking sound in the back of her throat. Aiden hooked his foot under the chair and with very little effort, sent her thumping onto her back. She grunted and then swore, and the globule that would have been aimed my way instead went high, and landed in the middle of her chest.

Aiden made no move to right her chair. He simply crossed his arms and said, "Try anything like that again, and I'll add additional assault charges to the attempted murder ones."

Her only response was another low growl and, just for an instant, her features became more wolf than human. But she didn't fully change, and it took a moment to realize why. The chair she was tied to wasn't plain metal; it was silver coated. It was a metal that was deadly to wolves; if embedded into their flesh, it ate away at skin and muscle even as it poisoned their blood. It was part of the reason why silver weapons were banned in reservations, and why some even went as far as banning combs and jewelry.

But aside from the whole poisoning issue, silver could also be used as a restraint, as it prevented the wolf from shifting from one form to another. While Larissa was clothed, her bare arms were tied behind her, which meant her skin was pressing against the silver-coated backrest. The silver obviously wasn't strong enough to immediately poison her, but it *was* preventing her from attaining wolf form.

Which was a damn good thing, given her expression very much suggested my throat would be the first one she'd rip out.

But why? That was the puzzle needing an answer right now.

I met Aiden's gaze. "I can try a truth spell, if you'd like. It can sometimes be hit-and-miss, depending on the mental strength of the recipient."

"Do it. If it fails, we can always try the rat option." Though his voice was flat and oh-so serious, humor sparkled in his eyes. "Do you need a hand with anything?"

I shook my head. "Just step back a bit to ensure you're not caught in any backwash."

He immediately did so. I took a deep breath to center myself and to gather energy. Once calm had descended and the awareness of those watching had faded somewhat, I slowly circled the fallen Larissa, softly murmuring the incantation, building up the layers of magic and then pinning them to the chair. Spell stones would have provided a more secure anchor, but the silver coating on the chair was a reasonable enough substitute. The spell might fracture if she moved around too much, but given how tightly she was trussed, that hopefully wouldn't be a problem.

I closed off the spell and then stepped back and activated it. The air shimmered briefly and energy pulsed, a soft heartbeat that told me the spell was successful.

I glanced at Aiden. "Ask your questions."

He stood next to me again, got out his phone, and hit the record button. "Did you kill Aron Marin?"

Larissa's face screwed up as she fought the spell. She opened her mouth, shut it again, and then all but growled, "No, I fucking did *not*."

A murmur of disbelief ran around the room. Aiden's expression didn't change. "You threatened revenge on his family, did you not?"

"Yes, but why would I kill Aron? He didn't have anything to do with it. If I was going to kill anyone, it would have been his bitch of a mother." Her gaze cut across to the elders. "She's the one who stopped me from marrying Garrett."

"And yet you were seen with both Aron and Marlinda the night they were both murdered."

"Of course, but I wasn't alone—a whole bunch of us went out for dinner."

"Was that where you discovered that Aron and Marlinda were lovers, and you became so enraged that you killed them both?"

"Why would I care if they were fucking each other?" Larissa bit back. "Not that they would have been. Marlinda was a lesbian. She wouldn't have touched Aron with a ten-foot pole."

"She was having an affair with Luc, so she wasn't a lesbian," I commented.

Larissa shrugged. "So she was bi—who really cares?

The fact remains, she wouldn't have done Aron."

"And yet the autopsy results show that they did indeed have sex before they died."

"Again, so? I didn't kill them, Ranger." She struggled against her restraints, causing the spell to shimmer in response. It held, but I wasn't entirely sure how long it would continue to do so if she kept fighting to be free. "I swear on the life of my mother, they were both alive when I left them."

Another murmur ran around the room, and this time it held an almost unwilling edge of belief.

"Then who did, if not you?"

"I don't know what killed them. I don't."

Meaning, I thought with a half smile, she *did* know *something*.

"It's interesting that you say what rather than who," Aiden drawled. "Because it shows an awareness that neither they nor Teresa White or Gerry Schmidt were taken by a human hand."

Just for an instant, fear flashed in her eyes. Fear, and a growing sense of horror. There was no doubt she knew what was going on.

"So while you might not be personally responsible for their deaths," Aiden continued conversationally, "by inviting a soul eater into the reservation to do your dirty work for you, you are nevertheless accountable for their deaths—and any others that occur until this thing is stopped."

"No! I swear, it wasn't me! I'm not the one—" She clammed up again, her expression a mix of mutinous determination and fear.

"Did you hire a witch to call forth the dark spirit?" I asked.

Her gaze shot to mine. "No, I didn't. Might consider doing so to get rid of you, though."

"That's going to be a hard thing to do from inside a prison cell," Aiden commented. "And I can't see your poor mother stumping up the cash for that sort of thing. If she did, well, she could be an accessory to attempted murder."

"You leave my mother out of it," Larissa bit back, with something close to fear in her eyes. "She has nothing to do with anything."

I flexed my fingers and silently bolstered the power of the spell, this time leaving an open connection so I could tighten it again if necessary. Doing so meant it would eventually start taxing my strength, but we needed answers. Larissa might be answering the questions truthfully enough, but she still wasn't telling us all that she knew.

"How did that spirit get here if not through another witch?" I asked, as the air shimmered around her with renewed vigor.

Her face reddened as she fought the order, but she had no choice now but to answer. "It was meant to be a bit of fun. We didn't mean for any of this to happen."

"What was meant to be a bit of fun?" Aiden asked.

"Using the Ouija board."

I swore softly. Why on earth did people consider Ouija boards to be nothing more than a bit of harmless fun? They were a goddamn gateway to the spirit realm, and very dangerous if you didn't know what you were doing—and most people didn't. Hell, most people didn't even take any sort of precautions. They just opened the gate willy-nilly and expected only harmless spirits to come through. Witches had spent years—if not decades—trying

227

to educate the masses, but it seemed the message still wasn't getting through.

"So who was there, and what happened?" Aiden asked.

"We were at Frankie's place—"

"Frankie?" he cut in. "Has she got a surname?"

"Kastle. She was a bit weird, in a hippy sort of way, you know?"

"And her address?"

"It's a little weatherboard place on North Street." She hesitated. "Thirty-one, I think."

"Who else was there?"

"Aron, Marlinda, and me, of course," she said. "Lance Marin was there, as was Gerry Schmidt, and a woman named Janice, who was one of Marlinda's friends. I've never met her before."

"You weren't told her last name?"

"No, but she wasn't a wolf."

Aiden grunted, and looked at me. "Would a dark spirit hunt down those who called it into being?"

"They're called dark spirits for a reason. And given these fools probably didn't take the proper precautions before using the board, they'd be easy prey."

"We drew a fucking pentagram on the floor," Larissa growled. "We aren't *that* stupid."

"What color candles did you use?" I snapped back. "Did you create a basic circle of protection, or a more advanced one? Did you beseech protection from the right gods?"

She scowled. "How the fuck do I know? It was just a pentagram."

"There is no such thing as *just* a pentagram—"

"Why did you decide to use the Ouija board?" Aiden

asked, lightly touching my arm in warning.

I took a deep breath and tried to calm down—a hard task in the face of such stupidity.

"We were all drinking and bitching, and I was going on about not being allowed to marry Garrett, and then Janice suggested I get a little supernatural payback."

"And Aron didn't speak up against this?" Aiden said, surprise evident.

"He did, but Janice convinced him it was just a bit of fun and no real harm would come of it."

"So that's when the Ouija board came into play," I said.

She nodded. "None of us took it seriously, not even Janice."

Which was their first mistake. Not taking things seriously was a good way to piss off the good spirits and invite in the bad.

"So what happened?"

She hesitated. "Nothing at first. Then the planchette began to move in this weird figure-eight pattern. We kept asking questions, but it was like it wasn't interested in helping."

"That's because it wasn't," I said. "It was trying to control the board."

"What happened after that," Aiden said, with another warning glance at me.

I crossed my arms and returned his gaze evenly. He'd asked for my help, so he was damn well going to put up with my questions and comments as well.

"Nothing much," Larissa said. "Janice started accusing us of moving the planchette and trying to scare her. She demanded that we stop."

"And did you?"

"Yeah. It was getting weirdly cold and dark in the room, so we just gave it up."

"Did you close the connection first?" I asked. "And did you wrap both the planchette and the board up in separate cloths and store them apart?"

"I don't fucking know. I left not long after that."

I swore again. "So it's possible we're dealing with a still-open connection."

"Meaning what?" Aiden asked.

I raised my gaze to his. "If we don't close it, a soul eater could be the *least* of our problems."

CHAPTER
eleven

Aiden rubbed a hand across his chin. In the sharp silence of the hall, it sounded like rough sandpaper. "What do we need to do?"

"Immediately find that board and close the connection down."

He swore and returned his gaze to Larissa. "When did all this happen?"

"Three days before Aron was murdered."

"And you went into hiding two days before then," I said. "Why?"

"Because I got a call from Frankie saying something weird was happening in her house, that it felt as if something was there with her, trying to get her, and she was scared." She paused, and something close to fear crept into her expression again. "She said we'd let something bad in when we were using the board, and that she needed someplace to stay while she got the place cleansed."

Which wouldn't have done one bit of damn good if the Ouija doorway was still open. "And your response?"

Larissa's gaze came to mine. For the first time, horror rather than fear lurked in the golden depths. "I said I'd pick her up after work. I wasn't going to lose money because she was suddenly spooked."

Yet more evidence that Larissa still didn't understand the true direness of the situation she was now in. "What happened?"

"The front door was open, so I went in." Color leached from her face, and her voice shook as she added, "Frankie was in the lounge room with a man I didn't know. They'd had sex—I could smell it in the air. She was sitting astride his body, but leaning over him, her mouth open and a couple of inches away from his. She looked to be drinking in this weird sort of sparkly mist that was coming out of his mouth. He was shaking, you know, like it hurt, but his eyes were closed and I'd swear he was asleep."

"Did you recognize the victim?"

Larissa hesitated. "No. He wasn't a wolf, though."

"Did Frankie say or do anything when you arrived?" Aiden asked. "Did she even see you?"

"Hell, yeah." She shuddered. "Her eyes—they were dead, you know? Not just lifeless, but colorless. Black."

"And that's when you ran?" I asked.

"Wouldn't you? It was weird, you know? After her phone call, I wasn't going to take a chance. And then Aron and Marlinda were also killed, and I feared it might be coming after me next."

"Did she run after you?"

"Yeah, but I got outside and she didn't follow. She stood in the doorway and screamed at me to come back. I didn't. I just got the fuck out of there. It was pretty obvious that whatever we'd let in had taken her over."

Not just taken her over, but had dined on her soul *and* was in control of her flesh. "So why did you try to kill me?"

"I didn't want you dead," she muttered sullenly. "I just wanted you maimed. I'd heard you were looking for me, and thought if you were temporarily out of action, I could get enough cash and things together, and get the fuck out of this place."

"That wouldn't have stopped me from locating you." It wouldn't have stopped a dark spirit, either; not without some major form of magical protection, anyway.

Surprise flickered across Larissa's expression. "Don't psychic talents have a range limit of effectiveness?"

"Generally, no," I said. "You could have been on the other side of Australia and I would still have found you."

If—and it was a big if—whatever personal item I'd been using to track her had a strong enough connection. But I didn't bother adding that. I'd rather she think there would have been no escape.

"Do you have any idea where Janice lives?" Aiden asked.

"No, because she was Marlinda's friend, as I said. You might find something at her place."

Aiden grunted and glanced at me. "How urgent is closing off that Ouija board?"

"The longer it's left, the greater the chance of something worse than the soul eater coming through."

"I didn't think there could be anything worse." He shuddered, and then turned around to face the elders. "With your permission, I'll call one of my deputies to come and pick up Larissa."

"Will she be charged with attempted murder?"

"Yes. I'm not sure if we can make a case of her being involved in Aron's murder, but we'll give it a try."

"What the fuck?" Larissa said. "I ain't responsible—"

"You had your hand on the planchette, did you not?" I cut in.

"Yes, but I wasn't the one who—"

"Then you're as responsible for this mess as everyone else." I returned my gaze to Aiden. "Can I suggest you delay taking her down to the station for at least a few hours?"

He frowned. "Sure, but why?"

"With the way the gossip brigade works in town, it'll only take a couple of minutes for the whole place to know she's in custody," I said. "So if the soul eater *is* hunting for her, it might be wise to arrange full spirit protection around the station to protect your people once she's there."

"Can you do that?"

I hesitated. "The protections would be stronger if the RWA witch applied them."

"I'll contact him." He glanced back at the elders. "Can she be held here? And without too many people being aware of the fact, just to be on the safe side?"

"I'll place a blanket ban on anyone speaking her name outside the compound," Rocco said heavily. "And we'll gag the bitch, just in case she gets it in her mind to howl for help."

"Are you thick or what?" she said. "I'm trying to avoid that thing's attention, not gain it."

Something flashed in Rocco's eyes, something that was wild and barely restrained. I had to wonder if, when a deputy did arrive, there'd be anything of Larissa left to retrieve.

"Marcus, Jonny, gag her now." Rocco's gaze returned to Aiden's. "We'll guard her until this evening, Ranger. Any longer than that, and we might just be tempted to take justice into our own hands."

"Understood." He paused, and then added, "Is Lance Marin here at the compound?"

"No, he's working at the spa in Rayburn Springs, and shares a house with a friend there. I'll send you his contact details." The man who'd answered was shorter than most wolves, and rather stout in build. "Do I need to warn him he could be in danger?"

"It couldn't hurt," Aiden said. "Right now, my advice for him would be to stay home and out of sight until all this is over."

"Will that protect him, though? It didn't help Frankie, by the sound of it," a woman said. Lance's mom, I guessed, given her worried expression.

"He should be safe enough during the day," I said. "We can ask the RWA witch to go over and place some protections around his house for tonight."

"Is there anything he can do in the meantime? Just in case?"

"He can keep the lights on, and place a mix of cumin and salt across all the doors and windows," I said. "If he's got any cloves in the house, tell him to stick them onto a chain and wear it until all this is over."

She raised her eyebrows, but didn't express the disbelief so evident in her eyes. "I'll tell him."

"Thanks." Aiden glanced at me. "Let's go."

He cupped my elbow with his oh-so warm fingers, giving me little choice but to leave with him. Once the door was shut behind us, I said, "Would Rocco really take matters into his own hands when it comes to Larissa?"

Aiden's smile was grim. "He's done it before, so yes. But I suspect that in this case, he said it more to scare Larissa. She's not directly responsible for his son's death—Aron is as much at fault, given he was also there using the Ouija board."

"Surely that depends on whether Rocco believes a soul eater is responsible for these deaths, though. You said some of the elders don't."

"But Rocco isn't amongst their number." He frowned at me. "How's that leg feeling?"

"How's yours?" I retorted. "I'm not the only one she shot."

"No, but my wounds were healed by the two shape shifts. You don't have that option."

More's the pity. He didn't add that, but it nevertheless seemed to hang in the air. It was yet again another reminder that I could never be anything more than a temporary passion for him.

"I'll make it back down to your truck, Ranger, so don't be worrying about me."

"Oh, I have no doubt you can make it, but I'd prefer it if you did so without reopening the wound." He hesitated, and then added with a slight grin, "Belle will have my hide if you're bleeding when I drop you back at the café."

Amusement twitched my lips. "You're scared of her?"

"Hell, *yeah.*" His grin grew. "She's built like a goddamn Amazon—she could probably throw me across the room without resorting to magic."

"She does do weights. She claims it's so she can better protect me, but don't believe her. She just likes the admiration all those muscles get her."

"With good reason. She looks amazing." He raised an eyebrow. "And you? You're not tempted to follow her lead?"

"Hell, no. It's too much like hard work. I'll keep to yoga and going on long walks, thank you very much."

"That sounds like something you'd see on a dating site."

"And what would a werewolf be doing on a dating site?" I asked mildly. "I wouldn't have thought finding a lover to be all that hard."

"It was research for a case."

"Yeah. Sure."

"Seriously."

"Believing you."

"I can tell." His voice was dry. "However, given the implied urgency of the situation and the fact it's going to take us forever to get back to the truck at this rate, do you mind greatly if I give you a hand?"

He didn't wait for an answer. He just scooped me up and held me close as he strode down the road at a much faster clip. I grinned and draped my arms around his neck. "I should protest that I'm not an invalid, but it feels rather nice to be held like this. And hey, who knows when I'll get another chance to enjoy all this muscular warmth."

"Indeed." His amusement faded a little. "How dangerous is it going to be to enter Kastle's place?"

"Very." I wrinkled my nose. "It actually might be wise to get the RWA witch to meet us there. He'll be more capable of handling whatever might still linger."

"Do you know if he's still at the café?"

"Hang on, and I'll check with Belle."

The words had barely left my mouth when she

replied, *He sure as hell is. He's been drilling me on how we got the wild magic entwined in the protection spells.*

We didn't. Not deliberately, anyway. I suspected it was a result of me bolstering the spells so soon after the wild magic had interfered with my incantation at the cemetery—some leftover energy wisps must have been still clinging to me, and had wound up in the spell.

I told him that. He doesn't believe me. He says there's intent. Anyway, you want me to send him your way?

I gave her the address and then added, *Tell him we're dealing with an open Ouija board and the possibility of a soul eater.*

Will do. She hesitated. *Be careful.*

With an official witch on the reservation, I'm not going anywhere near the place until it's safe.

Yeah, you say that now, but curiosity will get the better of you, I just know it. Just remember what curiosity did to the goddamn cat.

I sent her a mental kiss, and then tuned out and glanced up at Aiden. "She's going to ask the witch to meet us at the house."

"Good. I'll ask him about protecting the station, and Lance, too."

Silence fell between us. I tried to ignore my growing awareness of his closeness—of the way his muscles played against my body with each and every movement, or how much better it would feel if we were both naked—and kept my gaze firmly locked on the path ahead. To do anything else might be ultimately dangerous to our need to get to Kastle's house in a timely manner, especially if he was as affected by our closeness anywhere near as badly as me.

It didn't take too long to reach his truck. He placed me back down, one hand lingering on my spine as he opened the door with the other. Once we were both seated, he reversed out and drove carefully back down the track and out of the reservation. He didn't look at me until we were back on the main road to Castle Rock. Fifteen minutes might have passed, but the heat of desire still glowed in his eyes.

"We seriously have to make a concerted effort to find some time alone," he said. "Because I'm not sure I can take this frustration much longer."

I laughed, even though I very much agreed. "I'm sure you can take matters into your own hands if necessary." I hesitated, but couldn't help adding, "Why has it been over a year, Aiden? I know you were mourning your sister's death, but cutting out sex seems an odd way of doing it."

"I think we were all so intent on making her last few weeks happy that we forgot about ourselves." He shrugged. "After she died, I was too consumed by the need for justice and revenge to think about a relationship."

"You don't have to have a relationship to have sex."

"No, but you do at least have to be attracted to the person you're planning to bed. Until now—until you—I just haven't been."

"Which is probably the nicest thing any man has ever said to me."

"*That* is a rather sad statement."

"Indeed."

Silence fell again, and though there was an edge of awareness running through it, it was still very much an easy silence—one that could only happen when two people had grown comfortable in each other's company.

It didn't take us long to get to Castle Rock. Aiden drove past the town center and then turned right onto Myring Street. After a few more turns, we were stopping outside a somewhat run-down, single-fronted, green weatherboard cottage. Aiden pulled up beside the Ford Ranger truck that was parked in front of the moss-covered garden wall, and then climbed out. I did the same.

As the sound of the two doors slamming echoed across the odd silence, a somewhat stout figure appeared from the rear of the house and strode toward us. If anyone had ever looked less like a powerful witch, then it was this man. He was wearing a Carlton football jumper, jeans with frayed knees, and sneakers so old a sock-covered toe stuck out of the left one. He was bald, his face well tanned and full of wrinkles, and his eyes were muddy silver in color. Despite that, the power that rolled off him—even from this distance—damn near stole my breath.

"Ira Ashworth, at your service," he said, as he drew close enough to offer Aiden his hand. "You've got quite a mess to clean up, Ranger."

"You've been inside?"

"Far enough to know what we're dealing with and to smell the stink of rotting flesh. If you've face masks in your kit, we'll need to borrow them." Ashworth's gaze switched to mine. "And you'd be Lizzie Grace. Not what I expected, and quite disappointing, I have to say."

That's a statement I'd heard plenty of times during the first sixteen years of my life, but it was rather surprising to hear it coming from the mouth of a complete stranger. "What were you expecting?"

"Certainly not someone who bears Marlowe looks but none of their power. You're a conundrum, lassie."

He held out his hand, and after a brief hesitation, I shook it. His magic swirled around me, testing, probing. The smaller of the two charms I was wearing flared to life in response, and that, I suspected, was exactly what he wanted. After a moment, he grunted and released me.

"A puzzle indeed," he muttered. His gaze returned to Aiden as he came back with three masks. "There's a darkness haunting the inside of that house, so you'll have to stay out here in the sunshine until we give the all clear."

"We?" I all but squeaked. "I don't know enough—"

"I can deal with the spirit," he cut in. "But I can't do that *and* close the board. I haven't got three hands, lassie."

A smile twitched my lips despite the coldness stirring my gut. He really *was* like my grandfather.

"That agate charm of yours *will* protect you from the spirit," he continued. "I did some prelim probing, and the spirit inside isn't strong enough to get past the spellwork on the charm."

"That doesn't mean it's not capable of finding other methods to cause me harm."

"Well, of course not, and this one does seem to have answered the call of anger, if its hellish response to my questing is any indication."

"Great," I muttered, even as part of me wondered what he considered hellish. The other, less sensible half preferred to live in ignorance and deal with events as and when they happened.

"It is indeed." He cracked his fingers, anticipation evident, and then grabbed two of the masks. "Shall we go?"

He didn't wait for an answer; he just turned and strode back to the house, leaving me with little choice but to follow.

"Be careful in there," Aiden called after me. "Remember that whole returning to the café bleeding conversation we had not so long ago."

I flashed him a grin over my shoulder. He was leaning against the front of his truck, his arms crossed and expression annoyed. The wolf did *not* like being left out of the action.

But as I stepped over the old concrete wall and limped through the longish grass, trepidation began to override amusement.

Not just because of the pall of darkness that had wrapped itself around the house like a blanket, but because of the stench of rotting flesh coming from within. If my very human nose could smell it from the middle of the front lawn, then it was going to be bad inside.

Ashworth stepped onto the front porch and squatted next to a small backpack positioned to the right of the open door. The hallway was wrapped in shadows, an oddity given there was no cover over the porch and the sunshine should have at least shone into the first six feet or so.

Ashworth pulled his athame, several potion bottles, and a couple of cloths from the pack. He handed me one of the latter.

"I've put a mix of cinnamon and patchouli oils on them. Tuck it into the mask before you enter the house, and it'll help with the smell."

Help, but not entirely kill, I suspected. "And the plan?"

"I'll go in first and corner the spirit in the living area. You check the rest of the house, and find that board." He hesitated. "It's possible that an imp or two has followed the main spirit through the doorway, so be careful."

Imps were lesser demons—or sprites, as they were commonly known—and were generally more mischievous than dangerous. But they did have a tendency to throw things around, and in such a confined space that could certainly get perilous.

Ashworth took a deep breath and released it slowly; almost immediately, his magic centered around him *and* increased in potency. That surge of energy hit my skin in increasing waves, until it felt as if I were being bitten by hundreds of tiny gnats. I shivered and lightly rubbed my arms. It had been a long time since I'd felt such power— not since we'd left Canberra, in fact—and the biting sensation was one of the many things I *hadn't* missed.

But somewhere deep inside me, in the darker recesses that gave me the prophetic dreams, stirred the notion it was something I'd once again have to get used to.

I hoped it was wrong. I really did.

And yet, for all that Ashworth's magic bit, it very much explained why he was out here rather than living in the cozy—if often chilly—comfort of our capital, serving the needs of the council and the government. He might be a powerful witch, but his magic was little more than a flickering candle compared to the output of the high-ranking members of the royal lines. The few times I'd caught my father or mother unguarded magically, it had felt like I'd walked into the middle of an erupting volcano.

With his arms held up in front of his body, he walked into the house, murmuring an incantation as he did. While I couldn't hear the words, the sweeping nature of his magic suggested the spell was one that would basically corner the spirit—and the sprites, if they happened to be near—in one small section of the house. Once that was done, he could then deal with it.

I put on the mask, blinking rapidly as the dual—and somewhat pungent—scents of cinnamon and patchouli hit my nose, and waited, shifting uneasily from one foot to the other, until his magic reached a crescendo and the confining net was completed.

I took a deep breath, half coughed as the scents caught in my throat, and then silently began a repulsion spell. As the threads of magic began to form around my fingers, I warily stepped into the house. Despite the mask and the odorous cloth, the heavy scent of putrefaction still hit, and I gagged. Somehow, I held it together, even though my stomach felt as if it had lodged somewhere in my throat.

I spotted a light switch on the wall and flicked it on. Nothing happened. I frowned up at the light as I tried again. Still nothing. Either the globe had blown or the power in this place was off for some reason.

I crept forward, but with every step the darkness got deeper, until the sunshine was erased and everything around me was black. I quickly whispered a light spell and tossed it into the air. It rather resembled the will-o'-the-wisps—or ghost candles, as they were more commonly known—that inhabited the forests around Castle Rock, but where their light was a cool blue, this was a warmer gold. But, like the sunshine, it wasn't doing a whole lot to beat back the darkness.

I continued to move forward. In the uneasy glow of the sphere, I could vaguely make out four doors. There were two to my left, one straight ahead, and another down the hall and to the right. That was where the pulse of Ashworth's magic was originating, so at least I didn't have to investigate it. Not until he'd dealt with the spirit, anyway.

I directed the sphere into the first doorway, and then followed it. Something skittered through the shadows between light and utter darkness, and dread stirred. There were sprites in this bedroom.

I resisted the urge to fling the repulsion spell their

way, and looked around for the nearest light switch. It, too, was unresponsive. One broken globe might have been accidental, but two looked deliberate.

I started searching through the drawers and wardrobe, although anyone with any sort of sense certainly wouldn't have kept a Ouija board in their bedroom. After finding nothing in any of those, I knelt down to check under the bed. Pain ran down my injured leg and I cursed softly—only to cut it off abruptly as movement caught my eye. A very large vase was flying at my head.

I immediately cast the repelling spell into the air, but not at either the vase or the sprites. Instead, I let it drape around my body like a protective curtain. The vase hit it and bounced away, and the spell faded into the darkness, remaining active even though it wasn't visible.

A low chuckle came from the other side of the room—a sound that hadn't come from a human throat. I dropped my light sphere to the floor, and quickly peered under the bed. No Ouija board; just more shadows that moved and flowed across the outer edge of the light.

I rose and limped out the room. The sprites would undoubtedly follow, but if they were annoying me, they were leaving Ashworth alone—a good thing, given he had a malevolent spirit to take care of.

The next room was another bedroom, but appeared to be used more as a storeroom. There were clothes piled up on the bed, an ironing board set up on the left side of the room, and a long row of cupboards lining the other. As I opened the first cupboard door, clothes rose from the bed and launched at me. The spell cloaking me shimmered brightly and threw rainbows of light across the darkness, catching the scaly tails of several sprites and making them squeal in pain.

245

If I'd had more time, I would have made more light spheres and chased the bastards with them. But it was more important to find the board—until it was closed, it was very much the greater threat.

The sprites soon ran out of clothes, and started chucking other loose items at me, ranging from the various clocks that seemed to be sitting around to the iron, and even the goddamn ironing board. I growled in frustration, which was met by more laughter.

Then I was hit again—this time by something far larger. Something that didn't fall away, but rather sent me sprawling sideways. Pain once again ran down my leg, but it was sharper this time, and accompanied by a warmth that suggested it was bleeding. I cursed them fluently, brushed my fingers against the floor to keep from falling over completely, and then swung around—only to dive sideways to avoid being hit by the mirror portion of the dresser. It crashed to the floor and shattered, and bits of wood and glass flew, thudding into my boots and slicing through my jeans.

I hit the bed and bounced back to my feet, but the room was becoming a maelstrom of flying furniture, and if I didn't do something soon, I'd face the very real possibility of injury. But even as another spell sprung to my lips, I felt it—the stirring of magic. It wasn't Ashworth's; this was fresh, light, and even more powerful than he.

Wild magic.

Sweeping into the room, coming to my rescue without being called or asked.

And, just as it had in the cemetery, it entwined itself through my spell, both enhancing and empowering it, making it something far greater than I'd intended. As the nearby wardrobe began to shudder and shake, I quickly tied off the spell and flung it upwards. Light exploded through the room—through the house—and the sprites squealed as they were cast from the protection of the shadows and burned by the light.

In the other room, a deeper, more powerful but very inhuman voice joined in on the chorus of pain. A heartbeat later, Ashworth's spell hit a second peak, and with surprising abruptness the deep sense of evil left the house. Only the sprites remained, and they were being burned into oblivion, their tortured screams filling the air and the scent of their cindering flesh overpowering even the smell of putridity.

Footsteps echoed, and then Ashworth appeared. "How the fuck did you just do *that?*"

I frowned. "It was a simple light spell—"

"There was nothing simple about that spell, lassie," he cut in. "And there was certainly nothing simple about the power it contained—power you *don't* have."

"No, but the wild magic does. The sprites were getting nasty, so I created a sunburst spell. The wild magic enhanced it."

He frowned and cast around magically, probing for the wild magic that was no longer here. His expression, when it met mine, was a mix of confusion and excitement—and the latter was the last thing I needed. "How did that even happen? There was no wild magic evident when I entered the place, and there's certainly none here now."

"No, because it fled the minute the sprites had been taken care of."

It was almost as if the wild magic—or rather, the woman whose consciousness now ran through it—wanted to avoid a direct confrontation with a full-powered witch.

Though I had no real idea why, I suspected it might have something to do with what Gabe had done. He'd admitted that his spell had come from the remnants of a very old one, but perhaps that hadn't been the entire truth. Perhaps those remnants had been nothing more than that—scraps on which he'd based an entirely *new* spell. One that hadn't been considered possible.

If that were the case, then ghost or not, the high council would be very interested in not only talking to him, but also gathering the exact details of the spell. Then they would attempt to replicate the spell's success. After all, what better way was there to protect the wellsprings of this world than to infuse them with the spirits of powerful witches?

But such an endeavor would never be without risk; all power had the possibility to corrupt. Even highborn witches were not beyond its reach, although it was a rarity and quickly dealt with when it happened.

"That doesn't answer the question as to why it came to your aid," Ashworth commented. "Did you call for it?"

"No." I shrugged. "But it does seem to have an odd affinity with me—it rescued me once before—"

"In the cemetery," Ashworth cut in. "Your friend claims that's the reason behind the unusual construction in the spells that protect your place."

I raised an eyebrow, a casual action that belied the sudden acceleration of my heart. "You don't believe her?"

"I believe something very weird is going on, both in this place and with you two. But enough of that for now; let's find that fucking Ouija board before your light fades and something else comes through."

He spun on his heels and marched out. I released a

somewhat relieved breath, and continued checking the rest of the wardrobes. Again, there was no sign of the board, and the only things under the bed were dust bunnies.

I left the room. I could hear Ashworth ferreting around in the living area, so as my sunburst spell began to lose its brilliance I quickly headed into the kitchen. And there, sitting on the counter next to the toaster, was the Ouija board. In the fading light gnarled, shadowy fingers were beginning to appear, gripping the edges of the board—a spirit ready to erupt the minute darkness fell. The planchette sat beside it, unwrapped and unprotected.

I didn't go any closer to it. I just stopped and told Ashworth I'd found it.

He hurried into the kitchen. His energy, I noted, was nowhere near as fierce as it had started out. But then, sending that spirit back to whatever hell it had come from certainly would have drained him—both physically and magically. His gaze narrowed when he saw the board and the shadowy talons gripping it.

"Step back, lassie," he said. "I'll deal with this."

"Good, because I'm sure as hell not going to."

His expression was somewhat startled as his gaze jumped to mine, then he laughed. "And why not? You've been trained, haven't you?"

"Only at a basic level." I gave him a pleasant if insincere smile. "They tend not to lash out on the training of half-breeds."

Which was true, even if it didn't apply to me.

He grunted, and returned his attention to the board. Whether he believed me or not I couldn't say—not without touching him and unleashing the part of me that could read emotions.

And that was something I had no intentions of

doing—if for no other reason than really not wanting confirmation that my fears about this situation and his informing the council of our presence here were based on reality.

I crossed my arms and watched as he quickly and efficiently threw a confining circle around the board. When that was done, he glanced at me, and said, "You want to go outside, grab the shovel out of the shed, and dig two holes? They'll have to be two or three feet deep, at least."

"You're going to bury them? I thought it was better to burn them once they were purified?"

"I haven't any mistletoe with me to counter the influence of any hellfire spirits that might be attached to the board, so we can't risk it."

I grunted. I knew mistletoe had uses other than being a reason to kiss someone if caught under it, but I had no idea it could be used as a counter against fire spirits.

"Go, lassie. I need to ready this board for removal before your sunburst spell totally fades."

I spun around and headed out the back door, my gaze sweeping the overgrown backyard until I spotted the shed in the right corner. As I walked toward it, footsteps came down the drive, and Aiden appeared around the corner.

"You're limping again," he said. "What the hell happened in there? It sounded like the place was being wrecked."

"There were sprites in the house as well as a dark spirit." I opened the shed door and stepped inside. Light speared in through a window at the far end, highlighting the dust and heavy strings of cobwebs. "The sprites weren't happy about being evicted and I jarred my leg in the process of avoiding the things they were throwing."

"And sprites are?"

"Minor demons. More annoying than dangerous." I spotted a shovel and limped across to pick it up. "We found the Ouija board. Ashworth's closing it down, but we apparently need to bury it to totally secure it."

"I'll do the digging. You've been through enough for one day already." Aiden took it from me, and then waved me back out of the shed. "Where do you want the holes?"

I hesitated, scanning the small yard again, and then finally pointed toward a vacant, somewhat stony area away from any trees or shrubs. "Over there would be good."

"And naturally she picks the toughest bit of ground around," he murmured, amusement in his tone.

He'd almost finished digging the second hole when Ashworth came out, the Ouija board and planchette wrapped separately in soft white cotton. His backpack was slung over one shoulder, and there was a plastic sea salt container tucked under one arm. He salted the bottom of the first hole, placed the Ouija board in it, then began murmuring a blessing as he covered the board with more salt, and then added some garlic cloves, lilac, iron nails, and a couple of agate stones. He then motioned Aiden to fill in the hole while he repeated the process with the planchette in the second hole. When that was also covered in, he said, "Right, Ranger, the place is now safe, although I might stick around for a little while, just case we missed any sprites."

Aiden nodded and glanced at me. "Do you want to drive my truck back? I'll pick it up later."

I hesitated, and then nodded. While the café really wasn't that far away, I didn't feel like walking. My energy levels were seriously starting to crash. "Do you need to take your kit out of it first?"

"Already done that." He handed me the keys. "Just try not to grind the gears too much this time."

"I'll certainly try, but there's no guarantee of it happening. I drive autos for a reason, you know." I hesitated, then stepped forward and dropped a kiss on his cheek. "Ring me before you head over, and I'll have a coffee and a meal waiting."

"I will. Thanks."

I glanced across at Ashworth. "You're also quite welcome to come back."

"Thanks, lassie, but I think I'll just go back to the hotel and rest."

I nodded and left the backyard, well aware that Aiden's gaze followed me. I jumped into his truck, adjusted the seat to enable me to reach the clutch a little easier this time, and did indeed manage to avoid grinding the gears as I reversed out and drove back to the café. Which, considering the hurt leg, was something of a miracle.

"Hey," Belle said, as I limped through the back entrance into the main area. "Drink this."

I accepted the rather large and overly green drink with something close to trepidation. It was thick and soupy looking, but didn't quite smell like a swamp. In fact, as far as her potions went, this one definitely fell on the pleasant side of odorous.

"Unlike you," she said. "I suggest you head upstairs and grab a shower, because the stink of death clings and it'll drive our customers away."

I gulped down the drink and then headed upstairs. After I'd showered, I rebandaged the bullet scrape and then, once dressed, headed back down to take over from

Belle. Given she'd been running the place with only Penny as help for the last couple of days, she more than deserved a decent break.

My leg was aching pretty badly by the time we were ready to close, but I took some painkillers and then basically ignored it. Mike approached me at the end of his shift, his expression one of remorse. "I heard about what happened up at the compound. I'm sorry—"

"How did you hear about it?" I cut in. "The elders were supposed to put the story on lockdown until tonight."

He nodded. "Anyone outside of immediate family members wouldn't have heard a whisper. The only reason I'm now mentioning it is because Meika wanted me to give you her apologies for Larissa's actions."

"What her daughter did is hardly either of your fault."

"Yeah, it is, because we're the ones who got you involved in the hunt for her." He grimaced. "I didn't even think she knew how to use a gun."

Curiosity stirred. "How would she have learned to shoot? It's not a sport werewolves generally participate in, is it?"

"No. If we want to hunt, we generally use nose and teeth. A rifle takes out too much of the fun." He shrugged. "But a month or so ago she started hanging out with a couple of ratbags who belonged to the rifle range. It's possible she went there with them."

"Then I'm guessing she got the rifle from them?"

"Or she stole it from the range itself."

Stealing it was more than possible given what I'd seen of her, but that still didn't explain how she'd learned to use the weapon so well in such a short time. Surely it took far longer than that to become proficient at hitting moving targets from a distance?

So did that mean Larissa hadn't been at the other end of the rifle, but someone else? Someone who was now letting her take the fall?

I didn't want you dead—I just wanted you maimed, were her exact words when we were questioning her, right along with, *yes, but I wasn't the one who…*. What if that comment hadn't been about Aron at all? What if she'd meant the attempted murder charge against me? What would she have actually said if I hadn't cut her off?

If that *was* the case, was the real shooter on the run, or was he or she still out there, waiting for the right opportunity to take another shot at me?

Trepidation stirred, and I rubbed my arms uneasily. "I don't suppose you know any of their names?"

"No. But Meika might. I can ask if you'd like?"

I waved the offer away. "I'm sure the rangers will follow it up." And if they didn't, I sure as hell would. "I was just asking out of curiosity."

He hesitated, and then said, "Do you think she's going to be charged with Aron's and Marlinda's deaths?"

"I don't know, Mike, but she will at least be charged with shooting at me and Ranger O'Connor."

And even if it turned out she wasn't the one holding the gun, but rather one of her new friends, she'd still be charged with being an accessory.

He cursed softly and ran a hand through his short, silver-shot black hair. "Maybe some time away will do her good and set her on the right path. Maybe."

I reached out and squeezed his arm. His regret stirred around me—not so much about the current situation, but rather that he hadn't been more involved in Larissa's upbringing.

"Do you need a couple of days off? We can call in a substitute if you want to be with your sister—"

"No." He grimaced. "It's not like I can do a real lot now, is it?"

No. And Larissa was an adult; it was way past time for her to take responsibility for her own actions.

"I'll see you tomorrow, as usual," he added, and then headed out.

I locked up behind him and then made Belle a cappuccino, and a hot chocolate for myself, complete with lashings of marshmallows. And because I was feeling the need for an extra dose of sugar, I put a couple of slices of the freshly made almond butter chocolate brownies on a plate.

Belle clattered down the stairs as I placed the tray on the table. She'd changed and showered, and was looking rather awesome in a silver dress that hugged her curves in all the right places while emphasizing her sleek, muscular body.

I raised my eyebrows. "I take it you're going out?"

She slung her coat over the chair, then sat down and put on her shoes. "Zak rang me half an hour ago. He managed to get a couple of tickets for tonight's opening of the new *Phantom of the Opera* down in Melbourne."

Which just happened to be one of Belle's favorites. "Are you staying overnight?"

She shook her head. "He's got a maintenance job in the morning. Besides, it's only an hour and a half drive." She took a sip of the cappuccino and licked the froth from her lip. "What are you doing?"

I shrugged. "Probably nothing. Aiden's got the mess at Frankie's place to deal with, Lance to talk to, and then he'll probably want to talk to Larissa some more."

Belle leaned back in her chair, and tapped the table lightly. "You know, something about all this doesn't feel right."

"I know." I reached for a piece of brownie, and bit into its gooey richness. It might not help the brain matter work any better, but it sure as hell made my belly a whole lot happier.

"If Larissa was angry enough at Garrett's parents to call forth a soul eater from the Ouija session, why has it instead gone after everyone else at the session?"

"It could be as simple as no one at that session having the power to control it, and it's going after them instead of the intended targets."

She was shaking her head even as I answered. "If anger called it forth, then that anger should have guided its actions."

"So why isn't it going after Aron's parents?"

"Maybe his parents were *never* the target. Maybe Larissa is merely the fall guy for something else entirely?"

"If that's the case, then maybe it revolves around Frankie and the man she was with, as they were the first to die."

"I doubt Frankie was anything more than a convenient soul to consume and use."

"Which still leaves us with Frankie's victim."

"Did Larissa know him?"

"No. She just said he wasn't a wolf."

"And you believe her?"

"Yes." I finished the brownie and licked the chocolaty almond remnants from my fingers. "She said he looked peaceful—like he was asleep—so she obviously got a good look at his face."

"If he *was* the target, then the soul eater is free to do

as it pleases."

"But why would it then go after Marlinda and Aron? Frankie had plenty of neighbors—it would have been far easier to go dine on them rather than taking the time to hunt down everyone else involved in calling it forth."

Belle shrugged. "Given they were using the board without any sort of protection, it would have some sense of their souls and that, in turn, would make them very easy to track down. Of course, it could also be nothing more than payback for being called into this realm."

Which was certainly possible. Spirits—or rather, dark spirits—were well known for turning against those who controlled them if they got the slightest chance. I stirred the half-melted marshmallows into my hot chocolate and then took a drink. "I might go across to Émigré and talk to Maelle. Larissa insinuated that Janet was a friend of Marlinda's, so it might be worth asking if I can search her apartment again."

Belle raised an eyebrow. "Wouldn't that task be better done by Aiden?"

"Probably, but I don't think our resident vampire would appreciate too much contact with the rangers. Besides, I did promise to update her, and I'd hate to be breaking that promise."

"Good point. Especially if, as we suspect, she's more than a little capable of magic."

"I'm thinking she wouldn't need magic to take care of either of us. She'd just take a lovely long drink when we were least expecting it."

"True." Belle finished her coffee, and then added, "Are you still wearing that charm I made?"

"Are you?" I countered, even though it was obvious she wasn't.

"Point taken." She grinned. "Perhaps in the next day or so, we need to combine efforts and make a deterrent that will go with all outfits."

"Yes." I hesitated. "Although it might be better to wait until this case is over and Ashworth is gone. He's suspicious enough of the two of us."

"He's a chip off your grandfather's block, though, isn't he?"

"Indeed." My voice was wry. "I'm a disappointment, apparently."

She laughed. "Like you haven't been told that a billion or so times in your life already."

"Yeah." My smile faded. "The problem is the wild magic. It interfered in another spell at Frankie's house, which only served to clarify his suspicions we are not what we seem."

"Meaning he's likely to inquire about us?"

"More than likely, I'd say." I grimaced. "Of course, it may not matter in the end. Not if the council decides to uphold the witch ban and chuck us out of the reservation."

The sharp blast of a car horn cut off any reply she might have made. "And that will be Zak."

I shook my head in mock sorrow. "It's a sad state of affairs when a date no longer comes to the front door, and simply honks on his arrival."

"It is indeed, and I don't care." She rose, gathered her coat, and then kissed my cheek. "Be careful with Maelle. I still don't trust that woman."

"She doesn't intend me any immediate harm."

"I like the lack of conviction behind that statement. It comforts me greatly."

I grinned as the car horn sounded again. "The natives

are getting restless. You'd better go."

She headed out. I finished my hot chocolate, then cleaned everything up and headed upstairs to grab my coat and purse. I caught a cab across to Maelle's, but had barely climbed out of the car when Roger appeared in the club's doorway.

"Lizzie Grace," he said, somewhat effusively, "such a pleasure to see you on so fine an evening."

I raised my eyebrows. "My, we're in a good mood today, aren't we?"

"Indeed." He stepped to one side and ushered me in. "The mistress has recently fed, so all is good in our world."

"I'm glad." If only because the last thing I wanted to be facing was a vampire in serious need of sustenance. Her hunger had been bad enough last time. "But if she had other feeders, why did she leave it so long to gain sustenance?"

"Because I have my favorites," Maelle said, as she appeared out of the shadows clustered around the dance floor. "And when one or more of them goes missing or dies, I mourn. Part of that process is not taking sustenance for a period of three days."

"Three days is a rather arbitrary number, isn't it?"

She shrugged, the movement elegant. Her outfit today rather resembled something worn by aviators in the 1920s, although the black boots were thigh-high rather than ending just below her knee. "It depends on the vampire, the depth of their loss, and the keenness of their hunger. The latter two were strong enough to allow three days, but no more. Do you wish a drink?"

I shook my head, but nevertheless moved across to the bar and perched on one of the stools. "I wanted to ask you a few more questions about Marlinda."

"Indeed?" She sat beside me and arched one defined eyebrow. "Have you found her killer as yet?"

"She was killed by the soul eater," I said. "The question you *should* have asked is, who bought the soul eater to the reservation?"

"And is that a question you can answer?"

"Partially." I quickly updated her on the events surrounding the Ouija board. "I was wondering if you were perhaps familiar with any of Marlinda's friends."

"Some," she said. "She was a free spirit outside the realms of this place, and I know she had a number of lovers."

"Did she by chance mention any of them?"

Maelle's smile was cool. "It is never wise to mention one lover in front of the other—especially when that lover is paying your rent."

A wry smile touched my lips. "Just because she didn't mention them doesn't mean that either you or Roger don't know about them."

"You are indeed correct, Lizzie Grace. I think I should be quite grateful that the rangers are not as perceptive as you."

"I wouldn't ever underestimate them, Maelle."

"Oh, I won't." She studied me for a minute, her expression suggesting she wasn't ever about to underestimate me, either. "What are the names of the people you are now seeking?"

"There's only one—Janice."

Her lips pursed. "It is not a name I'm familiar with. Do you have a description?"

I shook my head. "But Larissa implied Janice was one of Marlinda's lovers—"

"She wasn't involved with anyone by that name," Roger cut in. "Is it possible Larissa was mistaken?"

"Yes." I hesitated. "Can I go back into Marlinda's apartment? If I do a more thorough search, I might be able to find some clue as to who Janice is, and what her relationship with Marlinda truly was."

"Roger can take you over there now, if you'd like. What's being done about the soul eater?"

"The rangers have called in an RWA witch. He dealt with the open Ouija board and the other demons that were at Frankie's house, and he's the one who will be dealing with the soul eater."

"And the person who called this thing into being?" she asked. "Or do you truly believe its presence here is nothing more than an unwise decision made by anger and alcohol?"

There was something in her cool tone that had me frowning. "You don't believe that?"

The smile that once again touched her pale lips held nothing in the way of humor, and sent a chill running down my spine. "I've encountered these spirits before, and their existence and rampages have never been due to chance or foolishness."

"When you say you've encountered them, do you actually mean they've been sent against you?"

"Oh yes, and more than once. After all, what better way is there to get rid of one demon than to set another against it?" Ice touched her eyes, and the chill running down my spine got stronger. "Unfortunately for them, I had access to sources capable of greater magic. And I did so enjoy my revenge."

I batted away the bloody images that rose to mind. "Vampires aren't demons—"

"No, but we were considered so in the past. Even in today's enlightened age, there are many who still place us on the same level as those dark entities." She studied me for a second. "I find it highly unlikely that a consumer of souls would answer the call of six drunken fools dabbling with an Ouija board. If the board *is* the reason for its presence here, then it's likely that one of those who remain alive is responsible. Whether by chance or design is another matter entirely."

"One of them—Lance—is a werewolf."

"Which does not preclude the possibility of his guilt, although I grant that it *is* unlikely. But that only leaves you with one unknown—and the possibility that she is a witch."

"No witch in existence would ever use a Ouija board without some form of protection."

"That may be true, but the possibility that she's either a witch or has unregistered powers remains. Your High Council might demand all half-breeds be registered, but we both know that doesn't always happen."

No, it didn't, and untrained or undiscovered talents could be extremely dangerous, especially if they only manifested with darker emotions. Like hate. Or anger.

Larissa might have been drunk *and* angry, but I really did believe she wouldn't have sent the soul eater after any of her friends.

So was unknown Janice behind this mess? Or was there another reason for the soul eater's presence here? Had we—had *I*—been misreading this whole situation from the beginning?

Given how little I knew about dark spirits—and soul eaters in particular—that was totally possible.

"What you need to get is a description of the

woman," Maelle said. "Several of Marlinda's friends were frequent guests here, so it's totally possible that this Janice was one of them. If that is the case, then we would have caught her on the security cams."

"When was the last time she had friends here? Before or after her disappearance?"

"Before. There were five of them all told, and they drank up a storm." A furrow of displeasure appeared between her brows. "I am somewhat forgiving of bad behavior from my feeders, but my patience is not endless."

"Feeders? Plural?"

She nodded. "Marlinda is—*was*—friends with several of my other attendants. Aled and Molly were with her that night, along with two others I did not know."

"What sort of problems did they cause?"

She waved a hand, the movement sparse but elegant. "They were very loud, and annoying my other guests. As I said, I can tolerate some bad behavior, but this is my business and I will not allow anyone to damage its reputation. And they were warned of that previously."

"So this isn't the first time they've done this?"

"The second. There will not be a third one for them, let me assure you."

If they'd had any sense, there wouldn't even have been a second time.

Of course, if they'd had any sense, they wouldn't have become a vampire's food source in the first place.

"If I can get a description of this Janice, would someone be able to check the security cams, on the off chance she met Marlinda that night?"

"I don't know how it would help, but I'll ensure it is done. At the very least, we'll be able to see the two women interact, and that, in turn, might tell us if any animosity had developed between them."

Even if there was, it still didn't explain why Frankie and the unknown man were the first to die.

Her cool smile appeared, though once again it failed to touch her eyes. "You should also be aware that if this Janice is behind Marlinda's death, I will be tempted to take matters into my own hands."

That raised my eyebrows. "And what of the guarantee you gave the council to shed no blood and feed on only the willing while in the confines of this reservation?"

"Oh, I would not, in any way, break that promise. I did not, however, make any such guarantee for Roger."

I glanced across at the man in question. He smiled benignly, sending another round of chills up my spine. Roger, I suspected, had done his mistress's dirty work on more than a few occasions.

"Shall we head over to Marlinda's apartment now, Ms. Grace?" he asked.

"Sure." I returned my gaze to Maelle. "Thank you."

She inclined her head, the movement regal. "It's in my best interest to help you, young Elizabeth, but do be aware that this will not always be the case."

I couldn't help the smile that touched my lips. "Oh, trust me, I'm well aware of that."

"Excellent."

And with that, she slid from the stool and disappeared back into the shadowed confines of her nightclub. Another chill ran down my spine, though I wasn't entirely sure why. I slung my bag over my shoulder and headed out. Roger was a silent presence at my back.

It didn't take us long to reach Marlinda's apartment and, once we'd ducked under the police tape and slipped inside, he said, "What, exactly, are we looking for?"

"I don't really know. A photograph, letters, something that mentions Janice's name." I shrugged.

"Do young people these days bother to print out their photographs?" he asked. "Don't they just post everything onto social media or keep it on their phones?"

"Yes, but given she probably had her phone with her the night she died, it'll now be in the rangers' hands and therefore out of my reach." I shrugged. "It doesn't hurt to check for other possibilities—we might get lucky."

He snorted, but nevertheless started opening drawers and checking them. Given the disarrayed state of many of them, it was pretty obvious the rangers had already done all this, but I couldn't ignore the need to check—if only because my psychic senses might spot something ordinary senses had dismissed.

But after an hour of solid searching, it turned out to be a false hope. I stood in the middle of the room with my hands on my hips. "Is this the only apartment she had?"

"Yes." Amusement touched Roger's thin lips. "Maelle might indulge the whims and desires of her feeders, but she's not that generous."

"I suppose the rangers have impounded her Mercedes?"

"Indeed, although the car was leased by my mistress and merely used by Marlinda. I believe her vehicle is still in the parking lot down the road."

I frowned. "Why wouldn't the rangers have impounded it?"

"Probably because she was not driving it the night she died," he replied. "But you are in a better situation than I to have that question answered, given your somewhat close relationship with Aiden O'Connor."

I ignored the amusement lurking around his eyes. "Have you seen her keys around? It might be worth checking her car, just in case there's something there."

"She would have had her main keys with her, but I believe there's a spare set in the biscuit tin in the pantry."

"You really *do* know everything about her." I went to investigate.

"It's my duty to ensure Maelle's attendants are happy and healthy, and that they have everything they might need to keep them that way. As such, I must have intimate knowledge of their desires, needs, and secrets."

"Secrets?" I glanced at him as I opened the biscuit tin. "What secrets did Marlinda have?"

"Other than her fetish for feet—which is not a need my mistress is inclined to cater to—there were none. She was something of an open book."

"What about her other feeders?" I fished out the car keys and then put the tin back on the shelf. "And how do you, as a thrall, manage to keep them from your mistress, given she can read your thoughts and speak through you at any time she desires?"

"I have learned to compartmentalize my thoughts regarding the upkeep of her feeders. She does not intrude unless I indicate there is a matter that needs her attention." He turned and headed for the front door. "Over the years there have been many feeders whose secrets I have kept."

"And the current crop? Have they any secrets you're keeping from your mistress?"

"One has an illicit relationship with her half brother, who is wholly supported through Maelle's generosity."

"Why do you allow it to continue, especially given incest is against the law?"

"It didn't interfere with her duties, so it was of no

concern." He raised an eyebrow, a somewhat cool smile touching his lips. "Maelle is from a time when such behavior was not uncommon, and therefore does not have modern sensibilities when it comes to such matters."

Meaning she was even older than I'd imagined. I ducked back under the police tape, and then closed the door. The sound echoed across the silence of the small hall. "I can't imagine there'd be anything much darker than incest in the current crop's background."

"One has a gambling problem, but beyond that, you're right—there is nothing concerning."

"The one with the gambling problem—is he or she still employed?"

"Yes."

Which left him or her off the suspect list. We came out into the street again. The sky ran with color—reds and oranges mingling with dusky pinks and purples. The sun might be going down, but she wasn't about to do so without putting on a glorious show.

"How many feeders does she keep?"

"It varies." He led the way around the corner. "She did have six, but she recently had to let one go."

"Why?"

"Favoritism and bad behavior. Or rather, too much of the latter, and a lack of the former that consequently led to a rise of jealousy."

"Seriously? They're bitching about who gets fed on the most?"

I couldn't help the surprise in my voice, and his smile flashed. "Indeed they do. And it's not just the women, I can assure you."

"So she has feeders of both sexes?"

He nodded. "While my mistress's tastes do run to

women, males have greater amounts of platelets and leukocytes in their blood. It is beneficial for her to feed on them at least once a week."

We reached the small parking lot, which was two buildings down from Marlinda's. Not very convenient for carrying groceries back, I would have thought. "How often does she actually need to feed?"

"As one of the older ones, she does not need to feed more than once a month. But she does so four times a week." He glanced back at me, an amused smile touching his lips, but an odd gleam in his eyes. "Is it not always better to sip than to feast?"

"I've never been one to ignore a good feast," I replied evenly. "But in this case, I'm sure her feeders appreciate her restraint."

Not to mention the fact that there was less likelihood of her presence being noted if she avoided gluttony.

"Indeed they do," he agreed. "In fact, both she *and* her feeders enjoy the experience."

A shudder ran through me. Having been recently bitten, I could honestly say there'd been nothing even *remotely* pleasurable about it. "I don't suppose the feeder you let go was one of the ones involved in the recent fracas at the club?"

"Yes." He stopped beside a Ford wagon a good ten years younger than mine. "This is Marlinda's car."

I clicked on the remote and opened the passenger side door. "So is it possible that she got so pissed off about being fired that she's gone after her former friends?"

He laughed. "God, *no*. Molly may not be the brightest bulb in the batch, and she may have a somewhat unstable temperament, but I doubt even she would be that foolish."

"Why? You said it was a matter of jealousy; if she was

angry enough, it's certainly possible."

"No." His voice was flat. Adamant. "She'd know only pain and death would come to her if she was so foolish."

"You said she wasn't bright, so maybe she is." I sat down and opened the glove box. "And that soul eater was called here by anger."

"Yes, but it couldn't have been Molly." He opened the driver side door and started searching around and under the seat. "She hasn't a scrap of witch power."

"Are you sure of that?"

"My mistress is. She would have tasted the ability in her blood." Another of those creepy smiles touched his lips. "In truth, if she had been fortunate enough to have such power, she would have gained the one thing she'd desired—favoritism."

"Maelle can taste power in someone's blood?"

"Oh, yes."

His gaze came to mine, and left me in no doubt that his mistress seriously wanted to uncover the secrets that lay in mine.

"No fucking way on this earth," I said, without really thinking about it.

He simply smiled. "If there's one saying that has proven true time and again over the many years she has been alive, it's that all things come to those who wait."

"Well, tell her not to hold her breath, because she's going to be waiting a long damned time."

"Oh, she is well aware of that." He pulled something out from underneath the seat and snorted softly. "I told the fool to check under her seat for this, and she swore she did."

The item he was holding was an iPhone. "So that's Marlinda's?"

He nodded and hit the on button. "As dead as a doornail. The charger should be in the middle console."

I lifted the console lid and retrieved the charger. "Can I borrow the phone and check out what's on it?"

"Sure. It's her old phone, so who knows how relevant anything you find will be."

It still offered possibilities, which was better than what we currently had—nothing. "Was she a photo taker?"

"Aren't most of them? Selfies are so very important to the young and egotistical."

I snorted. "Can you give me a description of Molly, so I know who I'm looking for?"

He sniffed. "Dark brown hair, green eyes, pale skin with freckles across her nose. Rather well-developed in the chest area."

I raised my eyebrows. "You can say big breasts. It won't offend me."

"I think perhaps there is little that would offend you."

"Your mistress taking a bite certainly would." I shoved the phone and its charger into my purse. "I don't suppose you happen to know the lock code?"

"As I said, feeders hold no secrets, even when it comes to something so inconsequential." He gave me the code, and then added, "It's likely she has photos of not just Molly, but several of the other feeders as well. They did go out together more often than not."

"Good. I can show Larissa a random selection and see if any of them look familiar." I hesitated. "Would you be able to send me a full list of her feeders—both their names and addresses?"

"Why?"

"Because it would be handy to check whether any of them have had any interaction with the unknown Janice."

He studied me for a moment, his gaze slightly distracted. Checking with the boss. "It can be done, but please ensure you do not give the list to the ranger."

I frowned. "What if it turns out there is some sort of connection between Maelle's other feeders and these six murders?"

"If there *is*, I want a guarantee you will not mention where you got the information from, and inform us before you give the ranger their names and address."

"I can't do the latter, Maelle. We're talking about the murder of six people. I can't be responsible for you going after this woman before we've had a chance to talk to her. We need to find out how she summoned the soul eater so that we can deal with it."

Roger's expression remained distracted. After a moment, he said, in tones that were more Maelle's than his own. "A deal, then. I will not in any way react against this Janice until after you and the ranger have spoken to her."

"I want that same guarantee when it comes to Roger, or any other henchmen or women you might have tucked in your closet somewhere."

The smile that touched his lips was cool, dangerous, and every bit hers rather than his. "I will also guarantee that. In fact, I vow that neither my people nor I will move against this Janice if indeed she is responsible for Marlinda's death until after the soul eater has been dealt with. Is that good enough?"

I hesitated. Dealing with the devil was never a good idea, especially when by doing so I was guaranteeing another's death.

Maelle must have sensed my reluctance, because she

added, "Is it not the witch creed to cause not direct harm unto others unless the circumstances are dire or involve the forces of darkness?"

"Yes, but—"

"You destroyed the vampire without thought. If indeed this Janice *is* responsible for the soul destroyer's presence, she must be dealt with appropriately."

"I've a strong suspicion my interpretation of appropriate is very different to yours."

"If you do *not* agree," she continued, her tone without inflection and all the more dangerous because of it, "I will use every source within my power to find and destroy this woman, whether or not you have tracked down the soul destroyer or the person who raised it."

If she did that, we might never find the person responsible—never have justice for those who had died. Which really left me with little other choice. I reluctantly agreed, and Roger's gaze became his own again. "Excellent. We have a deal then."

"Yes, we do," I said, even as I wondered how the fuck I was going to explain the list to Aiden without mentioning Maelle and her connection to them all.

We continued our search. Other than the usual bits of rubbish that accumulated in cars—pens, drink containers, torn-up junk mail, and random bits of fruit peel—there really wasn't anything else of note.

Once we'd locked up and returned the keys to their hiding spot, we headed back to his car.

"Thanks for your help," I said, as the chauffeur stopped the car in front of the café.

"I would say you're welcome, but we both know I only help because my mistress desires it," Roger said. "I'll send the list later this evening, when the venue isn't as busy."

"You don't know them off by heart? I'm disappointed."

"I can certainly quote you every detail of her favorites, right down to minutiae such as their driver's license and passport numbers. It is only the details of those who are on a longer rotation that I cannot immediately tell you."

"I guess you'll have to work on that, then." My voice was dry. Hell, I couldn't even remember my own driver's or passport numbers, let alone anyone else's.

He flashed an insincere smile. "Indeed I will."

I slammed the door shut and, as the vehicle drove off, unlocked the café door and walked inside. Once I'd plugged Marlinda's phone into a power outlet, I headed upstairs to do some more reading. Belle had found the book mentioned in the side note, but hadn't—if the bookmark between the first few pages was anything to go by—had the chance to read very far into it.

I made myself a coffee, and then sat down and started reading. Two hours later, I had at least one answer. I still didn't know exactly what sort of soul spirit we were dealing with, but I *did* now know how to kill it.

The good news was, it appeared my instincts had been on the right track—the first step to ensure erasure was to lure the spirit into an inactivated pentagram, then pin it to the flesh it was controlling via a silver knife and a high-level containment spell. The witch could then activate the pentagram and deal with the spirit.

The bad news was, soul spirits were notoriously difficult to trap, and the best way to do it was to use live bait.

Not just the soul it might have been sent after, but

also that of a witch.

Which meant that if either Lance or Larissa *was* on the soul eater's tucker list, they'd have to be placed in the path of danger if we wanted to kill this thing.

And that either Ashworth or I would have to stand beside them.

I swore and scrubbed a hand across my eyes. In reality, the task would have to be Ashworth's. It was his job, after all, not mine.

And yet I couldn't help the niggle in the back of my mind that said the task would, at least in part, fall to me.

I shivered, and after bookmarking the page for Belle to read, put it back on the coffee table and got up. It was close to nine, and my stomach was rumbling a reminder that it was time to consume something a whole lot more nutritious than cake and hot chocolate.

I went down to the kitchen and made myself a chicken salad and a pot of tea, then headed back upstairs to watch some TV. Time rolled by and, as the clock downstairs began to chime eleven times, I gave up any hope of Aiden dropping by, and went to bed.

Only to be woken at twelve thirty by the tolling of a church bell.

CHAPTER
twelve

I scrambled out of bed, ran through the living room, and hauled open the sliding door. My leg twinged a reminder to be careful, but I ignored it and went out. The bell had fallen silent, but an ominous hunger now filled the air.

A hunger that ran with frustration.

Which hopefully meant Ashworth's magic was holding the spirit at bay, preventing it from doing its task.

I ran back inside, locked the door, and then grabbed my phone. Aiden answered on the fifth ring.

"Liz." His voice was croaky with sleep. "Sorry I didn't ring, but—"

"The soul eater is on the move again. The church bell just tolled."

"Fuck." Sheets rustled and bedsprings squeaked, and I once again fought images of him climbing out of bed naked. "I can be there in ten."

Meaning he was up at the O'Connor compound again

rather than his own home. "Have you got Ashworth's contact details?"

I hadn't thought to grab them myself, and maybe I needed to—especially if the soul eater eluded us yet again.

"Yeah. I'll ring him and get him to meet us at the café."

"Make sure you wear that agate charm I gave you."

"I haven't taken the thing off."

"Good," I said, and hung up.

I continued on into my bedroom. Once I was dressed, I grabbed my agate charm and Aiden's keys, and then clattered down to the reading room. I gathered four silk pouches, some ribbon to tie them up with, and a number of herbs—including angelica root, ivy, rowan, and blackberry—that had serious warding properties against evil spirits. Once I'd boosted those properties with a spell, I placed them in the silk pouches, and then charged each satchel with an incantation asking the Air, Earth, Water, and Fire to protect the souls of those who were wearing them.

I placed one around my neck and tucked it out of sight under my shirt, then gathered my backpack—it still held the silver knife on which I'd placed the containment spell, and a couple of warding potions—and headed out of the room. I left a pouch on the counter for Belle, along with a note to tell her to put it on as soon as she got home, and then walked over to the front door.

Aiden appeared a few minutes later, flowing from one form to another as he neared the café. He wasn't even breathing heavily, despite the fact he must have run all the way here. "Have you got any idea of location?"

I hesitated, reaching psychically for the foul caress that ran through the night. "It's not close."

"Suggesting it's not attacking Larissa."

"No." I handed him a silk pouch. "Wear this."

His nostrils flared as he accepted it, and only the slightest hint of trepidation touched his expression. "What is it, besides being rather pungent?"

"Oh, sorry—I forgot about your keener sense of smell." I wrinkled my nose. "It's a herbal mix that will help counter an attack by our dark spirit."

"Then I'll put up with the smell." He slipped it over his neck, tucked it under his shirt, and then glanced past me. "Here comes Ashworth. You ready to go?"

"Yes." I stepped back to grab my coat from the inside hook, and then slammed the door closed.

"What makes you think the soul eater is on the move?" Ashworth said, as soon as he got within talking distance. "I haven't felt anything along the energy lines."

I frowned. "You can't feel the foul frustration in the air?"

"No." He fell into step beside me as Aiden led the way around to the building to the parking lot.

"Then I suppose you didn't hear that church bell tolling at twelve thirty, either?"

"No, lassie, I damn well did *not*." I could feel his gaze on me, but I studiously ignored it as Aiden opened the truck's passenger door and ushered me inside. Ashworth climbed into the back seat, and then added, "But the fact you *did* is not a great sign."

Once I'd dumped my backpack at my feet and put on my belt, I twisted around to face him. "Why? We can't be dealing with a *Nachzehrer*, because they supposedly only go after the souls of their kin."

His eyebrows rose. "And how would you know that if you've done no formal training?"

"Because I can *read*," I bit back. "And there is this thing called Google search, in case you weren't aware."

"Yes, but you often have to search through mountains of chaff before you get to the wheat."

"Left or right," Aiden said, as the truck reached the end of the parking area.

I closed my eyes for a moment, studying the pull of evil. "Left. It's not in the immediate area. It's more distant than that."

"Meaning it could be after Lance." He glanced briefly in the rearview mirror. "Will the shield you placed around his house hold the spirit out?"

"Combined with the salting and the clove chain Elizabeth advised him to do, it certainly should," Ashworth replied.

"Speaking of which…." I handed him the final silk bag. "I made this for you, just in case."

Energy surged as he accepted it—his magic, testing and probing the protections around the bag and the contents within.

"You didn't find this spell on the Internet."

"You'd be surprised what you can uncover on the net if you sort through enough of the chaff." I hesitated as the trace of evil shifted. "Left again at the next street, and continue on the highway."

Aiden obeyed, then flattened his foot and hit a switch. Blue light flashed and the howl of the siren bit through the air. "Let's just hope we get there in time to prevent another murder."

Amen to that, I thought, and returned my attention to Ashworth. "So you think this spirit *is* a *Nachzehrer?*"

"I think it's likely to be a kindred spirit, so to speak. The *Nachzehrer* is but one regional legend, even if it is the main one that now appears in any search. The one thing they all have in common is the tolling of the church bell when it's hunting."

"Is it actually a church bell?" Aiden asked.

Ashworth shook his head. "It's a spirit bell, and it's said only those who can talk to the dead or who are about to get dead can hear its ring."

"Ah," I said, "that explains it."

And then felt like slapping myself. I didn't need Ashworth knowing anything about the true connection between Belle and me. Not when the realization that we were witch and familiar would lead him straight to my family's doorstep.

"Explains what?" Ashworth asked.

"Why I can hear the bell." I somehow kept my voice even. "It's a by-product of my psychic powers."

"I wasn't aware communing with spirits was one of your gifts."

Meaning he'd been checking up on us. "It's not a strong part of them, which is the reason Belle does readings rather than me."

"Interesting." There was something in his tone that suggested disbelief. But then, Anna hadn't believed me, either. The RWA didn't employ fools, even if they weren't the most powerful witches Canberra had ever produced.

"Left at the next street," I said.

Aiden frowned. "Meaning we're *not* going to Lance's."

Not when the road ahead led to a semirural housing development on the outskirts of Castle Rock rather than to Rayburn Springs. "Given the frustration, maybe he's given up on Lance and gone after someone else."

"Unlikely," Ashworth said. "If Lance was its target, it

would have kept assaulting the protections until it either got through or dawn came. It would have no other choice."

"Why?" I said. "I thought soul eaters were able to run amok once they'd obeyed the bidding of whoever called them into being?"

"They quite often do, but there's something else going on here," Ashworth said. "It's unlikely that frustration you felt was the soul eater's, as they simply don't do emotion. And that means whoever bought it here was close enough at the time to redirect its actions."

"Has the containment barrier you raised around the ranger station in any way been tested?"

"It hasn't twitched. Larissa's not the source of this deviation, nor, I believe, the one who called the soul eater into being."

I studied him for a second. "That being the case, do you believe the Ouija board was the soul eater's gateway into this world?"

"It's highly unlikely. I think the dark spirit we encountered at Frankie's was what they called into being, and our soul eater came from an entirely different source."

I frowned. "So the Ouija board was little more than a cover?"

"One that was essentially used to fudge who their true targets were."

"If that's true," Aiden said, "then they've damn well succeeded."

"Perhaps," Ashworth said, his tone noncommittal and his gaze on me. "And perhaps not."

"Left again at the next street," I said, ignoring his unspoken demand to say what I knew.

We bumped over an old train line, then did a sharp

left onto a much smaller road, the truck skidding sideways for a few seconds before Aiden brought it under control.

The beat of evil sharpened dramatically, and goose bumps crawled across my skin.

We were close. *So* close.

"Slow down. We're almost there."

He switched off the lights and siren, and then slowed. We crawled along the narrow road, passing a number of homes, until the sense of evil became so strong it damn near stole my breath.

"Stop," Ashworth said, before I could. "It's in the next house. And *fuck*, it's strong."

"Can you deal with it?" Aiden stopped the truck and hauled on the hand brake.

"Yes, but not without the proper preparations—"

"Do whatever you need to, but do it quickly," Aiden cut in. "I don't need to be dealing with another body right now."

"I can work magic, Ranger, not miracles," Ashworth bit back. "The more powerful the damn spell needed, the longer it will take."

"The only problem with that," I said, as the pulse of evil reached a crescendo, "is that we haven't got long."

I grabbed my backpack, scrambled out of the truck, and raced for the house.

"Liz, wait," Aiden said.

I didn't, because I couldn't. Not if we wanted any hope of saving the soul eater's target. But even as I neared the front door, a scream broke the night's silence. A scream that was long, fear-filled, and then abruptly cut off. At the same time, the crescendo of evil peaked and then fell away. I cursed and reached for the door handle, only to discover it was locked.

"Move." Aiden's voice was cold. Angry. Not at me as much as the thing that was no longer inside.

He raised a booted foot and kicked the door open. It slammed back hard, and plaster flew as the handle buried into the wall. The hallway beyond was shadowed and carpeted, and the air smelled faintly of cinnamon and toast.

"Stay—"

"Don't even fucking *think* that, Aiden." My voice was a harsh whisper. "I may not be much of a witch, but if this thing attacks, I'm far better equipped to deal with it than you."

He hesitated, and then nodded. "But stay behind me, just in case we're dealing with another man mountain."

That I was more than happy to do. He stepped cautiously inside, his boots leaving imprints on the lush carpet. I unzipped the pack, pulled out the knife, and then followed, making sure I kept the silver blade well away from him.

Even though he didn't say anything, he was obviously aware of its presence, given the way his back twitched. But then, he'd only recently recovered from being stabbed with silver, and as a result, was probably even more sensitive now to its presence than most wolves.

We crept past two doorways, but didn't stop. Though evil had all but fled, the last few remnants of its presence pulsed in the room at the far end of the hall—a room that—if the tiles were anything to go by—was a kitchen area.

Aiden drew his gun as we neared the door. He motioned me to one side, and then stopped on the other, his nostrils flaring as he drew in the heavily scented air. Whether he discovered anything, I couldn't say. He simply motioned that he'd go through first, started a three-two-one countdown, and then went in fast and low.

I followed—and discovered death.

A man was sitting at the kitchen table, a piece of toast still gripped in one hand, and a dark pool of coffee from an upturned mug surrounding the other. His death had been swift, but horrendous—something that was evident from not only his cut-off scream, but also his expression. Horror, fear, and agony had all been etched into his face during his dying moments.

"The soul eater?" Aiden asked, voice clipped.

"It's not in the house." I tucked the knife safely away. "But this man wasn't present when they used the Ouija board, and that means Ashworth is right—this really isn't about Larissa or her revenge."

He glanced at me sharply. "But you do think it's about revenge?"

I hesitated. "You don't call forth such a powerful dark spirit unless your intent is either revenge or murder in the most painful way possible."

He frowned. "Given we're dealing with a soul eater, I would have thought they were one and the same."

"Only sometimes," Ashworth said, as he stepped through the rear glass sliding door. "Remember, the souls of the first victims were taken while they'd been at rest. It's only the last couple who have suffered, and I daresay that's due to the fact you two keep walking in on it."

"And yet we're no damn closer to either catching this thing or uncovering the person responsible for its presence here."

"Its actions here suggest otherwise—there was no attempt at seduction this time."

"If you've got any ideas, Ashworth, damn well spit

them out. We don't have time to fuck around."

Amusement played around the older man's lips, though his expression remained cold. "Then perhaps you had best ask your girlfriend to stop doing so."

"Me?" I all but squeaked. "What in the hell do you think I'm holding back?"

"Did you not go back to Marlinda's apartment today?" he asked.

Aiden swung around to face me. "Why would you do that? And how did you even get in?"

"Maelle gave me the keys. I went to the club to question her about Marlinda, because if I'm right and the unknown Janice is the key to what's happening, then— given she's supposedly a friend of Marlinda's—that was a logical place to search for information about her."

"We already *did* a thorough search. There was absolutely no indication that Marlinda knew anyone by the name of Janice. We didn't even find a photo matching the description we've gotten from Larissa." Aiden's voice ran with annoyance. He certainly didn't like the unintended implication that he or his people hadn't done their job properly.

"Which is exactly the same as I found," I replied evenly. "I did, however, discover her old phone in her car. It was as dead as a doornail, but once charged, we might find some photos of the elusive Janice on it."

"And how did you get to her car, given we've impounded it?"

"You impounded the one leased by Maelle. Marlinda owned a wagon, which was kept in the parking lot down the road from her apartment."

"Then it's either unregistered or listed in another state, because it certainly didn't come up when we did a search." The annoyance in his expression, if anything, had increased. "And when, exactly, were you going to tell me all this?"

"I was intending to earlier tonight, when *you* were supposed to drop by." I thrust my hands on my hips and met his glare with one of my own. "It's not like I'm doing any of this for fun—"

"Enough, both of you." Ashworth's voice was curt. "We have a dead man to look after and a soul eater to worry about. Bickering isn't helping."

Aiden took a deep breath, and the annoyance disappeared from his expression. But not, unfortunately, from his aura. "Did you find anything useful on the phone?"

"No, because it was dead, as I said. I've got it on charge back at the café."

"Then bring it to the station in the morning," he said. "We can scroll through the photographs and see if any match the description we have."

"Fine." My gaze went to the stranger. "Do you know who he is?"

"James Morrison," Ashworth said. When we both glanced at him sharply, he raised an eyebrow and pointed to the stack of bills near the phone. "Or so it says on those."

"Wonder what his connection to the elusive Janice is?" And if his name would be on the list that Roger was supposed to be sending me.

"That I can't tell you." Aiden pulled a pair of silicone gloves out of his back pocket. "Is there any chance of that thing coming back here?"

"It's doubtful, considering it's completed its mission," Ashworth said. "But I'll hang around, just in case."

Aiden nodded and glanced at me. "Do you want me to call you a cab?"

In other words, go home. I shook my head. "I'm fine."

He frowned. "You can't walk back from here—"

"It's only a couple of kilometers. I'll be fine, Aiden."

"Liz," he said, in a voice that suggested he would brook no arguments. "Aside from the fact it's the middle of the night, someone has shot at you twice now. Be sensible."

He was, rather annoyingly, right. I rubbed a hand across my eyes and then said, "I will—"

"I meant right here and now."

"You don't trust me?"

"In this particular case—and knowing how stubborn you are—no, I don't."

I scowled at him, but he simply raised an eyebrow. I dug out my phone and called a cab, only to be told that the narrow street wasn't listed on their system. I arranged to meet them near the old rail line, and then met Aiden's gaze. "Okay?"

"No. I'll walk you down there and wait—"

"Aiden, you have a crime scene to attend to. It's not that far, and there's too many trees around here to make a long-distance shot practical. Besides, I can use a repelling spell on anyone—or anything—that comes too close."

He didn't look happy, but he obviously sensed it would be futile to argue. I bid them both good night, and headed out of the house. The night air was crisp but rather pleasant, and the moon a bright if incomplete globe in the sky. The power of it sang across my senses, sharpening them.

Someone was out there in the darkness, watching me.

Whoever—*whatever*—it was, they were keeping their distance. I had no sense of them beyond that vague awareness. Had no sense that they meant me any harm. If I'd felt anything else, I would have immediately gone back inside, but for all I knew, it was one of the neighbors out investigating what the hell was going on here.

Even so, I flexed my fingers and silently threaded an immobilizing spell around them. The air shimmered briefly, a warning sign that the spell was ready to use. Whether my watcher had caught it, or would even know what it meant, I couldn't say.

The trees lining the other side of the road arched overhead, cutting off much of the moon's light. There were no streetlights here, and little in the way of noise aside from the occasional chirrup of a cricket.

I clenched my fingers around the spell, gaining courage from the pulse of it as I walked down the center of the road. The presence remained distant, but it nevertheless followed. I wished there was some way to find out who it was and what they intended. Wished, not for the first time in my life, that I could read minds like Belle. But while some of our powers did leech between us, *that* had never been one of them.

Somewhere behind me a dog barked, and I used it as an opportunity to glance over my shoulder—and caught the briefest glimpse of movement as someone ducked behind a tree trunk.

My follower was definitely human, though they were too far away for me to be able to tell if they were male or female.

My phone beeped. I pulled it out of my pocket and saw it was a text from Roger. Inside was the promised list of addresses for Maelle's five remaining feeders—two men and three women. The man he'd mentioned—Aled Freeman—was there, as was our most recent victim, James Morrison. There was also a Dani Holgate, Leanne Jones, and Mandy Wilson.

Neither Marlinda nor Molly were on the list, which was unsurprising given one was dead and the other fired.

If this whole mess *did* have nothing to do with Larissa's anger but rather Molly's, then those three women needed to be found and protected.

It also meant Aled Freeman could very possibly be the man Frankie had killed.

And that, in turn, meant three things: One, that Ashworth was right in thinking the Ouija board was nothing more than a ruse to cover the true mission of the soul eater. Two, that Janice was very possibly the "not so bright and very recently fired" Molly. And three, that we did have another witch on the reservation somewhere—someone who was not only capable of calling forth and controlling such a strong spirit, but one who was very adept at hiding her presence from three other witches.

My finger hovered over the forward button for several seconds, torn between not wanting to cause any further problems with Aiden, and the desire not to piss off Maelle in any way. In the end, I chose Aiden over the vampire, and forwarded the message to him, along with a quick note stating it was a list of Marlinda's close friends. I didn't explain where I'd gotten it. I'd worry about that when the time came.

I shoved the phone away and walked on, well aware that the dark presence continued to shadow my movements some distance back. I needed to know who it was, but, given the distance between us, any move I made—be it magical *or* physical—would be spotted in enough time to allow them to escape.

But as the road began to curve to the right, an idea stirred. I increased my pace just enough to gain some ground on my watcher without being obvious about it. When I was far enough around the curve and out of their immediate sight, I ran into the front yard of the nearest house and squatted down behind a thick camellia bush.

My watcher drew closer. I couldn't see them, couldn't hear them, but I could feel them. Or, rather, feel their aura. It was sharp, bitter, and angry.

If it *was* either Janice or Molly following me, why was she feeling the latter when it came to me? Or was anger simply an overall part of her nature? If Roger's comments were anything to go by, she was either emotionally or mentally unstable, and being fired certainly wouldn't have helped either of those.

Given the fact that, according to Maelle, there was absolutely no magic in her blood, then Janice or Molly or whatever her true name was had to be working closely with the witch responsible for the soul eater and the magic I was sensing.

And that, in turn, meant the answers we so desperately needed could finally be had—but only if I could successfully capture the bitch.

She drew closer. While the energy crawling through the air was nowhere near as dark as the spirit it had called forth, it nevertheless scratched across my senses and itched at my skin. The closer she drew, the more I felt the need to shower.

I did my best to ignore the sensation, and held my position. A few minutes later, across the other side of the road, a shadow flitted from behind one tree trunk to another, and then paused.

I waited. Until that shadow came out from behind cover, there was little point in releasing my spell. Incantations designed to immobilize did have some pretty severe restrictions, the worst of which was the fact the whole spell had to hit them directly. If they moved at the wrong moment and were caught only by the edge, it wouldn't work.

For several long minutes, neither of us moved. Then the figure stepped out from behind the tree and raced along the side of the road to the next one, which was one house up from where I was hiding.

That figure was not only very human, but also very definitely female.

I rose and, once she was past my position, silently moved out to the road. The dark-clothed figure had almost reached the safety of the next strand of trees. I raised my hand and silently launched the spell at the biggest part of her body—her back.

At the very last moment, she must have sensed something was wrong, but instead of jumping sideways, she simply spun around. The spell thumped into her chest, eliciting a grunt of pain as the force of it knocked her off her feet. She hit the ground with another grunt, and immediately tried to scramble to her feet. But the threads of the spell spread across her torso like wildfire, forming a net that quickly attached itself to the ground. Though she writhed and fought, she couldn't escape.

She also *didn't* fit the description of Molly I'd been given.

I got out my phone and called Aiden.

"What's wrong?" he immediately said.

"Someone was following me. I just netted them."

"Where?"

"Just beyond the road's curve."

"I'll be there in a few minutes—Tala's just arrived, and I need to update her."

Meaning there was another way in and out of this area, because she certainly hadn't driven past us. I hung up, shoved my phone into my pocket, and approached the woman.

"You'd better release me, bitch, or you'll fucking regret it."

I raised my eyebrows but didn't immediately answer. The color was high in her cheeks and her eyes sparkled with rage and something else. Something that ebbed and flowed, changing her eyes from blue to green and back again.

Magic. *Concealing* magic, although the spell wasn't the strongest I'd ever seen, given the fracture that was revealing the true color of her eyes.

But the foul feel of magic I'd felt earlier was still very much in evidence underneath the pulsing of my net. It wasn't a part of her spirit or her soul, though, as both mine and Belle's was. This woman wasn't a witch.

And that, in turn, meant the concealment charm she wore had indeed been created by someone else—probably the same someone who controlled the soul eater.

I squatted beside her. Her foot jerked toward me, but was stopped abruptly by the net. There were two very thin layers of energy covering her from head to foot, which suggested there were two spells being used, not just one.

There no charms around her neck, which in itself was unusual given the dark forces these people were dealing with. My gaze drifted down her length, but it was only when it reached her worn leather boots that I felt it. I might not be able to see past leather, but I didn't really need to. Hiding charms under the arch of the foot was an age-old trick of witches, and the dark pulse coming from hers certainly confirmed *that* was where the source of this woman's magic lay.

My gaze rose again. "What's your name?"

"None of your goddamn business," she snarled back. "You are *so* dead. Just you wait and see."

"Wait for what? A visitation from the soul eater? Because it doesn't actually work like that. You can't keep adding names to the kill list willy-nilly. Not without paying a price."

"You obviously don't know fucking much about them, then, do you?"

"Maybe not," I said. "But I did help stop it from killing Lance this evening."

"Who cares—it was James we really wanted."

This woman really *wasn't* all that bright. She didn't seem to realize she'd just admitted her part in his death.

"We?" I asked mildly. "Who are you working with, Molly?"

Her eyes widened just a little, even as she said, "Who the fuck is Molly?"

"I think the more interesting question would be, why did you call yourself Janice when you were at Frankie's? What game were you and Marlinda playing?"

"I have no fucking idea what—" She paused as headlights speared the darkness, spotlighting us both. "Get me off the damn road—you're going to get me killed."

"Although I'm sure there are plenty of people who'd like nothing more than to see you run over multiple times, Ranger O'Connor isn't one of them."

She swore and began to struggle anew, again to no

avail. I swiveled around as the truck came to a halt a few yards up the road. Aiden climbed out, and he wasn't alone—Ashworth was him.

I frowned. "How safe is it to leave Tala in that house alone?"

"The spirit won't come back, but I left a surprise or two for it if it does," Ashworth said.

Aiden stopped beside me and stared down at my captive. "Who is she?"

"This, I very much suspect, is the missing Janice." I reached through my net and tugged off her boots. Something rattled inside them both even as the shimmer of magic rolled up her body and disappeared. The woman it revealed was well-built, with large breasts, a smattering of freckles across her nose, green eyes, and brown hair.

"She certainly fits the description Larissa gave us of Janice," Aiden said. "But who is she really?"

"Molly Brown, a friend of Marlinda's up until she was fired for bad behavior at Émigré."

He glanced down at me. "She wasn't on that list you just sent me."

"No, but Marlinda and James Morrison certainly were, and I rather suspect Aled Freeman might have been Frankie's unknown victim."

"He was." He squatted next to me. "Why do you want these people dead, Molly?"

"I don't. She's barking mad."

"Liz is many things, but mad isn't one of them. Why were you following her?"

"I wasn't. I just happened to be going the same way, and she attacked me."

"Then tell me why you were at James Morrison's."

"We're friends," she said. "Why shouldn't I be

there?"

"You were never *in* his house," Aiden replied. "The air ran with many scents, but your foulness wasn't amongst them."

Molly hawked and spat. The globule hit the net and became little more than steam, leaving only a few untouched droplets that fell onto her coat. She swore softly, but didn't repeat the offensive action.

"If you don't start talking, Molly, you'll be charged with the murder of seven people, whether or not you're responsible for the magic that brought the soul eater here."

"And what evidence have you got tying me to those murders, let alone to the appearance of some damn soul eater?"

"We don't really need actual evidence," Ashworth said mildly. "The suspicion of dark magic is more than enough to have you hauled up in front of an RWA panel, who will get the truth out of you and then assign an appropriate punishment."

She snorted. "I'm fucking human, *not* a witch. You haven't the right—"

"Oh, I certainly have, especially with seven people dead."

"I'm not responsible for that—"

"Indeed you are," Ashworth said. "You might not be the source of magic, but you're certainly the source of the foul anger that called this dark spirit into being."

"No—"

"Then tell us who is," Aiden said.

Her lips thinned. She wasn't going to give anything— or anyone—up very easily. I glanced up at Ashworth. "You'll probably have to use a truth spell on her."

"Yes, although I suspect we might actually be dealing with an embedded spell that prevents her from speaking, rather than mere stubbornness."

I frowned. "Embedded? As in, into her flesh?"

"Yes," he said. "It's rare, and generally only done when both parties are considered compatible."

"Meaning spiritually? Or sexually?"

"Either, depending on the people involved and the magic being called on." His gaze narrowed. "Why? What have you heard?"

"The source that gave me the list also told me that Molly was living with her half brother, and that they were involved in an incestuous relationship."

"And who might your source be?" Aiden asked

My gaze went to his. "I can't tell you that."

"Liz—"

"I got the information on the understanding that I didn't reveal where. I can't back out on that promise, Aiden. I won't."

He studied me for a moment, then nodded and rose. "Let's get her back to the station and deal with her there. Liz, is your spell portable?"

"Yes, but I'll need to come with you. Ashworth can no doubt unravel it, but it would be quicker and easier if I just came along." I rose and handed Ashworth her boots. "The two charms she used to mask her identity and mute the sounds of her movements are inside. You might be able to use them to track down their creator."

"Wouldn't it be easier and more efficient for you to use your psychometry skills?"

I shook my head. "The darkness of the magic involved would interfere with any sensation I could pull from them. Besides, for psychometry to be effective, the item has to have a longtime connection to flesh."

All of which he should be aware of. Maybe it was more evidence of how little he believed anything Belle and I said about ourselves.

"Ah, pity."

I turned to Molly, caught the ends of the spell's threads, and silently adjusted them. As I did, the net's ends pulled away from the bitumen and instead wound tighter around her body, until every part of her was cocooned except for a portion of her legs just below her knees. While she needed to be able to walk to the car, given her propensity to kick, I didn't want her being able to get too much of a swing up.

Aiden herded her toward the truck. She swore and threatened him every inch of the way.

"That is a rather nice mutation of a very basic spell," Ashworth commented.

I shrugged and headed for the truck. "When you're taught nothing more than basics, you do tend to experiment."

"So it seems."

Again, his disbelief was evident, although in this particular case, it *was* the truth.

It didn't take us long to get back to the station. Aiden hauled her into the interview room, sat her down in a chair, and warned her not to move. He then walked across to the media unit and activated it.

Once he'd done his obligatory spiel about her rights and informed her everything was being recorded, he added, "State your name and address for the record, please."

"You can just go fuck yourself, Ranger. I want a lawyer here before I say anything."

"You're on a werewolf reservation," he replied. "The rules regarding interrogation can be somewhat murky at the best of times, let alone when there's magic and murder involved."

"You can't interrogate me without an IIT officer here, at the very least," she said. "I know the rules and regulations, Ranger."

"But not quite as well as you think," he said. "It rather depends on whether you are deemed witch or not, and for that, we need an RWA representative present. Which we have."

"That doesn't preclude the necessity of having the IIT here, because witch or not, I'm still human, not a wolf."

"Sorry, love, but even the scantest suspicion of magical ability means you're my responsibility, not theirs." Ashworth's voice was positively jovial. "And I have to say, I'm quite looking forward to dragging answers out of your murderous soul."

She didn't say anything, but for the first time since I'd netted her, fear flickered through her expression.

"Do you want me to unravel my net before you get down to business?" I asked.

Ashworth nodded. "I won't be able to get a feel for the spell that's within her with your magic present."

I nodded and immediately deactivated the spell. As the last threads of my magic faded away, Ashworth's stirred. The spell he placed on her wasn't one I was familiar with, and it fell around her shoulders like a gossamer blanket. She didn't appear to know what he'd done, which again confirmed Roger's comment there was no magic in her. Once the blanket was in place, Ashworth leaned toward Molly and studied her through slightly narrowed eyes.

Aiden glanced at me. "For the benefit of the recording, what's Ashworth doing?"

"Magically probing the spell that's been placed on Molly to understand what we're dealing with and how best to deconstruct it."

Ashworth swore and pushed away from the table. "It appears that whoever placed this spell on this girl has something in common with you, young Elizabeth."

I raised my eyebrows. "Meaning they're underpowered?"

"No, because there *is* a greater sense of power in the threads that twist through her flesh, but there's also every indication that we're dealing with a witch who hasn't been *trained*. And that makes their magic even more difficult to deal with."

"Ha," Molly commented. "I told you—you're getting jack out of me."

"I said difficult, not impossible, young woman." Ashworth glanced at Aiden. "I'll have to get my kit and take all the usual precautions. There's also a risk that removing the spell could break her mind. It just depends on how deep the roots of it go."

"I had no idea this sort of magic was even possible," Aiden muttered.

"Most people don't." His gaze returned to Molly. "I don't think it wise to attempt anything until daylight. Spells like this are often fueled by the night and the moon."

"I don't like the prospect of wasting yet more time," Aiden said. "We need to track the witch behind all this down before the soul eater finds its next victim."

"Tracking him down won't actually stop the soul eater. It won't stop unless *we* stop it; even when all those who have been targeted by the witch are dead, it will simply start killing random members of the public."

"Which means it's even *more* important we find this witch ASAP," Aiden growled.

Ashworth blew out a breath, the sound one of frustration. "While I don't believe it's the right choice, I'll go home and collect my gear. It'll only take half an hour, at most."

"You know, there *is* another option besides magic." As the two men glanced at me, I added, "Belle's telepathic. Why risk breaking Molly's mind if we can simply raid it? I can't sense any form of magic that would prevent her thoughts from being read, and she's certainly *not* wearing an electronic means of doing so."

"They've invented a device to stop telepaths?" Aiden said.

I nodded. "Those two IIT officers were wearing them when they were here investigating the vampire rampage."

"Huh. I'll have to make inquiries. It'd be nice to know Belle just can't wander through my thoughts anytime she damn pleases."

"That's presuming she thinks you have thoughts worth investigating."

He blinked, and then laughed. "That sounds very much like something she'd say."

"We have been hanging around together for a long time. Sometimes these things bleed over."

"Concentrate, people." Ashworth's voice once again held a note of censure. "I don't believe the spell placed on Molly is in any way designed to stop her thoughts being read, so if Belle's available, it would certainly be worth her trying before we attempt anything else. Is she home?"

"No. She's out with Zak." I got out my phone and called her. While Aiden was aware we could share thoughts, I had no desire for Ashworth to discover it. He was suspicious enough of us.

Her response was immediate—and direct. *The phone? Seriously?*

It's camouflage, so just pick up the damn call. When she did, I added, "Where are you?"

"Not far out of Castle Rock—why?"

"Can you come to the ranger station? We've a mind we need you to read."

She talked softly to Zak, and then said, "We can be there in ten."

Thanks. I repeated her comment and avoided looking at Aiden. He wasn't saying anything, but my ruse with the phone would certainly be ramping up his own suspicions about us.

The older man pulled out his phone and then sat down opposite Molly. "I don't suppose you have any decent coffee in this place, do you, Ranger?"

"We have coffee. Whether you'll consider it decent or not, I can't say." Aiden glanced at me. "Would you like something to drink?"

"Tea, if you have it."

"We do."

"I'll have mine with milk and three sugars, thanks," Ashworth said, as Aiden headed for the door.

"I'll help you." I dumped my backpack on the nearest chair, and followed him down the hall to a small lunchroom.

"Why didn't you tell him the truth about you and Belle?"

"Because of that whole conversation we had about

running from Canberra and my parents. I don't want them knowing where I am, Aiden."

He flicked on the coffee machine, and then bent down to get three mugs. "I would have thought *not* telling him the truth would be even more dangerous. Surely if you intrigue him enough, he'll just make inquiries about you."

"He might." He *would*. "But I don't think he'll uncover much, given we're not registered."

And *then* there was the whole fact that we'd changed our names and magically covered our tracks to ensure we couldn't be traced.

"There has to be a register for half-breeds," he said. "Especially if, as Ashworth said, they're considered dangerous."

"There is." I paused and frowned. "I wonder if Molly's half brother is registered? If he *is*, then we'll at least glean some insights as to what he's capable of."

"I suspect that's the reason Ashworth asked for a coffee. He wanted us out of the room while he rang the appropriate authorities."

"Which is why you didn't stop recording when we left the room."

He glanced at me, eyebrow raised. "That's very perceptive of you, Ms. Grace. Let's hope Ashworth didn't notice the same thing, otherwise we'll be no wiser as to what secret witch business he wanted to discuss."

"Given they're an uncommunicative bunch of bastards at the best of times, we probably won't learn a whole lot."

"Obviously that's one skill you did learn in the brief period you were at witch school."

"Or I simply have good reasons for keeping certain secrets."

"Which I'm hoping you'll trust me with one day."

I half smiled. "I'm hoping to be given the time for trust to grow, and not be shunted off the reservation because of some misplaced belief that witches are bad and the magic in this place will cause no harm."

He grunted and poured boiling water into one of the cups. "As I've said, I don't believe you'll be evicted."

He handed me the mug and a green tea bag, and then made the two coffees—which smelled slightly burned and had me wrinkling my nose. "You need to turn the water temperature down a little on that thing to avoid scalding the coffee."

"We can do that?"

"On most of these types of machines, yes."

"Huh. I'll get the service guy to look at it. What temp do you suggest?"

"Ninety-three degrees Celsius generally avoids burning but still makes a hot cuppa."

"You are a font of information."

I grinned. "Of useless information, mostly."

"*I* didn't say that."

"You didn't have to." I turned and headed back out into the hall. As I did, a bell rang out in the main room. "That's Belle."

He handed me Ashworth's coffee. "I'll go let her in."

I nodded and returned to the interview room. Ashworth was just putting his phone back in his pocket.

"Any luck in Canberra?" I asked casually, as I handed him his mug.

He raised his eyebrows. "Why would you think I was ringing Canberra?"

I smiled and perched on the edge of the table. "Because that's what I would have done—contacted the records office and see if they have any record of Molly Brown's magical half brother."

A smile touched his lips. "Unusually powered you may be, but dumb you are not."

The fact he now considered me unusually powered rather than underpowered wasn't a step in the right direction as far as my ambitions to remain undetected went. Footsteps echoed in the hall, and then Belle stepped into the interview room, all silvery glamour and happiness.

"And here I am to save the day." Her bright grin faded as her gaze fell on Molly. "Whoa. There's a nasty piece of work if ever I saw one."

"Yeah, and she spits, so don't get too close with that dress on."

"Huh." She stopped beside me, her gaze narrowing a little. "I'm not going to have much trouble with this one. What do you need to know?"

Ashworth didn't answer. When I glanced at him, he was staring at us, his expression one of disbelief.

"What?" I said, as trepidation stirred anew.

He opened his mouth, shut it again, and then shook his head. "I've never seen anything like it."

What the fuck is he on about? Belle asked.

I have no damn idea, and there's a part of me that really doesn't want to ask.

Trouble looming, you think?

For certain.

Well, it's not like we can avoid it now. Out loud, she added, "Like what?"

He drew in a deep breath and then shook his head. "Now is neither the time nor the place for that conversation. Not in front of a suspect, anyway."

"Okay," Belle said, with an uneasy glance my way.

"But you still need to tell me what you need to know."

"The name of her half brother, a description we can use so our ranger can put out an APB, and her brother's current location if she knows it."

Aiden glanced at Ashworth. "Didn't you ask the records office for a description and name?"

"Yes, but despite emphasizing the urgency of the situation, I was told it had to go through the approval process before I'll get answers." He shrugged. "They did say the request would be fast-tracked, but this way will be infinitely quicker and easier."

"And fucking illegal!" Molly piped up. "You can't just read people's minds willy-nilly—it's against the law."

"Actually," Aiden said, "in circumstances that involve a noncompliant witness and a situation that is unresolved and dangerous, *all* law enforcement officers have the legal right to use telepaths if the witness has been given ample opportunity to answer questions. Which you certainly have. Belle, proceed."

"Right." She cracked her knuckles and then got down to the business of mind reading. After a moment, she said, distaste heavy in her voice, "Oh my God, he's your damn *brother*, girl—what the hell are you thinking?"

"It's none of your damn business what we do."

"In that, you may be right, but it's still damn disgusting. *And* illegal." Belle's gaze narrowed as she dug deeper into the other woman's thoughts. "His name is Jack Lea, and he lives off the money his sister makes working at Émigré."

"Sounds like a right charmer," Aiden murmured.

"What's her address?" Ashworth asked. "If we could get this creep caught tonight, it will make the task of tackling the soul eater that much easier."

"Hang on." Belle's gaze narrowed again. "Okay, she's attempting to confuse matters by throwing random addresses at me mentally, but they're living in the new terraces on Kennedy Street. Number three."

"It's interesting that Marlinda, Aled, and now Molly all live in houses that are worth well over six hundred thousand, and which both Marlinda and Aled, at least, bought outright, with cash," Aiden said. "They're obviously paying bartenders and waitresses a whole lot more than they did back in my day."

"Because you're *so* old and they were only paying pennies back then," I commented, voice dry.

His grin flashed, despite the tension I could sense in him. "We were paid the award. What I *meant* was, I couldn't have lived in the type of accommodation these two are on what I was earning. I certainly couldn't have afforded to support a second person."

I'm sure Molly wouldn't have been able to if she'd *only* been on bartender or waitress wages. But she'd been one of Maelle's feeders, and as such had been well looked after. At least until she'd allowed her inner bitch loose.

"I'm guessing," he continued, "you wouldn't have a theory about their apparent wealth, would you?"

"Rich parents, perhaps?"

He raised an eyebrow, annoyance evident. All he said, however, was, "Can you get a description of her brother, Belle?"

She nodded and, after a few seconds, said, "He's got Sarr blood in him, though his skin is more a light brown than the black of mine. He's got their black hair and silver eyes, though."

"Build?"

She hesitated. "Thin. He's got a rather large nose, and

big hands and feet."

The latter being the reason she was first attracted to him, she added silently.

She's got a foot fetish?

Belle nudged me lightly, sending the tea I'd all but forgotten about slopping over the edge of the cup. Thankfully, it hit my jacket more than my fingers.

No, idiot. Remember what they say about men with big feet? Well, apparently it's true in this case.

Eww. And he's still her brother, big dick or not.

She doesn't appear to have the same sensibilities as you or me.

Wonder if the same could be said about the rest of them, given they're willingly feeding and fucking a vampire?

I think you'd have to be more than a little left of center to even consider becoming a vampire's food source.

"Which gives us more than enough to go on. Interview suspended at," Aiden glanced at the clock and then said, "two forty-five. Suspect to be held until more secure arrangements can be made."

"I'm not going to fucking prison," Molly growled. "I haven't done anything."

"Including not answering questions." Aiden walked around the desk and hauled her upright. "Let's go find a nice little temporary cell, shall we?"

"I'll add an exclusion note to the magic protecting this place," Ashworth commented. "Just in case the bastard gives us the slip and attempts to free his sister."

Aiden nodded and led Molly out the door. I put my cup down and quickly followed, as did Belle. It seemed both of us were desperate to avoid the looming confrontation with Ashworth.

There were only a couple of cells in the station, and all of them had silver-coated bars bracing the doors. A werewolf might well be able to smash through regular metal cell doors, but they wouldn't go near ones braced with silver.

"How do you rangers get around the problem of the silver?" I asked.

"Special gloves."

He shoved Molly through an open door, placed her on the very basic bed, and retreated. Once he'd plucked what looked like a thick oven mitt from a holder to the side of the doorway and tugged it on, he then closed and locked the door.

"Ashworth," he said, raising his voice so that the other man could hear him. "You can release her."

He did, and she immediately launched at us. She didn't get very far—cells designed to hold werewolves were not going have much trouble containing a troubled young woman—but her language was thick, foul, and filled with threats.

I blinked. "Well, I've certainly learned a few new curses in the past couple of seconds."

"As have I." He lightly touched my back and guided me down the hall. "You two need to go home. Ashworth and I will go search her apartment."

"Neither of them are going anywhere until they explain what the hell is going on." Ashworth came out of the interview room and propped in front of the exit door.

I stopped and tried to ignore the sick sensation growing in my stomach. "With what? I don't understand—"

"I meant with the two of you, and you're well aware of it." He shook his head. "Taken as separate entities, you are, at best, very weak witches—"

"A point that's been well established, so what's the

problem?"

"The problem isn't a problem, as such," he said. "But it's certainly something I've never seen or even read about."

"If this has any sort of point," Aiden said, "can we get to it? We have a dark practitioner to capture and time's a-wasting."

"The *point*," Ashworth said, his gaze once again gaining that sense of wonder, "is that these two might be *separately* weak, but *together*, they're as strong as any single witch I've ever come across outside of Canberra's confines."

It was a comment that had relief stirring. At least he wasn't saying we were all-powerful—that would have been the quickest way ever to have Canberra scrambling to investigate us.

"That's impossible. No witch—not even those from royal lines—can blithely share powers."

Except that we're not ordinary witches, and we can and do share our physical *energy*, Belle commented. *In fact, we're something that's never happened before—a witch who has a witch familiar. Your parents and the council were so busy bemoaning your lack that they didn't even check what our situation might have meant for us jointly.*

But if Ashworth can see the immersion of our powers so clearly, why wouldn't have my parents, our teachers, and everyone else up in Canberra? Once you became my familiar, we were constantly together.

Perhaps it's been a gradual thing. It's been the two of us for such a long time that maybe this *is simply a development of the trust and friendship that lies between us.*

Possibly. Though it still didn't explain why my parents wouldn't have seen the possibility, given they were considered to be amongst a mere handful of the most powerful witches in Canberra.

"So the High Council would have everyone believe," Ashworth said, dragging my attention back to him, "but there have been rare occasions where it has occurred, even if on a temporary basis. This, however, isn't temporary. It's full-time, and it's something that has developed over time. Your separate energy outputs flow and combine in a way I've never seen. It makes the whole greater than the two parts."

Which basically confirmed Belle's thoughts, even if it didn't explain why no one else had noticed it before now. Anna certainly hadn't mentioned it, nor had any of the other witches—some of them powerful, most of them not—that we'd come across over the years.

"Even if they are combining in the manner you describe, that doesn't explain your comment about our overall abilities." I somehow managed to keep my voice even despite the uneasy certainty that this would bring my parents—or at least their representative—to the reservation. "No matter what way you look at it, two quarters does *not* make a whole."

"No, it shouldn't, and yet here, with you two, it does."

Meaning if we are *hauled up in front of the High Council, we could make your parents eat every damn mean word they ever said about you and me.*

While that's an admittedly appealing thought, I have no desire to either see them again or get dragged back to Canberra and be studied like lab rats.

With that last bit, I agree.

I glanced at her. *But?*

She half smiled. *But it would be nice to be finally free to see my family again.*

Guilt stirred. My inadequacy—and my fears about what my parents might force me to do if they found me again—was the reason behind her lost contact. It might have been a joint decision to run, but it was Belle who'd paid the greater price.

We couldn't have stayed there and remained sane. And I certainly could not have stood by and watched you get abused six ways to Sunday, Belle commented. *Even my mom agreed it was better for us to leave and go into hiding for a while.*

Which still didn't make it any easier on her. I returned my gaze to Ashworth. "I think you're seriously overestimating—"

"I have *never* doubted what I see or sense, and I have no reason to do so now," he cut in. "You two are a puzzle I very much intend to figure out—but not right now. We have a witch to hunt down first."

"Then go. Belle and I can walk back—"

"Seriously?" Aiden said. "You want to have *that* argument again?"

I hesitated, and then shook my head. "You will let us know what happens tonight when you get the chance, won't you?"

"Yes, of course."

"Then escort away."

"Here I was expecting an almighty argument," he said. "I'm gathering Belle talked you out of it?"

"No, although as I've said before, she is the more sensible of the two of us."

"That is a somewhat scary thought given what I know of her."

"You have absolutely no need to be scared," Belle said. "And Lizzie only goes off the rails once or twice a year; it's quite fun to watch when it happens."

"I think there's a story or two in that comment," he replied, amused.

"And not ones you'll be hearing anytime soon." I grabbed the backpack and then followed Belle into the main room.

"Unless, of course, you bribe me with chocolate and pink bubbles," Belle commented.

Aiden's grin widened. "I shall requisition them ASAP."

He locked the station door and then escorted us across to the truck. Ashworth climbed into the back seat while Belle and I claimed the front. The café was only a block away, so it didn't take us long to get there.

"I might not get to the café tomorrow," he said, as he pulled to a halt. "Just depends on the time we finish up tonight, and what leads we get."

I nodded, then leaned over to kiss his cheek. Except he moved, his lips caught mine, and the kiss became something far more intense—and far more delicious.

He broke away with a slight groan. "You'd better go, before I do something I might regret."

"I wouldn't have thought sex in a truck would be something you'd ever regret," Belle said casually.

"It's the audience rather than the truck I'm referring to," he said. "And please stop reading my thoughts."

She grinned. "I wasn't. I didn't need to, given all the—shall we say—body language?"

He rolled his eyes, leaned across, and opened the door. "Go. And make sure you lock all the damn doors."

We climbed out, but as he disappeared around the corner, magic stirred around us. *Wild* magic.

And it was filled with an odd sort of warning.

Belle frowned. "Why is it here, in the middle of the

town, of all places?"

"I don't know." I scanned the street, but couldn't see the threat the wild magic seemed to be hinting at. "But given the last time it randomly appeared someone shot out my tire, we might want to get inside."

Belle hastily opened the door, but neither of us immediately went in. While anyone intending us harm wouldn't have gotten past the spells surrounding this place, caution never hurt. The window blinds were partially closed, allowing little of the moonlight to filter in, leaving the café area a wasteland of shadows and darkness. But even so, the place was obviously empty, and there was no sense of trespass humming along the magical lines. We went in.

The wild magic whipped in after us, swirled around, and then moved back to the door. When we didn't move, it repeated the process, this time more urgently.

It wanted us to close the door.

I frowned, but did so. No sooner had I done that than something hit it.

Hit it, and went straight *through* it.

"What the fuck...?" I glanced up and saw the hole.

A bullet hole.

Holy shit... another shooter was out there.

I dove away from the door, hitting my hip against the wall and grunting in pain as I knocked Belle away and down. Then, as one, we scrambled on hands and knees around the corner to safety.

Another bullet ripped through the old wooden door, smashed through a small vase, and sent pottery shards flying everywhere before burying itself in the wall opposite.

"I'm getting a bit pissed off with people shooting up

our door and our walls," Belle said.

"At least this shooter didn't bring down the shelf holding all our cups. Any idea where he or she is?"

Her gaze narrowed as she telepathically searched the area. "He's on a rooftop across the street, but three buildings down."

"Can you get him?"

"He's just beyond my control range. I can sense him, but that's it."

"Is it our dark witch?"

"Why would a witch capable of calling and controlling a soul eater resort to shooting someone?"

"Why would Larissa attempt to kill me just because I was trying to find her? Why the fuck would Molly think killing her rivals would get her back into Maelle's good graces? It's pretty obvious we're dealing with several people who hid behind the door when the smarts were handed out."

"All very true." She paused. "He's a hired gun, I think."

"I don't suppose you can ferret out who hired him?"

"That requires going deeper into his mind, and I need to be closer to do that."

Or he needed to be closer. As in, immobilized and under our control. "Is there anyone else around?"

"No one that means us any harm."

"Right." I scrambled up and ran for the rear door. *Let me know if he moves.*

Be careful.

I have no intentions of getting dead just yet. I still have a ranger to seduce.

Speaking of, do you want me to give him a call?

I hesitated. While it was important he and Ashworth

find the dark sorcerer, it was also possible the shooter could lead them directly to him. *You'd better, just in case.*

I opened the back door and raced into the parking lot. The moon's brightness flowed in and out of a stream of clouds, providing a vague, intermittent light, but there was still enough about to see and avoid the various potholes in the old bitumen.

I ran to the other end of the parking area, hauled my ass over the fence, and then continued along the lane that ran along the side of the old theater. Once I was in Hargraves Street, I moved back to Mostyn and paused in the doorway of the Subway on the corner.

Any movement? I cautiously peered around. The street was quiet and the rooftops dark.

Nope. He's still in the same position. Not sure what he's waiting for, given for all he knows, we're settling in for the night.

I'm not liking the feel of this situation.

That makes two of us. She hesitated. *Maybe you should come back here and let Aiden—*

No, I cut in. *The wild magic is urging me forward, not back. I have no idea why, but we can't afford to ignore her.*

Given she's saved your butt a couple of times now, that's probably wise. Belle paused. *I'll go upstairs and turn on a light. Hopefully that will keep his attention on the café rather than anything else.*

Keep well away from the windows.

I'll hover in the stairwell. He won't even see me.

I waited until the moon disappeared behind a cloud again, and then raced across the road. I didn't stop once I was under the cover of the building's awning, but kept going up Hargraves Street. Once I'd reached the small laneway that led to the parking area behind the pizza shop, I paused and quickly scanned the lane, looking for a way up onto the roof. I found it on the second building—a small fire escape with a metal bin very handily placed right underneath it.

It's probably how our shooter got onto the nearby roof.

I'd say so. I very carefully stepped up onto the bin, reached for the ladder, and began to climb. It creaked slightly under my weight, and I froze. *Belle?*

No movement his end. You're safe.

Relief stirred, but I still waited another few seconds before I started moving again. I reached the top, pulled myself over the small wall, and dropped down onto the roof. Aside from a sprouting army of antennas, and an air-con unit that had seen better days, the area was empty.

I padded over to the wall dividing this building from the next, and carefully peered over. Aside from yet more antennas, there were also a couple of long lounge chairs on this rooftop. No bad guy holding a gun, however.

He's on the next roof.

I carefully climbed over to the next roof. Metal skittered from under one foot, and the noise seemed as loud as thunder. The wild magic stirred, this time holding both censure and urgency.

He's headed your way. Find cover.

There is no fucking cover. Nothing other than those damn lounges, anyway. With little other choice, I kept low and raced across to them.

Almost on you, Belle warned.

I dropped down and lay prone next to the lounge, hoping like hell the shadows were thick enough to hide my hair. But if the moon came out from behind the cloud, the crimson color would give me away in an instant.

I held my breath and waited. For several seconds, nothing happened, and then I heard it—a soft scrape.

Just that, nothing more.

Tension wound through me and for several seconds, I didn't dare even breathe.

Nothing happened. The moon didn't come back out, and the shooter didn't come over the wall to investigate.

Okay, he's moving back, Belle said.

I closed my eyes and sucked air into my burning lungs. That had been close.

But the danger wasn't over yet. Not for me, not for Belle. Not if the growing urgency in the wild magic was anything to go by.

Something was about to happen. Something bad.

Belle, get out of the café. Now.

She didn't answer but she *did* respond. Her fear surged through me, and though I couldn't see her, I knew she was bolting for the back door. I rose and padded toward the next dividing wall, remaining low and gathering the threads of an immobilizing spell around my fingers.

I'm out in the parking lot.

Even as she said that, two things happened.

The warning in wild magic peaked.

And the café exploded into flames.

CHAPTER
thirteen

For several seconds I didn't move. *Couldn't* move.

Shock held me immobile as the force of the explosion lit up the entire area and washed heat across the rooftops.

"You *bastard*!" Even as the words were torn from my throat, I thrust upright and flung the spell at him.

He spun around, and I caught a glimpse of something glittery at his neck. Then he raised the rifle and fired again.

I instantly dropped down; the bullet pinged off the top of the wall just above my head, sending concrete shards spinning. Then he was running—coming *at* me rather than away.

I closed my eyes and did the one thing I'd sworn not to do again—I reached for the wild magic. It would take too long to craft a spell powerful enough to get past the charm he was wearing—and, even then, there was no guarantee my magic or my knowledge would be capable of such a feat.

But there was little defense against the wild magic, as few witches had ever dared to do more than protect it. Those who *had* attempted to use it had either died or come close to it—such as my mother.

Why I seemed to be the exception, I had no idea. And, right now, didn't care.

It answered my call swiftly, almost joyously—a white-hot heat that surged through my body with such force that for a moment it felt as if I would tear apart.

In an instant, everything was sharper, brighter; I could hear his footsteps, smell the faint musky pine scent of him on the air. Hear the whisper of his breathing, and taste his anticipation of the kill.

This wasn't a result of the wild magic. This was Katie—or rather, her ghostly werewolf capabilities sharpening mine.

I waited until he was close; until his anticipation, amusement, and the certainty of an easy kill were thick and heavy on the air.

Only then did I set the magic free. "Pin him," I said, "and tear that gun from his grip."

From the other side of the wall came a strangled sound of surprise, then nothing but an odd sense of satisfaction.

I rose. The shooter was being held—arms and legs akimbo—three feet off the rooftop. His gun lay a good ten feet away from him and had, from the look of it, not only been made safe, but actually snapped in two. The wild magic—and Katie—was a little pissed at the shooter. I suspected the only reason it hadn't also snapped the shooter in half was because it couldn't react against life without being ordered to do so.

And I wouldn't order this man's death, no matter how angry I was. To do so could adversely stain the wild magic forever.

Belle, you okay? I climbed over the wall and strode toward our captive.

Yes, but the back half of the upper floor is on fire.

Is it bad?

Not at the moment, she said. *It depends on how soon the fire brigade gets here as to whether the damage will spread.*

Didn't your grandmother teach you a fire prevention spell?

Yes, but the key word is prevention rather than restriction. I'll try and adapt it.

I stopped in front of the stranger, reached up, and pulled the charm from his neck. Energy burned across my fingers even as it whispered its secrets to me. The spell that had been bound to the agate was powerful—possibly more so than anything I could conjure—but the practitioner had made one mistake. He hadn't protected it against physical assault.

I dropped it onto the rooftop and smashed it under my heel.

"Who are you?" I demanded. "And why the fuck are you trying to kill us?"

He spat at me. I sidestepped the globule and then said mildly, "Try that again, and the magic that holds you will rip you apart, just as it ripped your gun apart."

His gaze darted sideways, and a trace of uneasiness entered his expression. He remained mute, however.

I sighed. "Okay then, we do this the hard way."

I flicked my wrist and the wild magic responded, pulling his legs further apart. The minute he screamed, it stopped.

"Right, shall we try this again?" I crossed my arms

and studied him. And was aware that, over his right shoulder, the flames consuming our building were reaching even higher. I clenched my fists and fought the instinct to lash out at him. It was an instinct that was as much Katie's as mine. "Why are you trying to kill us?"

Sweat was now rolling down his face, and his expression was one of agony. But then, it was a rare man who could comfortably do the splits without hurting himself.

The sound of fast-approaching sirens broke the silence. I hoped like hell they could stop the fire before it destroyed the building and most of our belongings.

"You have one minute to answer. If you don't, I'll make you pay for shooting at me *and* destroying our café."

He didn't speak.

"Fifty seconds," I said, then, "Thirty—"

The wild magic stirred, and his legs were very briefly pulled wider apart.

"Okay, okay," he all but howled. "It was revenge. I was sent here for revenge."

I raised an eyebrow. "By whom?"

"The Fitzgeralds over in Pike's Peak."

Meaning Belle had not only been right, but my misreading of them had very nearly gotten us both killed.

Hey, neither of us really expected those bastards would have the courage to hit back like this, so don't you be heading down guilt road.

Easier said than done when I could still see the flames of destruction leaping high.

I've managed to corral them to the top of the stairs and the kitchenette. Everything else is safe, and the smoke is being funneled out the hole in the roof.

There's a hole in the roof?

From the explosion. She paused. *Aiden's just appeared.
And?*

He's pissed you went after the shooter without waiting for him.
She paused again. *Ashworth said he'd put out the flames. It'll
save us from water damage, at the very least.*

But not save us from losing customers and money at
one of the busiest time of the year. Still, we were both
alive and most of the café was intact, so we had a lot to be
grateful for.

All of which didn't ease the anger still bubbling
inside.

I returned my attention to my prisoner. "How did
you manage to set the café on fire when you didn't go
anywhere near it?"

"A couple of days ago, I was part of a team that was
cleaning out the guttering next door. It was easy enough to
lop an incendiary device onto your roof from there."

Which explained why our magic hadn't reacted or
stopped him—it didn't work against inanimate objects.

Something we'll have to fix, Belle said. *Aiden's on his way
over.*

*Well good, because he needs to get someone up here to arrest
this bastard before I'm tempted to do something nasty.* Aloud, I
added, "Why didn't you set the device off as soon as we'd
gotten inside?"

"Because it was only powerful enough to destroy the
top floor."

Suggesting he'd deliberately missed us in the hope
that we'd race up there. If Belle hadn't telepathically
hunted him down, it might well have worked. "What if
we'd gone out the back door instead?"

He shrugged—or at least tried to. The movement was
severely restricted by his outstretched arms. "I would have

come back tomorrow night."

I crossed my arms against the chilling suspicion he might have been successful if he had. "Were you the one who was with Larissa up in the Marin compound?"

"Yeah, stupid bitch gave me the perfect cover, and didn't even realize it."

"Where did you meet her? At the gun club?"

"Nah, she was drinking in some pub on the outskirts of town, and I heard her bitching about needing someone to have an accident. So I kindly offered my services." He paused. "Look, I'm answering your questions—can you ease up on the whole splitting me in two thing?"

"Only if you keep answering questions." I paused briefly and let that sink in. "How did you force Larissa to keep your presence a secret and take the fall for you?"

He tried to shrug again. "I said I'd kill her mom if she didn't."

Which explained the fear in Larissa's eyes when we'd mentioned charging her mom. It wasn't so much our threat, but rather his that she'd reacted to.

"Was it also you who shot out my car's windshield?"

"Yeah. Not sure how you controlled that fucking thing given the speed you were doing. You should have slid straight into the trees."

I would have, if it hadn't been for a good dose of luck and the wild magic.

"Which of the Fitzgeralds hired you?" I asked. "Because I gather you *are* a contract killer."

He didn't immediately answer. The wild magic twitched in response, and he hissed through gritted teeth before saying, "It was the brothers—Cary and Michael."

Who were not only behind the plot that had run us out of town, but the owners of the Psychic, Taro, and

Spiritual Cleaning center that had suddenly become overrun with rats. I'd known they'd be angry—who wouldn't be?—but I really hadn't expected them to react so violently.

"And your name?"

"Bryan," he replied, somewhat reluctantly. "Bryan Redfield."

Footsteps caught my attention, and I turned around to see Aiden running toward me. He slowed the minute I spotted him, his gaze running from me to my prisoner and back again.

"You okay?" He stopped and touched my back lightly, though I wasn't entirely sure whether it was meant to comfort him or me.

I nodded and motioned toward the shooter. "Meet Bryan Redfield, the man who took a pot shot at us in the Marin compound. Larissa took the fall because he threatened her mom."

"Really? Did he say why he was trying to kill us?"

"Not us—me. And it has nothing to do with the soul eater. The Fitzgerald brothers at Pike's Peak contracted him to enact a little revenge."

"They're the two who suffered the rat infestation, aren't they?"

"The same."

"Which," Ashworth said, as he huffed towards us, "was rather stupid of them. Harsh penalties apply to those who react in such a physical manner against another witch."

Aiden raised his eyebrows. "Meaning it would have been okay to act in a magical manner?"

"Of course. Duels of magic are *not* a thing of the past, no matter what the government might have you believe."

He stopped beside me and studied my prisoner through narrowed eyes. "Why is there a feminine feel to the wild magic containing him?"

"I couldn't tell you," I said, and silently bid the magic to release the shooter and leave.

It did so with alacrity. As Bryan crashed to the ground and rolled into a ball of relieved agony, Aiden stepped forward, pulled Bryan's wrists behind his back, and secured them with the ever-present cable ties.

"There's also an unusual amount of intelligence in the magic of this place that needs investigating." His gaze came to mine. "As does your connection to it."

"How about we secure the wellspring before we worry about any of that?" I glanced at Aiden. "Once this bastard is secure, you need to get back to hunting the witch. I've a bad feeling the shit will hit the fan if we don't stop him tonight."

"We will, but I had to make sure you were okay first."

His words warmed something deep inside. "And I appreciate it, but you can't delay. It might be deadly if you do."

He frowned. "Have you had another of your visions?"

I hesitated. "No. It's nothing more than a gut feeling."

He grunted and glanced at Ashworth. "I've learned to trust her gut. We'd better go."

The older man nodded and left. Aiden stepped over his prisoner and then stopped beside me. "Ashworth's put out the blaze, but the fire department still has to inspect the building and declare it safe before either you or Belle will be allowed back inside. Have you anywhere to stay for the night?"

I smiled. "With all the hotels around the area, I'm sure we can find something."

"I'd rather you be somewhere safer than a mere hotel." He pulled his keys out, disconnected one of the smaller rings, and offered me the two keys and small remote. "They'll get you into my apartment in Argyle." He gave me the address, and then added, "There're two beds in the spare room and linen in the closet near the bathroom."

"Aiden—"

"Please," he said, shaking the keys. "I'll find it easier to concentrate on the task at hand if I know you're out of the way and safe."

I took the offered keys and raised my eyebrows. "Out of the way doesn't sound too gentlemanly."

He smiled and touched a hand to my cheek. "You know what I meant."

Indeed I did. I resisted the urge to lean into his touch, and simply said, "What about my prisoner? What do you want me to do with him?"

"Can you immobilize him? Mac should be here in ten minutes."

"I'll wait for him, then."

"Be careful." He hesitated, then leaned forward and lightly kissed my lips. "I'll see you in the morning."

"You will."

I watched him leave, then returned my attention to Bryan. "If you so much as twitch the wrong way, I'll break something vital."

Fear skittered across his expression, but he didn't say anything and he certainly didn't move.

Mac arrived spot-on ten minutes later. He had the typical rangy build of a werewolf, with brown skin and hair that suggested he was from an outside pack.

"And you'd be Lizzie," he said, holding out his hand in greeting. "What have we got here?"

I gripped his hand briefly and said, "The bastard who tried to kill Aiden and me over on the Marin compound."

"Well, that was daft." He walked over to Bryan, roughly hauled him to his feet, and then sliced off the cable tie. "I'll get you to go down the ladder first, Lizzie. That way, you can zap him or something if he tries anything stupid."

A smile touched my lips. "With pleasure."

I headed back across the rooftops. As it turned out, Bryan wasn't daft enough to attempt an escape. Once his hands were re-cabled, Bryan hauled him over to the waiting SUV while I returned to our café.

To discover it wasn't just the roof that had a hole in it, but part of the corner wall. I walked over to Belle and wrapped my arms around her. For several minutes, neither of us talked. We just took comfort in the fact we were both still alive.

"So how bad is it?" I said eventually.

"It looks worse than it is, I'm assured. Despite the hole, the two walls are stable. They've asked the State Emergency Services people to come over with a tarp to cover the gap until we can get it fixed." She glanced at her watch. "They should be here within the next half hour."

"And the damage inside?"

"I'm told the stairs and upstairs kitchenette will need replacing, and the electrics will have to be checked, but that's it. The café hasn't suffered any damage; it just needs a good clean and airing to get rid of the smoke smell. We're lucky Ashworth was able to put the fire out, otherwise, it could have been far worse."

"At least once everything's been checked, and the building declared safe, we can open the café again."

"Yeah. I'd hate to be losing too many days—not this close to Christmas." She glanced at me. "What do you want to do next?"

A smile tugged at my lips. "As much as I want to do nothing more than go to Aiden's and collapse onto the nearest bed, I think we need to detour past Maelle's and update her."

She sighed. "Not something I really want to do right now, but I agree with the need to avoid antagonizing her. I've already called a cab."

I raised an eyebrow. "Do they actually work at this hour of the morning? We're not exactly in the middle of a major city."

"Apparently it has only happened since Émigré opened all night. And that," she added, as a car horn tooted out the front of the building, "will be him."

"Should we give our contact details to anyone?" I said, as I followed her down the lane.

"Already have," she said, over her shoulder. "And the firies will lock up when they've finished."

It didn't take long to get around to the club. Once I'd paid the cabbie, we climbed out and headed for the door. Two large bouncers immediately stepped in front of it and said, "Sorry, miss, but no jeans inside the venue."

"I'm not here for pleasure. I need to talk to your boss."

"I'm sorry, but that's not—"

The door behind him opened and Roger poked his head out. "Gentlemen, these two ladies have all-hours access to this club and to our boss no matter *what* the time. Or," he added, with a somewhat disparaging glance at my clothes, "how inappropriately they might be dressed."

I grinned as the two big men immediately stepped aside. "I can strip off to my singlet, if you'd like. It has sparkly stars all over it."

"Thanks, but no. Please." He opened the door wider and waved us in.

We stored our coats in the check area, but I kept a grip on my pack. While Maelle might not like being in the same room as either holy water or a silver knife, they were at least tucked securely away rather than out in the open. I wasn't about to leave them behind—not when that vague sense of wrongness was beginning to ramp up again.

Apparently, fate hadn't already flung enough shit our way.

The music was loud, the place was jumping, and the bar absolutely packed. Even so, Roger moved through the crowd like a prince in his kingdom, with people flowing around him—and us. It was a wave that never touched or in any way threatened to make him pause, even though I wagered most of the people here didn't even know who he was.

I glanced up at the dark glass-and-metal room that had been built into the ceiling at the point where all the arches met. Though Maelle wasn't visible, I had no doubt she knew we were here—Roger wouldn't have appeared with such alacrity otherwise—and that she watched us.

She might be out of sight, but in this place, no one was out of hers.

He led us around the upper deck until we'd reached the ornate wrought iron door that was an intricate mix of vine leaves and skeletal spines. There was an inconspicuous keypad situated on the right-side wall; once Roger had entered the code, the door slid aside and revealed a set of black glass stairs.

"My mistress awaits," he said, and waved us forward.

I took a slow, deep breath and then stepped inside; blue light flared to life as I did so, a muted chain of spots that led the way up the circular stairwell.

At the top there was another metal door, but it opened as we approached. The room beyond was filled with shadows despite the bright array of lights that constantly swept across the darkened windows. A black glass table sat in the middle of the room, and there were two plush-looking chairs at the front of this. A third sat behind.

Maelle stepped out of the shadows to our right. I stopped immediately, as did Belle.

"This is indeed a surprise," she said, her voice a low purr that sent chills down my spine. "I take it you have information?"

"Yes, and you're not going to like it."

"In that case, I suggest a drink. Champagne? Or something stronger?"

"Whiskey, on ice, if you have it," I said.

Maelle raised an eyebrow as she glanced at Belle. "And you, lovely lady?"

"The same, thanks." Belle glanced at me. *Okay, so she's gay?*

Yes, and you've obviously tickled her fancy.

She's not getting anywhere near my fancy, let alone anything else.

I somehow restrained my snort of amusement, and nodded my thanks as Maelle handed us our drinks.

"Please, ladies, sit." She waved us toward the two chairs at the front of her desk.

"I'd rather stand, thanks," Belle said.

Maelle raised an eyebrow, her expression amused. "I'm sensing some discomfort coming from your direction."

"Yes, and I'm sorry, but it's instinctive."

"I appreciate your honesty." Her gaze flicked to me and hardened somewhat. "Now, that news."

I took a drink, waited for the alcohol to fire up my courage, and then said, "It was Molly who—through her half brother, Jack—summoned the soul eater."

Maelle didn't move. She didn't react. Not in any way. Not for several minutes, at least.

And yet the room was suddenly darker, and *she* a whole lot more dangerous. Pinpricks of fear scuttled across my skin, and I took another drink. The burning strength of the alcohol eased neither the fear nor the desire to run.

Holy fuck, Belle commented, a tremor in her mental tones. *This bitch is even scarier than I'd imagined.*

And even more so when you remember she's undoubtedly controlling her emotions and scare factor right now.

One finger twitched on Maelle's left hand. Just one finger, but it sent the image of her wrapping a hand around Molly's neck and squeezing the life out of her, breath by agonized breath, racing through my mind.

"She did this because I fired her."

It was a statement, not a question, and I nodded. "I believe she thought that if she got rid of some of the others, you'd be inclined to accept her back."

"I knew she was not overly endowed with intelligence, but I would not have expected such stupidity even from her." Her gaze rose to mine. The pale gray of her irises had surrendered completely to the white, and it was a god-awful, frightening thing to see. "Have you captured her?"

"Yes, but not Jack or the soul eater." I hesitated, and then somewhat reluctantly added, "You cannot, in any way, act against her or her brother as yet."

Belle glanced at me sharply, something I felt rather than saw.

"And I will not, as I have promised, until this matter is well and truly finished." She paused to take a drink of her champagne. "What of my other feeders? Do I need to worry about them?"

"Yes." I hesitated again. "I'm afraid Marlinda is not the lone casualty. Aled and James have also been killed."

"That is dire news indeed."

Meaning, I suspected, that the method Maelle would use to kill Molly just tripled when it came to the agony factor. "I gave the list Roger sent me to Aiden. I believe he is arranging protection."

"Will it be enough?"

"Yes, because the RWA witch will place protections around them."

"Will? So it has not happened as yet?"

"He hasn't had the chance. It's been a rather difficult night for us all."

She studied me for too many uncomfortable seconds. While I knew she couldn't read minds, I nevertheless had the vague feeling she was pulling forth secrets and memories, and examining their content.

"Is the ranger aware of how you got that list?"

"No."

"Good." She took another drink. "Until the ranger and the RWA representative are able to protect my feeders, are there any common precautions I can advise them to use? And are you able to go to them now and arrange something more appropriate?"

Saying no was not an option, her expression—or lack thereof—suggested.

I gave her the same advice I'd given Lance's parents, and then said, "It's not strong magic, by any means, but it's better than nothing until we can get there."

"Indeed. I'll get Roger to contact them immediately."

"Good." I downed the rest of my drink and stepped forward to place the empty glass on the table. As I did, awareness surged.

The dark witch was here.

The soul eater was with him.

And the church bell was tolling.

"Holy fuck," Belle whispered. "He's *strong*."

Stronger than me. Possibly even stronger than the two of us combined. *Can you immobilize him telepathically?*

She hesitated. *No. There's magical interference of some kind.*

"Who is strong?" Maelle said, voice curt.

"Jack. He's here, and so is the soul eater."

"Which makes no sense," Belle said. "Not when the whole point of the attacks up until this point has been to erase the competition for Maelle's attention."

"Maybe he's decided to erase a different type of competition—us. After all, we're the reason his sister is now sitting behind bars."

"The *why* behind his presence here is not important right now," Maelle commented. "What do we need to do?"

I swung off my backpack and hurriedly zipped it open. "How sensitive are you to holy water?"

A cool smile touched her lips. "Are you intending to throw it at me?"

"No, of course not. But we need to set a trap for the

soul eater, and to do that, we'll need to confine it within a protective circle—"

"Made of blessed water," she finished, and nodded. "I would have thought a pentagram would have been of more use."

"It would, but it's not like we have candles or our athames with us right now."

"Given he is strong enough to control this spirit, will not he sense the formation of your magic?"

I hesitated. "Perhaps. It would depend greatly on how much training he has and just how instinctive his magic is. Many half-breeds get the ability without the instincts."

Which was what ultimately made half-breeds so dangerous—if you couldn't see and sense magic, either your own or another's, you really couldn't master it.

Given his control over the dark spirit, he has to have inherited some instincts.

Not necessarily. There's been many nongifted people over the years who've successfully controlled the destructive nature of the dark ones. I mentally shrugged. *Either way, our priority has to be the soul eater.*

"And once you have done the circle?" Maelle said. "What then?"

I pulled out the knife, tucked it into my belt, and then grabbed the potions and holy water, handing the latter to Belle. "Then, hopefully, we'll pin it within whatever body it's using and kill it."

"Hopefully is *not* the most encouraging word you can use in this type of sit—" She stopped and cocked her head sideways. "Roger informs me that Leanne Jones—one of my feeders—desires to see me urgently."

"Could you ask Roger if he notices anything different

with her? Particularly with her eyes?"

She nodded, and after a moment said, "Her eyes are black. Solid black."

"Meaning the soul eater has taken her."

"I will," she said, her voice holding as little emotion as her expression, and sending yet another round of shivers down my spine, "truly enjoy tearing this bastard apart."

"Let's deal with soul eater first," I bit back. "Unless you want your remaining feeders to end up as soul eater breakfast."

The deadness in her gaze zeroed in on me, and just for a heartbeat, I saw death.

Maelle was not someone I ever wanted to make an enemy of, because *that* death would come for me.

Then she blinked and smiled. It did nothing to ease the trembling inside. "Indeed I do not. Proceed."

I swallowed heavily and then said, "Invite her up, but tell Roger to take her the long way around. We need ten minutes to set up."

"Jack's just walked into a vampire's base intent on destruction," Belle said. "That means he's either insane or extremely confident in both his skills *and* the strength of the spirit he controls. Either way, it makes him as dangerous as his creature."

"I know, but we can only deal with one threat at a time." I returned my gaze to Maelle. "Can you also ask Roger to ring Aiden? We need to get the RWA witch here ASAP."

Maelle nodded. "And my customers? Should we not evacuate this place?"

I hesitated and glanced at Belle. She shrugged. "He'd have to be wearing some form of concealment charm.

Evacuating the club will just give him cover to escape."

"And yet," Maelle said, "the minute you deal with his creature, he might well leave anyway."

"Let's hope he does, because it'll make dealing with him less dangerous for everyone else here." I hesitated. "Push far enough away from your desk so that we can walk between you and it; once we've done so and the containment lines have been drawn, don't go near them or in any way break through them. Not until the soul eater is dealt with."

"If you're intending to confine me to this room, you will not succeed. That door is not my only way out."

"I'm not trying to confine you, just the soul eater," I said, even as I tucked away the handy information that this room had a second means of escape.

She sat down, calmly picked up her drink, and then pushed back from the desk. Only the utter whiteness of her gaze gave any indication of the murderous fury she was controlling.

No matter what happened in the next few minutes, Jack Lea and Molly were not long for this world.

I glanced at Belle and, as one, we began the incantation. Belle walked one way, I walked the other, both of us murmuring the same words, building and layering the threads of our magic together as we slowly drew a circle around the desk with the holy water and the warding potions. We didn't close it, however, but walked instead to the open doorway and stood in the shadows clustered on either side of it.

With the unfinished spell threads gathered around one hand, I carefully pulled the knife free with the other. Just for an instant, a spark of energy flared along its edge, an indication the spell I'd placed on it remained active.

In the narrow stairwell beyond the doorway, footsteps began to echo. I took a deep breath and glanced at Belle. "Ready?"

"No, but it's too late to run screaming from this place now."

That it was. I briefly closed my eyes and tried to get some sense of the woman who was drawing ever closer. But there was nothing. The person she'd been had been totally consumed by the spirit that was now in control—and *it* was fierce.

Fierce, angry, and ready to kill.

If Jack ever lost control, Maelle wouldn't get the chance to tear him apart. The dark spirit would do it for her.

The footsteps slowly came closer. My grip on the knife's hilt became so strong my knuckles practically glowed.

The footsteps faltered, and then stopped just outside the door, just beyond sight. If she breathed, I wasn't hearing it. But then, the woman who was Leanne Jones was dead, and the spirit who controlled her didn't need air. It just needed her flesh to complete its mission.

I glanced at Maelle. She immediately smiled and said, "Leanne? Please, come in."

For several seconds, nothing happened. The controlled body didn't answer, and it certainly didn't move. The anger I sensed now ran with awareness.

It knew we were here.

Magic stirred, magic that was as dark as the spirit who controlled the body standing the other side of the door. Our dark sorcerer was trying to force the spirit forward.

But it wasn't *that* that had my gaze shooting across to Belle's. She'd been right in her assessment of Jack—not only was he far stronger than we'd thought, but with that strength came utter belief in his own ability. This was *not* the first time he'd controlled dark spirits, which was why Molly had been so damn confident we'd never capture him.

Obviously, there was a whole lot more to these two than any of us—Maelle included—had figured.

"I seriously do *not* intend to have any conversation with you when you're standing out in the stairwell," Maelle said. "So please, come in and tell me what's on your mind. Otherwise, depart. I'm not in the mood to play games today."

The press of magic grew, and the soul eater was forced into action. It took one step, two, and then it was in the room with us. It didn't look left or right—it didn't need to, given it would feel the presence of our souls. And if Jack was aware of our presence, he certainly didn't seem to care. He just kept his creature marching forward. For whatever reason, Maelle was his intended target tonight.

As one, Belle and I crossed over, completing the spell, and locking us both in the same cage as the soul eater.

The minute it was done, I stepped forward and plunged the knife into the dead woman's back.

The soul eater reacted instantly—a fierce, inhuman howl erupted from the woman's throat. As it echoed through the darkness, energy began to crawl across the woman's body, a bright, fierce net that would finish what the knife had started.

This time, there was no last-minute escape for the soul eater.

It howled again, and then spun and lashed out with a clenched fist. It caught me on the side of the face and sent me flying backward. Belle caught me with a grunt, holding me upright as the dead woman frantically tried to pull the knife from her flesh. But dark entities could not touch silver—especially when that silver had been blessed by holy water.

It roared again, and then turned and dove for Maelle. She didn't flinch. She just raised her champagne glass and took a sip. Leanne hit our barrier, and with such force that it actually bent around her.

But the threads didn't break.

The spell held.

I grabbed Belle's hand. Magic pulsed between us, a force that grew in strength as we began the banishing spell.

The soul eater—or perhaps even the witch controlling him—must have sensed the rise of magic, because the dead woman spun around and charged at us. Without breaking our grip or stopping the incantation, Belle spun and lashed out with a stiletto-clad foot. The blow smashed into the woman's nose, and the ultra-thin heel speared into her left eye. As the dead woman staggered backward, I followed Belle's action with a kick of my own—this time to the dead woman's knee.

She went down. We kept going with the spell, and the air began to shimmer and burn. But it wasn't so much from the force we were raising, but rather from the dark sorcerer. He was trying to enforce his will, to make his creature rise and attack.

But it was too late for that.

As our spell neared its peak, the woman's body began to twist. It almost looked as if there were hundreds of huge worms inside of her, seeking a way out, trying to escape. Her skin became an ocean of heaving waves, and her battered eyeball plopped out onto the floor and rolled toward us. My stomach churned, but I closed my eyes and kept uttering the words of banishment.

The spell reached a crescendo; the dead woman screamed.

Then, as the soul eater was sent back to the realm from which it had been drawn, she exploded.

CHAPTER
fourteen

L eaving us covered in blood, flesh, and bone.

It felt like slime. Warm, red slime.

I vomited.

A heartbeat later, so did Belle.

"Well, *that* was unexpected."

Maelle's voice vibrated with an edge that spoke of hunger. The gore explosion might have been contained within the boundaries of our magic, leaving her untouched, but I very much suspected it would not remain that way for long. That once we'd left, she would strip off and bathe in the bloody remains of her feeder.

"Yes, it was." I stripped off my sweater, and then used the inside of it to wipe away the worst of the gore from my face and hair, gagging as I did. "And it's not over yet. We still have to hunt down our witch."

But the sense of him was fading from this place. He was on the run, and that meant we had to get out there, and fast, otherwise we'd lose him.

And if we *did*, he'd have time to summon another soul eater. Or maybe even something worse.

"You cannot go into a room half-filled with werewolves reeking of a slaughterhouse," she said. "It will cause the very problem we are trying to avoid."

"I can't just let him go, either—"

"I'm not for a second suggesting that you do." She glanced past me. "Roger, please provide the ladies replacement clothing, and then escort them both outside via the tunnel."

I raised an eyebrow. "You have a tunnel?"

"One never lives to my age without taking all manner of precautions. Go."

We deactivated the containment spell and then followed Roger from the room. The door was closed and locked firmly behind us. No one was getting in to disturb Maelle's blood bath.

I gagged at the thought, but there was utterly nothing left in my stomach to regurgitate. About halfway down the stairwell, Roger paused and pressed his hand against the wall. A scanner kicked into gear, read his prints, and then a door opened. The room beyond was small, and filled with all sort of armaments, from medieval-looking things right through to modern. There was also a selection of clothing, and, of all things, a refrigerator. I did not want to know what sort of liquid it might be chilling.

Roger gave Belle a quick look, and then pulled a pair of slim jeans and a loose top from one of the racks. "These should fit nicely. There's a towel to your right that you might want to use first."

As she stripped off and cleaned up, he moved to a drawer, pulled out a pair of flat shoes, and handed them to her. Like the jeans, they fit perfectly.

"Thanks," she said.

"Once upon a time, I was a tailor. I haven't really lost the knack, even though it's a cover we've sadly not used for many years now." He repeated the process for me and, once we'd both changed and had brushed as much gore from our hair as was possible, added, "This way, please."

He led us through another door and then along a small, dark corridor that had obviously been built between two rooms. The club's music vibrated against the wall to our right, but there was nothing but silence coming from the other side. Maybe it was a storeroom. Or maybe it was some sort of safe room for Maelle. She'd have more than one of them, of that I had no doubt.

After a few more twists and turns, a heavy metal door appeared. Roger again placed his hand against the reader to open the door, and then stepped to one side and waved us through. "Happy hunting, ladies."

I didn't bother replying. I just dug my phone out of the pack and ran for the front of the building. There was no immediate sign of our dark witch—not on the street, not in the air.

"He's on the run, and already a couple of streets away," Belle said. "Or so say the spirits."

"Can you ask them to keep track of him for us?"

"They are. They're as pissed off as us at what just happened."

"It's not like they were the ones who got exploded over."

"No, but they said that sort of happening does tend to give spirits in general a bad name." She paused. "Are we going after him? Or are we waiting for the cavalry?"

"If we wait, we risk giving him the chance to

summon something else. I'll call Aiden. You lead the way."

As she raced off, I grabbed my phone and contacted Aiden. Roger might have already called him, but Aiden needed to know what was now happening.

"We're twenty minutes away," he growled, before I could say anything. "Wait for us."

"We do that and we risk losing this bastard for good."

"Then keep the line open and keep me updated on where you are."

"Hurry," I said, rather unnecessarily.

We swung around the corner and pounded up the empty street. I kept up a running commentary for Aiden's benefit, but I had a gut feeling he wasn't going to get here in time. That this bastard was ours to deal with, whether we wanted it or not.

Jack's essence began to stain the air, as did the gathering energy of magic. But it was low-grade—underpowered—which suggested he might have used most of his energy and strength controlling the soul eater.

Belle's guides directed us left, onto a street lined with large houses on acreage. Perhaps he was hoping to lose us in the bush. The thought had barely crossed my mind when there was an odd pop of sound. Belle swore and cannoned into me, the force enough to knock the breath from my lungs and the phone from my hand. We hit the ground, but she was up in an instant and all but dragging me to a nearby tree.

"The bastard's armed."

Given he wouldn't have gotten a gun into Maelle's, it could only mean he'd either stashed a weapon up here previously, or that the low-grade run of magic I'd sensed was him summoning a weapon from somewhere. "If he's resorting to a gun, he's been weakened. This is the best chance we'll have of getting him." I looked around. "Can you see my phone?"

"No." She paused, her head cocked sideways. "He's cutting through the next property, heading back toward Richards Road."

I drew in a deep breath, attempting to calm the churning in my gut and the quiver of nerves, and then said, "Right, we need to split up. Ask your guides to follow him, and let me know if he changes direction. If we can come at him from two directions, we might have a chance of at least pinning him."

Belle nodded and moved to the right. I went left, weaving my way through the scrub and climbing carefully through barbwire fences. Somewhere ahead a dog barked, but it was quickly cut off.

I kept on running—though it was becoming increasingly harder given the growing ache in my leg—and tried to remain as quiet as possible. I just had to hope that, for once, fate played into our hands.

In the distance up ahead came the glimmer of a streetlight, which meant I had to be nearing Richards Road. I went the long way around a darkened house and slowed as I neared the road.

Belle? I said. *Where is he?*

He's just hit the road. I'm a few minutes behind him. She paused. *He's headed your way.*

I flexed my fingers, but didn't dare gather magic. Weakened or not, he'd probably sense it. Instead, I picked up a sturdy-looking branch from the base of a broken tree and hefted it lightly. I certainly wouldn't want to be clobbered with it. Hopefully, it *would* stop a man in his tracks.

I found a tree that was close enough to the footpath for me to launch at him, but wide enough to hide behind, and stopped. After a minute or so, I heard him—his footsteps were heavy and his breathing was a harsh rasp that cut across the night. I hoped that meant he was at the point of exhaustion. Hoped the two of us could cope with him.

I fought the ever-increasing urge to reach for magic as his footsteps drew closer. Further out in the darkness, magic stirred, but it was true wild magic rather than the magic infused by Katie's spirit. It would make spelling dangerous, but it wouldn't stop me if it came down to a choice between it and survival.

But at the last possible moment, he seemed to sense my presence. His footsteps abruptly faltered, and his harsh breathing fell silent.

Belle, distract him.

"Oi," she said immediately, "who's that moving around out there?"

He swore softly and walked on. I raised the branch, and when his footsteps indicated he was close enough, quickly stepped out from the tree and swung my weapon with every ounce of strength I had.

It smashed into his left arm and with such force that my branch shattered. He staggered back for several steps, curses flowing across the night as his arm swung like limp spaghetti from his shoulder.

I raised the remains of the branch and stepped closer—only to see the gun in his right hand.

A gun he was pointing right at me.

He grinned. "This is going to feel so good."

Something shot out from the darkness to his right. Something that was all silver fur and fury.

Aiden, in wolf form.

He launched at Jack a heartbeat before as the trigger was pulled, and the shot that should have blasted a hole through the middle of my body instead clipped the branch just above my head and sent a rain of bark and leaves falling around me.

The gun went flying. As man and werewolf fell to the ground in a growling, tearing, screaming tangle, I raced across to the gun and picked it up. Magic surged, and I spun around, only to see Aiden torn from Jack and flung against the nearby tree. He slithered to the ground and didn't immediately move.

Jack, however, was up and running.

I reached for a tripping spell, but before I could either finish it or launch it, Belle stepped out of the darkness and smashed a clenched fist into Jack's face.

He was out cold long before he hit the ground.

She shook her hand, and then glanced at me with a wide grin. "Told you all the boxing classes would come in handy one day."

I laughed even though tears stung my eyes. We'd survived. Against all the odds—and a half-breed witch who was probably stronger than either of us—we'd not only won, but had come through relatively unscathed.

I lowered the gun and limped across to Aiden. His form changed as I approached, and he pushed upright, holding on to the tree with one hand. There was a half-healed cut near his right temple, and blood seeping down the side of his face.

His gaze, when it met mine, was slightly unfocused. "Why do you smell of raw meat?"

"Long story. And you'd better sit down before you fall down."

"I can't. I need to stop Jack—"

"He's been stopped." I grabbed his arm as he somewhat unsteadily launched away from the tree. "You, my dear ranger, are concussed. So sit down and do what you're told for a change."

He snorted but nevertheless obeyed. "There's a case of the pot calling the kettle black if ever I heard one. You were supposed to be headed to my place, not out here chasing down bad guys."

"And if we'd obeyed, the soul eater would have claimed another victim and our dark witch would have escaped."

"*That* is also true."

I smiled and carefully sat on the ground beside him, my shoulder lightly pressed against his. "Want to lend me your phone? I'll call in your people, and an ambulance."

"I've already called Tala, and I don't need—"

"Maybe not, but I'm guessing Jack hasn't got many teeth left after Belle's blow."

"Obviously my fear of her left hook was justified."

"It was my right, actually," Belle called out. "And you've nothing to fear from me as long as you treat Lizzie right."

"*That* I have every intention of doing." He winced and gingerly rubbed his head. "When this goddamn ache goes away, that is."

"Well, I do have the keys to your apartment now. There might be no getting rid of me."

His gaze met mine, and a slow smile spread across his lips. "How do you know that wasn't my intention in the first place?"

"You offered me a single bed in the second room."

"Any decent hunter knows you have to lure your prey

into a false sense of security before you pounce."

I patted his knee gently. "I'm afraid pouncing of any kind is off the menu for you until your concussion symptoms are resolved."

"I'm sure a gentle kiss or two won't hurt." He unlocked his phone and then handed it to me. "But do me a favor—next time you decide to run after a bad guy, try not to lose your phone. If we hadn't already been close enough for me to chase your scent, this might have ended very differently."

"I know." I dialed the emergency number and asked for an ambulance. "But I didn't actually lose it—it was thrown from my hand when Belle saved my ass from a gunshot."

"A statement that not only emphasizes the need for more caution on future escapades," he said, his tone dry, "but brings us back to the point that if you'd waited for help, like a normal, sane person, you wouldn't have been shot at yet again."

I flashed him a smile. "In case you haven't noticed, I'm not a normal, sane person."

He twined his fingers through mine. "And I can't say I'm sad about that, even if it sometimes frustrates the hell out of me."

"Good, but let's not talk about frustration. Not until we can do something about it, at any rate."

His soft laugh ended in a wince. "Damn, don't make me do that."

"Are you sure you want us to stay with you?" I asked, amused. "Isn't that like putting a plate of meat in front of a ravenous dog, and asking it not to eat?"

He grinned. "I would never call you a mere plate of meat."

I raised an eyebrow. "Then what would you call me?"

"A banquet. One I intend to consume slowly, over many hours."

My pulse leapt at the thought. "I was hoping for days, not mere hours."

"You have a café to run, remember?" Amusement and desire danced in his bright eyes. "And we do have to sleep sometime."

I tsked. "It's a sad state of affairs when a werewolf has so little stamina."

"That sounded like a challenge. Consider it accepted."

"Good," I said. "I look forward to it."

The following morning Belle and I headed back to the café. It was a goddamn mess. The explosion and subsequent fire might have been confined the first floor, but there was debris and dust everywhere—even in the most unlikely of places, like the freezer.

With the power out—and unlikely to be restored for a couple of days thanks to the damage done to the meter box in the explosion—we were left with little choice but to throw out or give away anything stored in the fridges. The local gossips caught on to *that* news with great alacrity, and we had a steady stream of people happily taking cakes and slices off our hands.

Mike, Penny, and Frank all pitched in to help clean up, and by the end of the day, the café was in good shape. At least when the power was restored, we could begin trading straight away.

Once the three of them left, I went upstairs to

retrieve the bottle of Glenfiddich whiskey I had stashed for emergency situations—such as bloody dreams of death and destruction, which thankfully didn't happen all that often—then grabbed two glasses and poured us both a drink.

"Here's to surviving another dark spirit."

Belle tapped her glass against mine. "And to learning that we are, indeed, as special as we always thought."

"To be honest, I'd rather we weren't." I downed the whiskey in one gulp. Though it burned all the way down, it didn't calm the stirring trepidation. "It's going to cause us grief, Belle. I can feel it."

"Probably, but like everything else, it's pointless worrying about it right now." She paused, and wrinkled her nose. "Ashworth's approaching."

I got out another glass, poured him a drink, and slid it toward him as he strode into the room. "Thanks," he said, surprised. "What are we celebrating?"

"Survival."

"Amen to that." He took a drink and then added, "Thought you might like to know that the High Council has called for nominations for the position of reservation witch."

I frowned. "That sounds like it could take some time, and I'm not sure we can afford it given we have an unprotected and very large wellspring here."

"Which is why I volunteered to remain until the position is filled."

"Oh, I'm sure the reservation council will be so pleased to hear that," Belle murmured.

"Positively joyous, I'm sure." He downed his drink and waved away my offer of a refill. "I did warn you two that I intended to figure out the puzzle you present. This gives me the chance."

Great. Not.

Better Ashworth than some unknown monkeyface from the council, Belle reasoned.

I somehow managed to avoid choking on my whiskey, and croaked out, "When you *do* figure us out, be sure to let us know."

"Oh, I most certainly will." He gave us both a nod, then spun and headed for the door.

As he left, Aiden walked in.

"What the hell are you doing here?" I asked. "You're supposed to be home, resting."

"I was. I got lonely, and then I got hungry. I figured I'd cure both by picking you up and taking you out to dinner."

I raised an eyebrow. "Are we talking about a date? A proper date?"

"It's about time, isn't it?"

"Hell, yeah," Belle said. "And I just won fifty bucks."

"So glad we could help boost your bank balance." Aiden's voice was dry. He glanced at me; the heat in his eyes had my pulse skipping a beat. "You ready to go?"

"Given I've been cleaning all day, and have grime from one end of me to the other, no, I'm not." I crossed my arms and gave him a mock glare. "Remember that whole conversation we had about giving a girl a little warning?"

"I do, and my reply is much the same." He held out his hand and wiggled his fingers. "Come along—I have a cab waiting."

I shook my head but nevertheless placed my hand in his. "Where are we going?"

"There's an evening jazz concert in the park. I have a

blanket, a picnic basket, and champagne waiting—the latter being yours since I'm not allowed alcohol at the moment." He tugged me close and dropped a kiss on my lips. "I'd much rather go somewhere secluded, but that's probably not a good idea given the concussion and the orders not to exert myself."

"And I do want exertion," I murmured. "When the time comes."

"Hopefully, time won't be the only thing coming."

I laughed, kissed him, and then stepped back. "Let's go get some culture."

"Have fun," Belle called after us. "Don't do anything I *would* do. Not for a couple more days, anyway."

It was safe to say we didn't. But fun was nevertheless had.

This wolf not only made me feel more alive than any other man I'd ever met, but also infinitely safer.

And that was dangerous. Very dangerous.

But right now, on a glorious summer night, wrapped in the warmth of his arms as we listened to the mellow strains of jazz, I couldn't have given a damn.

About the Author

Keri Arthur, author of the New York Times bestselling Riley Jenson Guardian series, has now written more than thirty-seven novels. She's received several nominations in the Best Contemporary Paranormal category of the Romantic Times Reviewers Choice Awards and has won RT's Career Achievement Award for urban fantasy. She lives with her daughter in Melbourne, Australia.

CPSIA information can be obtained
at www.ICGtesting.com
Printed in the USA
LVHW040249010819
626131LV00001B/5